"Heller's protagonist, Zachary Post, i
Jones, but with a far n;
—The New

"*Slab Rat* is a wickedly nifty debut b
talent, a story about a young magazii
niscent of Wilfred Sheed's *Office Politics* and Calvin Trillin's *Floater*,
but with a zesty appeal and style very much its own. It's one hell of a
fun read, and genuinely sexy, or as the magazine people it killingly
depicts would put it, *hot.*"
—Christopher Buckley

"Unkind and hilarious . . ."
—Celia McGee, *New York Daily News*

"Dead-on comic aim . . ."
—Mark Lozzo, *Los Angeles Times*

"Diabolically witty . . . terrific writing. . . . The appeal of *Slab Rat* is
universal. It's a wicked fantasia for the frustrated. And you don't have
to be a young Jay McInerney . . . to dig this book. You just have to be
a mammal—preferably one hip to the horror of twentieth-century
integrity giving way to twenty-first century ambition."
—Bob Mack, *GQ*

"Slyly satirical . . . sparky Gen-X take on the classic office-life versus
love-life screwball comedies of yore."
—*Elle*

"Howlingly funny . . ."
—Ian Martin, *The Toronto Sun*

"A riotously scathing satire."
—David Daley, *The Hartford Courant*

"An acutely accurate exposé of back-stabbing banality in the world of
Condé Nast, Tina Brown, and fashion shoots. . . . Cut-to-the-quick
social satire."
—Melinda Wittstock, *The Memphis Commercial Appeal*

"Wicked . . . wonderfully engaging . . ."
—Karen Heller, *The Philadelphia Inquirer*

"Black comedy at its best . . . deliciously absurd. . . ."
—Geoff Edgers, *The Raleigh News and Observer*

SLAB RAT

A NOVEL

TED
HELLER

SCRIBNER PAPERBACK FICTION
Published by Simon & Schuster
NEW YORK LONDON TORONTO SYDNEY SINGAPORE

SCRIBNER PAPERBACK FICTION
Simon & Schuster, Inc.
Rockefeller Center
1230 Avenue of the Americas
New York, NY 10020

Copyright © 2000 by Ted Heller

First Scribner Paperback Fiction edition 2001

SCRIBNER PAPERBACK FICTION and design are trademarks of
Macmillan Library Reference USA, Inc., used under license by
Simon & Schuster, the publisher of this work.

Designed by Brooke Zimmer
Manufactured in the United States of America

1 3 5 7 9 10 8 6 4 2

The Library of Congress has cataloged the Scribner edition as follows:
Heller, Ted.
Slab rat : a novel / Ted Heller.
p. cm.
1. Periodicals, Publishing of—Fiction. 2. Publishers and
publishing—Fiction. 3. New York (N.Y.)—Fiction.
4. Young men—Fiction. 5. Editors—Fiction. I. Title.
PS3558.E47625 S57 2000
813'.6—dc21   00-028469

ISBN 0-684-86496-7
0-684-86497-5 (Pbk)

For friends, family, and dog.

I wish to sincerely thank Jake Morrissey, my editor, and Nan Graham at Scribner for keeping their promises (so far). And Chuck Verrill, my agent, for rescuing me from oblivion. And Jill Pope and Robin Sayers, for their advice and encouragement.

PART I

1

SLEEK, GLOSSY art deco chrome, everything is sparkling silver and black and white. We're at a noisy restaurant downtown and I can see my reflection in everything—the walls, the floor, the plates and food, even the wait staff. Grilled swordfish and lumpy potatoes for twenty-five dollars, nine-dollar shrimp cocktails with only four shrimp and at this swank place they make sure not to cut the little beady eyes off. About fifty of us sitting at long rectangular tables, fifteen people to a table. Willie Lister sits directly across from me, draining glass after glass of white wine, a film of sweat coating his long sloping forehead.

From the brilliantly lit Important Table, a spoon suddenly clanks against a plate and then there is an abrupt hush. Nan Hotchkiss (endless legs but the face and ears of a bloodhound) stands up and makes a toast, holding the overstuffed Filofax that seems surgically attached to her left wrist. "Let's all drink to Jackie and wish her oodles of good luck," she says.

We raise our glasses. *Good luck, Jackie. Oodles of it.*

A few moments later, Byron Poole, the art director, and one of his androgynous assistants have put on wigs and lipstick. They sing a very off-key version of "Sisters" from *White Christmas*, Jackie Wooten's favorite movie.

("Which one's supposed to be Rosemary Clooney and which one's Virginia Mayo?" I whisper to Willie.

"You mean Vera-Ellen," he whispers back. He's right.)

Coffee and dessert are now being served. At the head of the Important Table, Betsy Butler stands up a bit woozily, adjusts her seven-hundred-dollar eyeglasses, and taps her spoon against a glass. The din is reduced to intermittent coughing.

"As you all know," our managing editor says, "this is Jackie Wooten's last day with us . . . she's going on to bigger but hopefully not better things . . ."

The short speech goes on and I cannot bear to listen to it and so I soak up every word. Jackie Wooten has been moved way, way upstairs, going from associate editor at *It* to senior editor at *She*, the equivalent of skipping from fifth grader to high school senior. It makes me feel like an absolute turd, this Bob Beamon-like vault of hers. Betsy continues: Jackie's been this, Jackie's done that, she means this much to us . . . blah blah blah.

"So, Jackie, we all chipped in and we got you this . . ."

Jackie stands up and takes a box from Betsy. It's half the size of a carton of cigarettes and is wrapped in light blue tissue.

Jackie has worked with Willie Lister for about five years; they've been sitting across from each other all that time. Spitting distance. She's broomstick-thin and her lips are barely visible. She went to Mt. Holyoke and her father is a noted pediatrician who, from all I've heard, I wouldn't let within ten feet of any child.

Jackie is thirty-one years old and headed big places. Willie and I are being left in her Chanel-scented dust.

She tells us she would like to thank us one by one but time doesn't permit. Time does permit her, however, to thank the most important people: Regine, Betsy, Byron, etc. She opens the box and it's from Tiffany . . . it's a gold desk plate that says: JACKIE WOOTEN, SENIOR EDITOR GODDAMMIT! It costs over $500.

"I love it!" she says with an excited weepy voice that suggests if she does love it, she doesn't love it very much.

I have nothing that costs over $500 except the apartment I live in.

It's breaking up now. People are table-hopping or slumped over in their chairs, exhausted and full.

Marjorie Millet slips her prodigious figure out the door alone and I wonder if I should follow but I know I shouldn't. And I don't want to anyway. Or maybe I do.

"I'm going to miss you, Zeke," Jackie says when I hug her. I tell her I'll miss her too and that it's been great working with her. You do a great job, I say. My voice sounds, if not all choked up, then mostly choked up.

"We'll have lunch sometime, right?" I say.

She nods.

Jackie Wooten feels like a skeleton when I hug her.

The next day I'm at the office sitting with Willie . . . I'm on the empty desk facing him, formerly Jackie's. There's nothing there now, not the little round mirror she would look in every half-hour to check her makeup, not the always freshly polished silver vase she would look into every five minutes to check her hair.

"Do we know who's replacing her yet?" I ask Willie.

"Some guy named Mark Larkin . . . I think he's at *She*."

"Mark Larkin? That name means nothing to me."

Someone from the art department, a tall pale neuter type named Charles, comes over with a 10 x 13 manila envelope; we're supposed to open it, throw in a few dollars for the Tiffany present, check our names off, and pass the envelope on to the next person. By the time it reaches us, it's already pretty stuffed.

"It'll be different without Jackie here," Willie says. He squeezes the envelope as if it were a plump giggling baby. "I hope I get along with this Mark Larkin guy." Willie has clear blue eyes, straight shoulder-length blond hair, a strong sincere face. I think he really does want to get along with whoever Mark Larkin is.

I take the envelope and undo the red string.

"Do you feel like having lunch out today?" I ask Willie.

"Lunch would be nice. So would a new tie."

I look into the envelope, a jumbo salad of fives, tens, and twenties. I take out two tens, pocket them, and pass the envelope to Willie after checking off my name. He takes out the same amount and reties the red string.

"You know, I never really liked Jackie," he says.

"No. Neither did I."

2

My name is Zachary Arlen Post and I was born and raised in Oyster Bay, a very well-to-do town on Long Island's North Shore. Gatsby and Nick Carraway summered in West Egg, Tom and Daisy Buchanan in the more upscale East Egg; well, Oyster Bay is one Egg geographically east of them and, socially, if I may say so, An Egg Too Far.

The house I grew up in was an imposing, exquisite three-story Georgian behemoth—once occupied by a cousin of Rutherford B. Hayes—perched high on a chain of rugged bluffs and staring out over the tranquil buffalo-shaped bay like a diligent sentinel. In every room—and there were quite a few of them—you could hear the rhythmic lilt of waves rolling in and out, sounding like cymbals tickled by a feather, as well as the occasional belch of foghorn; during yachting season the water blossomed with reds, blues, yellows, and oranges as sails billowed and darted and danced across the shimmering sea. We were surrounded by seven acres of perfectly manicured landscape; azaleas, irises, lilacs, sunflowers, and zinnias bloomed every spring and summer, and sycamores and elms brooded over the greensward, breaking the house and the land into a fragrant backgammon board of sun and shadow and sending serpentine stripes zigzagging down the bluffs to the sea. Arlen was my mother's maiden name; she hails from the Rhode Island Arlens, who came over in the seventeenth century and made a killing in real estate and, some time later, in steel.

My father was R. J. (Robertson James) Post, the brilliant but temperamental (i.e., psychotic) architect who designed summer houses for the filthy rich from Maine and Cape Cod down to the Florida Keys. If you have passed through Kennebunkport, Maine, or Naples, Florida, you have no doubt seen his work, the best of which was done in the 1950s.

A monograph on him published in the mid-seventies states that several of his more brilliant projects were never realized because he often had affairs with the daughters of the men who were paying him. Some of these girls were fifteen years old.

He was fifty-five when I was born and died when I was in my early teens. I have no brothers or sisters.

My mother now lives among the upper crust in Palm Beach, trying on and then usually buying expensive clothing and jewelry, eating delicate pastries, driving around in a golf cart with the Mercedes logo on it, going to auctions and dog shows, and playing an usually savage brand of bridge. She's had four facelifts, I hear, and is seeing some Greek playboy, the nephew of a feta cheese magnate. She and I never speak. She has six Afghan hounds and five bichon frises and when she dies, all the money will go to them.

I attended a now-defunct boarding school in Oak Park, Illinois, modeled after England's Winchester College, and studied Latin and Greek there and read Macaulay, Burke, Carlyle, and Pepys and was captain of my debating team; I read and sometimes translated Ovid, Racine, Virgil, Pliny, and Livy and I won an obscure award for a translation of some of the early satires of Plautus.

I went to Colgate, then took a year at Liverpool University and wrapped up my education at Berkeley.

I am a five handicap and have convinced myself that were it not for a bone spur in my left elbow, I might have turned pro.

A friend of mine from Colgate landed a job at *Newsweek* and got me work there, writing and researching and doing little editorial things.

I stayed there for a forgettable year and applied for work at Versailles Publishing, Inc. The opportunity I'd been waiting for.

I started at *Here* magazine, a century-old monthly devoted to architecture and interior design. I believe the fact that my father was R. J. Post

(I did mention that little tidbit on my interview) helped me land a job as an editorial assistant.

After a year and a half (I was now an editorial assistant at *Zest* magazine) I heard there was an assistant editor position opening up at *It*. I applied, had a boozy, flirty lunch with Regine Turnbull and Betsy Butler at Cafe 51, and got the job. Within a year I was promoted to associate editor.

{ }

OKAY, now the truth.

My real name is Allen Zachary Post but the ZAP monogram was too irresistible so I pulled the switcheroo when I was fifteen; on the scrawny side, riddled with zits, addicted to Classic Rock, Green Lantern comic books, and Yodels, it seemed the thing to do. I never changed it legally but Zachary Allen Post is the name on my driver's license and all my bank accounts (all two of them).

My mother's first name is Sally and her maiden name was Huggins. She's a bookkeeper in the garment business and lives alone in Queens now, in a chestnut-colored building overlooking the BQE. There's an immense advertisement for a toaster company on her building; a slice of white bread toasted golden brown is popping out of a svelte chrome toaster. The ad is about eight stories high and the toaster company went out of business more than thirty years ago. My mom's bedroom window is right on the crust. So perhaps she really does live among the upper crust after all.

She reads *Soap Opera Digest* and watches reruns of *Murder She Wrote*. She gets stuff from the Home Shopping Network.

My father is still alive. (My parents are divorced.) With his brother Jimmy, he owns two swimming-pool supply stores on Long Island (The Wet Guys I and II; they sell chlorine, bathing suits, rafts and inner tubes and waterwings, electric bug zappers, pool ladders, beach towels, bulky bags of Frog-A-Way repellent, algae remover, etc., and in the winter they scrape by, selling snow shovels and sleds). His name is Bob Post and he walks around in white shoes and blue slacks, wearing a New York Islanders jacket and a Mets cap. He remarried six years ago. His wife, Sheila, is a receptionist at a beauty parlor in Rockville Centre and—this won't be too surprising—they met at a bar in a bowling alley. He sometimes smells like chlorine and she sometimes smells like hair spray and the combination working together isn't very pleasant.

I've never played golf. Not even mini-golf.

I grew up in Massapequa, not far from the railroad station. I shared the downstairs floor with my younger sister (she's a physical therapist now, living in Houston and engaged to another physical therapist); there was a living room, my parents' bedroom upstairs, a kitchen and adjoining dining room. There was a small lawn in the back and the smell of car fumes was everywhere and the grass grew in brown and limp. A next-door neighbor who used to give me yo-yos and Slinkies turned out to be a lieutenant in the Genovese crime family and was found murdered in the back of a Lincoln Continental with his head on his lap.

People who grow up in Massapequa and Massapequa Park desperately want to leave, if only to escape to a town whose name they can spell correctly. (I've never been to Oyster Bay and my mother pronounces it à la Ed Norton in *The Honeymooners*: Erster Bay.)

When I was a kid my father drove a brown Impala. Now he has a blue Cutlass. Blue, the color of a swimming pool.

We didn't have a pool. "Those who sell, don't have," my dad said more than once, summing up this natatorial irony. We did have one of those round tubs you filled up with a hose and then stashed in the basement for the rest of the year where it would overgrow with mildew, the gray-brown residue of our dysfunctional plashings and strained wet merriment.

My parents, though, are decent, honest people and I speak to them regularly. But if either of them ever dropped in on me at work, I'm afraid to say that I would have to go after them with the nearest scissors or three-hole punch, with intent to kill.

They're very proud of me.

I've never been to Colgate or Berkeley or Oak Park, Illinois, or to Liverpool University. I chose those places because hardly anybody at Versailles Publishing has been there either. Harvard and Yale were way too risky, as were Oxford and Cambridge, as were Andover and Choate. Even Berkeley was a little dicey and I'm always ready to make a run for it just in case someone tells me he went there or knows someone who did.

I don't know if I can even bring myself to say where I did go to college. It's almost too sad to relate.

After college I spent three years at a little residential newspaper in Manhattan called *East Side Life*, a tabloid given away for free, placed in piles in apartment building lobbies, magazine stores, in banks near automated teller machines, and in coffee shops near the cash register. Half of the newspaper is restaurant reviews and local color (or, as we called it, local pallor) and the other half is ads for real estate, escort services, Middle Eastern movers, and Asian futon stores.

With my one good suit and an utterly false résumé in hand, I went to my interview at Versailles. If they called up Colgate, Berkeley, or Liverpool U., I wouldn't get the job. Fine. I had nothing to lose. And they couldn't call up that boarding school in Oak Park where I translated Ovid and Pliny because there was no such place.

I did have a friend at *Newsweek* and I gave Versailles Human Resources his phone number. He worked in the traffic department and I had alerted him that someone might call. He went along with the story.

I was in.

It's true that I worked at *Here* for a while and it was boring—mind-numbingly, lethally boring, except for the fact that I was constantly on my toes lest someone discover that I didn't really belong there.

(The only thing lower than wasting away at *Here* is working for Versailles' sister publication company, Federated Magazines, which puts out magazines for Boy Group-obsessed teens [*Teen Time*], gun enthusiasts [*Bullet and Barrel*], and people waiting in salons to get a haircut [*Do's*]— they're in another building and I think that building might be in another city. Nobody ever talks about them—it's a superstition. I don't even want to mention them.)

My boss at *Here* was a sixty-year-old French woman named Jeanne LeClerque; she had painted-on yellow eyebrows that resembled the McDonald's arches. At *Here* I did . . . *things*. I read things, opened things, wrote little things, passed things along, and collected the biggest paychecks I'd ever seen up to then.

Here, though, is where you either begin or end up. But being transferred there is so ignominious that usually you just quit instead; it's like being a baseball manager for twenty years and then finding yourself a first base coach.

I live in the low Twenties between Second and Third Avenue, in a drab and dreary brick building whose facade has been called brown, black, orange, red, gray, and white, depending on who is looking at it, the time of day, and the weather. They're all correct somehow . . . it really isn't any particular color at all, except maybe the color of a dirty old rubber ball with no bounce left. I'm the youngest person in it and I better move the hell out before that changes. If you don't get out by the time you're thirty-five, it seems, you're going to die of old age in it.

When our toilets don't flush or when we see mice, tenants ask each other, "Hey, do you know if the super's still alive?"

But it really isn't so bad. The rent is cheap. I probably should feel worse about living here than I do.

{ }

YOU CAN usually judge people by where they live, what their apartments or houses look like, how they dress, by the company they keep, how much they make, who they're going out with or are married to, where they sit in an office and with whom they sit.

I lose on most counts.

I share a cream-colored cubicle space, the size of a very large closet, with Nolan Tomlin, a North Carolinian and graduate of Emory University. He's a real loser, with an insufferably boring wife who invites me over to join them for dinner—I did go one time and, during the soup, expertly feigned a terrible migraine and excused myself. Unfortunately, Nolan's desk and my desk face each other so I'm stuck looking at him nine hours a day. Unless I do something very obvious like turn my desk around so that I face the wall point-blank, I'm forced to look at him.

Nolan holds the same position I do; we're both associate editors of "In Closing," the breezy, shallow ten to fifteen page section that follows, in order, the table of contents and masthead, the contributors page, the monthly letter from the editor-in-chief (which I occasionally write), the "Starters" section, and the meatier features section. And of course, the two-and-a-half pounds of ads.

Nolan is always writing short stories and novels and sending them out and getting rejected everywhere. When he has spare time at work—which is a lot of the time—he'll write what he calls his "fictions." He'll conspicuously swivel his computer screen around so nobody else can see it and he assumes a hunched-over, conspiratorial pose—he looks a bit like a squirrel pecking at a nut when he does this. When I have to go over to his desk, he'll click his mouse quickly and make the screen go blank.

But maybe he isn't writing . . . maybe he's playing Donkey Kong.

At first I read some of his fictions. Why Nolan cared about what I thought of his work, I don't know (he might as well have shown it to one of the security guards in the lobby downstairs). I went from telling him his work was good to saying it wasn't bad and then finally: "It's really somewhat interesting." "Really somewhat interesting" seems to have worked—he's never shown me anything since.

His most annoying habit (and he has lots of them) is trying to incorporate long literary-like sentences into everyday speech. But in a fiftieth-floor Manhattan office where sentences are seldom more than six words long, flowery Southern prose tends to stick out and he ends up sounding like an actor reading a hundred-year-old letter in a Ken Burns documentary. About Regine Turnbull, *It*'s terrifying editor-in-chief, Nolan once said: "Her skin is as soft and creamy as freshly mashed potatoes but there is an inner hardness to her more akin to cold steel than satin or silk."

(I know exactly what he's doing: he's test-driving his fictions on me. If I raise one eyebrow, he leaves the sentence in. If I raise two, it will get some reworking. If I raise no eyebrow at all, it's out. I'd have the two most powerful eyebrows in literature today, if only Nolan would ever get published.)

I've always regarded him as somebody who has been injected into my life only to be suddenly pulled out of it, a *Star Trek* extra who gets zapped out of the script within twenty seconds.

But what I'd like to know is, what the hell is taking so long?

Okay, I went to Hofstra University. Hofstra, which seemed to be all parking lot and no classrooms, all teaching assistants and no professors, all cars but no students, not quite a junior college and not quite a real one either. Sitting in a classroom there was like being in the bleachers at a Friday night Mets game except perhaps a little noisier and windier. One of the most commonly dreamt nightmares is of the dreamer suddenly finding himself in a classroom; he has not attended the class all semester, has forgotten he was even enrolled in the class and has not studied one iota, and is suddenly facing a final exam. But this nightmare is precisely how I spent three years of my waking life.

So there.

Pretty pathetic, isn't it?

But I'm trying to change all that.

{ }

I'm desperately trying.

And just when things seem to be going smoothly . . .

It is wrong and impolite, I know, to judge people by first impressions, but when I am being introduced to Mark Larkin and shaking his cold clammy right hand, my exact thoughts are: "This guy is a really serious asshole and a lot of people are going to hate him."

Betsy Butler introduces him to me. It's his grand tour of the office — I'd taken mine on my own first day at *It* about three and a half years ago, also with our managing editor as a guide. Betsy introduces you to every editor, every art person, every associate editor and editorial assistant and editorial associate, every ad sales and marketing person, etc. Within five minutes you've met seventy impeccably dressed, bright, splendidly mannered people and within ten minutes you can't distinguish any of them.

"This is Mark Larkin," Betsy, a fleshy divorced forty-five-year-old mother of two, says to me. "He'll be joining us." It's a bright morning in late June and through the windows behind them the sun crests over the Chrysler Building.

I size him up: wavy light brown hair, puffy reddish skin, thick glasses, rubbery lips, maybe queer, maybe not, maybe a quarter Jewish but probably not and if so, he wouldn't admit it under torture. But Harvard, definitely.

But the thing that strikes you right away is his uncanny resemblance to Teddy Roosevelt, as if they had poured the slurry of Mark Larkin's liquefied flesh into a Teddy Roosevelt mold. Mark Larkin is about twenty-seven years old but he looks like the older presidential Teddy, not the younger one who wrastled with buffalo, bears, rattlesnakes, and nasty guys named Black Bart.

(No one ever has to say to Mark Larkin, "Hey, you know you're the spitting image of Teddy Roosevelt." Because you don't have to; it would be like telling a Siamese twin, "Hey, did you know that you have another person who looks exactly like you attached to your hip?")

"Mark's been at *She* for what? . . . a year?" Betsy says. "He was an assistant editor there."

"A year and a half," Mark Larkin offers, pronouncing half like "hawf," not quite English and not quite American but something geographically in between . . . maybe this is the way they sound in the Azores.

I nod and say, "Oh . . . *She*." As if I don't know this already, as if I, having heard a week before that he'd be joining us, haven't done my research.

(*She* magazine, our biggest seller; circulation: 2,250,000 but slowly falling. Women's fashion, an occasional serious article about something not too serious, some book and music reviews, beauty tips, a lot of gossip and a horoscope, etc., and tons and tons of ads [clothing, wrinkle cream, perfume, cars, cigarettes].)

"Will you be working with Willie Lister?" I ask Mark Larkin, feigning ignorance. I notice Betsy looking at me through the lower part of her bifocals, gauging first reactions.

"Yes, l think I will be," Mark Larkin says, feigning same. This is the first time he flashes his blinding Teddy Roosevelt smile to me and it's big, like a donkey's teeth in a cartoon. His shirt collar is a different color than the rest of his shirt (as it often is) and he wears a red bow tie and suspenders, trying to affect a mild foppish look. That is his look: bow tie and suspenders (he probably refers to them as "braces"). All that's missing is a walking stick and floppy white hat.

I wonder: Has Willie already met him? After a sentence more from Betsy I slip away and make my way down a few hallways, moving through the Black Hole for a shortcut. Willie is reading a magazine, his feet up on his desk, his tie loose. Willie is also on my level, an associate editor, one notch below an editor, two below a senior editor, but basically only a notch above the gutter and two above being a proofreader. And like me, he's going nowhere. But—as he's been at *It* two more years than I—I'm getting there faster than he is.

"Oh my God, guess what?!!" I say to him with all the breathlessness of "The president's been shot!"

I notice a yellow-brown leather envelope, some magazines and a pad and some pens on Jackie Wooten's old desk, the first sign of human life, Post-Jackie. And the computer is on.

"What? Teddy Roosevelt?" Willie sneers. He puts down the magazine he's reading . . . it's the new issue of *Her*, another glossy Versailles woman's magazine, one of about six or seven of that ilk we churn out every month; on the cover of this one a young blond model, clad in yellow, is sucking on a banana that's been dyed black. The cover line is: IS YELLOW THE NEW BLACK?

"You met him, I take it," Willie says. "An asshole. From head to toe."

"You said it."

"He's the kind you have to worry about. In a year he'll be running this place."

"Oh, maybe he won't be so bad," I say, thinking: Yeah, he will be that bad.

Wordlessly Willie and I take in the empty chair and desk. The leather envelope looks dangerously evil to the both of us, pulsing and growing like a tumor. Mark Larkin will be sitting there, eight or more hours a day, five days a week, facing Willie, maybe for the next ten years. The portfolio is like the discarded cocoon he's just been hatched out of.

"Good luck," I say.

∫ ∫

BEFORE lunch that day Betsy Butler ambles over to my desk. She's *It*'s second in command and often must tend to squabbles, hissy fits, long-running feuds. It's a disagreeable business for her but is something she was born to do.

"I hope you and Mark Larkin are going to get along," she says to me, tapping a pen against my computer monitor.

"I hope so too."

"But you know, I just can't see it happening."

"Me neither."

"Make it happen, okay?"

About an hour after our introduction I'm coming out of a small meeting in a windowless beige conference room and I see Mark Larkin, his face flushed, his lips trembling. He's rubbing the top of his head, looking like a monkey trying to work a pocket calculator. I know what the panic is about: coffee.

In a flash I remember my first days at *It*. When I was the New Boy.

"I'm warning you, Zeke, you're going to be getting Regine her coffee for a while," Willie had said to me then.

"How does she like it?"

"A little milk and about a pound of sugar. That's how her hair stays so frosty."

So for three weeks—until a Newer Person finally came along—I got Regine her coffee. There being no coffee machine on our floor (there is a refrigerator; inside are usually thirty bottles of mineral water, lined up perfectly like soldiers about to parade), I had to go to the coffee-and-dough-nuts guy in the lobby, fifty floors down. This happened four or five times a day and I realized after a week that this was why there was no coffee machine on the floor, so that Regine could pull this demeaning little stunt. It was her cozy little welcome mat, a bear trap hidden in the fuzzy pile.

But I don't think that anybody has warned Mark Larkin and I doubt he's ever worked a menial job in his life. It must be quite a little jolt, him writing one-page pieces about models and actresses and penning little movie reviews and now going down fifty floors to get a cup of coffee—which Regine never finishes anyway.

"Where's the coffee machine up here?" he asks me.

The whites of his eyes are throbbing and vast and his red ears resemble freshly dissected tomatoes.

"Why?"

"Regine wants coffee."

"She's having you get coffee? And you're actually *doing* it?"

He shrugs, shifts his position a little.

This might be fun.

"Who told you," I ask, "she wanted coffee? Was it Velma?"

"Yes."

"Velma's just joking around. Don't get any coffee."

I've got him by the nuts. I happen to be feeling a little triumphant anyway now; Regine and Sheila Stackhouse have just agreed that the one-page piece I'm writing for the "Starters" section about Leroy White, the TV actor, should be a feature, maybe even a cover story for a future issue. I've never had a cover story at *It* . . . this is always a jewel in anyone's crown.

"What if Velma rawlly meant it?" Mark Larkin asks. Even though he's petrified, even though his voice quavers, he somehow keeps up that Azores accent.

"She didn't. Maybe Velma wants the coffee and she's just telling you that Regina wants it so that you'll get it."

He makes a crude remark with an exaggerated redneck Southern accent, with Velma Watts the target (something like "Well, I'm certainly not getting a nigra her coffee!"), meant to ally himself with me. He looks around first, not yet knowing that Velma is the only black person on the floor.

"You shouldn't say shit like that," I advise him.

"Please tell me where the coffee machine is . . ."

"There is none. You have to go to the nice Arabian gentleman in the lobby. A spot of milk and a pound of sugar. That's how her hair stays so frosty."

He trots off—almost spastically—toward the elevator to get Regine her coffee.

At the end of his first day he and I wind up going down in the elevator together. When the elevator doors open and the lobby spreads out before us—women in white linen, men with their jackets draped over their shoulders, messengers in Day-Glo bike shorts, all scattering and crossing paths—I ask Mark Larkin where he lives and when he tells me it's in my direction, I tell him I'll be walking home (I don't want to get stuck taking the subway with him). His bow tie and suspenders are still perfectly in place but I imagine the underarms of his pale green gabardine suit are soaked; first days at new jobs are like that and this is June and about 85 degrees outside.

"I sure owe you one," he says to me on the corner when we're splitting up. "For the coffee."

He sure owes me one, he said . . .

But what exactly did he mean by that?

I slowly walk a few blocks downtown to Grand Central Station and then go down into the subway, figuring he must be well on his way home by then. When I get on, the car is crammed, airless, and sweaty, one of those rickety number six trains from the 1920s, the kind that Dick Powell sang "I Only Have Eyes For You" in. Through the vapor of slack, haggard faces I spot Mark Larkin. I see only his profile . . . he's mostly turned away from me. Coming out of his leather envelope are magazines like *The Economist, The Spectator, The Nation,* and maybe even *Jane's Defense Weekly.*

If he actually reads all this, I figure, rather than just makes sure he's seen carrying it around, he might be someone to reckon with. Pretty formidable.

A few days after this I run into Tommy Land, who used to be an associate editor at *It* but has, thanks to some masterful brown nosing and a deft marriage (to a *Her* editor), swiftly ascended through the ranks.

"Do you know someone named Mark Larkin?" I ask him.

"I sure do," Tommy says, sticking a newspaper under his arm. "He's the kind who's going to go places quickly."

And then Tommy slips away, quickly going someplace himself.

{ }

BEING THE New Boy or New Girl is hell—there is no colder, more impersonal, more unfriendly place to work than at Versailles. In my first week at *It* Betsy Butler smiled at me and she looked like she'd just fractured her big toe. Once in a while I slip up and smile at someone in a hallway. When they look at me as though I'm complete lunatic, I quickly remember where I am.

I felt like a phantom (and a very poorly dressed one) my first few weeks at *Here*. I didn't know what to do and nobody told me anything. Things would be dumped in my lap and I had to guess how to proceed; should it be photocopied, faxed, thrown out, passed along? One time an editor threw a black patent leather belt in my in-box. Was I supposed to *edit* it??

I gathered enough nerve to approach her at her desk.

"Marguerite?"

"Yes?" She wasn't looking up at me.

"You dropped a belt off in my in-box?"

"That's right, I did."

"What am I supposed to do with it?"

"Take it to a leather repair shop, get it fixed, and then put a T and E slip through with the receipt in my name," Marguerite said, her eyes never once looking up from the copy she was either editing or obliterating wholesale.

(One of my fantasies, if I ever become a senior editor, is to dump a black patent leather belt in Marguerite's in-box. But there would be no payoff—she wouldn't recognize me, never having seen me in the first place.)

Yes, some people have become good friends, some couples have even met there, married (and divorced), but genuine warmth is another thing entirely. And it's not just taking belts in to be fixed; it's telling the New Person to make copies and send faxes, to get coffee, to run some personal errand, to make restaurant reservations or cancel them, to clean their desk, to get their feet off their desk, to call a messenger, to arrange for dry cleaning to be picked up or even to pick up dry cleaning.

New People, after four weeks of this, aren't so new anymore.

} {

"How do you use one of these infernal contraptions?" Mark Larkin asks me with a smile, not one of his blazing supernova jobs but more of the trying-to-be-buddies type, but still condescending in its own way. I'm at a fax machine, about to send a letter, and he looks very lost.

"You really don't know?"

"At *She* there were others to do it." He pauses and arches his eyebrows. "There are African Americans there."

(What is it about me that makes him think I'm such a racist? Or is it just him, one white male talking to another white male, playing the percentages?)

"You can get in trouble with Human Resources for that kind of talk," I say.

He shrugs. Perhaps by now he already suspects I'm not too serious about my work.

I guide him through the faxing process, half-expecting his tongue to be dangling out of his mouth like a child practicing penmanship, but when it's his turn to send the fax—it's a request for a quickie interview with an infamous art forger now dying of cancer in a Rome prison—he balks.

"I don't believe you," he says.

He doesn't believe that you put the paper in the machine facedown.

"You're right," I say sarcastically, "I'm just playing a joke on you."

So he faxes his letter face up. I gloat guiltlessly in my own mischievousness.

A week later, I notice, he's still faxing things the wrong way.

He didn't get much accomplished the first few weeks and he never landed the interview with the forger.

But I did.

3

It's 9:30 and I've been at work a half-hour already—I always make sure to get in before Nolan does so I can experience the delight of being here without him for a while.

"I just came up in the elevator with Gaston," he drawls.

(Not even a good morning out of him—but I don't say good morning to him either.)

"Really?" I don't look up from my newspaper.

Nolan urgently wants me to perk up but I refuse. It's important at Versailles to not be impressed by anything or anyone; if the news came across the wire that North Dakota had just bombed South Dakota off the map, you'd be expected to say, "Hmmm, curious, that" and then just get on with your work.

Over an ecru cubicle wall, a tuft of wild wavy red hair barely restrained by a violet scrunchy bounces past. Marjorie Millet. I see that and swallow hard and the violet scrunchy makes a sharp turn and the blazing red tuft vanishes.

"He was alone," Nolan says.

Gaston Moreau is always alone. Versailles' legendary elderly (and semiretired) creative director and I have never spoken to each other, he being the most important person in the building, me not being remotely close to being so.

Nolan jams a corn muffin into his mouth and crumbs fall like hail to the stack of newspapers and magazines on the desk.

"How was his breath?" I ask.

"The whole elevator reeked . . . like a fetid mound of two-week-old garbage in a back alley in the middle of an Alabama August."

A young woman, about twenty-two years old with very pleasant angular features and heavy-lidded eyes, comes by and places a small brown package in my in-basket, already teeming with unread, untouched stuff (articles, layouts, newspapers, magazines and more magazines). She smiles and goes away. She has long wavy brown hair and, at about five-foot-eight, falls easily into the preferred Versailles height range for women: five-foot-six to six-foot-one. She's cute and this is the first time I've seen her. She must be very new . . . the smile betrays her.

Something catches my eye: the little gray splotch of oil on the cubicle wall where Nolan rests his head. Perhaps it's good he works across from me because his bad manners always make my own pale in comparison. Hitler to my Mussolini.

"He looks unhealthy," Nolan continues. "The bags under his eyes are really heavy. And he's got these huge brown spots, like buckwheat flapjacks burning tar-black on a dry griddle. He might be on his last legs."

"If Gaston were going to die, he'd have done it already. Besides, being semiretired *is* being dead." According to rumor, the man went into his office every day, closed the door, drew the blinds and killed the lights, and napped.

I stick my hand in the already-opened brown package, having a vague idea of what it is: a book in galleys.

It's the new novel by Ethan Cawley, called *Badland*. It smells fresh, like wet ink and glue, and the cover is bright yellow and sticky. A brief note from someone in the publisher's publicity department says: "With the complements of the author." (Jesus, even people who work for book publishers can't spell! But this is from the publicity department so it doesn't count.) I'd given Cawley's last book a bad review, which certainly the reclusive tough-guy author hadn't read or given a shit about.

There is a Post-it note stuck on the cover. It says in small loopy purple handwriting: "Review. For this issue. RT."

Okay, Regine Turnbull. "For this issue" means I have to hurry.

I see something else in my in-box. It's from Sheila, my boss.

"We're holding this for the next issue," she's written on a Post-it note attached to my Q & A with the dying forger in Rome.

But by the next issue the man would be dead.

Sheila Stackhouse, a senior editor, sits just behind our cubicle wall, in a large office with a door, chairs, and a window. She has potted plants near the window (when she goes away I have to water them, but I usually wait until the day before she gets back) and pictures on her desk of her children and husband, three bubbly kids with blond bangs and blue eyes and a bald swarthy man with a heartbreaking frown and distant, forlorn gaze. Her window looks east and on clear days you can see airplanes taking off and landing; sometimes the sun shining down on the Chrysler Building is orange and brilliant, turning it into a lit match.

I walk into her office and stand near her desk while she leaves a message on someone's voice mail.

"We're holding the forger piece?" I ask when she hangs up. My mission is futile but I want her to know that though I'd take it lying down, I might not be flat on my back.

"There's just no room for it," she says.

"The man is on his last legs . . . if it doesn't run now . . ."

"You know how it is. We're close to shipping the issue."

"Maybe it could go into 'Starters.' " "Starters" is where Willie and now Mark Larkin work, another breezy shallow ten-page section.

"Ask Betsy Butler," Sheila says. "Maybe they have a page to bump. But things are very tight."

If the piece somehow gets into "Starters," though, I lose the smarting but somewhat pleasurable sensation of having been rejected for something, of having been treated shabbily. Which is better, getting the piece in or enjoying the hurt of being fucked over?

Suddenly there sounds a loud clattering of clogs and high heels. Heads bob past, voices murmur and mumble, paper is crunched. I stand up and follow the horde.

A meeting.

We are in a corner conference room (a very long room with everything beige except for the long glass table) and Betsy is leading the meeting, holding a pointer and looking like she's diagraming a pick-and-roll play. The Important People are here (not Regine, though; she no longer comes to these meetings) and so are the semi-important people, including Willie, Nolan, Mark Larkin, and myself. Nan Hotchkiss, a features editor so somehow still an important presence despite her aura of disinterest, slurps a light coffee and scribbles in her Filofax, which has come to resemble a triple-decker roast beef sandwich. Byron Poole, *It's* art director, and Roddy Grissom, Jr., the execrable photo editor, stand around a few pieces of paper that have been taped to the wall.

This is the next cover of *It* and we're supposed to come up with something clever and catchy, something that jumps off the page so that the issue follows it and jumps off the stands. The picture is of Anne Touchette, a Hollywood big-shot producer (and currently the most powerful woman in that town), bathing in a solid gold tub brimming over with dollar bills. The photographer exposed about a thousand pieces of film in two hours and Byron and Roddy have narrowed it down to these two pictures; in both, Touchette holds her arms up triumphantly, just a little flab dangling off, but her mouth is open in one shot and closed in the other. The bold italic, scarlet *It* logo is already there in the mock-up; all we have to do is come up with some words or sentences to make it complete. This is a monthly ritual and more often than not is exhausting, sometimes dragging on for hours and even days. (It took five days to settle on BEST BETTE for Bette Midler and WHO ARE YOU KIDMAN? for Nicole Kidman. It seems the worse the cover line, the longer it takes to concoct: HANKS FOR EVERYTHING for Tom Hanks, ELLE ON WHEELS for Elle MacPherson, STONE ALONE for Sharon Stone had taken about a week each.)

Betsy points out to us the one difference in the two shots, something that, given the generous size of Anne Touchette's gaping mouth, is pretty evident.

"Okay," she says, snapping the pointer against her thighs à la Erich von Stroheim or Bobby Knight, "so what do we do with it?"

I look at Willie, who is already sneaking a peek at me. Mark Larkin, yes, wearing a bow tie and suspenders, sits on his immediate right. I know what Willie is thinking: How, with so many pictures to choose from, with paying Harry Brooks (the photographer) over ten grand for the shoot, how with a makeup person, a caterer, a stylist and a hairdresser and a solid gold bathtub, *how could only two pictures be worthy of being on the cover?* Were the rest out of focus? Was Harry's thumb over the lens? A kid with an Instamatic taking pictures of his hamster had better chances.

"Annie Get Your Money," Liz Channing, an associate editor, throws out.

"Soaking in It," I say.

"You Never Touchette Anymore," Willie says. I'm the only one who giggles.

"Anne of the Thousand Ways," Mark Larkin suggests, leaning back and rubbing his chin. Some of the people present look at each other and nod impressed, almost awestruck nods and Willie bites his lower lip until it changes color.

"That's not bad," Nan says.

"Maybe we can do better though?" Betsy Butler says, scratching the cleft in her chin.

"Avenging Annie or something like that" Oliver Osborne, yet another associate editor, throws out, his heart not in it.

"A Touchette of Class?" I suggest. It seems just as dreadful as "Anne of the Thousand Ways," so why not? I realize that Mark Larkin is ahead at this point and I'm determined to not let him win.

Roddy Grissom, Jr. (his father is the publisher of *She*; were it not for that, not only would Roddy not be present, he might be in a lunatic asylum) says, "What's that on her chain?" Byron and Roddy now edge closer to the picture and Betsy follows, so that now nobody else can see anything but their bending backs.

Anne Touchette is naked in the tub but is wearing a gold chain around her neck. The dollar bills end safely above her nipples.

"It's one of those Jewish things," Byron says, looking back at us with dismay, like a doctor finding something disturbing in an X-ray.

"What do you call them?" Roddy says. If anybody knows the answer, they don't want to admit it.

"It's called a *chai*," Willie Lister says. "I think it's Hebrew for life." Willie, with his Episcopalian and Presbyterian bloodlines going back ten generations, can admit to knowing such a thing. His ass is covered.

"Oh, shit," Betsy Butler groans, tossing her pen onto the long glass table so it clangs.

You can't very well have something like that on a cover—nobody says it but everyone knows it, and while I sit here vicariously enjoying this game of parlor anti-Semitism gin rummy, I silently recall the story of when Jeremy David, the clothing designer, insisted on wearing a Jewish star at a Richard Avedon shoot for us . . . but Regine had finally persuaded him, with the promise of discounted ad space, to take it off.

"I didn't even know that, like, Anne Touchette was *Jewish??*" an assistant fashion editor puts in. Somehow anything someone who works in the fashion department says, like, comes out sounding like a *question??*

"Her father is indeed a member of the illustrious long-suffering Hebrew peoples," Mark Larkin tells us. "Her real name is Turtletraum or Teitelbaum or something convoluted like that. He's a lowly Chicago accountant."

Betsy asks Byron if the *chai* is evident in every single picture and Byron looks at Roddy Grissom, Jr., and they both shrug. *How could they not have noticed this?* everyone in the room is thinking. *Why didn't they or the grossly overpaid stylist, makeup person, and hairdresser notice it in the studio? Couldn't the caterer have said something?*

"If it is in every single one of them," Sheila Stackhouse says, "we can always take it out. We can do that, right?"

Byron and Marjorie explain that, with their Photoshop wizardry (they're going to work on her teeth anyway; there's some green gook from the $1,500 worth of catering) they can cover it up with more dollar bills. Roddy says he'll look at the other shots to see if there are any other good ones, ones wherein the offending *chai* isn't rearing its ugly gold Hebraic head right at the potential buyer or subscriber.

So we resume.

"The Magic Touchette," I say. "Queen Anne. Princess Anne. Lady Anne. Living *Chai* on the Hog. A Touchette of Splendor. Anne Overboard. Queen Anne's Face. The Coward *Chais* a Thousand Deaths. A Good Anne Is Hard to Find. Beautiful Touchette. An Anne, a Plan, a Canal. Anne *Alive!* The Right Anne for the Job. Let's Get *Chai*, Man. Bathing Beauty. You Can't Keep a Good Anne Down . . ." It's just coming out of me and I cannot stop but it's clear that Mark Larkin has won the day.

"That asshole," Willie mutters to me, walking out of the meeting. Five yards in front of us Mark Larkin walks between Nan Hotchkiss and Betsy Butler.

"Anne of the Thousand Ways," Willie fumes. "Christ! That sounds so . . . *precious!* I'm becoming ashamed to tell people I work here, which I probably won't be doing soon."

"It is really bad," I say. "I wish I'd come up with it."

"We're all gonna drown in a sea of our own twee-ness. Teddy goddamn Roosevelt."

Willie drinks some water, then angrily crunches the cup. We look at Betsy, Nan, and Mark Larkin walking down a corridor. Betsy casually drapes an arm over his shoulder.

"We're all dead meat," Willie says.

{   }

A FEW minutes after the meeting breaks up, I'm circulating around the floor. Actually I have nothing to do, which happens often, sometimes for as much as four hours a day. I'll walk around in a hurry, to the fax machine, to one of the five copiers, or just around and around, striding my way with no goal in sight except to kill time and appear very busy.

After a few turns I see Marjorie talking to Leslie Usher-Soames, an assistant designer, in front of the women's room. They both are wearing black. Leslie holds a small bottle of mineral water and Marjorie one of those plastic coffee cups that look like space capsules from the Mercury program. Marjorie stands a good four inches taller than Leslie.

"There's a New Girl," Marjorie informs me, raising her thick auburn eyebrows. "Have you met her? She's at Regine's copier."

"I think I've seen her," I answer.

I don't want Marjorie to see me being interested in the New Girl. She's dangerous enough without being provoked.

"Her father is Jimmy Kooper," Marjorie says.

(Jimmy Kooper is the top lawyer in the company and has somehow managed to make himself feared and loathed by people who have never met him, including me.) "So that's how she got the job," I say.

And a few minutes later . . .

With one hand Ivy Kooper is trying to pull a ripped piece of paper out of the jaws of a copier and with the other she twirls a long strand of wavy brown hair.

The New Girl.

"You need help?" I offer with a shy-looking smile.

"I'm making copies for Regine. Or at least I'm trying to . . ."

"She wanted you to copy a shredded piece of paper? Not very thoughtful of her."

She makes a funny face and tells me that it's ripped *now* but wasn't when Regine's secretary had handed it to her.

She's an editorial intern, having recently graduated from college, one of the ten colleges that everyone important who works in the company has been to. She wears a maroon skirt and beige cotton top and her hair is just a touch on the stringy side. She doesn't look the Versailles part yet (which would be: wearing all or mostly black, having hair you could see your reflection in, flashy but not garish lipstick, and being five pounds skinnier). With a pair of Converse sneakers on, she certainly isn't wearing the right shoes. And what really betrays her: she's friendly and has a sweet disposition.

I open up the copier and tighten something. Some women, I've learned, detest having men fix things for them; others positively wet themselves over it. I've got Ivy pegged for the wet-themselves type but I wouldn't bet on this six months down the line.

I shut the copier door with a bang and sail the paper through. (Regine is ordering a case of expensive wine for Donna Reems, the photographer; that was the paperwork.) Marjorie and Leslie Usher-Soames suddenly wheel around the corner. Marjorie smiles teasingly when she sees me with Ivy (Leslie's face stays emotionless) and I feel my face turn red, as if a brother of mine had caught me sniffing his daughter's panties.

They turn another corner and vanish.

I ask Ivy how she likes working at *It* after all of two hours and she says she likes it a lot.

"Honestly? Are we talking about the right place?"

"Well, it's kind of strange here."

"Hardly anybody says hello or anything, right?"

"Where did everybody go just now? Was there a fire drill?"

It takes a moment but I gather that, with everyone in the cover meeting, she must have thought the place had been completely emptied out. All she saw was vacated chairs and blinking computers . . . nobody had told her a thing and so she'd just sat down and waited for people to reappear.

"And," Ivy tells me, "so far, like, twenty women have told me how to fix my hair and do my lipstick and eyes."

"This is normal here. On my first day some guy told me my tie just didn't fit in. I told him I liked it. But when I got home I burned the thing."

She tells me it's the first job she's ever had in her life. That doesn't surprise me, she being Jimmy Kooper's daughter. I tell her I was at *It* for three weeks before everybody finally became convinced I wasn't a messenger wandering around looking for the bathroom.

Marjorie comes back, pokes her head around a wall (bending over like that, her breasts swing like a sack of potatoes), and says, "Zack, there's a meeting . . . if you can tear yourself away from her?" Then she goes away again.

Willie Lister comes striding down the hallway, headed toward the meeting. I notice his fists are clenched, which means he's torturing himself over something. Then a few seconds later Mark Larkin, adjusting his bow tie like Franklin Pangborn in a Preston Sturges movie, struts by, sees us, and nods.

I suggest to Ivy that we go out sometime for a quick lunch so that I can explain the inner workings of the place and the copying machine. (I prefaced it with: "Usually people who ask other people out on their first day are mashers or psychotic stalkers . . .") In a way I want her to gently blow me off but she doesn't. And the way she smiles so sweetly strikes me as somewhat sad. Sweetness didn't belong in this company or in the building, not even on a quick visit.

So now I have a "date" to look forward to, I guess.

Nightingale-Bamford. That's where Ivy Kooper had gone to high school. Nightingale-Bamford. Like Brearley and Birch Wathen, it's one of those twenty thousand-year-old super-Waspy girls schools in Manhattan that costs a few million dollars a year to attend and churns out debutantes, anorexics, Prozac and Valium addicts, charity-ball givers, horse breeders, interior decorators, boutique owners, self-hating Jewesses, manic-depressives, and obsessive-compulsives who vacuum the same carpet corner every twenty minutes.

Nightingale-Bamford! Nightingale-Bamford. Brearley! Birch Wathen! Birch Breargale. *It Was the Bamingale.* Galingbrear Nightwath. A Nightingbirch Breared in Bamgale Square . . .

After Ivy told me she'd gone to Nightingale-Bamford it was several days before I could stop singing it and jumbling it over and over again in my head.

And besides, as I said, she has a sweet disposition.

⟩   ⟨

TOWARD THE END of that day—maybe ten minutes before I left—I walk over to Willie's desk to talk something over. Since Mark Larkin moved into Jackie Wooten's space, I haven't been coming over so much. There's just something about him.

Neither Willie nor Mark Larkin is there. They're probably in a small meeting with Betsy Butler. I think of Willie sitting in a room with Mark Larkin, Willie's legs shaking nervously, wanting to throttle his new coworker.

I see something in Mark Larkin's in-box. The sharp corner of a bright yellow rectangle covered neatly with paper and magazines. I walk over to the desk and slide the papers and magazines aside.

It is *Badland* by Ethan Cawley, in galleys, wet and sticky. There's a small note from the publicity department. "With the complements of . . ."

Is Mark Larkin reviewing the same book?

How many people does Regine Tumbull have on this one thing?

For the rest of the day I keep thinking about that half-inch of yellow. I toss and turn in bed for half an hour before falling asleep—usually I'm asleep the second my head hits the pillow—my thoughts wavering between Wathingford Nightgale and the sight of that small mustard-colored corner, the shape of an arrowhead, which for a few minutes seemed sharp enough and hard enough to stab me through and through.

{ }

THEY GOT rid of the green gook and gave the eyes a fleck of turquoise where there was only brown, wiped out two blemishes off her cleavage, and covered up the *chai* with some more dollar bills.

They went with "Anne of the Thousand Ways" and Anne Touchette never noticed or never complained that something had been taken out of the picture.

4

I DESPERATELY want to marry Leslie Usher-Soames.

A few months ago she was the New Girl. I remember Marjorie introducing us and an innocuous thirty-second conversation. I don't remember where we were, what we said, or anything else other than Marjorie's comment to me afterwards: "You touch her, I'll cut off your scrotum." She was holding an X-Acto blade at the time and actually made the surgical gesture. I winced.

I do remember where I was when I first met Marjorie Millet. (Rhymes with "spill it." Her father changed his name from Morris Millstein to Martin Millet in the 1950s. He worked at Versailles many years ago—when lots of other heterosexual men did too—and learned his lesson.) I was coming out of the men's bathroom and, as sometimes happens when I'm wearing a suit, I was so preoccupied with properly tucking my shirt in, I'd forgotten to zip up. There's this statuesque woman, about five-foot-nine, in a black skirt, black tights, and a red silk top with three big black buttons and she's got the wildest hair I've ever seen, fire engine red and bubbling out of her scalp like champagne; she's holding, of course, a bottle of mineral water and she sees me come out of the bathroom and the door hasn't even closed behind me and she says, "Your fly's open, Buster."

The door closed and hit my backside and I looked down and she was right! But it wasn't as if half my shirttail was sticking out of my fly like an elephant's trunk. You could hardly see any trace of the actual zipper.

"Hi. I'm Marjorie Millet," she said. "I work here now."

I reached for her hand to shake it. She was unbelievably built and her hair was crazy and beautiful but her skin was a little bit craggy and her slitted green eyes were set too closely together.

"Did you wash?" she asked me as my hand waited for hers.

"Yeah."

"Well, then, I'm not shaking your hand," she said with a smile. She walked away. That was three years ago. I remember everything about it.

But back to the present . . .

I'm in the art department and Leslie and Marjorie are talking to Byron Poole, the art director. Not much is going on and people are relaxed (Regine is in Paris, at some fashion shows). I'm barely listening to anybody but all of a sudden I hear Leslie say:

". . . and my grandfather was fairly good friends with Winston Churchill."

I'm facing away from them when she says it and it's a good thing because I feel myself change color.

I compose myself and turn around and look Leslie in her pearl gray eyes. She's sitting at her desk, her computer screen washing her little nose in sapphire blue, and I say: "You're kidding, aren't you?"

"Ackshilleh, I'm not kidding a'tall."

And that was it: Winston Churchill.

Not that she doesn't have lots of other things going for her. She's intelligent and a very talented designer and pretty, although a bit on the skinny side. I think her best feature might be her skin but what you can do with skin, when it gets down to it, it's hard to say. She's about five-foot-four and has—permit me this one crudity about my future wife (I'm serious about this marriage thing)—small perky breasts that point up like faces looking at a man about to jump off a building.

The accent helps too.

She's British, of course (about a quarter of the company is British, the other three quarters wish they were) and she has that delightful, remarkable way that some British women have of gliding two inches over the ground.

Her family owns a mansion in the Boltons in South Kensington. I imagine that the outside of the place is the same color as her skin. I suppose there's also a big Manderley-type house in the country somewhere, with a name straight out of an E.M. Forster book, and that the walls are hung with paintings, as tall as giraffes, of her ancestors going back twenty generations.

And her accent . . . she sounds a little bit like a BBC reporter reporting from an exotic trouble spot, surrounded by Chechen rebels or Tamil Tigers, and a little bit like a lead singer with Pepto Bismol–pink hair from a new wave group in the 1980s.

It's all perfect.

"Did you ever meet Winston Churchill?" I ask her. Others watch and listen but they fade out.

"Oh no. He was long gone before I happened along. Quite gone. But he did sleep in my room a few times. Daddy says if you breathe in deeply enough you can smell his cigar smoke."

I stand a good three thousand miles away from that room but still I'm tempted to draw in a long deep breath.

Leslie doesn't show much of herself at work, in terms of her body and her personality. She's either very demure or reserved . . . or it's possible that there's just not that much to show. All you can see are her thin wrists and hands and maybe two inches of some calf, on a good day. And her face, which is as white and soft as a cloud. A brunette (with some henna highlights), she has the ultimate Versailles Publishing, Inc. hair: silky, soft, and manageable. It's always—and I mean *always*—in a ponytail.

That second when I heard her say her grandfather knew Winston Churchill . . . it was a momentous occasion in my life, as if a five-ton bronze sculpture in the shape of a slash mark had descended from heaven to split up one part of my life from the next. In one second I realized several things: I want to get married. I'm not getting any younger. I'd like to marry Leslie Usher-Soames. It would be good for me to marry Leslie Usher-Soames, professionally. I must now dedicate my life to marrying her. I must not be vanquished. I am Captain Ahab and Dr. Richard Kimball and Inspector Javert, she is the Great White Whale and the One-Armed Bandit and Jean Valjean.

But Leslie Usher-Soames will not marry me. Not the way things are right now.

So I must change the way things are.

• • •

But to think that merely by my knowing her, only three people (she, her grandfather, Winston Churchill) separate me from the following Twentieth-Century All-Stars:

Franklin Delano Roosevelt, Joachim von Ribbentrop, Neville Chamberlain, the king that abdicated for the woman he loved (Edward something or other), Eisenhower and JFK and Harry Truman, Queen Elizabeth, Lord Beaverbrook, and Joseph Stalin.

And I am four people removed from Gladstone and Disraeli and Queen Victoria and Adolf Hitler!

Shit, I will never get this close to these people again!

I have to be careful though. The quickest way to Leslie is Marjorie, her boss (Marjorie is associate art director; Leslie is an associate designer) but I can't trust Marjorie. If she knew I needed a dose of medicine to save my life she would give it to me but she'd make me crawl naked over electrified barbed wire first.

Leslie alluded to a boyfriend once, I think.

I said something to the effect of, "I might have to go to London on a story."

(This was an outright lie.)

She said, "Well, you simply *must* meet Colin then. I insist!"

Colin can't be her brother because wouldn't she have said, "Well, you simply *must* meet my brother then!"? And she doesn't seem like the kind of person to call her father by his first name. (Maybe it's a dog and she said "my Collie.")

I don't know if I can compete head-to-head with anybody named Colin; that's about as bad as going up against a Jean-Paul, a Klaus, or, most impossible of all, a Giancarlo . . . but if her boyfriend lives across the ocean, then the playing field is level—even if he has forty hyphens in his name and eighty Turnbull and Asser shirts in his closet.

My first instinct, after hearing about Colin, was to run right over to Marjorie and ask, "So who's this Colin guy?"

Marjorie would tell me he was Leslie's boyfriend, adding he's a millionaire stock broker and a male model and the heir to a dukedom, whether he actually was or not.

Then she'd go over to Leslie and say something like, "Zachary Post is interested in you. Be careful. He's a great guy but he's one open sore away from the tertiary stage of syphilis."

Leslie Usher-Soames comes equipped with a hyphen. I could use a hyphen, even if it's only a vicarious one. But she also comes with a very important comma.

Her father is "European Director, Business" at Versailles. He lives and works in London; I imagine he must earn $400,000 a year, but I could be underestimating by half of that.

Commas are the current rage. There are Vice Presidents, Creative and there are Executive Managers, Fashion and Managing Editors, Style. On its masthead *Appeal* lists an Associate Director, Makeup; perhaps soon it will become as absurd as Creative Editor, Fade Cream.

I don't have a comma. Associate, Editorial just doesn't cut it on a masthead. It sounds about the same as Getter, Coffee or Sender, Fax.

Colons are the next thing. Gaston Moreau, who used to be called Creative Director, is now being referred to as Director: Creative.

Before I latch onto Leslie's hyphen, I might have to get myself a comma. And I also have to hope she doesn't move up. If she becomes Designer: Art and I'm just an associate editor, I don't stand a chance. It would be like a nurse marrying the X-ray guy instead of a surgeon.

{ }

"THEY'RE NOT running my piece on Rachel Carpenter," Willie laments. It's morning, hardly anyone else is in the office. On his desk are five faxes; they're written in handwriting so sloppy you can almost smell the champagne, there are whole sentences in different languages, perhaps even in a recently invented one: it's Boris Montague's column.

"They killed it? The whole thing?"

(Rachel Carpenter is a young director, an *enfant terrible*, who recently won something at Sundance with her first feature.)

"Yeah. Piecemeal. Dead."

"That's too bad."

"I don't get it." He takes a long drink of his sugar-saturated coffee and we watch two editorial associates of questionable gender push a rack full of expensive clothing down the hallway in front of us, headed toward the fashion department. "No," Willie says, "I *do* get it."

"What's going to run in its place?" I ask.

"Teddy Roosevelt did some two-page puff job thing on Thad Wright."

Thad Wright . . . it takes a while to place the name. A hotshot artist with no talent but for self-promotion . . . a little splash among the Schnabel and Salle crowd in the seventies and early eighties . . . then nothing.

"He's still alive?" I ask.

"He's not but he came back from the dead just to screw me. What's up with your Leroy White thing?"

"It's in limbo. Regine said it could be a feature but every time I bring it up with Nan, something gets in the way."

"Meanwhile, I have to get *this* together by tomorrow morning!"

He waves the faxes at me—frightened of them, I back away; it's like waving garlic at a vampire. Boris Montague is a gossip columnist whose column runs in the back of *It*; Boris—nobody at *It* has ever met him face-to-face—writes about royalty, millionaires, playboys, jet-setters, countesses and cads. He doesn't have a home, not that anybody knows of; he just travels from Paris to London to New York to Lucerne to . . . to all over, staying at millionaire friends' houses or on their yachts. Mercurial, opinionated ("Isn't it time that Contessa Sophia Cappobianco—and, oh, how it kills me to call Her Royal Thighness a contessa—be banned from showing her unsightly visage in public?"), politically incorrect (sometimes he's The Man You Love to Hate, other times he's just the man you hate), Boris then either exalts his hosts and friends in print or stabs them in the back, writing down a couple of sentences and sending them to Willie (who then has to make some sense of them), and then moves on to another drunken spree in a villa overlooking Lake Como, a castle in Cornwall, or at a masquerade ball in St. Remo. His columns are usually long, involved insults punctuated with ellipses, things like: "If Armand St. Clair Stringcheese, once one of the finest polo players in Europe, were not such a fantastic drunkard and despicable whoremaster, he might still be a friend of mine but . . . My head is splitting now and will thoroughly explode unless I get some sleep . . . I hear that Marie-France Galliard, one of the great beauties of her day, is disgracing herself again with the company of that impotent toadying thief Teddy de Putanesca, a man I would not trust looking at a knothole . . ."

When Willie has to piece together a Boris Montague column, his mood can turn, understandably, very black. But nobody can take it away from him.

"Do you need my help?" I ask Willie.

"No, but I—"

Mark Larkin now walks in, puts his fat blue goosedown jacket around his chair, sets his *Times, Wall Street Journal,* and *Economist* down on his desk. He is wearing a bow tie and a red-and-green vest. He tries to come across as if he has tons of class but still he's wearing a Triple Fat Goose jacket . . .

"Hello, Zack," he says. "Will."

("Will" is Willie's masthead/byline name, but Mark Larkin is the only person who calls him that.)

"Mark."

Willie looks up from a Boris Montague fax and glares at Mark Larkin.

"Your Thad Wright article is bumping something I wrote," Willie says to him. "Did you know that?"

"Oh, that's too bad. I am awfully sorry." With his thick glasses and his face so puffy and pink, you never can really read his expressions. "I really mean that," he adds, which proves to me he doesn't.

"All's fair, though, right?" Willie says in almost a hiss.

He's starting to really hate him. This might be fun.

{ }

"WHERE ARE we with the Leroy White article?" I ask Nan Hotchkiss in her office. "I think I ought to know."

I tell her that *Boy* magazine is thinking of running it as a feature, if *It* doesn't (this isn't the truth). Nan is a space up the masthead ladder from Sheila Stackhouse and has a much nicer office, or maybe it just seems that way because there are no pictures of a husband who looks condemned to death. As I stand a few feet away from her, Nan is doing the Versailles thing, looking down at pieces of paper and not looking up at the person she's talking to.

"You have more important fish to fry right now," she says.

"Me? I have nothing important to fry."

"Oh *yes* you do."

Then she looks up at me and smiles for a moment. Something is up, I sense, sitting down.

"I'm leaving here, Zack. I'm telling Regine this Friday. And I cannot fucking wait!" The way she says it, the way she put the *g* on the end of fuckin', it sounds so forced.

But this is great news. An editor slot will be opening up. Could it be?

The comma I need to get the hyphen—this might be it? The path to the colon!

"Where are you going?" I ask her. But she could be going to work at a Burger King—it doesn't matter as long as she's going.

I take a few guesses at where it is—senior editor at *Appeal* or at *Ego*, maybe something in Europe—but she won't say yes or no, telling me it's neither here nor there (both of which, in fact, are the names of Versailles publications).

"I'm going to put in a good word to Regine for you," she tells me as she jams some paper into her Filofax. "I'm going to recommend to her and to Betsy that you get this job." She jabs her desk with her index finger. "I don't see why you shouldn't have it."

"Wow. Thanks, Nan. Really." I'm ready to grab her by her big doggy ears, stuff her Filofax into her mouth, and drag her right the hell out of her office that very moment and move my stuff in. "But why me and not Willie Lister or Liz Channing?"

"Why *not* you? I think you're just as qualified as they are. You're a team player. You belong."

"Yes, I guess I do." For a second, I'm pretty impressed with myself.

But then it gives me an uneasy feeling in my stomach, the fact that I belong.

{ }

I'M JEALOUS of Willie not because he's a better writer and editor than I am—which he is—but because not only did he go to Harvard but he was a starting outside linebacker there.

Once in a while, usually when he's had a few, he breaks out a videotape. The Harvard-Yale game is on some local New England channel and it's raining and the field is mud and clumps of sod and slime. Willie will fast-forward through the tape until he gets to the fourth quarter; while he's doing this you see this hulking figure in red wearing number 99, blond hair coming out of the back of the helmet and whipping like a racehorse's tail, mud flying all over like shrapnel. Willie is knocking people backwards, knocking them out of their senses, he's batting down balls, he's tripping runners and getting a yellow flag.

He'll stop fast-forwarding and the camera cuts to number 99 sitting on the bench while the Harvard offense is on the field.

"That big old buckin' bronco number 99, Willie Lister," the faux–Keith Jackson play-by-play man intones, "has really dug his sharp crimson claws into the sore hide of the Eli's today, Dan."

Willie — covered with mud and sweat, caked with brown, green, and black and obscured by the mist and the lens beaded with rain — lifts a hand up . . . there's a cigarette in it. He's got his helmet on and he's smoking a cigarette on the sidelines during the Harvard-Yale game!!

"Oh, he shouldn't be doing that," the color commentator says.

"I'm fired."

Willie is worrying again, digging his fingers into his forehead, making himself sick over everything.

"No you're not." But I stopped listening about five minutes before this.

"No, I'm gone. Dead meat. I'm flank steak. Chopped chuck, ground round, that's me all over."

His couch smells of dust and there's a rusty spring coming out of one end of it, where my feet are. Half the stuffing is gone and I feel a little like I'm spread out on an inflatable raft, drifting across a pool.

"I mean, look at everything," Willie says, sitting at the wobbly wooden kitchen table near the window, black with grime. "I'm rapidly being phased out. All the signs are there."

"You've been saying this for a year."

"Yeah, well, it's just taking a long time to rapidly phase me out." Willie scratches his chin . . . there's a triangle of golden brown stubble there. Willie's facial hair grows quickly and his five o'clock shadow begins to lengthen every day at about three; Regine once even told him to do something about it. (Willie has told me that story — I don't know if it's true or not. Miserable people are usually prone to exaggeration. But one day I accidentally wore mismatched socks to work and Regine kept sending me humiliating e-mails about it.)

"You've got the new *She*, I see," I say, desperate to change the subject. There's a copy of *She* on the table. A radiant, emaciated sixteen-year-old model with a frozen stare lies in satin sheets on the cover, her skin almost blue, and the cover line says: THE DEAD PERFECT LOOK. Is it a luxurious bed or the inside of a coffin? Is she very horny or just dead of undernourishment?

Willie flips the pages and a blast of perfume flies at me. Allergic to some perfumes, I sneeze and the room spins.

"Mark Larkin's got a book review in here," he says.

"I've gotta micturate again." I have no desire to hear him getting started on Mark Larkin. What with my fish to fry, soon I will rank one considerable rung above the puffy pink snot and he'll be inconsequential to me.

I sit up and look at the rusty spring, the color of a dying marigold. Some yellow-white stuffing is also coming out of the couch.

His bathroom is a toilet, a sink, and space enough for two average-sized feet. His shower is in the kitchen and looks like the battered hull of an old battleship. Willie's studio—which he shares with his girlfriend, Laurie Lafferty (an *It* fact checker)—is up five flights of stairs, a serious climb for Willie, who is about fifteen pounds overweight (but he's six-foot-three, so it doesn't show that much), or for anyone.

I notice a gritty cluster of small hairs on the back part of Willie's toilet, where the porcelain meets the pipes. Laurie, who's now at her weekly "book group," has always struck me as a clean person but maybe I'm wrong.

Walking back into the room, I see Willie thumbing through *She*. I sit back down on the couch, set my tweed coat on my lap, and say I should get going. "Do you think I should try dropping in on Marjorie?"

"You can still do that?"

"Probably not." Willie was one of the few people who knew about Marjorie and me, and I hadn't told him—he'd guessed.

He's found what he's been looking for in *She* and leans back in his chair.

For some reason I ask him if he's ever been to Marjorie's apartment.

"Never seen the place," he says, "never having been there, not being nearly important enough." One more negative in that sentence and he would have evaporated.

He holds the magazine up, opened to a page with a lot of text and two small color photos. Opposite it is a Chanel ad.

"Oh, wow . . . Mark Larkin's reviewing Ethan Cawley's new book," he says.

So that was why Mark Larkin had the book in galleys a few weeks before—Regine hadn't assigned it to him too, thank God. He was making a few extra bucks . . . and also more of a name for himself, freelancing for other magazines, something we all did.

"He likes it," Willie says. "Wow . . . He *really* likes it!"

Something about Mark Larkin liking the book makes me a little nervous. The book is due out any day and at that moment I've forgotten if it's called *Dakota* or *Badland* or *Kansas*. I'd savaged the novel and its author in the two paragraphs they allotted me in *It*, which always has a page of brief book reviews for people who read reviews but not too many books.

"Marjorie might not be home," I say, trying to appear nonchalant. But I'm thinking of the Ethan Cawley novel. It was an agony to finish. So I didn't finish it. It isn't the first book I've reviewed that I didn't finish and if you think every book reviewer reads every single word, then you can skip to the last paragraph of this one right now. In the case of *Dakota* or *Badland* or *Nebraska* or *Kansas*, I read the first 100 pages, quickly skimmed the middle 150, and dashed through the last dozen or so to see how it ended. I said that this book was nowhere as good as his previous one (called either *The Great Plain* or *Sage*), which I also hadn't liked (and also didn't read all of) but which others had said showed a "startling new direction" in his work; I also stated that with this, Cawley's tenth book, he had written the same novel ten times over, pulling a Vivaldi but without Vivaldi's talent.

"He writes," Willie says, "that it's a sure bet that Cawley will get nominated for the National Book Award and a Pulitzer. Jesus Christ, as if that Anglophile subhuman has ever placed a bet on anything in his life!" He throws the copy of *She*, which weighs about two pounds, at the front door and Laurie opens the door and the magazine hits her in her stomach.

"That's a fine way of greeting someone!" she says. She's very intelligent and sensible and they're the kind of couple about which some people say that she could do better and other people say that he could do better. So they're either perfectly wrong for each other or just perfect.

Willie asks her about the book group and she says it was okay. The book they'd discussed was *Emma*; since the group was dedicated to nineteenth-century women writers and had been meeting for two years, I'm a little surprised they haven't already knocked that one off.

We talk about office stuff for a little while. Laurie works in the dark airless room people call The Black Hole. It's the one area on the floor that isn't ecru or gray; proofreaders and fact checkers and other undesirables work there. Every magazine in the building has such an area: black walls, black carpetless floor, black formica desks, eerie fluorescent light. Near them are the freight elevators, the bathrooms, and the garbage-dumping room. The Black Holers can dress, talk, and act the way they want because they really aren't a "part" of us, they don't mingle and fit in and don't really count, and because of that they have it better, in a way. But they're usually people without any ambition, maybe keeping Marlon Brando's wise words about ambition in *On the Waterfront* in mind: "I always figured I'd live a little bit longer without it."

Ivy Kooper's name somehow is brought up.

"She seems really sweet," Laurie says.

"I know, that's her problem," I say.

"How can anything sprung from Jimmy Kooper's loins be sweet?" Willie asks.

I put my coat on and walk to the door. I ask Laurie what the next book is and she says *Persuasion*.

"You know," I can't help but comment, "it seems you would've done Jane Austen already."

"We have. We're doing her again."

Walking down the narrow stairs, it dawns upon me that Leslie Usher-Soames would probably never live in a building like this. She probably wouldn't even live in the building I live in. With every creak of the stairs I hear Nan's finger jabbing her desk, telling me there's no reason why the editor job couldn't be mine.

No, there is no reason. No reason at all.

Why is Willie such a nervous wreck?

Because despite his impeccable credentials and skills, he's stopped rising. And he's stopped rising because he knows everyone knows that he thinks the place we work in is full of shit.

Last year Willie wrote a four-page feature on the Chelsea Hotel for *It*. Donna Reems took the accompanying photos. Nan and Regine wanted to overhaul the piece, to make it more of a glitzy style piece, more about the famous people who had lived there; they added sentences and phrases that Willie wouldn't be caught dead typing, injecting magazine-speak (things like: arguably, at once, faux- and -manque-informed of, preternaturally) and overwrought phrases. He was furious and they knew it. He got down on his knees in front of Regine and Betsy Butler and begged them to let it run the way he had written it. "Four pages isn't going to kill us, is it?" he said. "Please, just this one time . . ."

And . . . they backed down. Twenty years ago Regine had started out at Versailles as I started out, as Willie did too, as a lowly editorial assistant; now she made over a million a year and her clothing allowance was more than my entire yearly salary. So she *was* smart.

It won an award for that piece but I don't think Regine and Betsy ever forgave him for making them back down.

} {

AFTER LEAVING Willie and Laurie's I get into a taxi and go straight up the avenue, to Marjorie's. There's a pay phone on her corner and I tell the driver to wait. Her building is on a quiet dark side street lined with bent skinny trees; it's a postwar white brick box with twenty-five floors, two elevators, and a doorman with white gloves, the tips of which are usually smudged gray with *El Diario*. Up until a year ago, I'd ring Marjorie's buzzer and more often than not she'd be naked when she answered the door, her blazing red bush looking crazed and electrified, a little bit like Bozo the Clown.

Marjorie's answering machine picks up now and I drone in my usual answering-machine voice, "Hi, it's me, are you there?"

Nobody picks up. I peer upwards . . . her lights are on. Everything in there, the sink, the shower, the tons of cosmetics, looks as if it's never even been looked at, and the furniture resembles the furniture in a TV drama; you didn't know if they were real or were props.

I taxi back downtown to the old grimy rubber ball I live in. Why had I even tried seeing Marjorie anyway? On the slim chance she'd sleep with me? I'm very angry with her suddenly, then I wise up and I'm angry with myself.

But I'm convinced she was home. Either she'll lie to me and say she wasn't (she's a very good liar) or . . .

"Did you get my message last night?" I ask her the next day.

"No, not until today," Marjorie says. We're on the phone.

"Your light was on."

"I know my light was on."

"Were you home?"

"I had some company."

"I had to go to the bathroom."

"Had you told me that, I might have picked up."

Which means she'd been screening. Sometimes she's not a very good liar. "Next time I'll mention it. Now I know."

"And you don't have to need my bathroom to call, you know."

We make office-related chitchat for a minute. She tells me some gossip about Byron Poole, *It*'s art director, and two Dutch guys he'd met in a bar. She instructs me not to tell anyone and I promise her I won't and I tell two people within the next two days.

Which is what she wanted me to do.

{   }

I WAS NEVER officially in love with Marjorie Millet and she was never officially in love with me.

All I know is if Marjorie Millet called me up in the middle of the night and said, "Come over, Slick, and let's do it," I would have. I would have if she was in Tahiti and I was in Iceland and I would have emptied out my bank account and if there wasn't enough in it, I would've begged on the street to get the rest to get there.

Something close to that happened once. She was in L.A. supervising a photo shoot with that week's *enfant terrible* director (in every issue of a Versailles magazine you can find the phrases *enfant terrible*, *wunderkind*, Peck's Bad Boy, and Young Turk) and I was in New York. It was a Sunday and I was home; it was about 11 A.M. in New York and I think she might have just woken up.

"You better be here tonight, Big Boy," she said. (Slick, Handsome, Big Boy, Buster, Big Fella . . . she's got this hint of Veronica Lake or Ann Sheridan to her and it drives me crazy.)

I gulped.

Now, there are women who, if they call you from Los Angeles and say, "You better be here tomorrow," you would say, "Okay, sure, I'm calling up American Airlines first thing after we hang up and buying a ticket." But then, when do you do hang up, you—as ultra-Brit Oliver Osborne might put it—toss yourself off. And then you realize, *Hey, man, I'm not going to California!* No way! (Airlines must lose millions and millions in masturbation moneys every year.) But there are women who, when they tell you to be there the next day, you'll toss yourself off and *still* make the trip. The semen won't be dry and you'll be on the horn to the airline.

Marjorie called me, I tossed myself off, I phoned the airline, and within ten hours her fingernails were scratching red lines up and down my back on a terrace overlooking the rush-hour traffic crawling along Sunset Boulevard.

It was as if she had me on a very tight leash, from her hands right to my groin. She'd call me up and tug on it and I'd be in a cab and then at her place, on the couch, on the floor, in the bed, in the kitchen, along the walls, in the shower, halfway out the window.

"You can go now, Handsome," she'd say.

Will Leslie Usher-Soames ever say, "Go down on me, Zeke, okay?" in a taxi cab? Will she ever say, "Let's go to the ladies' room and powder my pudendum" in a restaurant? Will she ever drop in on me unannounced on a Saturday morning at seven busting out of some lacy black Victoria's Secret get-up? No, I don't think so.

And are these things important? Probably only to shallow people. But they sure seem more important than what really is important and, while it's going on, you forget what is important, which *is* probably an important thing in itself.

And the noises, the yells and shrieks . . . it was unbelievable. One time when we were in her kitchen, the Venetian blinds dropped off a wall two rooms away. Sometimes she muffled it with her fist, sometimes with a pillow, which she would also punch while she bit it; she went through three pillows with me, biting and literally beating the stuffing out of them. At times she sounded like a driving instructor screaming at an inept sixteen-year-old student: HARDER! SLOW DOWN! LEFT! FASTER! TO THE RIGHT! TURN ME OVER! NOW! ALL RIGHT, THAT'S IT! STOP! And she did it with passion and belligerence, she sounded incredibly angry, even though I was doing everything in my power to please her. She wouldn't just say, "Do it," she'd say, "Will you fucking do it, goddammit?!"

She could make life difficult though.

There were a few times when she'd call me up and say, "Get over here . . . *now!*" And I'd be there in ten minutes but she wasn't home.

"I was at the A & P," she'd explain. "I suddenly had this craving for apple sauce."

But maybe she'd tossed herself off while I was brushing my teeth and she just didn't need me anymore.

"What's that noise?" I asked her once on the phone.

"It's my boy Buzz."

"Who's Buzz?"

"Buzz Eveready . . . my friendly vibrator. Here. Meet Buzz." Then she lifted the contraption to the phone.

"Hello, Buzz," I said, like an idiot.

"I knew you two would get along," she said.

(One summer weekend morning she dropped in on me in nothing but a raincoat, a black merry widow, thigh-highs, and sandals. It was pouring and thundering out and her long wild curly red mane was drenched and almost straight, the smoothed-out coils dripping silver drops all over the floor. She sat on the couch, spread her legs, and let Buzz Eveready do his thing. It took a minute and she was howling. When he was done she beckoned for me with her index finger. "Okay, your turn now. Take a whack.")

But there was a flip side to all this merriment, as there usually is, and it went bad. She was a lusty, big-boned, 36 D-cupped redhead but she was more important than I was at work; she, the associate art director, was slumming with me and I was in way over my head.

So—and this is a familiar pattern—it started with me going over to her place seven days a week (nights really) and not falling asleep until 6 A.M., then five nights a week and falling asleep at 4, then two nights and falling asleep at midnight.

And then no nights at all. But a lot more sleep.

I used to get e-mails from her like this:

TO: POSTZ
FROM: MILLETM
SUBJECT: precipitation probability

i am really really really horny and sopping wet

(For someone who works at a magazine, she isn't too strong with punctuation and capitals.)

To which I'd respond:

TO: MILLETM
FROM: POSTZ
SUBJECT: Re: precipitation probability

So what do we do about this?

TO: POSTZ
FROM: MILLETM
SUBJECT: Re: precipitation probability

stairway b alcove
please hurry darling

And two minutes later I'd be giving it to her from behind, her skirt hoisted up over her waist and her panty hose pulled down, me staring at the bold lettering on the sign: YOU ARE HERE.

(You get an e-mail with the words "please hurry darling" in it, it's something you never, ever forget.)

Her most irritating habit: making things up from the one brain cell of imagination she possessed, and then spreading it around.

It could be harmless but still it bothered me. A few months after we stopped sleeping together I mentioned how we'd once eaten at a particular restaurant together. She vehemently denied this ever happening. I just as vehemently said that it had and then told her everything she'd eaten that night; then it came back to her and she admitted that, yes, we had in fact once eaten there.

Then a few days later I brought up the fact that she had denied that we ate there. And she said that *that* had never happened.

She's very difficult.

Here are some things THAT NEVER ACTUALLY HAPPENDED OR WERE NEVER SAID BUT WHICH MARJORIE SAID HAPPENED OR WERE SAID:

1) I PLANNED ON STARTING MY OWN MAGAZINE, A KIND OF *Boy* MAGAZINE CLONE.

2) I TOOK DRAMA LESSONS AFTER COLLEGE AND I STILL WANTED TO BE AN ACTOR.

This is drivel, not even remotely true.

"Someone told me you wanted to act on the stage," Leslie Usher-Soames said to me one day.

"Who said that?!" I asked.

"Oh, I just heard it."

"It's not true."

"But you did take acting lessons, right? At the Royal Academy of Dramatic Arts?"

"How could that be? . . . I've never been to England."

"But you went to Liverpool University, didn't you?"

"Oh yeah, sure, but that was school, that doesn't count."

"Did you tell Leslie I wanted to act?" I asked Marjorie at her desk.

"Should I not have told her? Was that a secret?"

"Yes! I mean no, it's not a secret. It never happened."

3) I HAVE A $200,000 TRUST FUND.

4) I'M A MEMBER OF THE SOCIALIST WORKERS PARTY.

"I guess you won't be voting either GOP or Democrat, will you?" someone said to me once.

"What makes you say that?"

"You're some sort of pinko, aren't you? A fellow traveler?"

"Did you ever tell anyone I was a communist?" I asked Marjorie.

"Well, you *are* a member of the Socialist Workers Party."

"What do you mean?"

"This is what *you* told me!!"

"I never said that!"

"You *told* me you were a member. Maybe you were kidding."

"I wasn't kidding!"

"See! You are a member! And this just proves I'm right."

"How does it do that?"

"Well, do you hear yourself? Listen to how strongly you're denying it. If it really wasn't true, you'd admit it."

It could get pretty exasperating.

5) I HAD A GIGANTIC CRUSH ON REGINE TURNBULL.

"Why did you tell Willie Lister I wanted to do Regine?"

"I never did any such thing," Marjorie said.

"Yes you did. I know you did."

"What makes you think I told him?!"

"Because he began the sentence with 'Someone told me that . . .' and when that happens it's always you."

"Well, don't you want to do her?!"

"No! She barely comes up to my waist! She could be my mother!"

"You did tell me, Zeke, I know you did."

"So how then can you deny telling Willie I said it?"

"So you admit you said it!"

And here are some other gems:

I published enormous vanity-press sci-fi tomes under the pseudonym Lothar X. Criswell. I had lost my entire $200,000 trust fund betting on jai alai in Milford, Connecticut. I'd once tried to join the CIA but they found out I'd been treated in Switzerland for a nervous breakdown. A Kennedy girl had once tried to date rape me but her family hushed it up.

So when I set my sights on Leslie Usher-Soames my very first concern was: What the hell is Marjorie Millet going to tell her about me? Even if she sticks to the truth I'm in trouble.

{ }

WILLIE RUNS to my desk one afternoon, tells me to hurry up and get off the phone, which I do. I'm talking to my mother, who has strict orders not to call me at work unless she's about to die or is already dead. Willie says, "Follow me!" and we run, me behind him, to his desk.

A crate had arrived via messenger for Mark Larkin.

It's a painting—and a seriously ugly one—by the has-been artist Thad Wright. The subject of Mark Larkin's puff piece.

Mark Larkin has put it up on the wall behind his desk, so now Willie not only has to face him but also a horrible muddle of white and lime green paint going in all directions. It looks like someone was chasing Mylanta with Kaopectate and could keep neither one down.

"You know, I really miss Jackie Wooten," Willie says.

5

A COFFEE SHOP, three blocks from work. Finally I'm eating a meal with her. With a chaperone.

"I don't think I've read the thing in three months," Leslie says about our own magazine.

"You're not missing much," Willie barks out. He flattens his mashed potatoes with his fork, then forms slalom trails in it.

I keep sneaking peeks at Leslie's sea-shell gray eyes and lovely white skin, not a freckle, mole, or bump in sight. "I suppose that if I didn't work there I probably would care fuck-all about the thing," she says.

Accidentally her heel touches my ankle under the table. It's thrilling for a moment, just as thrilling as is her "fuck-all."

"Did you read Mark Larkin's piece on Thad Wright?" she asks.

Willie said he had. He can memorize every line in every issue, for what little good it does him.

"I didn't read it," I answer. I can't even remember which issue it ran in—was it in the one that was currently out on the stands, the one before that, or the next one, which hasn't come out yet? This is a problem I always have.

"It was unreadable," Willie says. (I have to take some blame for it; the headline "The Fall & Rise of Thad Wright" was my idea.) "After his three paragraphs on designer de jour Arnaud de Llama in the September issue . . . man, that was sickening."

"Yes, it was dreadful, wasn't it?" Leslie says. (I was hoping she'd say "dodgy." Whenever she says that word, I feel my heart pound.) Presently she's pecking at a salad but I've noticed something from watching her eat at work: she never finishes a third of her food. Sometimes she moves food around on the plate and takes two nibbles and that's it, shifting vegetables around for twenty minutes, like rearranging furniture in a doll house.

"You know, Mark Larkin got four free five-hundred-dollar suits out of that Arnaud de Llama article," Willie tells us.

"He has been dressing better, hasn't he?" Leslie says, pronouncing "been" like "bean" . . . which is strange since a bean is presently balancing on her fork.

Willie and I exchange disgusted looks, which Leslie, now temporarily occupied doing a CAT scan on a cherry tomato, doesn't see. My first thought is how unethical it is to accept presents from someone you're writing an article about; my second thought is: How come I wasn't picked to write it? I could use four new suits.

(The three of us are at the coffee shop to celebrate Willie's adventurous five-day European trek: he'd been sent a fax from a château in Andorra from Boris Montague, telling him to rush there right away so Boris could put together the remaining pieces of that month's column, which was fractured and incomplete. Regine and Betsy gave Willie the go-ahead and so he was off; he dashed to Crookshank's to pick up some clothing and then went straight to the airport, where he bought some luggage. However, when Willie arrived in Andorra the majordomo passed him a note from Boris, who had suddenly left; Willie now had to proceed to Honfleur. Willie called Betsy and she said it was okay, but when he arrived at the appointed location—a luxurious seaside hotel with more stars from Michelin than rooms—the concierge handed him a little note on hotel stationery [he showed it to Leslie and me at the coffee shop]: "Have gone on to Venice. The Cipriani. Room 20." In Venice Willie, exhausted now, finally hit pay dirt, sort of; though Boris was gone there was a piece of hotel stationery on the little night table in room 20. Willie picked it up and couldn't believe what he saw: it was covered with dots, with periods, hundreds and hundreds of them; it was all the ellipses—and nothing else—that Boris used in his column. Willie told us that it was too funny and he was too tired to be angry, and besides, there was a case of Cristal waiting for him on his desk when he got back. Courtesy of Boris Montague.)

"I think Regine loves him . . . he's really her blue-eyed, fair-haired lad," Leslie says, back on the subject of Mark Larkin.

I stop eating about now. "Fair-haired lad" . . . it sounds like an old Walt Disney movie about a lovable dog.

"Jesus, a few months ago he was getting coffee for her," Willie says.

"You once got coffee for her too," I remind him.

"I guess mine wasn't as good."

Leslie moves the radishes to where the arugula was and where the radishes had been she puts an olive. The olive has little dents in it, Leslie's teeth marks. She can't even finish that. Watching her rearrange her food reminds me I have to transfer money from my savings account into my checking account.

"He's another Tom Land," Willie mutters. "Except Tom has talent. Or he *had* talent."

"Who's Tom Land?" Leslie inquires.

"Just someone," I grunt.

"Did you know that Regine and Mark Larkin had dinner together last week?" Leslie asks us with an impish grin.

Willie and I look at each other again, this time more with astonishment than disgust, and his fork falls to the table for a clunky exclamation point that everybody in the coffee shop hears.

This is news. Regine rarely associated with anyone from work outside the office, not unless they were very, very important.

"How do you know?" I ask.

"Byron told me. He was there. It was at the Four Seasons."

The salt shaker falls over on the table, probably as a result of Willie shaking his legs a mile a minute.

Mark Larkin and Regine Turnbull having dinner. It's outrageous! He's an associate editor. So am I. So are Willie and Nolan and Liz Channing and Oliver Osborne and two or three strange people in the magazine's fashion department we don't ever talk to. I quickly remember teaching Mark Larkin how to use a fax machine and how terrified he was when he couldn't figure out how to get Regine her coffee.

And now they were having dinner together!

The coffee shop window is fogged up, it's cold outside and fuzzy gray shadows swim in and out of view. We're sitting near the window and I scrawl a sad Kool-Aid face on the glass, then cross it out. Leslie's glass of water has a small stain of her burgundy lipstick on the rim.

And then I notice something. A roiling wave of disgust turns the lunch I've just eaten to lava. It's . . . an engagement ring! A big gleaming diamond engagement ring that probably really isn't so big and gleaming, but it sure seems that way. How could I be such a blind idiot not to notice it before?!

She looks up at me, asks what's wrong.

"Nothing . . . What makes you think something's wrong?"

"You look sort of ashy." (The soft charming way she says "ashy" . . . making it sound like the name of an ancient Egyptian god or some kind of Indian food.)

I drink some water. She's noticed my ASHEE-ness!

I signal for the check and she excuses herself.

"Can you believe this?!" Willie fumes. His eyes look like a bull's, about to charge and topple over every table inside the restaurant.

"What?" I'm still brooding about the ring and gloating over the whole *ashee* thing; were my life the eleven o'clock news, these would be the opening and closing stories.

"Mark Larkin! Dinner with Regine!"

"You wanna have dinner with Regine, Willie? Come on!"

"He's becoming a malignant tumor on my life."

I shrugged. Mark Larkin was surely hateable but if he was the best thing you had in your Arsenal of Lousy Things to make yourself miserable, you were in tough shape.

"He's going to get us all fired," Willie says. "I tell you, in a year he'll be an editor-in-chief somewhere and we'll be spit-shining his penny loafers."

Leslie returns and I stand up, put my coat on.

I say to Willie: "Just 'cause he's moving up in the world doesn't mean we move down. If some guy in Tokyo gets a new liver, it doesn't mean another guy in Tierra del Fuego dies."

"It does if it's his liver."

Leslie, Willie, and I are out on the street now and smoke hangs on our breath. Thanksgiving is coming up but it's unseasonably cold, almost January weather. Leslie pulls on her small black leather gloves . . . it's a miracle she can get them on, they're so tiny, and I can make out the ring through the leather. Willie had Mark Larkin for a tumor—this ring was now my own threatening lump. How had I not seen it before?! She's wearing a furry emerald green overcoat and looks pretty in it and in the November light her eyes are grayer and prettier and the cold air brings out a lovely apple-colored glow to her cheeks. Or maybe she had applied more blush in the bathroom.

The tall slab we work in is two blocks uptown, a black monolith sixty stories high, thirty of those floors for thirty different magazines (from *Appeal* to *Men* to *Zest*); seen from the street the whole structure brings to mind an immense transistor battery, recently polished. Crookshank's (a men's clothier since 1899, the sign claimed) is directly across the street.

Every two weeks Willie and I go to Crookshank's so that he can look at ties, jackets, socks, and such. At thirty-three years old his body is now at the point when it has to decide what it's going to look like in middle age. A year ago he had no double chin and wore a 48 regular. Now he has to buy new shirts with a wider collar and he teeters between a 50 and a 52, depending on his last meal. He often secretly drifts over to browse in the portly section, along with many other men who once played football in college.

"Coming?" Willie asks.

"I'm heading back," Leslie tells us.

I tell Willie I have work to do and can't go either. He must realize I want to be alone with Leslie since he knows I've got no work to do. (I haven't yet told him of my plan to win her hand—lump and all—but now, right that very second when I abandon him, I think he catches on to something.) So Willie leaves us and I feel momentarily exhilarated. Finally: two blocks worth of non-work-related time with Leslie Usher-Soames.

But I feel a terrible pang of guilt watching Willie crossing the street. I like him a lot . . . there's something touching in the way he wears his churning innards on every stitch of clothing. What if his worries were coming to pass . . . what if he *was* getting fired?

If nobody would stand by Willie, who would stand by me?

Walking back to work Leslie tells me she has some shopping to do. I can tell she wants to do it alone and just like that, my hopes are dashed. It occurs to me to run to Crookshank's to meet Willie but I'm stuck too deep in my slouch to go anywhere.

In the Versailles lobby I see Gaston Moreau, alone as ever, getting into an elevator and I forget about being abandoned by Leslie and abandoning Willie.

What Nolan had said was right: his face really does resemble a burnt pancake. Not only does Gaston look terrible, he looks unusually terrible. This is a dying man.

⟩ ⟨

"I THINK you might be in trouble," Marjorie warns me.

"Me? What did I do?"

Our feet are up on her coffee table. The TV is on with the sound down—an unfunny, highly rated sitcom about a newspaper that seems to have only five people working for it.

"It's that book review, Zeke."

I've been waiting for a minor shit storm, half-hoping to just get it over with, the sooner the better, but also hoping Regine Turnbull might let it pass. Words like "masterful" and "brilliant" had been used by other reviewers and the book was poised to crack the best-seller list, a first for Ethan Cawley. So far I was the only one around who hadn't liked it. In the *New York Times* Sunday book section, there was a two-page ad with all the rave reviews and the words just leapt at you: mesmerizing, hypnotizing, spellbinding, bewitching, enchanting—who was this guy anyway? *Svengali?!* In most of these ads you can usually find *It* among the typical array of reviewers (the *Times,* the *Washington Post,* the L. A. *Times,* etc., and now Mark Larkin too, writing for *She*) but not now. And it's all my fault. My vision is of myself alone in some dark woods, running like a scared deer, twenty thousand book groups coming after me with broken, jagged wine bottles and hair clips drawn.

"What book review?" I stall.

Our ankles are crossing, on top of another. We're "friends" and can do this now. But still the thought of jumping her is never too far from my mind.

"That book you panned," she says, flicking the channels. She's lying back on the couch, a cushion over her stomach and her red hair is up and tied to one side. It's a wonderland, her hair, waves, coils and curls, long, viny and thick, and it goes on in every direction. She has no makeup on right now and there are faint blue bags under her narrow green eyes.

"Ethan Cawley, you mean," I say. "I just didn't like it."

"Did you finish it?"

"Of course I finished it. It was a while ago, in galleys."

"Because I remember you never finishing books you reviewed."

"That's not true. Sometimes I finish them."

"You told me you *never* finished them."

I don't want to let her go off on this so I say nothing.

"Anyway, this doesn't make you look very good," she says. "Also, you may have struck a personal chord. There's this story that years ago that when Regine was at *She*, she'd written a complete pan of *Chinatown* and then got the daylights yelled out of her by Sophie Vuillard."

"What if I'm right that it's a bad book? Maybe it got thirty good reviews because it got two good reviews and then nobody wanted to give it a bad one . . . ?"

She readjusts herself on the couch. A year ago she would've hit me on the head with a cushion right about now. Then we would have wrestled and tumbled onto the floor . . . her neighbors wouldn't bang on the walls because they loved to listen to it, and sometimes when I left the building her doorman would wink at me.

"So you and Leslie had lunch last week," she mentions slyly.

"We went out with Willie. That's all. It was payday."

"Hands off. She works for me."

"Leslie? I don't think she likes me that way."

"She doesn't."

I know very well that if Leslie *did* like me that way, Marjorie wouldn't tell me.

"How do you know that?"

"I just do." Did she? "Anyway she has a filthy rich boyfriend in London. He's got a hyphen too, Zeke."

So he *was* rich . . . but Marjorie would tell me he was rich even if he was on the dole and living in a cardboard box. And he had a hyphen. I knew his name was Colin but I called him Collie to myself and pictured his face looking just like Lassie's.

"Of course they *do* fight a lot on the phone," she says. "Long-distance bickering."

"Over what?"

"You're interested. I can see that."

"Just curious."

"Over stupid stuff. Couples stuff. The kind of stuff that made you break up with me."

"I never broke up with you."

"Yes you did."

Marjorie comes to a channel with basketball on it and I ask her to hold it there. She immediately turns the TV off and says, "Ha!" She often goes far out of her way to be annoying but really, she doesn't have to.

I try to snatch the remote control from her but she pulls it away. I do my best not to notice her nipples jutting through her blouse . . . they look like two men in ski masks about to hold me up.

"You like her, don't you?"

"Who?"

"Leslie."

"She's too skinny. You know my type, Bubbles."

"Nobody's too skinny."

"You're right. Not where we work."

"Besides," she says, pulling out a scrunchy and a barrette and letting her hair fall and spring out in all directions, "I think she has a thing for Mark Larkin."

} {

The People v. Zachary Post.

Regine Turnbull, in a handsome glen plaid skirt suit, is a grand-standing district attorney. And man, is she ever in a foul mood. I'm on the witness stand, slumping over in the face of certain defeat, and we're on Court TV. The whole country is watching.

Regine holds up a copy of Ethan Cawley's novel and yells, in her perfect Boston accent: "So did you or did you not give this book a bad review?"

The light catches the big gold burst on the cover: PULITZER PRIZE WINNER! NATIONAL BOOK AWARD WINNER! NUMBER 1 BEST-SELLER!

Me: I can't really recall the nature of—

Regine: You can't recall? You can't recall?! Two paragraphs and you can't recall?! Can you recall that you're under oath?

Me: I'd say the review was . . . mixed.

[She hands me a copy of It *and enters it as Exhibit A. Several words are highlighted in purple, her signature color.]*

Regine: Mr. Post, do you recognize this?

[I nod and the Judge—the same unpleasant man who presided over the trial of the men who tried to kill Hitler—tells me in loud cackling German not to nod.]

Me: Yes, I recognize it.

Regine: *[At the jury box, where her $500 Frederic Fekkai hair-sculpture barely makes it over the wooden bar]:* Read the highlighted words for the court, would you, please, Mr. Post. *[She says my last name as though she's spitting it.]*

Me: "Pretentious . . . tired . . . bland . . . silly . . . no conception of how women really think and talk . . . the same novel ten times . . . Vivaldi . . ."

Regine: And this is *mixed?!* If this is mixed, Mr. Post, I'd hate to see one of your *negative* reviews! *[The all-black, all-women, all-Nazi jury is in hysterics, to the strains of a Vivaldi concerto.]* I have no further questions for this mismatched-socked shitheel.

{   }

Nan Hotchkiss doesn't get the royal send-off that Jackie Wooten got. She's been appointed to be editor-in-chief of *Ego, U.K.,* which hasn't even published its first issue yet, and there is a small gathering in the big beige conference room, with a dumpy ice cream cake and two bottles of Cordon Negro sparkling wine. Regine isn't there, which is par for the course with her; if you're going, you're gone. But even Betsy Butler doesn't show up and so Velma Watts, Regine's emissary, presides over the dismal ceremony.

And there's no present from Tiffany. A manila envelope had gone around and we put money in it and bought her a gift certificate to some department store, Stern's, I think.

Her plane to London leaves tomorrow morning. It's the Concorde . . . no surprise there. Nan has even had a five-minute meeting with Gaston Moreau and he wished her the best of luck.

I want to pull her aside and wish her luck too, then get right to the point: "Did you put the good word in for me to Regine? Remember? I had important fish to fry! Did you?" But I don't. It's only three o'clock . . . I have a few hours left to ask her that question.

Oliver Osborne and I stand against the wall as Velma carves the rapidly melting cake.

"Do you know who's getting her job?" Oliver whispers to me. He's British, a graduate of Cambridge, and stands about six-foot-six. He has black bangs and wears slightly oversized Clark Kent glasses.

"I have no idea."

"Come on. You must know. Is it you, Zachary? You've become features editor now but you're not allowed to tell anyone until the announcement?"

A few minutes later Liz Channing stands next to me, holding a glass of sparkling wine. She's a Californian by way of Yale, thirty-four years old, a tall and slender blonde, married to a lawyer.

"Is this the worst Versailles party they've ever thrown or what?" she says to me.

"If one of the messengers quit, they'd throw a better one."

"The rest of her life's a breeze."

It would be; as top dog at a Versailles magazine, she'll never have to worry about anything again. Even if she gets fired, by the time she made it home there would be twenty messages on her machine with new job offers, all of them tempting.

"Who's getting Nan's job?" Liz asks. "Do you know?"

"I don't."

"If you ask me, I'd say Willie's getting it. He's been here longer than us." Liz is a smoker (she's always trying to quit) and has a raspy voice but whispering like this, she sounds like a car failing to start in the cold.

"What if they bring in an outsider?" I ask.

Mark Larkin, talking to Byron Poole, crosses our path.

"What if Theodore Roosevelt," she says, appalled at the notion, "*is* the outsider?"

I notice that Nan is on the verge of crying . . . whether from putting the last ten years of her life behind her or because of this bleak tribute to her, who can say.

We leave the room somberly but are glad to be out of there, like leaving a funeral.

When I get to my desk, some e-mail is waiting for me.

TO: POSTZ
FROM: LISTERW
SUBJECT: CRIME RATE SOARS!

Suddenly I hear yelling, the yelling of a maniac . . . it sounds like a hysterical mother watching her baby being fed to a wood chipper. At first I assume it's Roddy Grissom, the photo editor, yelling at one of his staff . . . But it's a woman screaming.

"Who has it?! Who has it?!" Nan Hotchkiss shrieks at the top of her lungs. "That's my whole fucking life in there!" Furniture is being thrown around, drawers are flung open. "If I don't find it, I'm going to rip this whole fucking place inside out! I'm going to kill the cocksucker who's got it!!"

Some mischievous devil has, it seems, made away with her Filofax.

This is the last I see and hear of her. She storms out after a futile two-hour search, her jowls jiggling like Jell-O, strings of saliva hanging from her lips, and I don't have the guts to pull her aside. She would have bitten me.

So I still don't know if she ever put in the good word.

} {

THE FINAL sentences of my Ethan Cawley book review for *It* went like this: "Cawley is attempting to do for the Great Plains what Sam Shepard did for the American West. The question is: Has anybody bothered to ask the Great Plains if it really wants this done? This is one pretentious yawn."

Mark Larkin's rave in *She* contained heavy-handed grad school sentences like these: "Ethan Cawley at once de-mythifies and re-mythifies, deconstructs and reconstructs . . . informed of its time and place . . . a crazy-quilt concoction of Zane Grey and James Joyce . . . turning American literature on its head, then standing it back up again . . . arguably the finest American writer writing today . . . This virile, poetic Peck's Bad Boy of American letters is doing for the mythic Heartland of America what Sam Shepard did for the American West . . . One can only sit back and exclaim, 'Bravo!' and then 'Yee-ha!' "

Based solely on my writing versus his writing, isn't it obvious that the book must suck?

} {

WE'RE IN one of the dark, short-on-oxygen and long-on-squalor bars that Willie spends a little too much time in, dank and seedy and hardly anybody else in there. The air is full of sludge, smoke, and Perry Como.

"So let's whip it out, Zeke. How much do you make?" Willie asks me. "I know you make more than I do."

This talk of money and salaries bothers me, probably only because it's *supposed* to bother me.

"How do you know so much?"

"A little birdy down in Accounts Deplorable told me." He gulps his drink, then tells me his salary. "And that does include the paltry bonus. You, on the other hand, make . . ." He tells me my salary, to the dollar. "And I don't begrudge you this, my good friend. You're Versailles timber. Me, I'm just timber, probably about to be felled. Now, it doesn't go by seniority because I've been there longer than you."

I finish my drink and wait for him to get to the point.

"Mark Larkin . . ."

This is the point.

"I don't know if I really want to know this kind of stuff." I lean back and the wood in my chair squeaks. The Giacometti-esque silhouette of the bartender is reading *The Daily Racing Form* and a Jerry Vale song comes on now. Where does Willie find these places? The one I'm in now I've passed by a thousand times and never once noticed. Maybe there was a guidebook: *LET'S GO: Squalor*, or *The Rough Guide to Dark Low-Life Bars with Watered-Down Drinks and Songs by Dead or Forgotten Italian Crooners.*

I give in.

"All right, how much does he make?"

Willie leans forward, actually licking his lips. The number he tells me is six thousand dollars higher than my salary. "Now is that criminal or what?"

It's amazing how the sound of a few words—or, in this case, a few numbers—can make a human being feel very sick in his stomach.

"That's terrible!" I spit out.

"It sure as shit is." But he's enjoying this . . . it really burns him up that Mark Larkin makes more than he does, it eats away at his insides. It annoys me too . . . but I wouldn't lose sleep (not more than thirty minutes) over it and I don't get a perverse thrill out of it. Willie, though, would be lucky if he got to sleep at all that night.

"Anyway, this could all be . . ." he breaks off.

"All be what?"

"I have big news," he says. "About me."

Maybe Willie is quitting, I wonder. He should quit—he's not really going anywhere. But I start picturing life in that building without him and it's not very pretty.

"I think I've got some important fish to fry . . ." Willie says. "Or so I've been informed . . ."

Fish to fry? To use an expression from my old zitty, classic rock days in Massapequa, my Spidey senses are tingling.

"Have you heard about Nan Hotchkiss's job? Who might be getting it?" he asks.

"Dame Rumor flies every which way."

I've only had one drink but what I'm hearing almost has me reeling.

"Anyway," he continues, "Nan pulls me aside a few days ago and tells me she's going to put a good word in for me with Regine. She says the job is as good as mine."

Did she jab her desk when she told him so?

"Well, that's great," I stammer. "Wow."

Do I tell him that Nan had told me the very same thing, that I have more important fish to fry too? She probably told Oliver Osborne about his fish, and Liz Channing too, and maybe even Mark Larkin had some important fish. Maybe all the messengers and the freaks down in Repro were walking around with dead trout in their pockets.

But I keep quiet.

"Congratulations," I say to him. "When you're frying that fish, make sure the smoke don't get in my eyes."

"It'll never come to pass . . . I'll never even get my freaking flounder in the fucking frying pan. They'll fire me first."

Probably not, I think, walking home that night. But whose freaking flounder would it be?

{ }

Velma Watts is Regine's secretary. She was once her live-in nanny but Regine so trusted her that she brought her into the company, despite her penchant for mangling people's names (I've gone from Zack to Jack to Jeb). She's five-foot-three, four inches taller than her boss, and weighs about 150 pounds, not an ounce of it fat. She's always reminded me of a fullback about whom the announcer says: "He's got that real good low center of gravity," the kind of player that gets only three carries a game but barrels forward for fifteen yards each time.

Velma smells strongly of perfume and I sneeze a lot when I'm around her.

"Shirley [she means Sheila] and I would like to have a talk with you," she says to me as I emerge from the men's room. She's from Detroit by way of Alabama and has a creamy voice, pronouncing some words like a blues musician; kids is keeds, hurt is hoit, help is hyep. "We'll meet in Sheila's office at twelve-thirty."

"Okay. Twelve-thoity," I echo, completely unintentionally, concentrating on her nail polish, the kind of dark red that shows a wound is more serious than originally thought.

At about 11:30 that day I approach Ivy Kooper and ask her out and she says yes.

(That is good timing on my part; had I been fired in an hour, she might have said no, should have said no.)

"Can it be dinner instead of lunch?" I ask her. My voice sounds pathetic to me . . . I almost can't make it to "lunch."

"Okay. Sure."

"Do you know anything?" I ask Marjorie at her desk. She's tilting pictures around on her computer screen. Leslie sits a few yards away, probably doing much the same thing.

"About?" Marjorie asks.

"About me. Velma and Sheila want to have a talk."

"It's the book review. It has to be."

"Yeah. I guess it is." Mark Larkin walks by and smiles his Teddy Roosevelt smile at me. If I had a pistol I would plunk every one of his teeth out.

"I wouldn't worry," Marjorie says. "It'll probably just be a good old-fashioned paddling. You like that, right?"

"No, if I remember right, you do."

I sit across from Sheila and Velma sits on my right, her powerful calves crossed. It's unusually sunny out for November; looking out the large window behind Sheila I see airplanes taking off and landing, the tram slinking slowly along to Roosevelt Island, two bridges brilliantly glinting in silver and gold.

"Regine . . . she's real mad," Velma begins. "It's that book."

Sheila leans forward. She has very broad shoulders yet still wears tops with shoulder pads. "You do realize what's happened?"

"I think so." I know exactly what's happened: I had said a book was bad and everybody else had said it was good because they thought that everybody else would say it was good.

"This book might win the National Book Award or a Pulitzer," Sheila says.

"It doesn't have my vote."

"You don't get to vote, though, do you?"

"No, I don't." Thanks, Sheila.

Sheila's bubbly blond kids and her sad bald husband are staring at me. Sheila is over six feet tall (she has to buy clothes at specialty stores for big women, places like "she-man shops") and has white-blond hair that goes up in a 1950s haircut—some people say she resembles Peggy Lee. In her twenties she was a "career girl" and was kept, she once told me, in a Greenwich Village studio for a while by a much older publishing man with a house and family in the suburbs; I picture her as one of the gals in *Three Coins in the Fountain.* Now in her early fifties, she's a senior editor who's peaked—she'll never go any higher in the company.

"You have to be much more in touch with what's going on, Zachary," she advises me now.

"Well, I think I am. I try to keep in touch." I'm surely more in touch than she is: she lives in Short Hills, New Jersey, and probably hasn't read a book in fifteen years. And the only movies she goes to are the movies her kids want to see, movies with explosions, morphing manimals, and action figure tie-ins.

"It looks bad, Jeb, that's all," Velma says. "That book might win some award and folks will recall that *It* didn't like it."

"You know very well," Sheila adds, "Ethan Cawley always gets good reviews."

Perspiring, beginning to melt into the leather beneath me, sneezing a lot, I readjust myself in the chair. Queens and Brooklyn fade out to a blue square the size of a postage stamp.

"He always gets good reviews," Velma says. Sheila looks at her out of the corner of her eyes. She doesn't need Velma in here and knows she's only serving as Regine's ambassador and goon.

"Had you written the same piece," Sheila says, "for *Him* or *Boy* or *Now*, that would've been fine. They can be negative and edgy. But it's not a good fit for *It*."

"Then why didn't you, Sheila, as my immediate superior, tell me this then or have me do it over or simply shitcan the whole measly two paragraphs?" I don't say this but I think it very loudly.

I say instead: "I understand."

"So this is what you're going to do," Velma says. "You're going to South Dakota and you gonna interview this Ethan Cowling."

"I *am* . . .?"

What an inspired, devious, novel form of punishment! Regine Turnbull is a genius! But my stomach is turning over.

"Yes," Sheila says. "It's going to run in the January or February issue."

"He'll shoot me!" I say. "He's into guns . . . he hunts. He probably pours pure grain alcohol onto his breakfast cereal. I'll show up on his property and he'll blow my head off."

"That's just what Regine said too," Velma says.

{   }

THE same day.

A large staff meeting; editors, assistant editors, editorial assistants, and, from the art department, the art director, designers and assistant designers, and the entire fashion department and photo department, all "brainstorming" for the upcoming two or three issues, coming up with ideas for stories, assigning stories, pictorials, and smaller articles to freelancers.

"Mark's going to London to finish his story on the Duke," Betsy Butler, chairing the meeting, tells us at one point.

I'm not aware he had started such a piece and neither are too many other people, judging by their expressions. I even whisper to someone: "Why are we doing an article about John Wayne?"

"The Duke . . .?" Liz Channing asks, equally dumbfounded.

"Do you want to explain it?" Betsy says to Mark Larkin.

He clenches his jaw, lifts it an inch or two. He explains how an aging, sick Brit—a mere lord and not a duke—is facing complete financial ruin yet refuses to part with his priceless collection of Corots, Canalettos, and Constables, and his sprawling villa outside Siena. As Mark Larkin explains all this, rubbing his thumb clockwise against his index finger and middle finger, and as people sit around either utterly rapt or disgusted, I realize I've already read this same story, not once or twice, but perhaps ten times. If it wasn't an English lord, it was an Italian count or a French marquis. And the story usually ended the same way: Lord Whatshisface holds out, then dies, leaving no immediate heirs. Then some fifty-year-old chain-smoker with an Hermès ascot, $400 shoes, and a full head of salt-and-pepper hair steps forward and claims to have been the man's boyfriend since the age of thirteen, when he was plucked off the beach at St. Tropez or the slopes at Gstaad, and then . . . well, the story never does end, it just dies in litigation. It's the kind of article that you read the first two pages of, then when it says *continued on page 181* you don't turn to page 181. And if by chance you do hit page 181, you still don't read the rest of it.

Betsy asks Mark Larkin: "Is this going to interfere with your story on Muffy Tate?" (Muffy Tate is a high-powered literary agent about whom I also had no idea Mark Larkin is doing a story.)

"I shouldn't think so," he says.

Betsy mentions what stories Tony Lancett and Emma Pilgrim, *It's* star freelance writers, are working on, then she turns to me and says: "We're going to hold your Leroy White article."

I nod a slow resigned nod. It's the one thing I'm working on that I care about, but they shouldn't know that.

"Are you reviewing a book?" she asks me.

The people who aren't looking at me look at me and the people who are, look down. This must be what actors feel like when they're on stage and forget what play they're appearing in.

"Something will come along," I say. "I have a big pile on my desk I'm sorting through."

"Well, make sure you pick something you like this time, after you're through sorting," Betsy says.

I tell Betsy I want to do a piece on a young sculptor for "In Closing." Nobody in the meeting has ever heard of him, which is good, because that's what the section is supposed to be about.

"Is his work any good?" Nolan asks, thus completing the first half of his usual two-sentence contribution to a meeting.

"He's handled by the Raymond Dunston Gallery on Wooster Street," I say. "He's starting to sell really well." I have no idea if he's selling anything; I'd received some press clippings about him from the gallery thirty minutes before and until I opened the envelope had never heard of him either.

"Okay, we'll see," Betsy says, not willing to commit to my sculptor or to me.

It's clear how much I've damaged myself with Ethan Cawley: if I thought something was bad, it must be good. If I thought something was good, then it was probably terrible. It was as if I were a TV weatherman predicting a sunny glorious day and so everybody goes out with umbrellas and galoshes.

"Have you heard of Daffyd Douglas, Zachary?" Mark Larkin says. Daffyd Douglas is a British author—his first book has just come out and it's assumed he'll be shortlisted for the Booker Prize.

"Yes," I say. "Of course." I have heard of him but feel as though I'm lying.

"What about interviewing *him*? He could be very hot very soon. Muffy Tate's probably going to get him on her list."

"Sounds good," someone says.

But since when does Mark Larkin hand out story ideas to others, especially me?! *I had once told him where and how to get Regine's coffee!* I told him where the bathrooms were (I'd given him wrong directions on purpose). Now he's telling me I can't interview my sculptor—who wasn't really mine until about a half-hour ago—but have to interview some Young Turk fresh out of a coal mine by way of a rave club or heroin clinic, whose novel and accent are probably indecipherable.

Now, I have no objection to interviewing Douglas other than the fact that it's Mark Larkin's idea—he wouldn't be any worse than some of the other people I've wound up writing about. But I just don't like the position I'm in and my temples begin to throb.

"Ho, no," Velma butts in suddenly. "He's not doing any such thing. He's goin' to South Dakota to interview that Ephraim Gillies."

The ceiling is coming down on me . . . this is humiliation, pure and simple, and now they're all looking at me . . . I hear some giggling coming from the Fashion Department, the shallowest, stupidest people on the floor. Of course everybody would eventually find out about the Cawley interview . . . but to announce it like this! I'd rather have stood up and said, "Hey, everybody, I still suck my thumb and wet my bed!"

"Really?" Mark Larkin says with a big donkey grin. "I like the symmetry. The punishment should fit the crime, I suppose."

"Yeah," I weakly joke, "but I think it's a little unfair to make me walk to South Dakota."

Nobody laughs.

TO: POSTZ
FROM: LISTERW
SUBJECT: The Asshole

ML only brought up the Douglas interview so that Velma or someone else could humiliate you don't you think

(Like Marjorie's, Willie's e-mail is seldom punctuated.)

I write back:

Maybe. What about this possibility: ML knows Muffy Tate's signing him so ML's trying to get him some free publicity to get on her good side?

Willie responds:

did you notice the one time i tried to open my trap at the meeting, ML started speaking he won't even let me speak

But I hadn't noticed it. He goes on:

I think I just ought to get a hacksaw and slice the guy into a multitude of little pieces

To which I reply:

Make sure you shove that bow tie up his ass too, okay?

And he answers me:

you got it pal!

⟩ ⟨

At about five o'clock that day, after not moving from my desk because I'm still so embarrassed (my bladder has been killing me), after sitting and marinating in my own bile for the whole afternoon, I finally pluck up enough courage to tend to my social life, which—since it involves dating an intern—really doesn't amount to too much.

> TO: KOOPERI
> FROM: POSTZ
> SUBJECT: dinner
>
> You sure you still want to have dinner with me? I'm the outcast of Park Ave. Or do you want to bask in my refracted shame?

She was at the meeting too and had seen me shrivel and cringe.

> TO: POSTZ
> FROM: KOOPERI
> SUBJECT: Re: dinner
>
> We're still on. I'll bask.
>
> Hey, this is the first e-mail I've gotten here that doesn't have to do with getting someone coffee!

Ah, the old days of just getting coffee and faxing! If someone dropped a black patent leather belt in my in-box that moment, I'd start mending it myself . . .

{ }

Ivy and I take the subway downtown and have dinner at a cozy Italian place on Second Avenue in the East Village. I pay, of course. (*It's* interns don't make a dime; still, as Jimmy Kooper's daughter, she's probably doing better than I am.) I don't really feel like being out with her that night—or with anyone—after all that's happened. I'm fuming and would have liked to have gone home and pulled a Willie: stare at the ceiling and wait for either it or my head to explode. Despite her urge to bask, Ivy probably isn't so crazy about the idea either, most likely thinking she's having dinner with the biggest loser in the company.

"You know, I don't really have to walk to South Dakota," is the first thing I say when we sit down at our table.

She unbundles the checked black-and-white scarf from around her neck and says, "But you do have to walk back, right?"

She isn't model-beautiful but she's willowy and has dark eyes, very brown, deep and mysterious, and the small table candle flickering in them brings out a lovely on-and-off chocolate luster.

I explain everything, not stopping to take a breath, telling her of interoffice politics and rivalries, gamesmanship and favoritism, and it feels good to get it out. Every sentence of this tirade is prefaced with "You're new and I don't want to manipulate you but . . ." and then I try my best to manipulate the daylights out of her. I tell her of a rumor that Byron Poole had rubbed Alpo over himself and had sex with a Great Dane, that Sheila was an alcoholic and kept a bottle of Heaven Hill in her desk, that Marcel Perrault, the fashion editor, was on the take and got two grand in cash every month from Ralph Lauren, that the Fashion Department had orgies on the nights of paydays.

It's all a ploy to get Ivy on my side.

She's so innocent . . . she believes everything, I think.

Not by design I've left her very little time to talk about herself and when she does, she doesn't say much, either because she's shy or simply doesn't have much to say. This can be a problem with people under twenty-five years of age; not having that much experience under their belts, they just don't have that much to dislike, which means they don't have that much to talk about.

But I don't know what it is—whether it's what I'm saying or the way I'm saying it—but she . . . she *takes* to me. We walk (it's windy and her wavy brown hair blows in her face and lashes against mine; she buttons up her long tweed coat and hugs herself to keep warm) toward the Astor Place station and then she asks me if I want to get a drink.

"Do you mean now?" I ask, still thinking I've made a leper of myself, talking about all the other lepers.

"Sure . . . unless you don't want to."

A rejection now might blow any future chance with her, so we walk back to the East Village and sit down in a booth in a tiny dark Ukrainian bar. It's her turn to speak and so I let her, but I have no idea what she's saying: it's college stuff, friends (Kimberly, Daphne, Susy) stuff, family (Daddy, Mommy, her brother Brett or Chad) stuff. So I sit and nod and say, "Really?" and "Why's that?" at the appropriate times. She's sharp, intelligent, nice looking, it occurs to me, and I'm glad she doesn't have silky, soft and manageable Versailles hair; she has a breezy way of carrying herself, resting her chin on her hands, smiling and pursing her lips, tilting her head to laugh, playing with a napkin—maybe this poise and polish is Brearingale Birchford in action. One thing I do notice, despite my not listening to her too carefully, is that she's incredibly sweet. Despite being a New Yorker, despite being Jimmy Kooper's kid, despite her classy 100 grand education, she doesn't seem to have a mean fiber in her body. It occurs to me, as she goes on about Tiffany and Daphne and Brett or Chad, that she's not at all suited for Versailles Publishing, Inc., that either the place will eventually shred her to little bits or bend her to its will like putty.

"And so why do you think that is?" she asks me.

Huh? I'm caught . . . I have no idea why *it* is or what *it* is in the first place. Her last five sentences to me could have been spoken in Chinese.

"I don't know," I say. "You know, I guess I just don't know."

She looks at the Stolichnaya clock over the bar.

"I'll take you back to the subway," I say.

"I'll take a taxi."

Of course. She's Jimmy Kooper's daughter. They lived on Park Avenue in the Sixties. Why should she ever take the subway?

It's very cold out now and I'm exhausted, exhausted from airing all the steam out and by pretending to be interested in her, although by the evening's end I am a little interested in her, I must admit.

(If only sweetness were more interesting! Why is someone like Marjorie Millet—TROUBLE in boldfaced italic 68-point scarlet—ten times more fun to be with than someone like Ivy Kooper?)

Outside, Ivy asks me what I'll be doing for Thanksgiving.

"My mom lives in Palm Beach. But we don't speak."

"Why not?"

"It's a long story."

"And your father?"

"Oh, he's long gone."

"So you have no place to go?"

A taxi stops and Ivy looks at me, white and green streetlights and red car lights flashing in her dark eyes, her hair again blowing in her face.

That was it right there. That's what did it for me.

Being pathetic . . . I tell you, it works almost every time.

AN ELEVATOR, just Mark Larkin and me inside, going up to work. He's graduated from the Triple Fat Goose jacket he was wearing weeks ago and is now wearing a pricey camel hair coat and carrying his beat-up tangerine-colored leather envelope. I don't know if he knows how much I dislike him. And my dislike is slowly turning into hatred . . . every day it gets more intense, like a deadly virus inside a test tube getting bigger and uglier, overflowing like beer foam over the brim of the tube. Willie hates him too but thrives on hating him; I don't want that to happen to me . . . I don't want to need an object to hate.

"Too bad about yesterday," he comments.

"Yesterday? What happened?" But I'm playing dumb.

"That Ethan Cawley business. Rough, Post, rough."

"Oh yeah. That. Well, *your* review is certainly all over the place."

"It is, isn't it? And I couldn't stand the book. But if I'd said that, my review wouldn't be all over the place, would it?"

The elevator stops and a tall woman in black leather pants who looks like a stiletto gets on—this is the floor of *She* magazine, considered the flagship publication of Versailles. She presses the next floor up and gets off there, at *Her* (circulation: 1,500,000, often called "*She*'s poor kid sister"), a magazine aimed at women who wish they were rich and snotty enough to live the *She* life.

"But I guess it's one of those chalk-it-up-to-experience things," he resumes. I notice his bow tie, black with tiny yellow dots, is a clip-on job, not the real do-it-up-yourself article. Proving he really doesn't have all that much more class than the average joe.

"Yes, now I know how to handle myself. What was up with suggesting I interview Daffyd Douglas? Did you read his book?"

"In galleys, yes. Muffy Tate sent it to me. Regine and I had discussed it, your interviewing him."

We get off the elevator and walk past Pat Smith, the seventy-year-old receptionist, who everyone calls Smitty. (For some reason she's allowed to smoke in the building and nobody ever complains about it. She always has a cigarette going and looks like a skeleton with a thin coat of white paint sprayed on, and her voice croaks like a lawn mower.)

"Anyway, old boy, I'm sure everything will turn out fine in the end. It always does." He raises his eyebrows, flashes the T.R. smile, something he can't do for too many seconds without looking like a piano keyboard.

(I think it was that day that Willie realized who else Mark Larkin was the spitting image of: Joseph Cotten as the eighty-year-old Jedediah Leland in *Citizen Kane*, the one going on and on about cigars and nurses.)

It isn't until I reach my desk that I realize Mark Larkin had called me "old boy." Equally horrible is: (1) him saying things always turned out fine in the end and (2) the fact that he and Regine were discussing what to do with me. That is what really gets me.

Who is he, my guidance counselor?!

Maybe, it dawns on me, it was Mark Larkin's idea to send me to South Dakota. That donkey-mouthed, camel-hair-coated son of a bitch.

} {

"OKAY," I say to Sheila in her office, "I called and bought the plane tickets to South Dakota."

"That's good. I'm really sorry about this. But you know Regine . . ."

"You know, the weird thing is that when I saw the galleys on Mark Larkin's desk, I thought he was being assigned that too."

"Assigning the same thing to two people?" Sheila says. "That's unheard of."

} {

IT ISN'T just Ivy—I'm really racking up the pity.

"I'm terribly sorry, Zeke," Martyn Stokes says to me. We're on line at a deli near work, getting our breakfasts, on the Monday before Thanksgiving.

"About?" (This time I'm not playing dumb.) Martyn is the editor-in-chief of *Boy* (circulation: 1,000,000 and soaring), the Versailles magazine aimed at twenty- to-thirty-year-old males, telling them how to dress, what music to like, what actors to adore. He's a South Londoner now living on Beekman Place and he bears a slight resemblance to a robust Errol Flynn. Everyone knows Martyn is destined for great things; when Gaston Moreau dies, it's assumed, either he or Regine will become Creative Director (or Director: Creative) of the whole place, landing the coveted million-dollar-a-year job (that doesn't include the co-op apartment and the $50,000 clothing allowance) that entails doing very little.

"The whole book review thingy," he says. "I hear there was quite a row." (Row. Thingy. Dodgy, telly, naff, bits, wanker, bap, snog . . . I'm convinced Brits use cute words just to be different. Yet they call something as simple as cookies "digestive biscuits" and Martin is Martyn. It's hard to figure out.).

"It happens it was a lousy book."

"I'm sure it was." Does he believe it or is he just being nice to me? He probably doesn't read too many books; more likely he goes home, reads magazines and then more magazines, watches shows like *Dawson's Creek*, *The X-Files*, and *Xena: Warrior Princess*. Martyn could have been a male model, an actor, or, with his broad shoulders and square jaw, perhaps even a heavyweight boxer, but for some reason he chose the magazine world. Once a week Martyn, the best-dressed man most people have ever laid eyes on, makes the gossip columns—he's constantly caught canoodling with models and starlets and any other females he can get his long manicured paws on. We've always gotten along; he's printed several freelance pieces of mine including one three-page feature about a can't-miss off-Broadway playwright who, it turns out, missed.

We walk toward the Versailles building together and for two blocks I'm way out of my league. It's possible, of course, he wants to ditch me. But maybe not. I try to sell the Leroy White piece to him but he says it's too "old" for his publication. He asks why *It* hasn't printed it and I explain that it might be too "young" for them.

"So you're going to West Dakota?" he asks me. (I guess he hasn't really ever mastered American geography.)

"East Dakota," I correct him.

"Not much out there, I imagine."

"Mount Rushmore."

"Really? I thought that was in St. Louis."

I ask him if *Boy* had given the Ethan Cawley book a good review.

"We didn't even review it," he says. "It wasn't assigned. So unfortunately I don't have anybody to humiliate."

⟩   ⟨

I PUT WHAT I think are the final touches on my Leroy White article . . . for the third time. This is the third variation on the same theme: it had started out as a paragraph on *It*'s "Ones to Watch" page, then was a one-pager and now is a feature; hopefully a Donna Reems or Harry Brooks photo shoot would be in order. For a change I was writing about a subject I'm genuinely interested in: an actor who appeared in practically every lurid 1970s black exploitation movie (*Shaft in Africa*, *Foxy Brown*, *The Mack*, etc.) but was a Juilliard acting-school alumnus who had played Othello, Macbeth, and Hamlet in off-Broadway productions. Often in those movies, White was wearing a leopard-skin coat, shooting a sawed-off shotgun, and driving a pimpmobile, or wearing tall Lucite high-heeled boots with barracudas swimming inside them. He had completely disappeared in the eighties, working as a redcap at JFK Airport, but was now the star of a highly respected cop show and had won two Emmys. It was inevitable that he'd be abandoning the show for good for either the screen or the stage or both.

With the article in my hands, I walk past Velma and enter Regine's office. The goal is to drop it in her in-box and exchange a few words and tell Regine the White thing was done. (I have a great cover line: WHITE IS THE NEW BLACK.) But Regine isn't in and so I don't put it in her in-box. I walk around the office a few times, then go back in. But she still isn't there.

"Regine's gonna be back after lunch," Velma shouts to me. Regine often has lunch at some very fancy places with some very fancy people and "after lunch" for her sometimes means six in the evening.

Carefully, I set the article on the top of the pile.

I see Velma stand up, put her coat on, and leave. This gives me the opportunity to do something I've always wanted to do: check out Regine Turnbull's Rolodexes. There are three of these bulky overflowing mammoths right near her telephone, itself a leviathan (she has a hundred numbers on her speed dial). One Rolodex is currently open to *PoW* and there are a few London phone numbers written on the card. It is, I realize, the Prince of Wales. This is under the *R*'s, for Royalty, and there are about eighty cards in this section . . . princes, princesses, dukes and duchesses from countries, principalities, and breakaway republics that either nobody has ever heard of or that overthrew their monarchies a hundred years ago.

I flip the cards to *P* for politicians.

C&C comes up, with a few Washington, D.C., phone numbers. That's the President.

She has *PMUK* and *PFr* (Prime Minister, United Kingdom, and

President, France, I guess) and she has *SotH*, which, given the area code, I assume to be the Speaker of the House; and *SoS*, the Secretary of State. Every senator and every Cabinet member is in there and she has their home phone numbers and addresses too.

On another smaller Rolodex are the fashion people and the writers, agents, photographers, models. Here are the many home phone numbers of John Galliano and Calvin Klein, the many car phone numbers of Giorgio Armani and Karl Lagerfeld; here are Ralph Lauren and Donna Karan's beeper numbers. The remaining Rolodex (and the largest) is for entertainment people. Mixed among every single living luminary and his or her agent and publicist and personal assistant are the phone numbers of very famous dead people . . . but, because of their notoriety and of her sentimentality, I suppose, she keeps their cards: Cary Grant, Fred Astaire, Audrey Hepburn, etc.

She has the phone number of practically everyone who was anyone since 1945 and if I were more mischievous I could prank everyone from Jimmy Carter to Steven Spielberg to Donald Trump to Prince Albert of Monaco to Madonna to Yasser Arafat.

When I return to my desk I flip my own anorexic Rolodex to a random card.

Sal's Pizza on Forty-fourth Street comes up.

Passing by Regine's office as I'm about to leave for the day, I see no sign she ever came back from lunch. Sometimes the lunches get so long and involved—she has a phone by her table for these things, I hear—that she simply goes home afterwards.

I look for my article in her in-box. But the pile is now twice as high—a tower of articles, proofs, memos, magazines, clippings from newspapers, letters, and photos—and it takes a minute or two before I can finally find the thing.

I put it on the top and leave.

{ }

ANOTHER BIG meeting in the big conference room. Sheila Stackhouse, pointer in hand and wearing a tent-like black linen dress, is in charge (a temporary role she might be relishing a little too much for everyone's taste), Betsy Butler being unable to attend.

Michael Thorne, the young, dangerously high-checkboned movie star, is on the cover. In the picture Thorne smokes a huge cigar and the HOLLYWOOD sign is behind him and the sky is full of stars. Under each arm (he's wearing a four-thousand-dollar Armani suit, which he gets to keep) a busty blonde pops out of a low-cut gown. There have been rumors about Thorne for years, whispers that he likes boys who look just like him but a few years younger, rumors that he's so gorgeous he has convinced his male co-stars—often happily married men—to perform oral sex on him; this cover is his, his publicist's, and our way of putting these rumors to rest.

"I think it's the best bloody cover photo we've had in months," Roddy Grissom says. He says this every issue.

"Yeah, since the last one," only Liz Channing has the *cojones* to say.

Eager to get it going I say, "Thorne in His Side."

Liz is writing these chestnuts down—this often was Nan's role, but at this very second Nan might be yanking all the pews out of Westminster Abbey, still looking for her personal bible.

"Around the Thorne," Oliver Osborne suggests.

"Come Blow Your Thorne," Lizzie says. Everyone giggles, given the nature of the rumors.

"I Like Mike," someone says.

"No, not that," Mark Larkin says.

"Every Rose Has Its Thorne?" Nolan Tomlin suggests. Putting it in the form of a question, he sounds as if he's been transferred to the fashion department.

"Wait!" I say, practically jumping up. "I've got it! Thorne of Plenty!"

People look at each other, impressed and content. They seem to like it. Okay, it's not "What hath God wrought?" but we've run much, much worse cover lines than that, ones that nearly hurt your teeth if you said them aloud.

"Hmm," Sheila says. "Did you get that one, Liz?"

Liz nods and shows us that she did write it down.

Nobody has any other suggestions so we move on to other topics. Roddy leaves the room as do Marjorie, Leslie, Byron, and the other art people. It seems I might have won this round, and Willie winks at me approvingly.

Sheila looks at her list of items and goes around the table, making sure we're all up to date on what we're working on.

Before the meeting breaks up two things happen.

Sheila says, at the end of a long round-up of what's going on in the next few weeks: "And Boris Montague will be in Paris next week and will be faxing Mark some of his column, is that right?"

"Yes," Mark Larkin says. He leans forward uncomfortably, braces his entire body as if about to be kicked in the stomach.

"*What?!*" Willie says, aghast.

"Mark is going to be editing Boris's colum . . ." Sheila says with a loud swallow.

"*Since when?*" Willie says, his face the same shade of red as his huge quivering fists.

Nobody says a word. Everybody wishes they were miles away from this room.

"Regine didn't tell you?" Sheila asks.

"No. Regine didn't tell me. Regine didn't tell me anything. I never see Regine."

"I thought that she told you," Sheila says. "I'm sorry."

"She should have told you," Sheila says to Willie.

"I can't believe this!" Willie says.

It occurs to me that this is why Betsy Butler didn't attend this meeting. Regine never intended to tell Willie he was being replaced as Boris's editor, and Betsy didn't have the heart or guts for it. So this was their way of doing it, by pretending that it already had been done.

"Why? Why is this happening?" Willie says to no one, to everyone.

"I think Regine feels that we could use a change," Sheila answers feebly. She cannot look him straight in the eyes . . . even if she can, I don't know if Willie would see her.

"I can't believe this," he says again.

Mark Larkin says, "I'm going to give it my best shot. I don't think anyone will notice a difference."

But that's not the point! And everyone knows it.

"This is just unbelievable," Willie says. "I've been doing this for years." It almost sounds like he's crying. He turns to Mark Larkin, whose body is still braced for punishment, and mutters: "If you edit his column or so much as talk to him on the phone, I'll kill you."

"I have to do what I have to do," Mark Larkin says.

After ten long seconds of silence Sheila says, "Okay, okay . . . I'm not so sure about this cover line. Thorne of Plenty is good but is there anything else we can think of?"

Mark Larkin looks up from his lap and says, "How about: Oh, For the Love of Mike!"

Nobody says a thing. Nobody's face changes.

"Hey! You know, I think that's pretty good!" Sheila says. "Thorne of Plenty and Oh, For the Love of Mike! We'll decide which one to go with."

Slowly and quietly, like tired aching football players shuffling around after a game, we stand up and leave the room. Willie remains by himself alone, still red, still clenching his fists.

{ }

"I'M REALLY worried about Willie," Laurie Lafferty says to me.

She is as far from the typical Versailles employee as you can get; she wears jeans and sneakers, her hair is the hair of a human being and not a Barbie doll or Breck model, and she's friendly and warm. The guards downstairs often stop her and make her show her ID and even then they don't believe her.

"What's up?"

"He thinks about Mark Larkin all the time. It's becoming an obsession."

"I can kind of understand it though."

She rolls her eyes. She doesn't know what kind of competition Willie and I are up against; she doesn't understand the stress and doesn't know how frightening and vicious failure can be, that it lingers long into the night and filters into the lonely pale hours of the morning when you've got nothing else for company but the growls of garbage trucks and your own filthy bitterness. But maybe, since they spend a lot of time together, she does know.

"When's the last time he's had anything longer than half a page in the magazine?" I ask. "It's got to be months now."

"Six issues ago . . . the article about that lawyer who sued himself. And before that, the Chelsea Hotel article."

She says: "I'm afraid he's going to do something really stupid." (We've never had a conversation this serious before.)

"He'd never kill himself."

"I didn't mean that."

"Why doesn't he just quit? With his connections and talent, he could be someplace in a week."

"Because then he wouldn't have Mark Larkin to think about. Maybe when he gets Nan Hotchkiss's old job, maybe he'll be better then," she says.

"There's been no announcement yet."

"He says it's a done deal. You know what makes him smile? He imagines becoming a senior editor and then shitcanning—to use his and your word—every idea and word Mark Larkin comes up with."

"That would probably make me smile too."

When I get back to my desk gloom hangs all over the cubicle, dripping like motor oil, darkening everything but the spot that Nolan's greasy hair has made on the wall.

I want Nan Hotchkiss's job. If Willie gets it, though, I can live with it. It seems to be the only hope. My mind works, going in impossible directions: Willie, by nature of his seniority, gets the job, gets Mark Larkin fired, Willie moves up, then I move up.

Just when things begin to look brighter—but only in my imagination—Ivy Kooper walks by and dumps something in my in-box. Snapping out of my reverie I see it's a mock-up of the next *It* cover . . . Michael Thorne, the two busty blondes, the Hollywood sign, the stars and cigar. And written across the bottom in sapphire blue is: OH, FOR THE LOVE OF MIKE!

I put my head in my hands and stay that way for a while.

What was I doing there?

I didn't know.

Did I want to be anywhere else?

No fucking way.

I go into e-mail.

TO: KOOPERI
FROM: POSTZ
Re: tonight

Free tonight? Dinner? Not free? A drink? Anything? Please?

{ }

IVY AND I GO out to dinner again, the night before Thanksgiving. She's upset because she has little to do at work except file, put things in in-baskets and take things out of out-baskets, sort some mail and make copies and send faxes, and do an occasional demeaning personal errand—the previous day she'd picked up a prescription from Byron Poole's veterinarian, then brought it to his dog walker's doorman. She had probably assumed that right away she'd be writing articles and interviewing writers and actors. I thought the same thing too when I started. (I envisioned myself writing Joseph Mitchell–style *New Yorker* pieces about the lost and forgotten; these hopes were dashed when I fully absorbed the typical *It* cover: MICHELLE (Pfeiffer) MY BELLE!, A (Gwyneth) PALTROW SUM! (Ethan) HAWKE SOARS!, GOLDIE (Hawn) GIRL!, A LOAD OF (Sandra) BULLOCK!, etc.)

On the subway to the restaurant Ivy invites me to Thanksgiving dinner with her family, still pitying me for having no place to go, but I politely decline. Having dinner with the abominable Jimmy Kooper isn't my idea of a nice Thanksgiving evening and it's probably not his family's idea either. When you see his name in newspapers or magazines, the words "pit bull" usually manage to appear in the same sentence. He might sue me for taking too much stuffing.

Besides, I'm going to have a $11.99 Thanksgiving dinner with my mother at a coffee shop a few blocks away from her place in Queens, that building with the giant toaster.

"But thanks anyway," I say to Ivy.

We kissed for the first time that night, our second date. In a doorway on Twenty-eighth and Second Avenue, not too far from Marjorie's apartment building. It was icy cold out but the skin on her face was very warm and very soft. I remember brushing a finger along her eyebrows, feeling the little fuzz flick back up as I moved back and forth.

I was going too fast and she liked me too much.

Getting involved with her would be a big disaster.

I just know it will be.

⟨ ⟩

TO: POSTZ
FROM: TURNBULLR
SUBJECT: IDEA

I just want you to know that we think it's a truly splendid idea you gave to Sheila.

TO: TURNBULLR
FROM: POSTZ
SUBJECT: Re: IDEA

What idea?

TO: POSTZ
FROM: TURNBULLR
SUBJECT: Re: IDEA

Assigning the same article to two different people. There's nothing wrong with a little competition, is there?

You're really thinking on your feet.

6

"I CAN'T stand most of these people!" Liz yells to me, three inches away. "I hope you know that!"

"I was hoping you couldn't stand them!" I yell back.

A four-room apartment in a postwar doorman building on East Fifty-sixth Street, jam-packed and buzzing, very little space to move around in . . . about 150 people, most of them are John's friends, John being Liz's husband of five years, most of them are lawyers and lawyers' husbands and wives. But a few of us are here: me, Willie, Oliver. The music and chatter are very loud and you have to scream to be heard.

"How much longer are you going to stay?" Oliver asks me.

"I don't know if it's possible to leave!"

Liz pleads: "Please get me out of here!" But does she mean it? She is the hostess after all and she's all decked out; her satin top and pants combination looks like a pair of pajamas but must have cost one whole paycheck and her shoes don't look very cheap either. A large Christmas tree in a corner is blinking red and green and there are lights strung along the walls and ceiling but behind the slithery trains of people going every way you can hardly see any of it.

Willie is drunk, Oliver Osborne is drunk too, and Liz is well on her way.

"I wish everyone would just *leave!*" she snarls to me before going off to greet some new arrivals.

"Liz has fine legs, don't you think?" Oliver says. His bright blue eyes are looking a little lopsided and dark to me.

"Here. Have more," Willie says, sticking a glass of something in my hand.

"Are you guys having a good time?" It's John, wiry and tall, close-cropped hair, a dimple in his chin that could hold a quarter . . . he looks like an astronaut and Willie has always referred to John as John Glenn or Astro-Boy.

"This is the best party I've ever been to," Willie tells him, puffing an arm around his shoulder. "I mean that. Did you know I was conceived at Truman Capote's Black and White Ball? Lemme tell you all about it . . ."

John warily edges away and Willie mumbles to himself for a few seconds.

Liz rejoins us and says, "Look, if you guys go, tell me where you're going and maybe I'll join you." Then she steps away, joins a passing train of party goers.

"Those calves, Zachary, there ought to be a museum for them. I've never quite noticed it before."

"Let's hop in a taxi and go to Mark Larkin's joint and throw tin cans up at his window," Willie says. "Let's ring his doorbell and run. Let's ask him if he's got Prince Albert in a refrigerator and if his submarine races are running in the can."

"*You're here?!*" Marjorie says to me, suddenly appearing a foot away.

"Pretty much."

"Some of John's friends are pretty nice for lawyers." If this is said to arouse anger and jealousy in me, it works . . . the thought of one of these bullying belligerent overpaid assholes getting his rich slimy paws on her . . . I feel a fiery twinge rise up from my toes to my scalp.

"Then go ahead and grab one, Margie." And she slips off to do as ordered.

"She's certainly a handful, isn't she?" Oliver says.

"Tell him, Zeke, tell him," Willie urges with his elbow.

"Tell me *wot?*" Oliver asks. He's the tallest person in the room, almost touching the ceiling, and his square glasses are falling off his nose.

"Ah! You know, old flings and stuff," I say.

"Marjorie Millet?! Good god, man!" he says.

"You people work at *It?*" It's one of John's friends and he doesn't even look old enough for law school.

"No, that's a downright lie! Who told you that?!" Willie says. He shoves his chest against the poor kid, who bounces a yard back into a crooked line of people and falls. Drinks are spilled.

"Shagging Marjorie Millet?! She must be a can of dynamite!" Oliver says to me.

"Does dynamite come in cans?" I ask.

Willie is helping Lawyer-Lad off the floor . . . the kid's shirt is drenched with several streaks of different beverages.

"Tide, Lestoil, and a dash of turmeric," Willie tells him, "are good for getting out highball stains."

"Can we get out of here?" I say. "I can't breathe."

"You've got to tell me more about this. When were you with her? I want to know the how, why, where, and when."

"Ever the get-tough journalist, Ollie, old chum," Willie says. "I think you're arguably the best damned reporter we've got. But you're in too deep on this story and I've got to take you off." He's slurring his words, bending over a little, and his eyes are sinking.

I say to Oliver, "Willie wants to go to Mark Larkin's house and ask him if Prince Albert's submarine's in the can. Are you in? 'Cause I'm not long for this place."

"Let's do it. I'd love to rip apart that cunt."

I look around for Liz but she's lost and I get a little dizzy from the air, rife with alcohol, tobacco, body odor, and perfume. I see Marjorie in profile talking to a lawyer and she peeks at me for a fraction of a second and raises an eyebrow, rubbing it in. She has black tights or stockings and garters on and her calves look sleeker than they really are. I'd give every penny I have just to lift up her black skirt and loft my face up there, maybe spend the rest of this lonely chilly weekend that way.

"Is Mark Larkin getting Nan's job?" Oliver asks me. He's clutching my shoulder and staring right down at me.

"Who knows?"

"Don't you care?"

"I sure do care. But I don't know."

"Is there any chance I'm getting it? I have some fish to fry, I do, Zeke."

Oh no . . . more fish.

Oliver continues. "If Willie gets it, that's all right."

"Why hasn't he gotten it already then?" Willie is right near us but is too drunk to hear us or make sense of the conversation.

Liz is with us again and Willie tells her she's arguably at once the best damned preternatural reporter we've got but is in too deep on the story and he's got to take her off it and although she was a Young Turk-Manquè she too informed of her time.

"We're going soon," I say. "We're going downtown."

"You lucky fucks! *Where?* I swear, I can get the fuck out of here." I've never heard her curse like this (her father is a successful banker but her mother once slung hash at a San Francisco greasy spoon).

Willie names a bar downtown, one I've never heard of but can picture perfectly: choked with damp darkness and smoke, brown everything, stale smells.

We're in a taxi going downtown, Ollie, Willie, and myself, crunched tight into the backseat.

"You've got to tell me more about Marjorie."

"That's water under the bridge, Oliver," Willie tells Ollie.

"What else is going on in our little club that I don't know about?"

"Ted Tarrant is putting the bricks to Annie Williams. He's been doing it for years." Ted Tarrant is *It*'s publisher, Anne Williams was once an ad sales person.

"But didn't she die two years ago?"

"You'd be surprised how few people care about such trivial things, Ollie. No, let's talk about the new *objet* of Zeke's affection, Miss Leslie Usher-Soames."

"BLLLLGGGH!" Ollie yells with mock disgust and even the taxi driver turns around for a second.

"What do you mean: BLLLLGGGH?" I ask him.

"She's as cold as ice! I know *her* type."

"Ah, you never know."

Stores and buildings flicker like cards shuffling and the taxi bounces and it feels like we're going over waves.

Willie says, "Zeke thinks that underneath the massive white glacier of Leslie there churns a seething volcano just waiting to erupt in a violent spasm of heat, lust, and desire."

"You think that?" Oliver asks me.

"Yeah, I do."

"I really would doubt that. Underneath that massive white glacier there churns another massive white glacier."

"I gotta hit the head," Willie says, adjusting something.

"Can you last till we get downtown?" I ask him.

"If not, it's just a pair of slacks."

"What about Lizzie?" Ollie asks.

"She's got John Glenn."

"I know, but what *about* her?"

"Do you have the hots for her?" I ask Ollie.

"Oh no. Not a'tall. But she looked pretty tonight, didn't you think? What's that her hair she, her style the way she . . .?" He's having a lot of trouble communicating. "A mignon?"

"A chignon."

Willie doubles over, trying to keep his bladder in check. "Oh God Jesus, I really do have to go." He asks the driver what he does when he has to go to the bathroom really badly and can't find a restaurant or bar that will let him go. The man, whose last name might be BLLLGGGH, passes back to us a plastic jar of something . . . it's empty but smells faintly of piss. Willie unzips his fly and urinates into the container.

"I have seen everything now," Oliver mutters, his hands over his eyes, shielding himself from all this. The taxi is bouncing along and Willie rolls down the window and turns the jar over and his pee leaks all over Lexington Avenue and probably the door of the taxi too. He passes it back and thanks the driver.

"Whew! That hit the spot," Willie says. He's not doubled over anymore but he's not sitting up perfectly straight either.

We walk into a dark stale-smelling dive and only one person is inside other than the bartender and to my amazement, it's Liz Channing. She's sitting at the bar, a man's navy blue coat, probably Astro-Boy's, falling loosely over her shoulder.

"What took you so long, fellas?"

"How'd you get here so fast?" I ask.

"I left before you did. What will it be?"

We get some drinks and move to a booth.

After we talk about work for a half-hour Willie says, "Okay, let's try not to talk about work."

For three minutes nobody can think of anything to say.

"What are you doing for Christmas, Willie?" Liz asks. "We can talk about that, right?"

"What am I doing? Work. Hating my job, hating myself, hating the man and that ugly painting across from me."

"You're not going home?"

"No. I'll be around here. You?"

"New Hampshire, John's lovely Republican God-fearing family. Zack?"

"I gotta go to West Dakota, remember?

"That sucks. That really bites the big one," Willie says. He slaps me on the back so hard that I spit out the vodka and tonic that's swishing around in my mouth.

"I dread meeting this rugged reclusive ranchero rough-and-ready writer."

And then for an hour more we talk about work, how much we hate it, how miserable we are . . .

"Oh, sometimes I do so wish I were a New Girl," Liz sighs.

We're standing across the street from Mark Larkin's building, a five-story brownstone on East Thirteenth Street somewhere. It must be close to two in the morning and it's very quiet out . . . in some windows Christmas trees flash on and off. Liz has closed the buttons of her coat but it really does look like she went outside in her pajamas and high heels.

"So what do we do now?" someone says.

"We just wake him the fuck up," Willie says.

"What does that get us?" Liz asks, her chignon fraying.

"Nowhere. But what does not waking him the fuck up get us?"

"I've got a plan. If we really want to take the piss, why don't we ask him . . ." Oliver says, and it looks like he's really straining and reasoning. "Why don't we ask him if he wants to come out with us?"

"But what if he *does*?"

"Oh yeah. Right . . ."

"No, this calls for something really drastic," Willie says. "But I just can't think of anything really drastic right now."

We're standing around on the empty street, standing around and wobbling in the frigid air, a car occasionally winding by.

"Maybe he's not even home," Liz says.

"Maybe he's asleep," Ollie says.

"He's *supposed* to be asleep, fool!" Willie snaps.

"Maybe we all should go home," I say. I'm thinking of Marjorie in the black dress, then not in the black dress, of her in black pantyhose . . . I'm thinking of burying my head in her chest and her biting my ears and scratching my back. When I get like this, when imagination takes over like fever and all reality and common sense vanish, her pouting stomach flattens very quickly and her craggy skin softens and we get along simply splendidly.

"You think your party's still going on, Liz?" I ask. Maybe I can whisk Miss Millet away.

"I hope not . . ."

"This is such . . ." Willie begins. He sits down dejectedly on a garbage can . . . his shirttails are out and his hair is stringy. "This is like the biggest anticlimax since . . . since . . . since Nagasaki, maybe?"

"I really don't see how Nagasaki was an anticlimax, Willie," Oliver says.

In the sky a frosty full moon pulses behind a water tower.

Willie shrugs. "Can't we think of anything?"

"Maybe we should all go home," Liz says.

Willie and I put Liz and Oliver in a taxi . . . they both live uptown. Before it drives away, Ollie rolls down the window and sticks his gigantic square head out, his Clark Kent glasses dangling off his nose at an impossible angle. "I just don't understand the Nagasaki metaphor," he says and the taxi carries them away.

We go into Mark Larkin's lobby (it's just the little dusty vestibule with the buzzers on the wall and Chinese food menus on the floor) and we find his name on the buzzer. Willie presses it and we wait a few moments. I try to remind him that revenge is a dish you eat cold but in my current stupor I tell him something like cold revenge is a dish best heated up sweet.

"Hello?" cackles Mark Larkin's groggy voice over the little speaker.

"Chinee foo downstair!" Willie says.

"Huh?"

"Chinee foo downstair! You sen out for Chinee foo!"

"No I didn't. Go away."

"I have you co noodles and moo shoo pork. You sen out for Chinee foo!"

"Go away, you yellow slant-eyed mongrel!"

Willie has walked me to my building. My nose is running and so is his and his face is flushed with the booze and cold.

"That wasn't it," he says. "That's just not going to do it."

"Mark Larkin?"

"I'm in dire straits, man. So are you but you're too sane to realize it."

I put my key in.

"Valorous, extreme action, Zack. That's what this situation calls for."

I open the door and smell the many rancid snug smells that are the dreary bounceless rubber ball I live in.

"We could try to get him fired," I suggest.

"I don't think that's going to do it either. We've got to doing something really drastic. Something serious and final. Our world would be a better place without him in it."

"I don't know," I say. "There's no—"

But he's not listening . . . he's losing himself in whatever thoughts are taking over. He shakes his head, snaps himself out of it, and then begins his cold walk home by himself.

PART II

7

A CONVERSATION WITH ETHAN CAWLEY

Ethan Cawley is a man of few words, but what words he has are decidedly precious. *Badland*, his tenth novel (Lakeland & Barker, $29.50) and almost certain National Book Award nominee, takes place in what by now is familiar territory for Cawley readers: the harsh Badlands of the American West. But Cawley, who has at once been compared to both Vivaldi and Sam Shepard, boldly breaks new ground here as he (in the words of one reviewer) "deconstructs and reconstructs, de-mythifies and re-mythifies." It's no wonder that the rights to film *Badland*, Cawley's first number-one best-seller, were snatched up by Robert Redford for a reported two million dollars. *It* met the reclusive rough-and-ready Peck's Bad Boy of American letters on his sprawling 80-acre ranch somewhere in South Dakota (Cawley, who wore a Banana Republic denim shirt and Tommy Hilfiger jeans for the interview, craves his privacy) and asked him about his life, his art, and his fragrance.

It: Why do you live out here?
Ethan Cawley: I want to.

It: Does it ever get boring?

EC: Yeah. Not really.

It: What do you do to keep occupied, other than write?

EC: Sleep. Eat. Take walks.

It: Have you begun your next book?

EC: Maybe.

It: What's the last book you read?

EC: Probably the last one I wrote.

It: Who are some contemporary authors you admire?

EC: Hmmmph.

It: Who do you envision playing Jake Hardin [the lead character in *Badland*] in the movie?

EC: Nobody. Anybody. Could be Marlon Brando.

From the next room, Corinne Cawley [the author's second wife] calls out: "How about that Jeff Bridges? Or Clint Eastwood?"

It: If you win the National Book Award or the Pulitzer Prize, will you accept it?

EC: Sure.

It: Why?

EC: Good for sales.

It: Is there a constant theme running through your work?

EC: Life is tough, and don't step in the cowshit.

It: What's your fragrance?

EC: Calvin Klein's Obsession for Men.

{ }

A CONVERSATION with Ethan Cawley . . .

That "interview" (squeezing orange juice out of Play-Doh was more like it) took place over Christmas and ran, I believe, in *It*'s February issue, but it might have been March. It almost didn't run at all but his book won some obscure, highly regarded French prize and Cawley landed a MacArthur genius grant.

"This isn't publishable," Betsy Butler told me when it was done. (It took days to even get it to look like the above!)

"This is what he sounds like," I said to her. "Or do you want to listen to the tape?"

"Well . . . no. No thanks."

Between my questions and his answers were interminable stretches of dead air, of guttural groaning, him spacing out and in and back out, of him moving around on his $6,000 couch, rubbing his jaw and grimacing and fumbling for something to say or forgetting that I'd even asked a question. Or he'd just look out the window at . . . at not much of anything.

To get a half-hour of dialogue I went through nearly three one-hour tapes. Even his silences were incoherent.

That was my punishment: having to go there for Christmas . . . I was being taught "a lesson."

But I really didn't mind the Christmas part, although had I told my overseers that they might have devised some more nefarious punishment, one that really might have stung. Christmas for me usually is: waking up late, taking a subway to Queens to my mother's house, taking her to her local coffee shop for the $11.99 Christmas Special, then a subway back to Manhattan and recovering from that, then taking a train out to Massapequa and having dinner with Bob and Sheila Post and my sister and her beefy Texan physical therapist fiancé. By dessert Dad has usually fallen asleep, Sheila drinks too much wine and starts talking about her girlfriends at the beauty parlor, Sister gets on my case for not helping her clean the dishes, and Beefy Texan Physical Therapist wants to get the hell out of there almost as much as I do, which is just about the only thing he and I have in common.

So flying first-class to Rapid City, renting a purple Dodge Neon, getting a decent meal allowance (no three-star joints out there in the frosty sagebrush but still, a free meal is a free meal), well, all that wasn't really much of a punishment . . .

(Driving out to JFK Airport via Golem Car Service, the car went past my mother's building. I could see the lights of her Christmas tree twinkling in the window, in the giant piece of golden brown toast.)

Except the interview itself. That was torture.

When the door is opened for me I'm met by a small man with a smooth, shiny face, ample and carefully tended gray hair, and bright blue eyes.

"I'm here to interview Ethan Cawley," I reach out my hand and say. "Zachary Post from *It*."

"Yeah. Ggrrr. Hmmmph."

I'd expected him to look like William Holden circa *The Wild Bunch* — a lanky wizened man, a creased leathery face with Ted Williams slits for eyes and a flinty blue stare, crow's-feet reaching to his ears and chin, sparse but wild silvery hair. That's what his book jacket photo looks like, an exaggerated topographical relief of the rockier parts of the moon. But Cawley looks more like Ralph Lauren than he does William Holden.

I set up the tape recorder on the Roche-Bobois coffee table in the living room. Looking out the windows I see endless empty plains, scrabbly and still, and snowcapped mountains on the horizon, foamy white clouds slicing through them. But no houses, no stores, no people, no buildings, no nothing. (In magazine-speak: "The place is at once preternaturally bleak and beautiful, as is Cawley's prose-poetry.") He's not merely living on the edge of nowhere, he's right smack in the middle of it, a long, lonesome drive from anything.

(No wonder every book he writes is the same: nothing ever happens to the guy. How could it? There's nothing around to happen.)

I expect to see a beat-up old Hermes typewriter or some kind of clunky Gutenberg hulk that sounds like a shotgun blast with each peck, but I notice a modern Power Mac 7200 and a high-powered laser printer. And there are no moose heads on the walls either, no bear pelts or caribou penises. Instead: prints of Monet water lilies and the framed covers of his books.

Cawley doesn't want me here and I don't want to be here but I am, so he makes it, I believe, as agonizing as he can for me. Unless he's always like this. With his groans, grunts, and grimaces, he's acting as though my being here is the biggest pain he can endure. Perhaps it is.

During the interview — in the middle of one of his zoned-out pauses — I see him snap to suddenly. He says, "There she is." I turn around and see fifty yards away a white Range Rover headed our away.

I'm expecting one of his sturdy Jessica Lange female characters to walk in (they say things like: "You're a loner, an outsider, Harlan. You been alone and outside your whole damned life"), so it's a surprise when a woman the shape of a jar of mustard waddles in. Corinne is his trophy wife, a trophy, perhaps, for finishing fifth in something.

I shake her hand and she asks — no, tells — her husband to make some coffee. Once again I find myself deceived; rather than a mug of jet black gut-scorching java, what I'm served is a cup of one of those instant International Coffee concoctions, something like Cinnamon Vanillaccino.

There's this story that Truman Capote once arm-wrestled Humphrey Bogart and not only won, he won three times and nearly threw him off the table in the process. I always found this story difficult to believe but I do believe it, and when I'm leaving the house my urge is to say to Ethan Cawley: "So do you want to step outside, cowboy, and try to take me on?"

Walking back to the purple Neon, the gravel crunching beneath our feet, Corinne Cawley tells me something, something I'd like to mention in the article but can't, of course, not for a harmless puff piece for *It*.

It is dark and cold out now and the stars look to be only a few feet away and I'm thinking of the two-and-a-half-hour drive back to Rapid City. It's Christmas Eve and the roads will be deserted; I'll be singing along with the radio within minutes—that's what I'd been doing driving out ("Brandy wears a braided chain of the finest silver . . .").

"He doesn't look at all like his pictures," I say to Corinne, putting my key in the car door.

"Oh, he just has that done," she says.

"He has what done?"

But she tells me nothing more, which is enough to pique my curiosity. She knows she probably shouldn't say any more, especially to some nosy big-city reporter such as myself.

I found out through Harry Brooks that—through airbrushing, computers, and some other devices—they put wrinkles, furrow, and crow's-feet into Ethan Cawley's unrugged, uncreased, unleathery face. And they add the flinty blue stare.

Mark Larkin does a feature on Arnaud de Llama and gets four new suits. He writes about Thad Wright and gets a free painting, albeit a Mylanta monstrosity. I do a Q & A with Ethan Cawley and I get a hundred grunts and a rented Dodge.

Is there something I'm doing wrong?

{ }

A RECURRING dream.

I'm sitting at my desk going over some copy. From a few yards away

Nolan Tomlin's telephone has simultaneously taken on the aspect of the crystal ball in *The Wizard of Oz* and a police radio. As nasal police-operator voices report various crimes and give addresses—a run-over body on the N and R tracks at Twenty-third Street, a baby charred to a tiny crisp in a pizza oven in Rego Park—I can see these gruesome events playing out on his telephone in glorious Technicolor.

Smitty, the skeletal chain-smoking receptionist, then appears in Nolan's magical gizmo and tells me that someone is in the reception area and has an appointment to see me. It's always someone very important . . . sometimes Steven Spielberg, sometimes Giorgio Armani, sometimes the President or Elizabeth Hurley. And I see them there, in the crystal ball, waiting for me on a couch, anxiously checking their watches.

I walk through the office hallways to get there but the place is now a maze of abrupt dead ends and sharp turns, and nobody else is there. Although it's difficult for me to get to reception, I'm getting closer and closer and although I'm no longer near my desk I still see—in that eerie split-screen way of dreams—the crystal ball, and my visitor is getting impatient.

And then: *poof*, I'm there.

I walk past Smitty, who now really *is* a skeleton, and I see that what I have always feared has come true: my father and his wife have dropped in on me at work, they're just sitting there, waiting to see me. Bob Post is holding a long net in one hand (like a pitchfork) and Sheila has her hair up in a bun.

"You're not allowed to visit me here," I groan to them as *Massapequan Gothic* stands up to greet me.

"Yes! I know!" my father says with a big smile. He's got his aqua blue Sansabelt slacks on and his blue Islanders jacket and his blue Mets cap . . . he looks like a swimming pool! He's shimmering and rippling and clear. *My father is a swimming pool!*

"You're not allowed to visit me here," I repeat.

"Which is why we did!" Sheila enthuses.

They're asking me how my holidays were, how West Dakota was, when I hear a door open and close behind me. My heart feels like an Alka-Seltzer tablet sinking through water. Someone at work is seeing me talking to my father and stepmother!

I turn around and see Regine Turnbull, all four-foot-eleven of her. She looks prettier than usual and she's wearing a Bob Mackey gown and a diamond necklace rented from Harry Winston just for this cameo role in my nightmare.

"Hey, we've never met your boss!" Bob Post says with that big chlorine smile of his. He sticks out his hand to shake Regine's (he calls her "Rogaine" by mistake) and there's a wad of green algae in it.

I look at Regine and it plays like the fun-house scene in *The Lady From Shanghai*: there are hundreds of her and they're warped and distorted into silvery obese Regines and silvery tall broomstick Regines and Regines that look like globules of mercury jiggling on a mirror.

"I've never met your parents!" all these undulant fun house Regines say.

"She's not my mother," I try to say but the words don't come out, I'm so petrified.

"Tell me, Mr. Post," Regine says, and now there's only one of her and it's the genuine frightening-enough article. "What is it like being arguably this country's greatest living architect?"

Bob Post's smile evaporates . . . he's no longer a pool.

"*Architect?*" Bob Post says. "Hey, I'm just a Wet Guy . . ."

⟫ ⟪

WHEN I walk back into the office after my humiliating Western sojourn, I make sure to get there extra early—I show up at 7:30. When you come back to work after a bad haircut or after you've been diagnosed with a fatal illness, every single eye is somehow looking away but also glued to you. I don't want that.

Walking past what used to be Nan Hotchkiss's office, I notice the door, which has been closed for about two months, is open now.

Two men are inside, maintenance men in navy blue work pants and our building's address in red script on their lapels. They're moving the furniture out, stripping the shelves off the wall.

"Hey," I say. "What's going on?"

"Someone's moving in today," one of them answers.

"Do you know who?"

They look at each other and shrug, then look at me and shrug.

"It's either me or you . . . I'm almost sure of it," Willie says.

"What makes you so sure?"

We're in Crookshank's, checking out clothing, killing time.

"Velma walks up to me this morning with a gigantic smile and tells me I'm going to like Regine's announcement today. I ask her if the announcement has to do with who's getting Nan's job and she says yes. I kept prodding her but she wouldn't really tell me anything. But she's got this million-dollar grin on her kisser."

"Sounds like it's you."

Willie eyes a pair of suspenders with a horce-racing theme, taken from a Degas perhaps, lots of pastel blues and oranges.

"You're not thinking of wearing suspenders, Willie. What's next, a bow tie?"

We move on to the socks and then the ties. The long picture window is covered with steam and nothing is visible beyond it. Willie relates that Velma had told him the person getting the features editor job is "strictly one of us," which means they aren't bringing in an outsider. Then Velma said, winking at him and trying to suppress her giggles, it's someone *very, very* close to him.

"Mark Larkin?" I ask.

"No. She knows that would be sticking a hot shish kebab skewer through my heart. The two people very, very close to me are you and me."

My mood quickly elevates. Which means I don't need to buy any clothing.

"Have you noticed anything strange? About Regine's office and meetings?" Willie asks me. "Or maybe you don't see it where you sit."

The door opens and frigid air whisks in with the sounds of cars and buses.

"There are a lot of meetings lately," he continues. "In Regine's office. Completely off-the-schedule meetings."

"So?"

He picks up a loud fuchsia tie with a golf theme: tees, clubs, balls, and golf bags. One of Crookshank's cadaverous salesmen hovers over us . . . they all look alike: sixty years old, gaunt, slicked-back dyed brown hair, sickly green complexions, and eyes that repulse light.

"They're not one-on-one meetings like you'd think, Zeke. You know, I don't know if this tie would even fit around my neck." He's exaggerating but it's true: he gained about five pounds over the long lardy Christmas break.

I feel a prickly feeling sneaking up from my stomach, my temples begin to throb, and I pick up a tie with a drinking theme: martini shakers and glasses. Maybe I *will* buy something.

"Well you know, it's probably just business stuff," I say. "Sales, marketing, and circulation."

"But editors are in there . . . Sheila, Betsy, and Byron too. And why are Tony Lancett and Emma Pilgrim in there sometimes? And Mark Larkin?"

I hang the cocktail tie on the wrong rack, over ties with little chubby *putti* shooting arrows at hearts, and Willie does the same with the golf tie.

"Mark Larkin's in there? With Emma Pilgrim and Tony Lancett?" (*It*'s star feature writers.)

"Tony and Emma are only there some of the time. But Jedediah Leland . . . he's there a lot." (Mark Larkin now divides his time equally between being Teddy Roosevelt and Joseph Cotten in *Citizen Kane*.)

"Do you ever listen in?"

"I can't . . . not when Velma's right there giving me the evil eye. But I can tell you this: our meeting to come up with the Michael Thorne cover line? It was total horseshit. I heard Mark Larkin come up with 'Oh, For the Love of Mike!' the day before in Regine's office. That's why I didn't even bother tossing in my measly two cents in that meeting. It's like the meetings we go to are . . . redundant."

"So that was why . . ." My voice trails off.

So that was why, although everyone had liked my Thorne of Plenty cover line, it had been so abruptly killed. Because they already had one . . .

So the meetings I was attending, I realize as I stare at hundreds of ties dangling off their racks like hanged men, were like sound checks or moot court or rehearsals for the understudies. My work life was a preseason game! The real crucial stuff was going on elsewhere and not only was I not invited, I didn't even know about it.

"You should make a point of strolling by Regine's office more, pal," Willie says. "It'll make you sick."

"Maybe I'll do that."

Fifteen minutes later we leave and, marked down from $600, my brand-new $250 sport coat fits me perfectly.

JACKIE WOOTEN. She got the job.

And it was Mark Larkin's idea, his "brainstorm."

That's what Velma tells us when we gather for the announcement. "After much soul searching and deliberation, we are at once pleased . . ." Velma, reading from a pink piece of paper with loopy purple writing, begins; the upshot of all this is that Regine apparently couldn't decide who should get promoted. Mark Larkin suggested they bring back Jackie and it was done. "A brilliant idea," Regine says, via her equerry Velma Watts.

Jackie had done her six-month apprenticeship at *She* as a senior editor and is now back home, "where I belong," she tells everyone in her brief speech.

("I had absolutely nothing to do with this," Betsy whispers to me. "Nothing. You tell Willie that.")

Oliver Osborne looks like he's going to vomit and Liz Channing's face turns ghostly white . . . it's the stench of their important fish rotting. And believe me, I smell my own fish too. Midway through this mass burial, Willie walks out of the room . . . I expect to hear furniture being thrown or walls being torn down. But he goes home for the day, probably for a shot or two of bourbon and then a sleepless, tortured night. (And I know what those nights are like now, though mine aren't as long or as intense as his: at 2:00 A.M. he sees himself becoming a fact checker in the Black Hole, at 3:00 he's being sent down to *Here* to work, at 4:00 he gets transferred to our sister company, Federated Magazines, somewhere in Cincinnati or Provo, Utah, working at *Bullet and Barrel* or *Do's*, and he's editing copy about two-in-one shampoo/conditioners.)

The real kicker is when Jackie, ending her glad-to-be-back speech, tells us: "And I look forward to working with Mark and everybody else here . . ."

"Mark and everybody else here," Oliver mutters to me. "That cunt." It's the first time I've ever heard Oliver Osborne refer to a woman as a cunt, unless he's talking about Jed Leland.

At the end of the day I manage to rise out of my disheartened, disgusted slouch and I limp into Jackie's new office to welcome her back. She has a new short flip haircut but looks older, more successful, this after only six months of having her salary and prestige doubled.

"Congratulations," I say to her.

She thanks me and tells me what a nightmare *She* was, how everyone fears and hates Sophie Vuillard, *She*'s editor-in-chief, how out of touch and close to senility Sophie is, how stale the magazine has become . . . but I realize that, on her first day at *She* she was probably saying the same things about *It*.

I mention my Leroy White article—this is why I've gone in there in the first place. Months ago she'd been very supportive when I recommended it be a feature and not merely a one-pager in "Starters" or "In Closing."

"I have so much on my plate right now, Zack, I don't know," she says now.

"Martyn Stokes wants it for *Boy* but . . ."

(I'm groveling . . . I'm the same age as she is and not so long ago we were at the same level.)

"Maybe," she says, looking down at paperwork, at her "plate." One day, I'm thinking, I'll bring a blowtorch to work and heat up every plate in this goddamn building . . .

"Hey, where's that Tiffany's desk plate we got you?" The one that said: JACKIE WOOTEN, SENIOR EDITOR GODDAMMIT!

"Oh, it's somewhere at home," she says, still not looking up. "It sounds so collegiate. *Jackie* . . . nobody calls me that anymore."

Now she is: Jacqueline Wooten. Jac-*leen*.

At four in the morning I'm home sleeping when the phone rings. I fumble for it, pick it up.

"It's me," Willie says, wide awake.

"What's up?"

"Can you sleep?"

"Yeah. I was . . . just now."

"I can't sleep. How can you sleep?! I'm wide awake."

"Is Laurie there?"

"She's at a friend's."

"You gotta get to sleep." But it had taken me more than two hours to drift off.

"*Mark and everybody else here*," he says, doing an exaggerated imitation of powerful new features editor, Jacqueline Marie Wooten. And then he imitates Velma: *Soul soichin' . . . A brilliant idea.* "I keep hearing it over and over again. We've become parsley, dude."

I picture that—maybe, in my half-asleep state, I even see it: there, on the plate, was the steak of Regine Turnbull and Betsy Butler and Byron Poole; on the side there were the nouvelle potatoes of Sheila Stackhouse and Jacqueline Wooten; and there were the buttery vegetables of Marjorie Millet, Mark Larkin, and Roddy Grissom; and there on the edge of the plate was the parsley—you're not even sure if it's to be eaten or merely looked at . . . Willie and I are desperately waving our thin leafy arms for help.

"You gotta—" I start to say. I was going to recommend counting sheep but I know that the sheep would morph into Mark Larkins jumping over computer terminals and the *baa*'s would become A *baa-baarilliant idea* repeating incessantly.

"I think I'm going crazy, I think," he says.

He hangs up.

Before falling back asleep—and it takes a while because now I start thinking again—I recall that a few weeks ago in his apartment, Willie had called himself dead meat, flank steak, or chopped chuck.

Now we've both been demoted to garnish.

✦{ }✦

"ARE YOU sure you want to do this?" I ask Ivy.

"Okay . . ."

"Okay isn't yes." I have to make sure.

"It's not no either."

"It's like a yes with a minus sign in front of it."

"Okay then. Yes." She smiles. "I think I want to do this."

"But that's not a real yes either. You *think* but you're not sure."

We're on my couch and my shirt is off and Ivy's is unbuttoned, one small but firm twenty-two-year-old breast exposed. Her pants are completely off and mine are unzipped. There's a nickel-sized rip in her pink panties near the delta of the V, a puff of brown hair coming through.

"I think I'm sure," she says. "Should we go to the bedroom?"

"I don't know." That would be a big move . . . it would mean penetration. The bedroom is three thousand miles away.

"You don't have a girlfriend I don't know about, do you?"

I could lie . . . I could lie and save our souls while there's still time. Or do I tell the truth and thus confirm my reservation for a crashing plane?

"No. There's no girlfriend. You're the first girl I've ever done this with."

"Oh. That makes me feel real special."

I say something like: "You're really something." And she is really something. I have to admit. She has a nice body, slender and delectable, and her nipples are as firm as pecans, the same color too. (One admirable thing about Versailles Publishing, Inc. Human Resources: they really do make an attempt to only hire attractive women.)

"So are you," she says, sounding as though she believes it.

But oh no, I'm not really something, not at all. I'm verging on pathetic, I'm only one step up from it, I'm on the "pitiful" stair. I went to miserable Hofstra Parking Lot University and I didn't even graduate. And now, with my dry-humping and sloshing around with this twenty-two-year-old New Girl in the first week of the new year, I'm doing something I know I shouldn't. All roads are leading to disaster, emotional anguish, terror, devastation, and damnation. She's going to fall in love with me, I can tell, and I'm not going to fall in love with her, which is probably why she's going to fall in love with me. At dinner there will be long leaden silences and she won't mind it or notice it but I will. I'll look at her as she reads or watches TV and I'll wonder: What is she thinking? *Is* she thinking? Her father will hate my guts or simply sue them. Her mother (a Brearingnight-Bamford alum and—stealing a page out of my own book—a descendant of Rutherford B. Hayes) will throw her finest china at me, she'll have to triple her Valium dosage, and she'll begin sobbing the second I walk into their house. *And everyone in the office will find out*—that's the worst part. They'll wink at me in the elevator and the lobby. Marjorie will find out and tell everyone, including Leslie Usher-Soames, destroying my chances with her and Winston Churchill forever. Marjorie will ask Ivy out to lunch and she'll accidentally let it slip that she and I were "involved." And with moist eyes Ivy will ask me, "So who else at work?" and I'll have to come clean about that New Girl what-was-her-name at *Zest*, a ditzy pigeon-toed airhead with dyslexia I couldn't stomach after the first time but did manage to stomach another five times or so (how did *she* make it past Human Resources?). And Regine will find out about Ivy and me and talk to Velma, and Velma and Sheila will talk to me and tell me to be careful, that I shouldn't shit where I eat (or is it the other way around?).

But what has me truly terrified is that Ivy Kooper will embarrass me at the office. We'll be in a big meeting and she'll raise her hand and she'll say something and it will be the lamest, most fizzled-out dud in the history of meetings. And the only noises will be cringing and grinding teeth and suppressed guffaws. Everyone will look over to me and they'll think: So why are you with this ditzy airhead chick anyway?

But the problem is — as I am presently on top of her and she's supple and very warm, those deep coffee-brown eyes brimming over with sweetness (yes, sweetness again) — the problem is that I'm on top of her and she's supple and very warm, etc. And I'm starting to like her! But not just for that — she's wonderful, a really nice girl. I mean that! I enjoy her company. She's smart, funny, clever, well-read. She reads the *Times*, for Christ sake, and the *New Yorker*, which in a good week I only skim. She's not an airheaded ditz at all! Hey, maybe she can move in! My mother would love her. Maybe, just maybe, when Ivy finally speaks up in a meeting it won't be so bad. Maybe it will be the best idea anyone's heard for years. Something revolutionary . . .

"Okay. Let's do it. Come on."

We stand up.

Hand in hand we walk three thousand miles to the bedroom.

What a big mistake.

{ }

I'VE BEEN seeing Gaston Moreau every now and then for years, hunched-over and doddering in the lobby or in an elevator, heaving his way out of the limousine that takes him to work every day. (When he's in that car, he looks like an iguana peering out through the glass of a terrarium.) Occasionally — but very rarely — I'll see him walking on our floor, a liver-spotted ghost mistakenly haunting the wrong home, searching in the wrong house for rooms, furniture, hallway, and people he once knew well.

There's a bank machine in the Versailles lobby, near the newspaper stand (Patel's Papers), in a small room of its own.

It's the second week of the new year and I'm at the bank machine.

Having taken Willie's advice, I'm fuming: I'd just strolled by Regine's office and seen Mark Larkin sitting in there with Emma Pilgrim and the fashion editor, Marcel Perrault.

There are two people in front of me at the ATM: a Stiletto from *She* in shiny black leather pants, heels, and a fuzzy rust brown sweater is getting some money, and right in front of me and reeking of an orange liqueur-like cologne, a few strands of straight white hair slicked back with a briny pomade over his crusty pate, is Gaston, or "Gassy" as insiders call him. He's wearing an expensive suit but on his lumpy eighty-year-old frame, it looks sloppy and tattered, oversized in some places (the wrists) and too small in others (the pants barely reach his ankles).

The Stiletto—judging by her makeup, she's probably Editor: Lipstick at *She*—gets her money and leaves, noticing Gaston behind her but too momentarily stunned to even smile.

So it's just me and him now.

He puts his card into the machine but the card is upside down. The machine informs him it cannot read the thing and spits it halfway out. But, since he's in his eighties and quite unaware of many things happening around him, he keeps pushing buttons.

"Mr. Moreau?"

"Yes?"

"Your card's in upside down." I'm surprised he even has to go to a bank machine. "Look . . ."

I pull the card all the way out and put it in the right way. Two smells—his breath and cologne—are beginning to make me dizzy. And there's a third smell too: illness.

"Okay, now try it."

He starts pushing buttons again but has forgotten to put in his password.

"Don't you have a PIN?"

"A *peen?*" With his combo platter of accents (French and upper-class English), he pronounces it "peen." "You have a *peen?*"

"A secret code?"

Gassy nods, smiles. His teeth are crooked and brown, pebbles soaked in ketchup.

"Who are you?" he asks me with moist iguana eyes, the liquid oily and dull greenish.

"I work at *It.*"

"*It?* Maybe you and I have meeting today, eh?"

Is he proposing we should meet?

He says: "Larkin . . . Are you this Marco Larkin fellow from *It?*"

"Yes. That's me. Mark Larkin. What time is our meeting again?"

"I sink at perhaps three."

I sink perhaps right now because . . .

Because Mark Larkin, the son of a bitch I told how to get Regine's coffee, the jaw-clenching shitheel who didn't believe you faxed paper upside down, the pompous toadying asswipe with the suspenders and bow tie, the bastard who called me "old boy" and (his newest thing) "Post," as if we'd been at Eton or Harrow together . . . because Mark Larkin, an associate editor (that's my title too!), is meeting the Magazine Maestro, Gaston Moreau, the Director: Creative of the whole vast operation, from New York to Hong Kong, São Paolo to Moscow, at three! How could this be?!

Wait until I tell Willie *this!!* He'll never sleep again . . .

"Yes, it's at three," I say to the hunched-over reptile. "I look forward to it."

"Regine tells me good sings of you."

He starts playing with the ATM buttons again.

"I might have to cancel due to your breath, Gassy. It's really putrid. Or maybe I'll interoffice-mail you some gum or mouthwash before we confab. I mean, guy, it's at once positively and preternaturally nauseating and lethal. You're gonna kill people with it."

"You impudent blackguard!" he spits out, liver spots twinkling. "How dare you!" Saliva bubbles on his lips.

"Your teeth look like a . . ." I can't continue—he's a sick old man and other than his meeting later that day with Mark Larkin, he's never done me any harm. I was trying to *peen* all my impudence and blackguardedness on my nemesis, but by the time their meeting came around, the old man would forget it.

I begin to inch away. A few twenty-dollar bills shuffle out of the machine and Gaston turns slowly around, like the turret of a damaged tank, and scoops the money out.

"What is zis?" he whispers. "Zis . . . zis on the money?"

I see the corners of the bills have some red ink on them.

"It's nothing. It's real, don't worry."

He puts the money in his wallet. The machine beeps.

"Don't forget your card," I tell him. I hand it to him . . . his spotted gray hand is quivering.

When I put my own card in, the machine tells me it has no more money to dispense. He and the Stiletto had cleaned it out.

A few hours later I'm in a small conference room with Betsy Butler and Leslie Usher-Soames and we're talking about a piece—a half-page article I'd written about an artsy-fartsy Swiss mime troupe (I got more talk out of mimes in ten minutes than I did from Ethan Cawley in three hours)—when Marjorie appears in the doorway and asks us if we've heard.

"Heard what?" Betsy asks.

"You mean you haven't? Gaston is dead. He died in his office."

We all look at each other. It certainly isn't the most unexpected news in the world. But still . . .

"But I saw him a few hours ago . . ." I say. It seems as if the next part of the sentence would be: ". . . and he looked great!" But there is no next part of the sentence.

Willie walks in and asks us if we've heard and our blank expressions answer him.

Then Mark Larkin appears, his jacket off, his shirt rumpled, his clip-on bow tie slightly askew . . . I have no doubt that he arranged this whole disheveled look for effect.

"I found the body," he says, feigning to be out of breath.

"What were *you* doing in there?" Willie asks him, cutting right to the point.

Mark Larkin doesn't acknowledge it.

"I walked into his office," Mark Larkin continues, "and he was just lying there." Faceup on the cold slab of his floor, he adds, Gaston's mouth and eyes wide open.

"It's a sad day," he says in a pithy tone. "The man changed the shape of the American magazine . . . no, the shape of publishing the world over. What was it someone once said of John Barrymore? . . . 'We were fortunate to have lived in his time.' "

"Hmmm," Betsy says, tapping a pen against a stack of papers.

"That was Charlie Chaplin," Willie says. "Someone said that about Charlie Chaplin."

"No, I think it was Jackie Robinson," I put in.

There's nothing to say. The man was a legend, it's true. One might say that we all owed our jobs to him, which is perhaps why some of us aren't too broken up about all this.

"What were you doing in there?" Willie asks Mark Larkin again. But again there is no answer.

"So does this mean we get a day off tomorrow?" Liz Channing asks me when I tell her the news.

TO: POSTZ
ROM: LISTERW
SUBJECT: The Asshole

what in the name of jesus was he doing in there anyway?

TO: LISTERW
FROM: POSTZ
SUBJECT: Re The Asshole

They had a meeting. That's what he was doing. I was going to tell you but didn't want you to make yourself sick over it.

TO: POSTZ
FROM: LISTERW
SUBJECT: Re The Asshole

i like making myself sick
next time tell me

It's nine at night and I'm still at the office, struggling and transcribing, trying my best to make sense out of the Cawley interview, fast-forwarding through gaps and rewinding past grunts. Some of the lights are off and there are only a few people around. I'd been trying to synchronize my departure with Leslie's, but she's slipped out already and so now I can leave too. Earlier I'd overheard her arguing on the phone, I assume with her fiancé, the rich hyphenated collie.

I put on my coat, then remember I have no money.

Mark Larkin comes out of the bathroom when I'm on my way out.

"Hey, can you lend me a few dollars?" I say.

"Now, now . . . don't you have that big trust fund?"

"I blew it all on jai alai. Come on, just ten dollars. I can pay you back first thing tomorrow."

He takes out his wallet and thumbs through a thick wad of twenty-dollar bills.

All of the bills have red ink at the corners and in a second it all clicks in.

"I saw you rob Gaston's corpse. I saw you." I swipe a twenty and watch his face break into splotches of red.

"What are you talking about?"

"Don't bullshit me. I saw you."

He purses his lips, takes a deep breath. I've got the company's rising young lad by his fair-haired nuts and he knows it. The tips of his ears are on fire and his cheeks swell up.

"Okay, Post, you've got me on this one. But mum's the word. I've had this bad cash-flow problem . . ."

"You probably thought he'd have at least a thousand in there, didn't you?" I swipe another twenty.

"Come on. You don't even have to pay me back. Here, take another . . ."

I don't take it. The whole wad could be mine but then all the dirt sifts onto me.

"Admit you'd have done it too," he says with a pathetic smile.

"Rob a corpse? No, I don't think so."

He contorts his face into a Teddy Roosevelt scowl. He's huffing and puffing but cannot find a way out.

And then the coup de grâce:

I pull out the little tape recorder, the one with the Cawley interview on it, and click the stop button.

"And now I've got it all on tape for posterity's sake."

"You wouldn't."

"I might, Larkin," I said, "old boy."

Walking toward the elevator, I gloated exaltedly, actually tee-heeing aloud to myself.

But I didn't have anything on him really. I had the tape recorder, sure, but I hadn't been recording.

But he doesn't know that.

＊{ }＊

TO: CHANNINGE
    OSBORNEO
    POSTZ
FROM: LISTERW

 SUBJECT: Obit

Gaston Runs Out of Gas

TO: CHANNINGE
    LISTERW
    POSTZ
FROM: OSBORNEO
SUBJECT: Re: Obit

Gaston Has Passed On

TO: LISTERW
    OSBORNEO
    POSTZ
FROM: CHANNINGE
SUBJECT: Re: Obit

Moreau Just Ain't No Mo'

TO: CHANNINGE
    LISTERW
    OSBORNEO
FROM: POSTZ
SUBJECT: Re: Obit

Director: Creative Dies of Colon-Related Illness

Imaginary headlines, via e-mail, for Gaston Moreau's death—this is how we pass the day after he died.

It's a variation on another game we play to keep ourselves occupied and sane: How would some Versailles magazines handle actual news?

Boy: SARIN NERVE GAS ATTACK IN L.A. BRAD PITT, WEARING

HUGO BOSS JACKET AND HERMÈS TIE, MILLIONS OF OTHERS FEARED DEAD.

She: ALIENS INVADE EARTH DRESSED IN SPRING PASTELS.

It: GENGHIS KHAN DO ANYTHING!

Men: LED BY PAPA HEMINGWAY, RUGGED ALLIES LIBERATE PARIS WEARING CLASSIC OLIVE DRAB AND DURABLE KHAKIS.

Here: SLEEK POST-MODERN WALL OF JERICHO TUMBLES.

Now: THE FIVE SEXIEST APOSTLES.

{ }

"DO YOU maybe want to go out?" Ivy asks me.

"Right now? It's kind of late."

We're lying down in the darkness and Ivy's hair is slung across her chest and she's twirling some of it.

I ask: "Out where?"

"I don't know. For dinner or to a movie. Or maybe just take a walk."

"Sure, I could do that. Maybe. It's cold out though."

"You're afraid we'll run into someone from work."

"It crossed my mind."

"But they'd think we're just friends."

"No they wouldn't."

"Why not?"

"They know me better than that."

"Why? Like, do you make a habit of this kind of stuff. What about the summer intern last year?"

"I never laid a hand on her." That's true. (If Marjorie ever finds out about Ivy and me, she'll surely tell her about the un-stomachable pigeon-toed dyslexic ditzy *Zest* intern, there's no doubt about it.)

"You're not ashamed of me, are you?"

I pull the comforter up to my neck. She has so much going for her. But the problem is I actually have to ask myself the same question: *Am* I ashamed of her?

{ }

"I SHOULD quit, just get knocked up and quit."

"Me too," I say to Liz Channing.

"Or forget the preggers routine . . . I'll just do freelance work."

We're in Max Perkin', a coffee bar two blocks from work, sitting at the window, which is covered with swirls of vapor. It's 2:30.

"I mean, I just don't know how much longer I can put up with this shit." She tells me she can write freelance pieces for *She*, *Her*, *It*, and *Ego*.

"Did you ever think that, just to spite you for quitting, Regine wouldn't publish you? And that she'd tell Martyn and Sophie and the others not to publish you too?"

Liz stares into the window a half a foot in front of her. The steam and water drip down in streaks and look like melting fingers.

The door opens and, along with a blast of frigid air, Tom Land and Trisha Lambert (sounds like "lamb-bear"), husband and wife and very much the couple of the hour, blow in. I cannot believe the coat Tom has on . . . it has to cost a thousand bucks. He's from one of the Five Towns in Long Island, which is almost as bad as being from Massapequa. An associate editor at *It* when I first started there, Tom was still doing New Boy things, getting people coffee, sending faxes for them, getting his nose as brown as he could get it while still being able to breathe. He hung around the more important crowd and was remunerated with good assignments and by simply being seen with the Important People, what Willie calls "gilt by association." Now he's the deputy editor of *Boy* but he's still getting coffee for the few people left who outrank him. Trisha (her sports nickname would be "The Human Spirograph") is tall and slinky with angles for eyebrows, ears, and a chin. Several times a year while thumbing through the taken-at-random "On the Street" photos in the *Times*, you'll come across her photo, in the winter bracing herself as her cashmere scarf waves in the wind, in summer sporting cool casual linens, in spring strolling gingerly with her Wayfarers on, in fall walking with determination and a classic brown leather bomber jacket.

"Hey, Tom," I say. Gone are the days when I can call him Tommy.

"Zachary," he says with a forced grin.

"Hello, Liz," Trisha says.

"We've never seen you in here," I say to them.

They shoot us a look that says: Well, now that we know you come in here, we might not ever come in here again.

I make a sarcastic comment about Gaston's death and they don't like my tone and Liz kicks me.

As a joke I say: "Maybe Mark Larkin will move all the way to the top.

It's like a 'Golden Bough' type deal . . . he kills the king so he gets to replace him."

"Well, I don't think he's ready for that just yet," Tom says. "And he hardly killed him."

"I was only kidding."

Trisha tells us they had Mark Larkin over for dinner last week. For some reason this stings a bit.

I can't help myself and ask, "Why did you do that?"

"Why?" Tom says. "He's a friend, that's why."

{ }

"So we'll go out then?" Ivy asks me.

"Yeah, sure."

"This Friday. For dinner? We *have* had dinner together before."

Yes . . . but that was before we started sleeping together.

"Why you're so crazy to have dinner with me, I don't know. I'm not some kind of scintillating raconteur."

"What about all those stories you made up? About Sheila keeping a bottle of Hamburger Hill in her drawer?"

"Heaven Hill. It's a bourbon . . . So you knew everything I was saying that night was a crock?"

"I sure did. So we'll leave from work, okay?"

"Why not meet at the restaurant?"

"Okay. And we can wear wigs and glasses with fake noses and mustaches."

Later the same night. She's getting dressed, about to leave. "Do you think I'm too quiet at meetings?" she asks.

"Too quiet? No, I don't think so."

"I just feel I'm being conspicuous by not ever saying a word. I think that I should start contributing, other than filing and getting coffee. I *would* like them to hire me. Betsy told me there's an editorial associate job opening up soon."

"Well, it's always good to make suggestions in writing . . . it cuts down on the sneers and rolled eyes you'll get in a meeting."

"But then I'm still a dead weight at a meeting. I have to start speaking up, that's it."

I sit up and stare at the wall.

"Are you okay?" she asks me.

"Yeah. I guess so."

{　}

A COMPANY-wide e-mail circulates around Versailles, asking us to remember Gaston's historic contribution to magazine publishing, not only in America but all over the world. Gaston, it says, was the first to do this, the first to do that, he did this with graphics and that with photography, he hired this editor, that art director. But how innovative was he really? Are you telling me that if Alexander Graham Bell hadn't invented the telephone, I'd be ordering my Chinese food with smoke signals?!

This is the thing that really bugs me about magazines: magazine people think they're doing something great, like curing polio or putting out something every month that rivals *Moby-Dick* or *The Portrait of a Lady* (we even refer to an issue of a magazine as "the book"). But come on! Half of a magazine is ads for $100 perfumes that cost fifty cents to make; ads for skirts and tops now available at Saks, Nordstrom, The Limited, Neiman Marcus, etc.; ads for jeans with anorexic, hollow-eyed, pock-marked teen models; ads for $400 shoes and $200 scarves; ads for $40 bras that cost a dollar to make; and page after page of ads for skin softener, anti-aging formulas, age mollifiers, eyeliner, mascara, lipstick, and then products to remove all these other products: nail-polish remover, blush remover remover, concealer concealer, and then products to cover up the remover: blush remover fade cream and on and on and on. When Salk and Sabin came out with the polio vaccine, was it brought to you by Revlon, Estee Lauder, DKNY, Polo, Gucci, Prada, and Calvin Klein? And I don't remember *Moby-Dick* having ads for Absolut, or *The Portrait of a Lady* having a four-color Mercedes-Benz ad on its inside back cover.

And the other half of a magazine is all (or mostly) unimportant nonsense (as thoroughly useless as the horoscope page in the back—which I often write), most of which could be faxed in from publicists and agents: promoting celebrities, exposing unimportant scandals, reviving dying careers or reburying or exhuming dead ones, and then page after page of cheesy fashion spreads with affectedly excited boy models who don't like girls, hugging affectedly bored girl models who probably don't like boys and who definitely don't like food. And then the interchangeable advice articles, always with numbers: 10 Ways to Get Back Your 2nd Husband, The 9 Myths About Cellulite, The 8 Sexiest Men in Hollywood, The 2-Minute Orgasm, and so on. If you work in the business the numbers and words come at you like the colors in a kaleidoscope: The 8 Sexiest 7 Cellulite Myths About Your 6 Husbands' 5 Golden Rings 4 French Hens . . .

So why am I in this Eye Candy trade?

Because it impresses the piss out of people when you tell them where you work.

But I have to act as if Gaston's death has saddened me. I have to pretend to everyone but Willie, whose first aside to me was: "Okay, who gets his job? Two to one it's Regine."

It's a good question and it keeps me up at night, entertaining the possibilities.

	Regine	_Martyn_
age	49	35
height	5 feet (with heels, hair spray)	6'4"
weight	90 lbs. sopping wet	245 lbs (in an Armani suit, free)
place of birth	Beacon Hill	Lambeth
education	Bryn Mawr	Cambridge (he claims)
hobby	works at a magazine	works out, reads magazines
sex life	married, two kids	active, very active
quote	"This can be done a lot better."	"I suppose this is good enough actually."

It seems to me that Regine Turnbull has the slight edge; the job calls for you to do very, very little. She already has a lot of expertise in that area.

If Regine gets the job, it means enormous changes at It. If Martyn gets it, it still could mean changes for us.

Here is a possible Tinker-to-Evers-to-Chance scenario:

> Regine becomes Director: Creative of Versailles
> Betsy Butler becomes Editor-in-Chief of It

> *Sheila Stackhouse becomes Deputy Editor*
> *I become Sheila Stackhouse, Editor, with my own office, a hefty*
> *raise, and, perhaps more important, RESPECT!*

This is so obvious a transition that it can't happen. But it isn't impossible so I do hope for it . . . it's the first thing I think of when I wake up. I'm sick of sitting across from Nolan and staring at beige cubicle walls, crooked towers of magazines, slab upon slab, piling up on my desk. I want an office, the Chrysler Building out my window, privacy and a lot less to do.

Here is another possible transition:

> *Regine becomes Director: Creative*
> *Betsy Butler becomes Editor-in-Chief of* It
> *Betsy fires Sheila and Jac-leen Wooten (to remove rivals)*
> *Willie and I get promoted*
> *We get Mark Larkin fired.*

This is also too much to hope for. It just seems too easy.

But even if Martyn gets Gaston's job, there is this possible chain of events:

> *Martyn becomes Director: Creative*
> *He fires Regine (a smart move on his part)*
> *Betsy, Sheila, Jackie move up . . .*
> *. . . creating a senior editor slot for yours truly.*

It's possible. If I'm Martyn Stokes, the last person I want eyeing the back of my neck is Regine Turnbull. When Jesus Christ comes back, is he going to rehire Judas?

> *Martyn becomes Director: Creative*
> *Some Asshole at Boy becomes Editor-in-Chief of Boy*
> *Betsy is shifted to Boy, filling Some Asshole's slot*
> *Sheila and Jackie move up*
> *I move up.*

Now that's more like it! It seems so unpredictable that it might actually take place.

"What's going to happen?" Willie asks me at the coffee shop near work. Leslie is with us again, moving olives and lettuce around a plate with her fork.

"It's like musical chairs," I say.

"I sort of hope Martyn gets the job," Leslie says. "It would mean less of a shakeup."

"You know, if Martyn gets it," I conjecture, "he then can make wholesale changes. He could fire Byron Poole or move him, then Marjorie is art director and *you* move up. Or he fires Byron, moves Marjorie to another magazine, and you're art director."

"That does sound nice." She has a pleasant bright smile but I notice that two of her teeth (way in the back) are a little on the fangy side.

"Or," Willie says, "he could fire me. Or Regine could fire me."

"She could fire you anyway," I tell him.

"Well, Martyn wouldn't fire me, I know that."

"Why wouldn't he?"

"Because he's probably forgotten who the hell I was."

(It's usually a bad sign when people talk about themselves in the past tense, I've found.)

I'm at a copying machine, copying the insipid Swiss mime troupe piece. I've described their performances as "exhilarating, exciting and uninhibiting" and said they were the new *enfants terribles* of performance art. (Or were they the Young Turks?)

Willie sidles up to me.

"Ready for this neutron bomb?" he whispers. "I think Mark Larkin's getting Martyn Stokes's job when Martyn gets Gassy's."

I think I have to actually strain to keep control of my more disgusting bodily functions.

"What makes you think that?"

"My birdy in Accounts Deplorable."

He's mentioned this unnamed source quite often. "Who is this birdy anyway?"

"Laurie knows someone down there. Martyn's getting a big—I mean *huge*—raise and Mark Larkin's getting one too. I can't be totally sure on this but it does look like it's going down."

The copying machine is trying to spit out my two paragraphs but the paper is getting jammed and ripping to shreds.

"What you're saying is that Mark Larkin is going from being an associate editor of *It* to being the big cheese at *Boy?!* It can't be! It's too big a jump."

"Don't forget, chum, that Martyn Stokes was a mere associate editor and then, boom . . . like that, he got the top job at *Boy.*"

"But he's Martyn Stokes!" I practically yell. "Of course that would happen to him!"

"Well, he wasn't always Martyn Stokes! That was when he *became* Martyn Stokes. And maybe this is where Mark Larkin becomes Mark Larkin."

"If Mark Larkin moves up, he'll do anything in his power to move us out."

Except now I have some blackmail on him—or so Mark Larkin thinks. I'm not the movable feast I once was.

"Is that the Swiss mime troupe?" he asks me.

"It's the worst thing I've ever written in my life."

"You didn't actually go see them perform, did you?"

"You gotta be kidding me . . ."

"Let's kill him, Zeke."

I don't know if he's serious or not. I look at him and I notice gray circles under his eyes. "How?"

"The only way I'm going to be normal again is if he's dead or fired."

"Well, he's not going to be fired, is he?"

As if we're all characters in a soap opera, Mark Larkin walks by just then, not seeing us.

"Some people should get killed," Willie says, "it's true. Hitler . . . if someone had killed him during the Beer Hall Putsch, would that have been so bad? George Steinbrenner . . . would it really be so bad if someone capped him?"

"So you really want to kill him?"

"It would make my life so much easier. Yours too, pal. Admit it."

"You're not capable of such a thing."

"It could be like a Leopold and Loeb thing, the both of us."

Except Leopold and Loeb got caught. The trick of it was in making sure I wasn't going to get buttfucked in Attica for the remainder of my life. But it's like the great, sinister speech in *The Third Man* in the Prater wheel, when Orson Welles asks the ubiquitous Joseph Cotten (the irony!) how much he'd take for every dot creeping around beneath them.

There was no question that I would pay someone to pick off the little troublesome dot that was Mark Larkin.

"How would we do it?" I ask.

"Out a window. Poison him. Strangle him. Slit his throat. One of those would do it."

"You've been thinking about this, I see."

"Five hours a night, every night for months."

"Are we really having this conversation?"

"No. I'm not talking to you right now."

He lumbers away, walks down the hallway, probably heading for the Black Hole to see Laurie. I look at the original, what I'd been trying to copy. SWISS MIMING . . . Revolutionizing The Art Form Turning Mime On Its Head *Enfants Terribles* Post-Modern Deconstructing Blah Blah Blah. The paper turns into a liquidy blob and against it I see Mark Larkin falling out a window, like Jimmy Stewart falling in *Vertigo*, spinning around helplessly and falling with a dull thud.

My hands are ice cold.

No, I don't have it in me. There's no way I can personally kill someone. No, not personally.

I look up and see Willie getting smaller and smaller and then vanishing as he walks down the hallway into darkness.

8

THIS HAPPENED recently:

I was in the photo department one day, looking over photos of an up-and-coming actress I'd written something about. Roddy Grissom, Jr., one of his assistants, and I stood around his light box, leafing through about a hundred transparencies, narrowing it down to a final cut. As usual with the work of a highly paid professional photographer, most of them were unusable.

Velma Watts barreled in and said, "Does anyone know how to get a passport real quick? It's for Regine. Hers has expired. She needs one to go to the Cannes Film Festival."

I said there were services for that kind of thing—you went to an office, gave them a picture and your old passport, then a few days later you had your new one.

Velma went away and came back three minutes later, saying: "She wants to know where she can get the picture taken."

"It costs like five bucks. There's a—"

"Zachary, I'll handle this," Roddy said. He picked up his phone and speed-dialed a number: "Hello, is Dick there?" he asked. "It's Roddy."

"Dick" wasn't there but Roddy was given a different number, which he promptly dialed.

"Hey, Dick, it's Roddy. So how *is* the world's greatest photographer? . . . Uh-huh . . . Uh-huh . . . Ha ha ha! . . . Hey, I have a very special assignment for you . . ."

I couldn't believe what I was hearing . . . it was one of those moments in life when you realize that not only are the rich very different from you and me, they are outlandishly, ludicrously, sickeningly different.

I listened while Roddy Grissom arranged for Richard Avedon to take Regine Turnbull's 2 x 2 1/2 inch passport picture at a cost of (including studio time, hairdressing, makeup) about $4,000.

When anyone looks at the face of Roddy Grissom, Jr., they're immediately reminded of a rodent. His hair is fuzzy and rat-colored brown and by the end of the day it's usually ruffled in three or four places. He has small beady eyes and hair grows out of his nostrils and ears. An unkempt slob of about five-foot-three, he managed to slip in under the Versailles door, some six inches under the tacitly understood height requirements, abetted unquestionably by Roddy Grissom, Sr., publisher of *She*. But nobody ever resented Roddy for succeeding via nepotism—they had too many other good reasons to despise him.

Everybody hates him. Regine hates him and wants as little to do with him as possible and thus has little to do with him. Ted Tarrant, *It*'s publisher, hates him and so do the messengers and the dwarf guy in the copying room downstairs. The security guards in the lobby recoil when he walks by; this doesn't surprise me as two or three times Roddy has yelled at them for some minor transgression regarding having his lunch sent up.

He's the only person at *It* who actually yells. When you're reprimanded at Versailles it usually comes in a quiet sober tone with the door closed. And it's so quiet in the offices that if someone even slightly raises his or her voice, you can hear it twenty offices away. Leslie Usher-Soames works about five cubicles down a hall from me, and when she argues on the phone with the hyphenated collie I can catch a word or two of it. ("Oh, you don't have to be such a prat abow-tit, Colin!")

When Roddy Grissom yells, everyone hears it. Laurie hears it in the Black Hole. Martyn Stokes hears it and *Boy*'s offices are on the next floor up.

He yells at his small staff and at nobody else. He has a photo assistant, Valerie Morgan, and a photo researcher, Nancy Willis. Valerie has been at *It* for a long time and how she puts up with Roddy's abuse, nobody can figure out. But nobody has ever been able to stay at the researcher job for more than eight months, thanks to Roddy's sadistic temper. If he doesn't humiliate his staff publicly by giving instructions to them in baby-talk, it goes like this:

"Are you a bloody fucking moron, Nancy?!"

"Valerie, can't you do *ANYTHING* right?!"

"You're an incompetent bitch, Nancy!"

"You're mentally retarded, aren't you?!"

In the time I've been at *it*, he's gone through about five researchers. They start out fine but in a month they have dark circles under their eyes and tremble all the time; in two months they're zombies, mouths open and eyes dazed, dead to the world.

As if Nancy Willis didn't already have enough trouble, her mother was diagnosed with pancreatic cancer a few weeks before Thanksgiving. So Nancy would dash up to Lenox Hill Hospital on her lunch break, spend a half-hour with her mother, then hurry back down.

Roddy would complain to Betsy about these lunches; if you worked in the photo department it was unusual to take anything more than a five-minute break. Roddy would make caustic asides about Nancy's hospital visits at meetings, sometimes with her present. "She's probably going to a tanning salon," he said once. *A tanning salon???* She was now a chalky color from her head to her hands, except for the brown bags under her eyes.

"No, you are *not* going, Nancy, to see your damned *dying* mother today!" he said to her one day, making it sound as though he was denying an eight-year-old the use of a toy. Later I came upon her curled up in a stairway, her face in her palms, crying.

"You're really going to get a facial at Georgette Klinger, aren't you?" he once barked to her in front of ten people. "What you really need is plastic surgery."

That one came close to the end.

One slow, quiet day at work, after just having shipped an issue to the printer, I hear a familiar booming: "NANCY, YOU CANNOT DO ANY-THING!! WHY ARE YOU SO INCREDIBLY STUPID?! TELL ME!

WHY?! I WANT TO KNOW. ARE YOU A MONGOLOID?! YOU LOOK LIKE ONE! I CAN'T BELIEVE ANYONE WOULD EVER FUCK YOU!"

I don't hear anything for a few seconds.

"I AM NOT LETTING YOU OUT TO SEE YOUR MOTHER TODAY!"

It's quiet again for a while.

"SHOULDN'T SHE HAVE DIED BY NOW ANYWAY?! JESUS CHRIST, WHAT IS TAKING HER SO BLOODY FUCKING LONG?!"

Then Valerie shrieks a blood-curdling shriek: "NANCY! NO!"

A piercing miserable groan sounds, a truly harrowing noise.

Valerie yells, "Oh my God! Oh my God! Oh my God!"

Everybody, myself included, runs toward the photo room.

It looks like a Madame Tussaud's wax exhibit of a famous crime scene, like the murder of Marat or the assassination of Julius Caesar. Valerie is frozen with one hand over her gaping mouth, Nancy is frozen and there's bright red blood all over one hand, Roddy is sitting on his stool, right near a light box scattered with shots from a recent Meg Ryan shoot . . . a big pair of scissors is stuck into his chest two inches above his heart. He has a stupid look on his face . . . he's still alive but he just looks so stupid, almost drunk. The blood is bubbling out his chest.

"Why did you do this to me?" Roddy asks Nancy.

"Because I wanted to, I guess," she says.

He looks down at the scissors. He doesn't know whether to leave them in or take them out. So he leaves them in.

For the next half-hour, until an ambulance comes, he goes about his business, the scissors sticking out. He even comes over to my desk and starts talking about photos for "In Closing," as if the scissors sticking out are a hideous tie he's inexplicably found himself wearing.

The police come and arrest Nancy and when the word spreads that reporters will be allowed upstairs, there's a frantic rush to the ladies' room to put on makeup.

Betsy Butler told me that when Regine—who was out of town when it happened—found out about it, the very first thing she said was: "Are the Meg Ryan pictures okay?"

Roddy was fired . . . but you can't really call it blaming the victim.

Regine knew that the next person would blow Roddy's head off with a shotgun, so she got rid of him now to avoid any future embarrassment. Valerie Morgan got Roddy's low six-figure salary job and Nancy Willis was quickly found not guilty by reason of insanity.

Betsy Butler announces Valerie's promotion at a staff meeting in the large conference room. Although everyone is very happy for Valerie, it isn't really a time for celebration, because we all feel bad for Nancy. Had Roddy Grissom been killed on a street corner by one of the $500-a-throw escorts he's said to pay to spank him while he sucks on a lollipop, there probably would have been champagne and pâté de foie gras.

"It's brilliant!" Willie says to me, imitating a Brit. "It's absolutely brill!"

"What is?"

"Nancy Willis stabs Rodent Gristle, Jr., Nancy gets put away, Roddy gets fired, Valerie gets promoted."

"You're not saying Valerie arranged the whole thing, are you?"

"No . . . but if she had, they ought to create a new Nobel Prize category for it and give her a hundred of them."

"I guess they should. Yeah. Brilliant."

{ }

I'M WALKING around the office with a harried, determined look (because I have nothing to do) when this tall slender gent in a navy blue raincoat and a pinstriped suit walks by me, looking very out of place. He's fair-skinned and has hollowed-out eyes, straight brown hair combed back (he bears a slight resemblance to a young Boris Karloff), and a square jaw.

It has to be him! Colin. Leslie's fiancé.

So I wait a beat or two and do an about-face and follow him.

Sure enough, Colin Tunbridge-Yates strolls into the art department and Leslie stands up and smiles. I go into the art department to make small talk with Marjorie. Leslie kisses Colin (on the cheek, a half-second peck) and gracefully lifts up one leg in a very annoying and affected manner.

"Have you met Colin, Zeke?" Leslie asks me. This is the first time she's ever called me Zeke and the fact that she's doing it in front of Colin isn't lost on me.

I give him an up and down. "No, I haven't had the pleasure."

I shake his hand, which is just as lifeless as his skin coloring, but my hand is clammy enough to instantly dilute the sham smile on his face.

"This is Zachary Post . . . he's an editor here," Leslie says. There's something in her tone now that suggests she likes me, but still it sounds as if she's saying: "Mr. Hamilton, meet Mr. Burr."

"An associate editor," I correct her modestly as he wipes his hand-shaking hand against the raincoat.

"Is that a new coat?" she says to him. (After all, they hardly ever see each other.)

"Yes, it's a Burberry. Got it in London. Six-hundred quid."

I interrupt. "The store on Regent Street or Haymarket?" (I know my magazine ads well.)

"Regent Street."

"You could have bought it for half that at Moe Ginsburg's. That old Jew really knows how to throw a sale." He gives me a very brief dirty look, which I eat up. I can't let this son of a bitch upstage me. I'm going to bring him down to my level . . .

"So what is it that you do again?" I ask him, summoning up some Massapequa.

"I'm a risk arbitrageur. In the City."

"In the city? But I thought you lived in London."

He rubs his huge chin and I say, "Risk arbitrageur?? And you don't have trouble getting a visa? I mean, the first word is a board game about world domination, and the second word you have to speak French to say."

Colin turns to Leslie and says, "Were we going to have lunch?"

They leave after another round of unpleasantries.

"Can I talk to you for a second?" Marjorie says sternly enough to give me a fright.

"Okay, sure."

Oh no! She must know about me and Ivy. This could get ugly.

We walk into Stairway B, of all places, me walking behind her (at the proper angle, her breasts are visible even when she's walking directly away from you), her crazy frizzy hair foaming with each step. Even though the jig is up about something, if she said, "Dive into me now, Big Boy," how could I say no . . .

So we come to our secluded little alcove on Stairway B. There are cigarette butts, spent matches, and ashes at our feet.

"You want Leslie, don't you?"

"Me?"

"You do! It's so obvious! You have a crush on her!"

"Why is it obvious?" I swallow.

She shifts—and everything quickly follows her—to an attractive akimbo position.

"Because of what you said to Colin." She's pointing a finger at me. " '*I haven't had the pleasure.*' Jesus!"

"And this means I have a crush on Leslie?"

"Yes. Because you would never say that kind of thing unless you didn't really mean it."

She has me dead to rights.

"And what's worse is," she continues, "you sounded as if you meant it. Which you didn't! And why didn't you mean it? Because you want Leslie. And the way you were goofing with Colin!"

I look up, I look to the right and left. I think about the times I used to spin her around (right here) and lift up her skirt, pull down her pantyhose, and . . .

"If you want me to help you out in this thing, I can," she informs me.

"*You're* going to help me, Marjorie! You told her I took acting lessons at RADA!"

"Well, you did!"

"No I didn't!"

"Then why did you tell me you did?"

"I never told you I took acting lessons!"

"Well, if you did take lessons, you should have told me so."

We're deep in the bowels of Argument Purgatory, the No Man's Land of which she is reigning empress.

She says: "You probably only told me anyway so I would tell Leslie . . . to impress her."

But she has the timing all wrong. "No, I would have told you that before we ever met Leslie!"

"Aha! So you *did* tell me!"

But I don't mean that. What I mean is that she accused me of telling her before—*oh, forget it!*

"I don't want your help," I say. "But thanks . . . besides she seems happy with Colic."

"Colin. And she's not that happy."

"Oh?"

"No. She wants him to move here but he won't leave his job there. She's sure he's seeing someone in London."

That's good news! For me.

She says, "If you change your mind, I'll help you." She stands straight up and everything springs back into place. The truth is that second I want her and only her, the old Tahiti-Iceland thing.

"Okay, I'll keep your offer in mind."

And then, surely just to torment me, as she walks away she does a thing she knows drives me crazy: she takes a scrunchy out of her hair and shakes her head and her hair falls, fizzes, and bursts out like waterfalls, champagne, and fireworks.

Whatever spirits I have that are aloft at that moment instantly plummet.

{ }

IVY AND I are walking outside on a weeknight, around nine o'clock. I'd caved in—we're coming back from Bandar's, an Indian restaurant on Lexington Avenue. It's a cold starry night and we're walking closely together.

"See, that wasn't so bad," she says.

I'm scanning around in all directions, looking for people.

"I think tomorrow I might speak up in a meeting," she warns me.

Oh no . . .

"What are you going to say?"

"That's the thing . . . I have no idea yet."

"Which meeting? The ten o'clock one?"

"Yep. The earlier the better, just to get it over with."

"I won't be there, I don't think," I say, trying to figure out where else I can be.

"You don't want to catch my big debut?" (She purposely pronounces it "de-butt" . . . she really is very clever and likable.)

"I don't want to cramp your style."

"Who knows if I have a style to cramp?"

To my horror, from across the street I hear: "Zachary! Zachary Post!" A female voice.

I turn to my left, feeling like a threatened animal—if I had stink glands the neighborhood would be reeking—and see Betsy Butler coming toward us, crossing the avenue.

"Ohhhh, you're going to kill me for this," Ivy mutters as Betsy approaches, probably coming from one of the ten dates a week she averages in her never-ending quest to remarry.

"At least we weren't holding hands," Ivy whispers.

"Hello, Betsy . . ." I cannot even muster up enough energy to pretend I'm surprised to see her.

"*Ivy Kooper??* Well! This is a surprise," Betsy says.

Please be tactful, Betsy, I'm thinking. Please be subtle, diplomatic, and . . .

"So are you two an item or what?"

"No, we're just friends," I say, seeing Ivy's eyes darting to me at the corners.

"Friends, huh?" Betsy says.

"Yeah, friends. Is that so impossible to believe?"

"Where are you coming from?"

"Uh . . . we just had dinner."

Ivy has a strand of her long brown hair in her hand and is nervously twirling it.

"Just dinner," Betsy says. "Yeah. Okay."

(Betsy Butler to Velma Watts to Regine Turnbull to Marcel Perrault to Byron Poole to Marjorie Millet and then back to me. And to Leslie. That's how it would go, I was sure of it. And it probably wouldn't take five minutes.)

"Well," Ivy says to me when I see her home that night, "I guess the next big nightmare for you is meeting my parents."

{ }

TO: ALL EMPLOYEES, WORLDWIDE
FROM: VERSAILLES EXEC. OFFICES
RE: TRANSITIONS

The Board of Directors of Versailles Publishing, Inc., is at once pleased and proud to announce that Martyn Stokes will be, effective immediately, filling the role of Executive Editor: Creative, a new position, and that the title of Director: Creative will be retired forthwith.

As you know, Martyn has been a loyal and dynamic force at VPI for seven years, and we are sure you all will welcome and applaud this appointment. During his four-year tenure at BOY, circulation increased from 250,000 to 1,000,000, and BOY won three National Magazine Awards.

On a sad note, Sophie Vuillard, Editor-in-Chief of SHE since 1943, will be retiring, also effective immediately. Her inspiring, legendary presence will be sorely missed.

The day this e-mail flashed onto my computer screen—and to thousands of others at Versailles offices from Scandinavia to Southeast Asia—Regine closed her door. She closed it with a furious, terrifying slam that she wanted everyone in our Stockholm and Singapore offices to hear.

People stayed out of her way for a while.

{ }

"OKAY, SO we're running the Swiss mime troupe in 'Starters' in either March or April. We've also got Zack's sculptor piece . . . that's a page, with a photo of the sculptor and probably another one of a sculpture or two . . ." Betsy is running through some stories for upcoming issues and it's a big meeting, with the edit, art, and fashion departments. "Anything else?" she says, looking up through her fashionable but old-womanish glasses. "The way I see it we've now got half a page free."

Then it happens.

Ivy raises her hand. My solar plexus, throat, and scrotum shrink to one-tenth their normal sizes and the air inside my lungs turns to an unbreathable gas.

"Uh, yes?" Betsy says to her with a hint of a condescending smile. Now her glasses are at the bottom of her nose and she's somehow looking up and down at the same time. She looks younger than her forty-five years but still strongly resembles one of Van Gogh's potato eaters.

"There's a German theatrical musical group called Neuro Euro-Rubbish," Ivy says. "They're kind of artsy-fartsy but with a sort of Brecht-Weill-Max Reinhardt cabaret approach to their work. They're huge now in Germany and France and they're going to be booked into the Public Theater for a few months this summer. They could be the next Stomp, Blue Man Group, or Cirque du Soleil."

Her voice sounds so composed, so steady, so graceful even, so professional . . . what I'm hearing, I know, is Nightingale-Bamford. It all had worked . . . *it had took!* But still I need to breathe.

"This sounds interesting," Betsy says.

Jackie asks if Ivy can interview one or two members of the group. Ivy said she could; her father knew the head of their management company.

"So having Jimmy Kooper for a dad," Mark Larkin says, doing something weird with his jaw (it looks as if he's trying to make his upper and lower teeth switch places), "does pay off, eh?"

"I'm sure it pays off in other ways too," Marcel Perrault says.

"Well," Ivy says, the hair on the left side of her head falling down with perfect timing, bounce, and aplomb, "you don't have to live with him."

She's a smashing success—a hell of a lot better than the first time I spoke up—and the Versailles Human Resources Department could videotape it and sell it as the prototype for all prospective employees.

The meeting breaks up. My Leroy White piece is still floating around in limbo, looking for an issue and six pages to land in.

I trot to the bathroom, going past Smitty, who croaks between puffs: "Where's the fire, Zachary?" and I close the stall door and slam the seat and cover down and sit down. I stay there for close to ten minutes, recapturing my breath and normal body temperature.

And this was without Ivy making a fool of me! What kind of condition would I have been in if she had?

Before Ivy made her big pitch, something else at that meeting happens.

For "Starters" Willie mentions a Louisiana-based writer he's been reading lately. His name is A. L. Fontenot and he's published five novels; all of them have received glowing reviews but sold miserably. A few months ago, Fontenot changed publishers.

Willie has an old friend at Fontenot's new house and they'd gotten the reclusive author to agree to an interview. Willie's piece would be two pages at the most, most likely one page. It's a given, he says to everybody, that Fontenot's "break" would come very soon, probably with the imminent release of his new book.

Willie really wants to do this story . . . his voice is loud and full of purpose. It's the most animated I've seen him for months. "He's a writer like Cormac McCarthy or Harry Crews," he says, "or—sorry, Zack— Ethan Cawley." He mentions Cawley not to embarrass me but just so an author's name will ring a bell with the staff, particularly the fashion department—they probably never read anything but the fabric content on labels.

"It might be good to get the jump on everyone else," Betsy says.

Liz Channing says she's read a book of Fontenot's and, though it was difficult, it was worth the struggle.

"I don't know," Mark Larkin says. "Are we going to do a piece on every writer who doesn't sell well?"

Without seeing it I know Willie's legs and feet are shaking a mile a minute under the long table.

"It's a once in a lifetime opportunity," Willie says. "He might never grant another interview again."

"We should, like, first make sure he's, like, tele*genic?*" a fashion department airhead says with a pretentious-looking squint.

"I've got news for you: this ain't television," Willie says. "The question is, is he photogenic? And I have no idea. I also don't know if Tolstoy was."

"He wasn't," Byron Poole says.

The story is put on hold. Mark Larkin comes up with three or four reasons why we shouldn't do it. Willie counters each one but after a while he simply loses his will to fight.

"Okay, we just won't do it," Willie says.

"I'm not saying we don't do it," Mark Larkin offers. "I just want to know *why* we should do it."

"No, we just won't do it," Willie says, looking exhausted.

When I get back from the bathroom and recover from Ivy's smashing debutt, this is waiting for me:

FROM: LISTERW
TO: POSTZ
SUBJECT: The Asshole

the rough rider just came over to my desk and said no hard feelings.

I ask him:

What did you say?

He tells me:

i told him to go fuck himself.
he's a dead man zeke a dead man.

It dawns on me to save this e-mail.

{ }

PROVING THE possibility of there being a God, Mark Larkin didn't get
the editor-in-chief job at *Boy*. Thomas Land, the Master Ass-kisser of Park
Avenue, did. (Now that bastard has fewer people to get coffee for, but I
bet he still gets Martyn Stokes a cup every now and then.) This in itself
was quite an unpleasant shock but still I was greatly relieved it wasn't the
puffy-faced, thickly-bespectacled, pink-cheeked toady on my own floor.
Tom is the same age as I am, we started the same year, he's not that much
smarter than I am. He went to Yale but then again I went to Berkeley and
Liverpool . . . right?

It was quite a shrewd career move, Thomas Land marrying Trisha
Lambert two years ago. Within six months Trisha became a senior editor
at *Her* and now he's editor-in-chief at *Boy*. They're just going to keep rising and rising until they either reach heaven or the whole marriage
implodes, baby and all.

With gritted teeth I sent Tom a six-sentence e-mail congratulating
him—maybe he would remember his old pal and ask me to come
aboard. It took about five business days for him to send me a thank you.
And that's all it was: "Thank you."

There's *schadenfreude* (damage-joy) when you're happy that someone else is doing badly, but is there a German word (success-grief, tri-
umph-misery) for when you've been made utterly wretched by someone
else's success?

For the hell of it, while I was on a groveling streak, I e-mailed Nan
Hotchkiss in London. I told her I was hoping everything was going well.
Who knows? Maybe there's something for me there.

I'm desperate.

After Martyn's promotion, Regine's door was closed for two weeks
straight and nobody dared knock on it, call her, send her an e-mail, or
even walk by her office.

It turned out, though, that she left the country . . . she hadn't been in her office anyway. (A picture of her ran in the *Times*; she's sitting front-row at a fashion show in Milan, wearing dark oval sunglasses that make her look like a bee.)

It didn't look like there would be an everybody-into-the-pool game of musical chairs. Everything would stay the same . . .

But one afternoon after Regine had returned from her beehive in Milan, Sheila Stackhouse had an announcement to make:

"I have cancer," she tells the art and edit staff, gathered in the big conference room to hear her. "So I'm going to take a leave of absence. Six months, maybe three months. I'll be back, though, guys. My number's not up. I'm going to lick this thing, you watch."

People start applauding and I join in. But it's like when you have to applaud after a lousy play because you don't want to hurt the actors' feelings. And it's strange: Are they clapping for her or for Cancer itself, because it's as if Mr. Cancer is standing right there with a big ugly smile, his hairy festering arm wrapped around Sheila's shoulder, taking her away to the horrible wastes of Cancer Land.

I have a feeling she won't be back. She's in her fifties and when she makes her announcement, the light in her once bright clear eyes is already somber and dull.

"Mark Larkin will be taking over for me until I return," she tells us, and my blood turns from a mild simmer to a furious boil in one second. "So let's all wish him good luck."

TO: POSTZ
FROM: LISTERW
SUBJECT: The Asshole

TO: LISTERW
FROM: POSTZ
SUBJECT: Re: The Asshole

LISTERW:	i can't believe this
POSTZ:	I can.
LISTERW:	but we've been here longer
POSTZ:	Yep.
LISTERW:	it's not fair.
POSTZ:	I hear you, chum.
LISTERW:	he'll fire you he'll fire you and NT will get a raise

POSTZ:	No. Nolan's useless. TR isn't stupid.
LISTERW:	i feel for you, dude. ML will be working a few yards away he'll be editing your copy, making wholesale changes, shooting down your ideas you won't get more than 4 hours sleep ever again
POSTZ:	There's something I should tell you, Willie.
LISTERW:	uh oh what? you have the big c too?
POSTZ:	I'm having an affair with IK.
LISTERW:	i knew that already buddy
POSTZ:	You did?
LISTERW:	everyone knows
POSTZ:	Who told you?
LISTERW:	oh you know the usual gossip mongers
POSTZ:	Was MM one of them?
LISTERW:	yeah does that shock you? she was the 1st who told me
POSTZ:	Christ! MM's going to tell LUS!
LISTERW:	she already did because LUS was the 2nd one who told me and she told me MM told her
POSTZ:	The world is ending. I had no idea it was going to end like this. It's dismal.
LISTERW:	but IK seems like a really sweet girl zeke you could do worse
	gotta go!
POSTZ:	Why? Who's there?
LISTERW:	your boss
POSTZ:	Sheila?
LISTERW:	no your new one
	jesus! he's already emptying his desk!
	vultures vultures vultures!

⁑   ⁂

I LEAVE work at about 5:30 on the day of Sheila Stackhouse's announcement. Everything is the same in her office except there are about two dozen red and pink roses that Velma's gotten her on behalf of Regine.

The next morning all the furniture is different, there's a new rug, the pictures of Sheila's family are gone, and Mark Larkin has his own personal effects up (a Harvard pennant, a framed sepia photograph of a huge white house on a wavy sea of grass, the kind of house that the great R. J. Post used to build).

And Mark Larkin is in there, in the splotchy pink flesh and the

Coke-bottle eyeglasses, in a Hugo Boss suit and one of his usual distasteful shirts with the collar a different color.

"Good morning, Post," he says. "I meant to tell you yesterday that I look forward to working with you."

He holds his hand out and I shake it. I want to say: "I remember you on your first day, you Teddy Roosevelt Cantabrigian fuckhead, pissing your bully pulpit pants in terror because you didn't know how to get Regine's coffee. And you had never used a fax machine before, you rich spoiled country-club son of a Jed Leland cunt, you thought it was something right out of the fucking Jetsons."

But I say: "I think we'll make a good team."

"Yes. I rother think we will. I know we've had a rocky road so far. But it's par for the course, I'm sure it was that way for you when you first started."

"I don't remember."

"I really hope we can pull together. Of course, that doesn't mean we couldn't stand a few changes around here though, does it?"

A chill sweeps over my skin. I notice the Mylanta-Kaopectate painting on the wall. So this was why Sheila's husband had looked so forlorn in the picture, because he somehow sensed that one day this acrylic-on-canvas disaster would be hanging right here . . .

"Changes?" I say.

But he doesn't hear me and launches into his next sentence.

"You know, it occurred to me coming to work: I'm the only editor here who's a male, other than Marcel Perrault. But he's a fashion editor and a cocksucker so it doesn't count. If you ask me, this place can use a good shot of estrogen."

"I think you mean testosterone."

"Yes, one of those hormones."

Changes? What changes?

Nolan shoves a muffin into his mouth and crumbs fall onto his desk and lap. My eyes note the oil spot on the wall where he rests his head. It's black now, the size of a dart board, but I could swear that recently it was light gray and very small.

"Sheila's bad news yesterday," he begins, "was like the mist swarming over a murky swamp like—"

"Please, not now."

He has the look of dead meat about him . . . flank steak, chopped chuck, as Willie would put it. He's a ground-round goner. The *Star Trek* extra in my life is about to be phased out of the picture.

"Did you send Sheila flowers?" Ivy asks two days after Sheila broke the bad news.

"I did."

"What kind?"

"Red roses. I sent them to her house in Short Hills."

"Did you write a card?"

"Of course. 'You're a great boss. I'm pulling for you.' That kind of thing. What do you think I am, an animal?"

She kisses me on my cheek and says, "You're not so bad after all."

"I guess I'm not," I say, looking around to make sure nobody had seen her kissing me.

The next morning I send red roses to Sheila. The card says that she's a great boss and I'm pulling for her.

The rumor is that when Sheila told Regine she had cancer, Regine snapped: "How could you?! At a time like this! We're shipping the March issue!"

The two dozen red and pink roses from Regine had come in a beautiful crystal vase. There was a card from Regine.

"Good luck and thanks for everything. Bye. RT."

That "Bye" means everything. It means the end, that Regine is kissing her off, no hospital visits, no phone calls, no cards, no more flowers, no appearance at the funeral, no anything.

And it was in Velma's handwriting.

{ }

"DO YOU know about the party next week? At Pernety?" Marjorie asks me one day at work.

"What's the occasion?"

"Promotions, retirements, death."

It's a "shuffles party," she explains, commemorating Gaston's passing, celebrating Martyn Stokes's great leap upward, Sophie Vuillard's retirement, and the promotion of whoever would be Sophie's replacement.

There's no doubt in anyone's mind that Martyn's first act in his new position was getting rid of Sophie Vuillard. She was the doyenne of fashion, culture, and taste . . . forty years ago. Now she's just a wrinkled twig with a failing mind and a cotton candy puff of saffron hair. The rumors are she often forgets her own name, but most worrisome of all, her circulation is down. *She* is Versailles' flagship and Martyn couldn't watch it sink. It shows he knows what he's doing, firing her. Gaston hadn't done it because firing her meant that he would have had to deal with her, which he hadn't done since 1963.

"Don't invite anyone else, okay?" Marjorie instructs me.

She means Willie, I imagine . . . or does she mean Ivy? Or does she not mean it at all?

"Well, I don't know if I can make it," I tell her.

"Why not? Something better might come up?" She twists her mouth suggestively and arches her back, making her chest swing violently to the left. Now she's talking about Ivy, there's no question about it. Go ahead, say Ivy's name to me, I'm thinking. Go ahead, you Big Overripe Strawberry, make a sarcastic comment, about her age, her father, her allowance, you wall-rattling howling dervish, whirling banshee, chandelier-swinging jackhammer.

"You'll be there. You know you will," she says.

She's right. I'll be there because, among other reasons, she'll be there.

TO: POSTZ
FROM: USHERSOAMESL
SUBJECT:

Will you be coming to the bash?

Oh my God! Leslie Usher-Soames has sent me an e-mail!

And somebody else in the building cares about punctuation and capitals . . .

This hasn't ever happened before. Leslie is reaching out to me. My heart is racing. It's excitement, raw and invigorating. She sits only a few cubicle walls away but it's almost like kissing a woman for the first time.

And it's right out of the blue, unsolicited.

As soon as my heartbeat slows down a bit, I reply:

Yes I'm coming. Haven't got a stitch to wear but I'll put something together. Is your beau still in town?

I wait for a reply. And wait. After five minutes I look away from my screen but I keep looking back up every thirty seconds. I log out and then reboot, thinking maybe that will help. Forty-five minutes pass and there's no response from her. This must be what it's like thinking you've won the lottery but then you find out you were one measly digit off.

I see Leslie walking down the hallway with Marjorie and Byron Poole and two people from the fashion department.

She must have sent me her message to me and then been pulled away.

TO: POSTZ
FROM: USHERSOAMESL
SUBJECT:

CTY is back across the Pond. No great tragedy there, eh? Look forward to seeing you It should be quite a piss-up. LUS.

It occurs to me that if Leslie Usher-Soames marries Colin Tunbridge-Yates, her monogram will be LUSTY.

(She'd left out a period after "seeing you," I notice. But maybe not on purpose.)

I try to think of something clever to reply but decide—though it's very difficult—to leave her hanging.

{ }

JIMMY Kooper seems like the kind of guy who: wakes up at 4:30 A.M., goes to his gym and runs and lifts weights with some lawyer buddies, hits a Turkish bath for two hours and then goes to the barber shop at the Plaza for a shave, gets a massage at some posh place that only twenty people know about, then goes to work, takes a three-hour lunch with clients or friends, goes back to work to intimidate his staff, takes a two-hour meeting with his stockbroker, money manager, or bookie, drops in on his mistress after work and either gets handcuffed or handcuffs her, and then goes home. He just seems like the kind of man who manages to extract sixty hours out of a twenty-four-hour day.

"You know, I think a client of mine lives in one of your father's houses," Jimmy Kooper says.

"Oh yeah? Where is that?"

He wedges some lettuce out from his teeth with a toothpick and makes a loud sucking sound.

"Naples, Florida. This house looks like a mausoleum."

"Well, that was his style all right."

Ivy kicks me under the table . . . I've told her the truth, that my father was not R. J. Post the architect but is Bob Post the Wet Guy. This hasn't prevented her from spreading the false news to her parents—which I find endearing—who sit opposite me now in a dark French restaurant on Lexington Avenue in the Seventies.

"Yeah, style," Jimmy Kooper says. He's gotten the lettuce out and is pecking at a different tooth for a different foodstuff. "You gotta have style."

Ivy's mother dabs her little mouth with her napkin. A pit bull and an Afghan hound, Jimmy and Carol Kooper are built in classical comedy-team style, the Big One (Hardy, Costello, Gleason) and the Skinny One (Laurel, Abbott, Carney), though not that exaggerated; he has shoulders like a sofa but isn't fat, she's like a coat hanger but isn't dangerously skinny. Looking at her, at the hefty sable coat draped over her chair, at her rich East Side face covered with powder, at her carefully coiffed blond hair, at her bright complexion (she looks like a wax pear) and little fishhook nose, she reminds me of someone . . . but I can't quite place it. Even the way she speaks and carries herself makes me think of someone else but I cannot remember who it is.

We talk about Versailles for most of the evening. Jimmy Kooper is the company's chief lawyer. He prevents lawsuits, initiates lawsuits, settles lawsuits, he deals with advertisers and employees, the insulted and the injured. With our millions of readers, lawsuits come from every direction; women sued because a mascara tip they'd picked up in *Appeal* caused an allergic reaction or because a combination of foundation and blush had, their lawyers claimed, caused their marriage to fail; men sued because a style tip they'd picked up in *Men* ("When Stripes and Checks Get Along") had gotten them fired. Even horoscope suits are filed against us time to time. Jimmy Kooper has to bully people into submission and he's sufficiently built for that, with his Rock of Gibraltar jaw and big hands. (And his voice booms—the ice in our glasses of water tinkles when he speaks.) Why he became a lawyer for a *Fortune* 500 magazine company, I don't know; usually his ilk (barrel-chested, fifteen double-breasted suits and camel hair coats, gray felt fedora, white silk scarf and million-dollar scowl) become *consiglieres* and attach themselves to men called Jimmy the Chisel or Vic the Whale.

"Ivy tells me that you grew up in a house," her mother says to me in between nibbles of her *coq au vin*, "that Rutherford Hayes' cousins once lived in?" She leans over her string beans and says to me: "Rutherford Hayes is a relative of mine."

She makes it sound as if he's at the next table, as if she knows him personally . . . and I notice she dropped the middle initial.

"Not that again, Carol," Jimmy Kooper shuts her up, thus turning my ten minutes of boning up at www.rutherfordb.hayes.com into completely wasted time. "She's always going on about this. Rutherford B. goddamn Hayes." Again he goes at the food in his teeth, making the kind of chirpy sucking sounds that, had you heard them outdoors and not inside a restaurant, you would have thought a group of bird watchers was close by. (Was *any* food making it past his teeth?)

They ask a lot of questions and—surprisingly—I only have to lie on a few occasions. Compared to the kind of nerdy or acne-riddled guys Ivy must have brought home in her college and high school years, I'm pretty serious stuff; this is one of the few occasions when being an associate editor at a magazine that sells over a million copies seems like quite an accomplishment. They keep prodding me, though, keep asking pointed questions, trying to discern what kind of future I've got, whether I'm a rising star or whether I've already peaked. It is here when I have to lie (but perhaps my plateau still shows).

It's a pretty uneventful dinner . . . except for when I excuse myself to the bathroom and Jimmy Kooper joins me a few seconds later. There are four empty urinals but he inexplicably chooses to use the one immediately to my right.

The four of us go back to their apartment. This is the first time I've ever been in an apartment building on Park Avenue, other than when I handed out piles of the free local newspaper I used to work for. I've never seen a place like this before. The apartment has cathedral ceilings, ornate molding, arches in the hallways, alcoves in the walls, four bathrooms for four people (she has a brother somewhere) . . . I can't believe it.

We sit down in the living room and have an after-dinner drink. I hit the automatic pilot button now, the wine I've had with dinner helping me, and I seem to be handling myself well. Ivy looks very nice; she has on a blue dress and her hair is in a braid. Her mother goes to the bathroom at one point, probably to sprinkle more powder on her face. With her gone, Jimmy Kooper's mood changes a shade and I get a little nervous; he starts talking about Douglas Davis (*Men*'s publisher), calling him "a dumb queer spineless fuck who needs to have his skull busted but good a few times." I sit back and wonder: How, with a vicious pit bull for a father and a courteous, powdery Afghan hound for a mother, did Ivy Kooper turn out so nice? Is it possible she has multiple personalities and that I never see the one that eats furniture?

Ivy takes me downstairs. Walking out I notice that the closet in their foyer — yes, they have a foyer and it's bigger than my bedroom — is stuffed full of furs . . . chinchillas, sables, foxes. I'm ready to move right in there, sleep on the floor, and let them tickle the top of my head.

We walk to the corner and she says, "Well?"

"I kept waiting for him to garrote me."

"No, he just met you. He was sizing you up. He'll kill you the next time."

"There has to be a next time?"

I make a move to kiss her good night but she buries her head in my chest. I hug her and stare out at the cars rushing both ways on Park Avenue, at smoke spewing out of a manhole, at luxurious apartment buildings with doormen in uniforms that make them look like czars, kaisers, and generals.

Where the hell do I belong in this world, I'm wondering.

On the bus I realized who it was that Carol Kooper reminded me of. It was my mother! No, not my real mother. She reminded me of the mother I'd invented for myself, that eccentric nut in Palm Beach who drives around in a Mercedes golf cart and is leaving everything to her dogs.

For some reason the bus home that night ends its route early and I have to get off on Thirty-fourth Street. It's not that cold out for January so I decide to walk home.

I find myself in Marjorie's neighborhood. It's impossible for me to go past her corner without thinking of everything that happened inside her apartment, the screaming, pounding, grinding, straining and pushing and pulling. If Thelonious Monk and Golda Meir can get streets named after them, if Willa Cather and W. H. Auden can have plaques up on the buildings they once lived in, then there ought to be a bronze plaque up on Marjorie's building:

MARJORIE MILLET
Associate Art Director of
It Magazine and
Sack Artist Extraordinaire
Lived and Had Sex Here

A light is on in her apartment, the living room light.

The notion strikes me like a bullet between the eyes: I'll call her up, invite myself over, she'll open the door, I'll drop to my knees, she'll savagely rub her hands in my scalp, and—

Even though I have no intention of doing this—even though I really want to—I start feeling around for a quarter.

Then Mark Larkin walks by me.

He's about ten yards away, crossing from the west side of the avenue to the east. He doesn't see me. He's wearing normal, non-work clothes: chinos (baggy and too short), his Triple Fat Goose goosedown jacket, Wallabies, and a Red Sox cap.

I just stand there, paralyzed by numbness, and the quarter teeters on my fingertips. A little traffic is going by and thin wisps of smoke hang on my breath.

Mark Larkin goes into Marjorie's lobby.

I let out a noise—I don't know if it's a squeak or a moan or a whimper or a squawk, I don't know if it comes from my mouth, epiglottis, or pharynx—but it's the saddest, most pathetic, loneliest, most desolate noise I'm capable of emitting.

(She couldn't possibly be calling him Big Boy, Handsome, Slick, Tough Guy, could she? Because he was none of those things. But then again, am I?)

Yes, I'm a dickhead; it shouldn't even have occurred to me to drop myself at Marjorie's threshold and bury myself in her thighs. Yes, I'm shallow; why should her thighs knocking my ears like policemen banging on a front door be the highlight of my life?

But this is how truly shallow I am:

That night, I went home and cried into a pillow.

9

THERE IS a fierce February snowstorm the night of the party and the higher reaches of the sky are so full of snow and spiral milky billows that the whole sky looks white and slate gray, like an eraser's smudges on a chalkboard. Pernety, on an anonymous sidestreet in the Flower District, is a small French restaurant on the ground floor with a large ballroom facility the next one up. Versailles always has its parties there.

I'd gone to Crookshank's and bought a new suit and shirt for the occasion, knowing that, as much as I spent, most of the people who would be there would spend much, much more. Is there a better-dressed company than Versailles Publishing, Inc.? Probably not, but Versailles people had *better* dress well, seeing as we're the Official Taste Merchants to the world. It would be like the editors of *The Wine Spectator* drinking Ripple.

I'm about to walk up the large staircase to the ballroom when I see Liz Channing sitting alone on the first step, assaulting a black high-heel shoe. Her hair is up in a chignon again and she's banging the heel against the wall, calling it a dirty son of a bitch. She's viciously going at her bubble gum (her way of quitting smoking) and blowing bubbles.

"You okay?" I ask her.

"Goddamn this thing!" she says. She looks up at me. "You don't want to go up there, believe me."

"Why not?" I take the shoe and examine it.

"It's the usual ritual . . . everybody wearing black and stinking of perfume and acting like we shit gold bullion." She looks at me checking out the shoe and says, "That thing's done for."

She takes it back from me and I ask her if she's going back upstairs and she says, "Yeah, right, barefoot!" I leave her on the stairway, cursing and beating the daylights out of her shoe.

The party comes to me in an immense wave, curling in and bearing down in slow motion. The place is packed (it was ridiculous that Marjorie asked me not to bring or tell anyone—there are people here who have no idea what party they're at) and there's very little room to move around in. It's dark inside except for some soft blue and red light playing on the black walls here and there. Fashion show catwalk music plays but does so at a low volume and although the floor shakes, it does so in a deadened, dull manner.

As I move through the crowd, an annoying editor from *Appeal* or *Zest* congratulates me on landing Sheila Stackhouse's job, mistaking my bad fortune for Mark Larkin's good, and I say thanks and move away. As usual at company events, Versailles employees who normally can't manage hellos or how-are-you's are eking out half-smiles and quarter-nods—for them this is the equivalent of Scrooge standing the Cratchitt family to a Christmas goose.

I get a drink and hope that Willie shows up so I'll have someone to talk to . . . he could disparage this whole scene with me. But I hadn't invited him. He must have heard about it though, but he just hadn't come. For that, I envy him.

Suddenly Laurie Lafferty is standing next to me. She's holding a drink and, in jeans and a flannel shirt, isn't dressed for the occasion. The two tiny squares of blue light reflected in her round eyeglasses make it look as if she's watching television.

"Are you here alone?" I ask her.

She says she's here with an *It* proofreader, a Black Holer people refer to as "The Phantom" because she's so quiet and pale.

I ask Laurie if Willie knows about the party and she says she has no idea. "We're not living together anymore."

"You're kidding!" I say.

"I'm not. I can't believe you didn't know this already."

"I didn't." I ask her who moved out, she or Willie.

"We take turns. Sometimes he stays at the Chelsea Hotel and I get the apartment, sometimes I stay at a friend's house."

I recall the night Willie phoned me at four in the morning, the day that Jacqueline Wooten got Nan Hotchkiss's job. He told me then that Laurie was staying at a friend's.

"He's talking to himself now," Laurie tells me.

"He talks to himself?"

She nods and says he does it all the time, that he was waking her up all hours of the night, sitting up in bed, facing the wall and mumbling incoherently.

"And what kind of things does he say?" I have to ask.

"Nonsense." She begs me not to tell him that she told me. I tell her not to worry.

"I was thinking," she says with a pleasant smile, "of maybe you and Oliver and Liz just coming over one night and having a talk with him, maybe trying to get him to seek help . . ."

"Like an insomniac intervention?"

"I know, it's ridiculous."

I try to reconcile the young linebacker in crimson, wearing number 99 and flattening anything that came his way, his blond hair flying around, the Harvard graduate who read *Finnegans Wake* and *The Man Without Qualities* and all of *Remembrance of Things Past* (in French!), with this paranoid nervous wreck who talks to plaster and paint from sundown to sunrise.

"He's thinking about getting a gun, Zack. He says it's easy, you just drive to Virginia, buy it, and drive back up."

"And what would he do with said gun?"

"He won't answer that question."

About ten yards in front of me Trisha Lambert, in a backless black satin dress and looking like an ad for Valentino, twists and turns through the crowd. She sees me out of the corner of her vulpine eye and then she quickly looks away. I'm about to say something to Laurie when . . . when I feel someone pinch my butt. It has to be Marjorie Millet, right?

But it isn't. It's Leslie Usher-Soames. And I've never seen her looking like this.

She's wearing a black dress and actually showing some of her outer epidermal layer and you can see what little cleavage she's able to piece together. (This is the most I've ever seen of her, other than her face, hands, and wrists.) And her back is on display, almost *all* of her back, and it's a great back, sleek and aerodynamically designed, with sharp shoulder blades right out of a clothing designer's sketch.

(*And she pinched me!* Let's not forget that.)

"Leslie! How dare you!" I say with mock anger.

Laurie Lafferty quickly disappears into the crowd.

Leslie is on the verge of being loaded, maybe one more drink would shove her over the borderline. Who knew that this Sloane Ranger with (most likely) the claret-drinking, *Spectator*-reading, tweed-wearing, Fortnum & Mason tea-sipping, fox-hunting father with the house in the Boltons and probably a country estate with a name like Festersore or Slatternleigh, even got loaded?

"You don't have a date?" she asks me.

What does she mean? Does she mean Ivy? I know that she knows but she doesn't know I know.

"No, I don't. And Colin Tunabrunch-Yeast is back in London?"

"It's Tunbridge-Yates and it's a bloody shame he's not here, izzen tit?"

"How often do you two actually see each other?"

She takes a sip of her drink—it leaves a glistening silver mustache for a second—and says, "Too often."

This is getting interesting—she's looking pretty and for the first time since I've known her, her hair is all the way down . . . no sign of her ever present ponytail. (It had occurred to me that, were she to need life-saving brain surgery, she would decline it since it would mean temporarily losing the thing.) She has the ultimate Versailles hair: luxurious, bouncin' and behavin', full of Silkience. All the Clairol and Breck ad copy applies.

"But you two are engaged."

"Are we?" She crinkles up her nose. "Yes we are. I think . . . I'm almost certain he's shagging some tart."

Within the space of four business days she's e-mailed me (unsolicited), goosed me, and now mentioned "shagging" to me; this and the little pinch of her cleavage, her vertebrae on display, and her hair all around her shoulders . . . it's a little too much and makes what I'm drinking twice as potent.

"What makes you think so?" I ask.

"Because he doesn't want to shag *me*. And we haven't seen each other for months. I just hope that whoever it is, she gives him the bloody clap."

The doors are slightly ajar so I kick them right the hell in.

"Well, you certainly seem shagworthy to me." *Ugh!* It's times like these, when I switch into Auto-Flirt, when I really do loathe the sound of my own voice. And for all I know, Shagworthy is her mum's maiden name.

"Yes, I *am* rather shagworthy, don't you think?" (Does she really want me to answer this question?) She finishes her drink and is loaded now, shaking her head absentmindedly to the music.

She knows about Ivy and me, I'm thinking, *she knows, she knows, she knows*. Why, why, why did I get involved and how do I terminate it bloodlessly?

But maybe Leslie is one of those types who are drawn to men who are with other women, especially women they know. Maybe beneath that perfect alabaster skin there frolics a naughty imp, and having Ivy Kooper for a girlfriend (is that what Ivy is?) makes me more attractive, like an expensive suit, a house in the Hamptons, and a $200,000 trust fund.

"I'm going to get another jrink. Whatever you do, Zeke, *don't* move!" She points straight down to the two black linoleum tiles I'm standing on.

"I'll be here," I say, sighing and buttoning my jacket to hide my sudden erection, which nobody but nobody would ever see.

"Do you have an erection?" Marjorie, sidling up to me, asks as soon as Leslie goes to get her refill.

"No, I don't." She hands me a drink.

"You got one simply from talking to Leslie, didn't you? I know when you sigh and button your jacket it means you're aroused. Remember . . . I used to arouse you."

You still do and you'll torture me when I'm ninety years old . . . your breasts wriggling free and the fire in your eyes will be the last images I see when the final ounce of life wheezes out of me. It could be what kills me next week.

I unbutton my jacket and she pinches my groin.

"See, I was right! I knew it." Her eyes widen.

Now, this is the first time her hands have journeyed to these parts in well over a year. It isn't helping any.

What if she wants me to . . . to "get with her"? What do I do? How do I say no . . . *why* would I say no? I can't afford to pass up such an offer. It's like someone handing out Rolls-Royces; you might not want one but you'd be an idiot to say no.

(And there was the added bonus: Wouldn't I really be getting supreme revenge on Mark Larkin? Even if he never found out—which was unlikely since it was Marjorie—I'd still have gotten the better of the bastard, my temporary boss.)

And what about sweet innocent Ivy Kooper?

Well, I've never pledged myself to her, nor she to me. I know that relationship has to die, most likely die a horrible death. She'll cry, get mad, and cry again, and I'll feel rotten for a while, maybe for a long while, but not forever.

"You can let go now, Marjorie."

She lets go. Too bad.

"How come your little chippy's not here?" she asks. So that little chunk of ice is finally broken.

"What chippy?"

"Jimmy Kooper's five-year-old kid."

"She's not five."

"Excuse me. Seven. You're going to break her precious little Nightingale-Bamford heart."

"I'm not looking forward to it."

"I guess she's not important enough to be here, is she?"

"Neither am I," I say.

"Hands off, Margie. I saw him first," Leslie says as soon as she joins us. My feet are still glued to the two black tiles.

"Not really," Marjorie says.

"Oh yes, you two were quite the hot item once, weren't you?"

Now, until this moment I've had no inkling that Marjorie had told her, though it figures she had, she being Marjorie. Everything—me doing Marjorie, Colin's possible infidelity with the tart, me doing Ivy, Leslie's hair and back, Marjorie's chest—is spilling out tonight. I can, if I really need to, play the Mark Larkin card at any time. But it's worth saving, I figure.

"A hot item?" Marjorie says with a snide laugh. "I wouldn't say it was that hot."

That I cannot handle. She just can't go around publicly badmouthing the most sublime moments of my life. It was the closest I'd ever come to paradise and here she is, slandering it!

So I snap: "Oh! Mark Larkin's better?! Tell me, does he speak softly and carry a really big stick when he does it?!"

Leslie's mouth drops open and some gin and tonic trickles out. She has to step back so it doesn't spill on her outfit.

"What the hell are you talking about?" Marjorie says, aghast and aglow.

"I'm talking about you and Mr. San fucking Juan goddamn Hill fucking each other!"

"WHAT?!" Marjorie says. She might toss her drink at me, I'm thinking, right at this new suit.

"I know about you two, okay? I know. Jesus, with that big Teddy Roosevelt grin, you could park twenty-six cars on his fuckin' teeth!" (At this point I'm not sure exactly how many teeth a human being has.)

"I am not sleeping with Mark Larkin."

"You're not?!" But she might be lying. (Once when confronted by Byron Poole about sleeping with me, she'd lied about that . . . or so she had told me.)

"No! What makes you think I am?"

"I saw him go into your building at night. Late at night once."

She shakes her head once or twice and says: "I'm not sleeping with him . . . I never *have* slept with him. He's . . . neuter. I think. He likes other neuters. Jesus Christ, he was returning something to me . . . a computer disk. He left it with the doorman. And what are you doing anyway . . . *stalking* me?!"

As I explain to her that I'd merely been in her neighborhood, Leslie empties her gin and tonic in one gulp. Her eyes are sparkling and her white skin is luminous but you can tell her head is taking its first spins.

I feel so utterly relieved that Marjorie isn't clawing the skin on Mark Larkin's back to linguini and clobbering his ears to bits with her thighs . . . it feels as though I'm ascending off the floor, lifted up by smiling little cherubim tickling my ears.

"Marjorie, would you, like, marry me? Tomorrow? Or tonight?"

"I'm going to have to say no to this offer. But really, you're *très* romantic."

"I understand."

"Now had you asked me two years ago . . ."

"Why? What would you have done?"

"Well, did it ever occur to you to marry me?"

"Lots of times," I lie. "Would you have said yes?"

"Never! Not in a million years."

She turns her back to us and moves away and it seems as she disappears into the crowd that each color she's wearing (red and black and green) goes in a different direction.

"Well!" Leslie says. "This is turning out to be quite some bash."

"So Cholera's really back in London? You're sure he's not sneaking around some bushes anywhere spying on you?"

She nods and sucks on a swizzle stick, looking like twelve-year-old jailbait with a chocolate malted.

"Are you doing anything after this?" I ask her.

She shrugs, purses her lips.

"Come out with me then," I say. "Okay?"

She nods. I sigh and button up my jacket again.

Oliver Osborne is at the bar, talking to a few people from *Men*, towering over them as he does over everyone.

I make small talk with the *Men* crowd, all of who are in their forties and on the scruffy side (elbow-patches on their jacket sleeves, rumpled shirts and faces), and with Ollie, who I know would give half his salary to work at *Men*, which might be literally the case: *Men* is not one of our better-selling books and the people who work there are paid accordingly.

"Those lucky bastards," Ollie says to me when they move away. "They go to work and when they go home they can actually look at themselves in the mirror without puking."

"Yeah, if they can afford a mirror."

Mark Larkin is coming up the long staircase. There is snow on his shoulders and his face is flushed from the cold.

"Can you give me the keys to your apartment, Zeke?" Ollie asks me.

"Huh?"

"I've got something going but I can't take her home."

He tells me that his roommate (another Brit), who works at our rival, Condé Nast, has some cousins staying over, about ten of them.

"You want the keys? To lay pipe in my crib?"

"If it's not too much trouble."

"You want them right now, don't you?"

"If it's not too much trouble."

"It's all right. But please, don't make a mess."

He promises he won't and I give him the keys and tell him to leave them under my doormat for me. He asks me how I'll get back into my building and I tell him I'd ring any old apartment, that nobody who lives there cares who they let in. He rushes off a second later—I try to see who the lucky girl is but the place is too dark and crowded.

Martyn Stokes makes a five-minute speech in front of everyone, saying he's "pleased and rawther pleasantly astonished ackshilleh" to accept his new position. It's a dream come true, he says, something he's wanted ever since he first opened his mum's copy of *She*, when he was five. (It figures it would be *She*.) He recites this speech as if it's completely ad-libbed, every touch of humble self-deprecation expertly executed, with perfect timing and perfect stop-on-a-dime pauses and even some clever stammering thrown in now and then. It's meant to disarm and charm everyone and it does and it's as if he's wanted to deliver this exact same speech since he was five years old too.

At one point he tells us: "Oh yes, my very first act will be to combine *She* and *It* into one magazine. I'll be calling it . . . *Shit*." People laugh and then he says, "I've been wanting to make that joke for years"—this also gets laughs, helped no doubt by the fact that he pronounces years "yares."

He can do no wrong. He could fire half the people in the room and they would laugh, slap him on the back, and congratulate him.

I realize, as I watch and listen to him win everybody over, that he's only six years older than I am. And now he's got it all. His clothing, his meals, his rent, his transportation . . . it would all be taken care of. He hardly has to do anything. Any worry he would ever suffer again in his life he would have to bring on himself.

This is a coronation.

And then Sophie Vuillard, practically bent over at a 90 degree angle, slowly lurches to the makeshift stage to say her *adieu*'s. It's the end of an era—that's what we're supposed to be thinking. But, to be honest, her era ended with the top hat, with fancy nightclubs like the Latin Quarter and El Morocco, with Walter Winchell and Checker cabs and Chesterfield cigarettes and the pillbox hat.

Yet some people weep openly as she says her good-byes (she speaks in a suspiciously hoarse whisper)—they have their hands over their mouths or hold cocktail napkins over their eyes. The high priestess of good taste, the "Grand Goddess of Glamour" (she's been called that for decades), once a creature straight out of a movie like *Laura* or *Funny Face*, now looks like a broken Q-Tip, a smudge of yellow ear wax on the cotton.

While Sophie speaks, Marjorie, about halfway across the room, has her eyes cast distantly into blank space . . . she's biting her nails, spitting them out to the floor. She's one of the few unmoved people in the house; she had started out at *She* and Sophie had once, over something very trivial, called her a dirty stinking Jew to her face. Standing close to me a black fashion editor from *Appeal* is in tears; doesn't she know that Sophie had refused to put a black woman on a *She* cover until only six years ago, or does she just not care? (And that black woman had to be light-skinned and photographed with two white ones.) Way on the other side of the room, Mark Larkin stands near Martyn Stokes, the former looking deeply moved, the latter too high in the clouds to be affected by anything other than a passing meteor shower.

Then Martyn announces Sophie's replacement. Her name is Alexa Van Deusen (you simply do not fail in life with a name like that) and the applause rumbles around the room. I recognize her immediately: she was the tall Stiletto in black leather pants in front of Gaston on his last trip ever to a bank machine; she's one of the many knitting-needle thin editors who try to pass off grimaces for smiles, who treat people they see every day for years like complete strangers or potential assailants.

She can't be older than thirty. Unless she's very incompetent or runs into some bad politics or dies young, Alexa Van Deusen will have the job for the next forty years.

"I love you, Sophie," Alexa Van Deusen says with tears that stain her cheeks with mascara. "I love you so much."

I've got to move up. Commas and colons and corner offices are up for grabs but going in every direction but my own. The Old Turks are dying in their offices or being pushed out, and the Young Turks, Peck's Bad Boys, *wunderkinder*, *kinderettes*, and *enfants terribles* are taking over.

What can I do? I've got to make it happen.

"Are we going?" Leslie on tip-toes whispers in my ear.

This was the answer right here, this was the answer, the way out and the way in. Here is my comma, my colon, my corner office with the Chrysler Building for a view. Here is the sweet-scented breath of an angel heralding the coming of splendid things.

Are we going? Yes, I hope we are.

Her emerald faux-fur coat is already on and her icy breath and the smell of gin send a shiver down my spine.

She's walking in front of me, not quite drunk enough to reel but certainly not cutting a very direct path to the staircase. I turn to my left and see Ivy Kooper, a dim blue light vibrating behind her. She's looking right at me, her tough guy father is on her left in a double-breasted suit with a white silk scarf, and a few executives stand on her right. She's wearing a lavender dress with long lavender gloves and looks very pretty, her slender curves and long legs and long wavy hair all on display. She smiles sweetly at me and I smile limply back, then she sees Leslie and she doesn't smile. And then I don't smile. Then I walk out.

∗{ }∗

LESLIE and I go to a bar on Columbus Avenue in the Seventies—she lives just around the corner. The snow falls in large downy chunks and a white spidery glaze curves across the bar's windows. There is hardly anyone else inside and we sit at a table.

We make small talk and after she makes short work of a gin and tonic she tells me to get her a "fizzy jrink."

"A fizzy drink? What's that?"

"Soda of some sort." She's slurring her words, leaning over the table, her eyes shifting back and forth.

I get her a seltzer and as I'm waiting for it, I look at her sitting alone in the booth. Her loose hair is falling over one shoulder and her skin is still luminous, like the supposedly poisoned glass of milk in *Suspicion*. Fizzy jrink? Euro-Disney, fanny packs, white socks . . . maybe foreigners are intent on remaining five years old. They hate Americans, which you can't blame them for, but then they also go days without showering, take Jerry Lewis seriously, risk public beheading to tape *Baywatch*, and wear lederhosen.

Leslie and I stay at the bar for over an hour and I keep seeing Ivy's smile change to a non-smile, the fuzzy blue light behind her draping over her like a shawl.

What do I say to her the next time I see her?

Once again walking behind her I go upstairs with Leslie. Like Marjorie's hair and chest, her back might become an obsession for me, but it will take some doing because, let's face it, backs really don't do all that much. It's a narrow spiral staircase and she drags her coat (it's from Saks, the label says) behind her on the steps and it's difficult for me to not step on it and stop her in her tracks . . . it's very tempting to fuck up that coat.

We're both covered with snow.

When she steps inside the apartment she removes her shoes with a quick kick of each leg, but she tries to catch each shoe and stumbles a little in the attempt. One shoe lands in the sink and she giggles drunkenly but it sounds almost witch-like.

There is framed artwork all over the walls (there are a few nineteenth-century fox-hunting scenes; was that a great grandfather in red atop a chestnut colt jumping over a puddle?) and a very expensive computer setup in the living room. The apartment is neat, comfortable, and Old World stylish . . . Daddy is definitely helping with the rent.

"I knew you fancied me," she tells me. Marjorie had told her. Of course.

We kiss for ten minutes before I leave.

For three of those ten minutes I'm trying to get her mouth open so I can put my tongue in it.

Ivy feels like a cozy warm comforter when you kiss her and Marjorie felt like a blazing fire with tendrils that pulled you into the source of the heat. Leslie feels like an ironing board.

We're against her front door the entire time and at one point she makes a "mmmmmmnnff" noise. This is very promising to me but it's possible she does this only because my wet shoes are standing on her bare feet.

"You should relax a little," I say to her.

"I am relaxed," she says.

Maybe this is Colin's problem. Maybe it isn't some tart.

{　}

I TAKE A taxi downtown . . . the wind has picked up and the snow is blowing through the empty night streets in warped whirls and waving wobbly sheets. In my drunken state it looks like we're flying and weaving through great snowcapped mountains.

I get off at Pernety and go back in. The crowd has thinned and Ivy is nowhere to be seen.

•　•　•

I take another taxi to Marjorie's place.

"I have to see you," I say to her from a pay phone.

"I'm about to go to bed."

"Please? It's imperative."

"How do you know I'm not with someone?"

"Are you?"

"No. But how do you know?"

"Please? For old times' sake?"

"Okay. But not for old times' sake."

I cross the street, plodding over tall white snowdrifts—mine are the first footprints in them—and wonder what she'll be wearing when she answers the door. She'd said she was about to go to bed so maybe it will be something a little kinky, but on her, even dowdy bathrobes and furry pink slippers take on new meaning.

She answers the door in a bathrobe, white with pinstripes. There's a hint of a familiar black camisole underneath (a tiny rosette is showing) and her mop of red hair is loose.

I fall to my knees and jam my face into her crotch.

I feel her hands in my head. She's pulling my hair.

"Get up! Would you please get up?"

She slams the door behind me and I stand up.

"What was that about?!"

"I don't know."

"Sit down!"

I sit down on her couch and so does she, but as far away from me as possible.

"Ivy Kooper saw you leave with Leslie."

"I know. But how do you know?"

"She told me. She wasn't looking too happy so I asked her what was wrong. And she told me."

"You didn't tell her about us, did you?"

"No. You did."

"No, I never told her about us."

"Well, she said you did when I told her."

"When you told her *what?* . . . when you told her about *us?*"

She nods and I groan, "Aw, goddammit!"

"Anyway, you can lie to her and just say you took Leslie home and that nothing happened."

"I did take Leslie home and nothing happened."

She pours me a glass of water and I try to get a better glimpse of the camisole but she keeps her hand over the top of her robe.

"So Marjorie . . . Who are you seeing? Anybody?"

"I have . . . suitors."

"Who? Buzz Eveready? You two were pretty tight."

"All the time. Woman's best friend."

"Who else? Anyone human?"

She curls up tightly until her heels touch her rear end.

"Okay, this is a secret, Zeke, and you can't tell *anyone*. You got that? Don't tell Willie or Leslie or Ivy. Especially don't tell Ivy." (This might mean: tell Ivy.)

"Okay? Hit me."

"I'm Jimmy Kooper's mistress. So there."

I'm sorry to resort to clichés but this really does feel like a sock in the jaw.

"You gotta be fuckin' kidding me."

"I'm not."

"But he's fifty! And he's an asshole!"

"He's nice to *me*."

"I bet he is." I don't say anything for a while. "You know, I did say, 'Anyone human?' "

She throws a couch pillow at me.

In a flash many different things come to me: the candlelight flickering in Ivy's eyes on our first date, how everyone had liked her when she spoke up in the meeting, Ivy in the darkness of my apartment with her head on a pillow, how nice she was but how uninteresting it could sometimes be; I think about Marjorie, her thighs and breasts swaying and shaking and her hair dripping with silver rain in my house on a wet weekend morning, how we sometimes hated each other but how I'd never been happier; and Leslie and Colin, who never saw each other but who were engaged and bickered long-distance; and now the corporate *consigliere* Jimmy Kooper, cheating on his powdered doughnut of a wife but doing it with the vixen-goddess, rock-'em-sock-'em blow-up doll Marjorie . . . Did *anyone* have it right other than supposed neuters like Mark Larkin and people who lived their lives stone cold alone?

"So, Marjorie, please answer me this question: with fifty-year-old, pit bull James Kooper, Esquire . . . do you pound on his shoulders and claw his back and yell until his eardrums pop?"

"I'm not going to answer that question."

"That means yes."

"Think what you will."

"Believe me, I'm going to. So, uh . . . why him?"

"Why not him?"

"What about him is so good? Can you answer me that?"

"Answer me this: What about you is so good?"

"I can't answer that question."

She walks me to the door.

"So you're sleeping with the father of the girl I'm sleeping with," I say. "Do you realize that?"

"This makes you my step-fucking-son. Or something like that."

She opens the door. But I don't give up that easily.

"Is that a camisole under the robe?"

She nods.

"Did I buy you that?"

"Yep."

"Could I see it?"

She closes the door on me.

The long hallway I stare at narrows and slants down into something like a sliding pond or garbage chute.

I'll never have Marjorie again. Unless I marry a very good friend of hers and Marjorie feels like having a little hot mischief an hour or two before the wedding. Other than that contrived scenario, there's simply no hope.

But she told me something interesting that night.

During all the shuffling, the Gaston-Martyn-Sophie-Sheila-Mark Larkin *Boy-It* musical chairs, it had occurred to Martyn Stokes to move me to *Boy* magazine. As, are you ready for this, a senior editor. *I could have been a senior editor!* My own office, a real view, a very hefty raise, and, most important of all, RESPECT!

But the idea was shot down.

Martyn had gone to Byron and Betsy (Regine was in Milan, doing her queen bee routine at the fashion shows) and asked them about moving me. They said it was okay. Then Byron and Betsy mentioned it to Jacqueline. She said it was okay.

Jackie mentioned it to Mark Larkin, my boss of only a few days. He nixed it.

He needed me, he said; he needed me under his new job title. It would help ease his transition, which he pretentiously referred to as an "interregnum."

He had stopped my promotion, my own great leap upward, my head-first dive in the pike position into the Pool of Respectability, so he could have me working beneath him.

Willie was right. The guy had to go.

When I get home everything is spinning and liquidy, as if seen inside a blender. Snow is in my hair and on my shoulders and my socks are wet. Outside my building I feel for my keys but cannot find them . . . I'm too drunk for a few moments to remember why not.

I press a few buzzers of some apartments and, sure enough, someone buzzes me in. The elevator wobbles up to my floor and I slump into my apartment. (The key is under the doormat.)

There's a note on the kitchen counter. Oliver has small anal retentive handwriting; it looks just like computer print, eight-point Palatino.

"Had a ball. No mess. Cheers."

I crumple the note and sit down on the couch and look at the wet footprints on the rug leading to me.

Had I lost Ivy but gained Leslie? Did I want that? In what direction am I moving?

I get undressed and listen to the old radiator in my bedroom spit, hiss, and rattle. It's loud and gurgling out heat but the place is ice cold . . . how can that be? What a building . . . this shithole could collapse any second into a million pieces and all the cat piss, beer, smoke, and grease smells would just float away into Ugly Building oblivion.

I'm drifting off to sleep in my bed when my toes rub up against something hard, something small and sticky.

I dig under the sheets and fish it out.

It's a black heel. There's a little wad of bubble gum stuck to it.

10

April is the cruelest month, arguably *the* great poet of this century conjectured, and then in ten or so different languages he rambles on to tell us exactly why. Something about lilacs and rats' alley. Something about false teeth and a gramophone.

But is April really so cruel? Aren't lilacs truly splendid little darlings, and wasn't that warm blanket of snow actually frightfully cold?

Every issue of *It* has a half-page Letter from the Editor by Regine Turnbull, accompanied by a blurry black-and-white photo of her (Regine is standing on top of five phone books in the shot, I'm sure of it). Regine doesn't write this letter. Oliver writes it, Liz writes it, Willie and I write it. You begin with a short paragraph or two about the month itself ("March might not have been so kind to Julius Caesar, but . . .") and then you segue—that's the difficult part—into the contents of that particular issue. Connecting Thanksgiving with a Nick Toomey piece about Claus von Bulow, or March coming in like a lion to a Tony Lancett piece about stolen Holocaust art, usually takes one strained out-of-nowhere sentence, but it can be done.

But if rainy April really is so cruel then how can it bring such a delightful downpour: Gabriella Atwater at home and on the set with Ethan Hawke, Emma Pilgrim in the White House and on Air Force One, Mark Larkin on the scandalous Miranda Beckwith, the Dallas demimondaine?

Somehow I always get stuck writing the April letter. For three years in a row I've managed to spin it around an April-is-the-cruelest-month routine. It's like a magician who only knows one dumb trick, pulling T. S. Eliot out of his hat. Nobody has ever mentioned this, nobody has ever complained . . . I have no idea if anyone has ever noticed. Maybe Regine doesn't even read it.

{ }

I have to call Ivy the day after the party, a Saturday, to get it over with. Beforehand I rehearse the conversation dozens of times, scripting it out; if she says, "So where did you two go?" I'll press the "Leslie was really bothered by something and I had to . . ." button. If she then says, "I don't know if I believe you," I'll push: "It's the truth. I don't lie." Then if she says "Yes you do," I'd play: "I know. But never to you." Which usually shuts people up.

I'm ready but still cannot call. How do doctors tell parents their four-year-old kid is going to die? Wouldn't they rather pluck a hot dog vendor off the street, stick a stethoscope around his neck, and pay him fifty bucks to do it?

After hours of struggling and napping and flipping through pointless Saturday TV drivel, I make the call.

Ivy's machine picks up. I listen to the greeting and hang up.

Knowing she has one of those machines that tells you what time the person called, I wade through another half-hour of Saturday TV and call again and leave a message.

"Hey, it's Zack. Give me a call. Okay?"

Now I'm stuck . . . the snow is already gray and turning black and it's cold out. But now I'm a prisoner. I have to wait for her call.

So I wait. Then I leave another message, at around seven.

Ivy calls at 8:30.

I don't pick up.

"Hi, it's me," she says. "I've been out all day with my friend Daphne . . ." She stops talking . . . she just can't think of another sentence and so the machine, thinking the call over, cuts her off.

This dismal one-man-show takes another turn when, a half-hour later, I call her back. I get her machine and leave a message.

Then I do something unbelievable. I look up her parents' number and call them.

It's about nine at night and the radiator is clanking and driving me crazy.

Her mother answers.

"Carol Kooper, this is Zachary Post. How are you?"

Has she forgotten me? Or does she now know, courtesy of a teary mother-daughter chat, just how loathsome I am?

"Yes, Zachary," she says.

"Is Ivy there?" I cut right to it.

"She's not here. She's out with her friend Daphne." (Carol Kooper doesn't sound to me as though she knows I'm loathsome. But she might sound this pleasant talking to a group of huns standing outside her front door with maces and axes.)

"Okay," I say. "Would you tell her I called?"

"Well, I don't think she's coming back tonight. She said she's spending the night at Daphne's."

"Okay. I'll call tomorrow then. Thanks, Mrs. Kooper." That sounds like Eddie Haskell, one part sugar, nine parts Brylcreem.

So she's with her friend Daphne. That's good.

I put on some clothes and get some Chinese food. It's dark out, the streets are virtually deserted, the sooty snow covers cars and sidewalks and trash cans.

When I'm paying the man at the cash register for my dinner I hear someone say to him: "She was lying."

It is me talking.

"What?" the Chinese cashier asks.

"She was lying," I tell him and myself. "Carol Kooper lied over the phone. She was home. Ivy was home all day. Screening. Then when I called the mother—"

He looks at me and nods, taking me for crazy.

She calls me Sunday night.

"Where have you been?" I say.

"I've been with Daphne. I thought I told you that."

"Yeah. I don't know. Maybe I forgot."

"You called my mother? Wow."

"I was getting worried."

"About me?"

No. About *me!*

"Yeah. Is everything okay?"

About us. It's dawning on me now that what I did—leave with Leslie Usher-Soames—will never be mentioned.

"Everything's okay. Daphne bgprblm blmng hrx bfrnd . . ."

She tells me a five-minute tale of her college friend and I tune out.

"So I'll see you tomorrow at work?" I say.

"I guess."

∗{ }∗

"I'M GOING to move Nolan Tomlin," Mark Larkin tells me in his office, leaning back in his swivel chair with his shoes on the desk. He's handling a silver letter opener with an ornate handle . . . is he going to give himself a manicure with the thing?

"Where to?" I ask. I sit opposite him, leaning over as if suffering from stomach cramps.

"That's really up to Human Resources, isn't it? Maybe *Zest?*" *Zest* is our women's sports and fitness magazine. People sometimes call it "Sweats."

"He's never done a push-up in his entire life."

He shrugs, and I say, "Who are we going to bring in to replace him?"

"The bowels of this building are crawling with candidates. I have some ideas. Betsy and I have been talking." He rattles off a few names, editorial assistants at other magazines.

"Do I have any say in this?"

"Zachary, do you want Nolan to stay?"

"No." But what if Nolan leaves and I walk in one morning and King Kong is sitting there wearing a Calvin Klein suit, writing copy, and eating a corn muffin?

"Then why complain? Don't you trust me?" I don't answer.

He says, "What about Will Lister? I heard you once say he was the best writer here."

"I may have said that."

"Do you really think he is?"

"He could be."

"Better than Tony? Better than Emma?"

I notice the first-name basis, flinch, and say, "Possibly."

"Better than me? Better than me, Zachary?" He tilts his head slightly back, moves it around slowly, as though gargling.

"He's not given a chance to write much anymore."

"We all have chances to write." He takes his feet off the desk, sets the letter opener down, the handle pretty close to me. "This is a lot like a democracy, don't you think?" he says. "It's a lot like capitalism. We all have a chance. Even down to the dumbest messenger. If you try, if you really try hard enough, you'll make it. I firmly believe that. I do."

I lean back in my chair—submerge into the cloth is more like it— partly to distance myself from the temptation of the letter opener, which I'd love to jam into his Adam's apple.

"But it seems that," I say, "this system benefits some people and fucks over others. No matter how hard they work."

"Yes. And it's the best system there is."

Days and days pass . . . the tension turns the air foul. It's like waiting for the hangman to show up in your cell at seven in the morning but he doesn't pop in until eleven at night. I sit across from Nolan, never telling him he's being moved. We construct bits and pieces of polite conversation—the weather, magazines, the news—and as always I find him annoying, but now there is a touch of pathos about it. That grease spot over his head is now officially the Sword of Damocles and any second now, the spot will chop his head off his shoulders.

(But when will that "any second" be?)

"You haven't shown me anything for a while," I say to him one day.

"What do you mean?"

"Your fictions. A short story or a chapter of a book."

Some muffin crumbs fall to the desk and floor.

"I didn't think you were interested."

I shrug and say, "It's always good to know what the person sitting three feet away is up to."

"Well, what are you up to?"

"Nothing."

"I've got something with a publisher right now. A novel."

Huh?! Was he about to be published?! Suddenly I don't feel quite so sorry for him . . .

"You have an agent?"

"No. I just sent it in. To a few places."

"Totally unsolicited?"

"Yes. It's been out for about four months now."

Whew! It's at the bottom of a pile, under a tower of other novels and memoirs and poetry, gathering dust and turning yellow.

"Well, I wish you luck."

He thanks me.

At the coffee bar with Willie and Liz I break the news.

"Nolan's out."

"How do you know?" Liz asks.

"A little bird told me. It was, you might say, a lark."

"You're certainly hobnobbing with the right flock," Willie says, "if your little birdy is a lark."

"Come on. Shut up."

"Who's in, if he's out?"

"Was I mentioned?" Liz asks. "Probably not."

"No. But Teddy Roosevelt said the bowels of the building are crawling with people."

"Jesus," Liz says, blowing a bubble and popping it, "I never pictured myself as a tapeworm before."

"Would you make the move," I ask Willie, "if they told you to?"

"I guess I'd have no choice."

Silently we finish our coffees and I think of Willie sitting across from me, from nine to six every day, for months and months . . . if he could last that long. He's my best friend. But is this something I really want?

"You haven't invited me over to dinner for a while, Nolan."

"You wouldn't come."

"How's Janet?"

"She had the flu last week. As sick as a mangy old dog sopping wet with rain, like a wet rag lying in a gutter."

I raise two eyebrows and say, "And she got over it?"

"Yes. She got over it."

"We should all go out to dinner."

"All? Who is all?"

"You know . . . you, Janet . . . me."

"Maybe."

This thing is fraying my nerves . . . If Mark Larkin is going to get rid of Nolan, *then do it already!* Especially before I'm stuck having dinner with him and his insufferably boring wife.

"Have you made up your mind?" I ask Mark Larkin one day in his office.

"About?"

"About Nolan?"

"Oh, Nolan's gone. Forget about Nolan."

"I can't! He sits closer to me than I do! What are you waiting for?"

"You think this is easy, Zachary?"

Yes. It *is* easy for him, I'm sure of it, it's easy and he's relishing it.

He mentions some editorial assistant—I swear the name is John Barsad (but isn't that a character in *A Tale of Two Cities?*)—that Human Resources is touting for the job.

"And Willie?" I ask.

"Nothing is for certain, old boy. I have some work to do now. So do you. All right?"

The following day I'm at a fax machine, on my knees replacing the paper. Suddenly a pair of dusty Wallabies appears right in front of me. Nolan Tomlin.

I stand up.

"You son of a fuckin' bitch," he says.

"What are you talking about?"

"I just got fired." He points at me.

"You were fired?"

"You son of a fuckin' bitch." He pokes his pointing finger into my chest.

"Why are you blaming me? I had—"

He stomps one of his Wallabies on my foot and it hurts.

"You knew I was gettin' fired. Didn't you?"

"No. I swear!" I'm so frightened that it occurs to me to tell the truth. "Mark Larkin told me he was moving you out. Like, to another magazine or something. He never said you were being fired."

"He offered me a fact checking job at Zeke Magazine, *Zest*."

"You mean *Zest* magazine, Zeke," I say. "And you said no? Why would *Zest* be so—"

He grabs me by the collar. "Of course I said no, you fuckin' son of a fuckin' bitch."

"But I didn't get you fired."

I grab his hands with mine, hoping maybe the cold sweat would scare him into releasing me.

"Mark Larkin said you dint want to work with me anymore, that I never did shit and was dead weight. He said it had nuthin' to do with him." In his fury his Southern accent is coming out . . . he's from Chapel Hill, North Carolina, but now he sounds like one of the inbred swamp mongrels in *Deliverance*.

"He's lying," I tell him. "He's lying. Can't you see that?"

He takes his hands off my collar, folds his arms over his chest, and I hope that Betsy Butler, the closest thing on the floor to a cop, will walk by.

"I think you're lyin'," Nolan says. "I think you're a lyin' son of a fuckin' bitch bastard."

Some things you can't argue with, but in this case he's a little bit wrong.

He storms away, heading back to his desk, I assume, to clear it out or maybe to confront Mark Larkin and weed out the truth.

I pick up a phone and call Oliver Osborne at his desk.

"Ollie, do me a favor," I whisper. "Nolan just got the ax."

"Yes, I know. It's all over the place."

"Bring me your coat. Bring it to the fax machine near the Black Hole."

"Is it cold there?"

"No, it's cold outside and I want to get out of here."

"Now?"

"Ollie . . . Just bring it."

"Why? Do you not like your own coat?"

"Hurry!"

I go to the large window and look out. Way below I see Crookshank's, the coffee shop, the tops of taxis and buses, people moving around in long wriggly threads. Someone is walking toward me. A shadow . . .

"Thank God, Ollie," I say, turning around to see a fist coming right at me.

Crumpling to the floor I begin to lose consciousness but somehow keep it, and the ceiling and the fax machine and the light coming through the window whirl over me and float away.

"Here's my coat, Zeke. I really don't see what's wrong with your mac," I hear a British voice distantly trill. "Oh, God."

"You fuckin' son of a fuckin' bitch bastard fuck."

I had a broken nose and got a few days off and fifty painkillers out of it. I had to wear a kind of a Hannibal Lecter mask for three days and my mother visited me at home and brought a salami sandwich and a six-pack of Dr. Brown's black cherry soda.

Lying at home zonked out on Vicodin, waking up in a daze and falling back asleep, I saw that there was a lesson to be learned from all this. Just as Willie had seen the lesson when Nancy Willis stabbed Roddy Grissom and Valerie Morgan landed Grissom's job.

Mark Larkin had lied to Nolan Tomlin.

Nolan Tomlin believed him.

Nolan Tomlin punched me out.

It was so simple and so economical, it was almost beautiful, like one simple three-letter formula that explained how the universe was created. You took a slightly unhinged person, a computer on the fritz, and you fed it bad information. Something was bound to happen: the person would snap, the computer would blow up.

It was gorgeous.

"Everything okay with you?" Willie asks me. He calls me every few hours from work, maybe because he cares, maybe because he's bored.

"I'm okay."

"Save some painkillers for me, dude."

"No refill though." He might use them on himself, all at once.

He tells me no one has been pegged yet to take over Nolan's job. He mentions the John or Chad Barsad guy and when I, still adrift on the opium fog, question the validity of that name, he seems skeptical too.

"You know," I say, "Mark Larkin said you couldn't handle Nolan's duties."

"He said that?"

"Yeah. I recommended you for the job but he didn't think you were up to it"

"That shitheel. And hey, I should have gotten Mark Larkin's job!"

Now that he thought Mark Larkin didn't think he was up to it, he really wanted the job.

He says, "I ought to stab that fucker."

I think about recommending using the letter opener but say goodbye instead.

Gorgeous.

I think I stopped taking the painkillers that day. I had about forty left and put them in my medicine chest. They might come in handy one day.

Ivy comes over once and she looks angelic—she looks so kind and caring behind the drug-laced curtain of gauze, yet I can barely make her out and I'm worried I might be imagining her. She sits facing me on the edge of the bed, one leg up and the other on the floor, and jokes that my broken nose might be an improvement. I pretend to be worse off than I really am . . . why not milk this thing for as many days off and as much sympathy as I can?

She tells me Betsy Butler had told her there was an editorial assistant job opening up, that there's a chance she'll get it. She's finished her piece on Neuro Euro-Rubbish and it's going in either the April or May issue. I reach out for her hand and she takes it. But a minute later I realize she's not holding it anymore.

I have to admit something. That day when I went through hell trying to reach Ivy on the phone—I called up Leslie Usher-Soames.

"Do you want to meet for a jrink?" Leslie asked me.

"Tomorrow night?"

"What about in twenty minutes?" She giggled and blood rushed to my groin. Maybe she isn't such a cold haddock after all.

"I'll be right over."

When I walked in I was stunned to see six other people there, two men and four women.

"These are friends of mine," Leslie said, opening the door. (It seemed like a surprise party for me except I didn't know them and it wasn't my birthday.) "And this is Zachary Post."

"Hello, everyone," I said, forming a shit-eating grin.

IF IVY WON'T bring it up, then I won't bring it up. We'll just forget about it or do a terrific job of pretending we did.

But I'm petrified that, in the middle of a work day, she'll appear at my desk, beckon me over to Stairway A, and have it out with me. "Is it her or is it me?" she'll ask.

And then there are other times—men are men after all and so they will be pigs—when I think: "Hmm, hey, wait . . . maybe I can have *both* in my life! Maybe I can actually get away with this. Leslie has the collie so I can do *her* and I also can have Ivy, whom the one lonely better angel of my nature seems to need desperately. Maybe I can pull this captain's paradise off."

But this is all broken-nosed, painkiller cloudiness, opium dreaming.

When I recuperate and return to work, a maintenance man is dabbing ecru paint on the grease spot on Nolan's cubicle wall.

"Good to have you back, Zachary," Mark Larkin says. "Your proboscis doesn't seem worse for the wear."

He briefs me on what's in the works for "In Closing" and on some other stuff. I've got a playwright to do a fax interview with, a new hip downtown nightspot to go to, two books to review and two pieces to assign and tons of copy to edit.

He says: "Oh! I nearly forgot. You're getting a new partner tomorrow."

"Yes, I thought so. So who is it?"

He makes a few tsk-tsk noises and clucks his tongue and says, "All in good time, Post."

It was Willie.

That same afternoon Willie comes over to me and tells me he's being transferred, that Betsy has just told him (and she added: "Don't tell anyone till tomorrow").

We make a few lame jokes (I call him "roomie," he throws an imaginary football, we talk of throwing a kegger) but after this jollity ceases there is a pervading sense of dread. I know and he knows this is a short-term thing. Like a rubber band stretching out farther and farther, neither of us can imagine it lasting.

When he moves his stuff into his new drawers the next day, I sit there and sneak peeks at him. He does something very funny: he opens and closes the desk drawers very loudly, opening them so they squeak, then slams them shut, as if this is a warning of how loud and annoying he'll be. He starts talking to himself too: "Hmm, now I could put my pencils *here* but if I do that, where do I put the three-hole punch? I need to create some kind of tension between the pencils, which are lively and vertical, and the three-hole punch, which is black and somber and more horizontal."

When he's putting stuff into the lower drawer, he's on his knees and the shirt he's wearing comes out of his pants and I get a glimpse of his stomach . . . it's red and blubbery. I realize that, if Willie were to show up on an interview with Versailles Human Resources right now, there would be no way he'd get the job.

Within a week Nolan has become like someone in my kindergarten class: I remember the name and a little bit of the face, but not much else. But Willie sitting there is very real and almost alarming, like finding yourself bumper to bumper on a small street behind a truck that says CAUTION: FLAMMABLE GAS KEEP BACK 20 FEET.

And Mark Larkin is in his office, not eight yards away.

"This is going to be hell," Willie says to me one day. (We can talk to each other face-to-face now, it doesn't have to be e-mail or on the phone. But we whisper.) "He's right in there and we're here."

"Quite a hand Destiny has dealt us," I muse.

He starts singing "The Gambler" by Kenny Rogers: "You got to know when to hold 'em, know when to fold 'em, know when to walk away, know when to run . . ."

Mark Larkin then passes between us, on his way to a meeting with the Important People and adjusting his bow tie.

"I didn't tell you this," I say to Willie.

"Didn't tell me what?"

I make it up quickly.

"The Rough Rider said you wouldn't last four weeks here. Too much pressure. He said you'd crack."

"He really said that?"

I nod . . . feel like a real rodent.

"You once told me to shove his bow tie up his ass," Willie says. "After I wasted the bastard . . ."

"Did I say that?" I'm momentarily shocked by my own coarseness.

"Yeah. You did. And I think it was a good idea."

Willie and I are sitting in Mark Larkin's office. The sun bursts in through the windows behind him, burning him into a white splotch and illuminating that horrible painting on the wall, turning it into churning white and green lava.

We go over a few things, mostly stuff from contributing writers we're editing . . . Mark Larkin is glad that I liked the book I reviewed (I didn't but I said I did) but he recommends some changes. "It can be a positive review, Zachary, but still be sharp. Positive doesn't mean dull."

I nod, tell him I'll retouch it.

He tells Willie *It* might publish his Rachel Carpenter article (Willie had spent an evening in Atlantic City with the Sundance Festival award-winning director). "This could be one page."

"Her movie is being released nationally," Willie says. "And it's going to be very big. How about two pages?"

"There's just something about it," Mark Larkin says. He puts a pencil in his mouth, curls up so that his feet press against the top desk drawer. "It's irksome . . . I just cannot put my finger on it." He taps the desk with the pencil, wet with his saliva.

"Is it that I'm in the article?" Willie asks.

"You? I don't know. I don't honestly know."

"I mean, it's not a straight Q and A. We hung out, we had drinks, we drove to Trump's Castle, lost every penny we had, and she told me everything about herself."

"That could be it." He snaps out of his semi-fetal position and puts his feet on the floor. "I usually don't go in for that gonzo sort of thing."

"This is hardly gonzo."

Mark Larkin looks up from the article and Willie smiles at him and I notice the letter opener, the handle twinkling in the sunlight, the blade pointing toward Willie.

"Well, it sort of is gonzo. Do you think it's gonzo, Zachary?" Mark Larkin says.

I'm ready. "I don't think it's gonzo-proper."

"Oh, you don't?"

"No. I don't."

Willie winks at me. It feels good, being somebody to go to war with.

"Listen," Mark Larkin says, "could one of you get me a cup of coffee? Light, no sugar."

We don't say anything for a few seconds, then Willie adjusts himself in his chair and says, "You want us to go downstairs and get a cup of coffee and bring it up to you?"

"Well, you don't *both* have to go get it! That would be a waste of man-hours, wouldn't it? We're quite ergo-dynamically sound here at Versailles."

"I'm not getting you coffee," Willie says.

"Too demeaning, eh? What about you, Zachary?"

"I don't think so. I never got coffee for Sheila."

"Perhaps you should forget about Sheila. If Regine heard you weren't getting me coffee, I think she would take my side on this, don't you?"

He's right . . . that's what's so terrible. Jacqueline Wooten gets coffee for Betsy, and Thomas Land is probably getting coffee for Martyn Stokes; it doesn't matter how high up you are as long as there's some thirsty asshole one inch higher.

"Meeting adjourned then!" Mark Larkin says, waving his hands as though they're wings and he's trying to fly out of his seat.

We walk toward the door and hear behind us: "I would like that coffee though. And you *do* want this gonzo thing in, don't you?"

BANG!

Willie slams his big fist down on the desk and a Krispy Kreme cup filled with pens and pencils bounces and falls on its side.

"I'm gonna wring that fuckhead's neck, man!"

"Maybe if we get him coffee?" I say.

"Where's your spine?"

"Where's your common sense?"

An editorial assistant walks by in the hallway, his hands full of paperwork. He's gawky, skinny, pale, and has straight strawberry blond hair. This has got to be Chad or Tad Barsad.

"*You there, son!*" Willie says to him in a grave, sonorous voice, sounding like Zeus.

"Me?" he says.

"Get me a cup of coffee, would you?"

"From downstairs?" He isn't any more thrilled than we were.

"Yes, son. From downstairs. Here. Keep the change." He hands the kid (he's about twenty-three years old) a fiver.

"You want two coffees or one?" the kid asks.

"One. Light, no sugar."

"Hey, wait," I tell the kid. "Get me one too. Black, no sugar."

"And I'll have one, regular," Willie says. "Lots of sugar. Thanks. And don't you ever, *ever* get anybody coffee again."

⟩ ⟨

THE AFTERNOON at Leslie's house was one miserable occasion; an idiot, I stuffed two rubbers into my wallet before hurrying over there and what I got I deserved for being so cocksure.

Colin's sister Vicki is there, visiting from London, and she looks just like her older brother, the cheeks, pallor, and hollowed-out eyes. When she speaks I can hardly hear her and she moves around stiffly, as though her neck were in a brace. The others present are all Versailles people.

And to my surprise, to my shock, Meg Bunch is there, sitting on the couch, the center of attention as always. Meg Bunch is the Executive Editor: Fashion of *She* and is (inarguably) one of the ten most powerful people in the fashion business.

"I didn't know you knew Meg Bunch," I whisper to Leslie as she and I cut up some limes in her kitchen.

"I don't really. My dad does. Whenever Meg is in London she has dinner with my family."

This really is a most eligible bachelorette . . . Winston Churchill had slept in her bedroom and her parents had dinner with the absurdly eccentric (she wears bubblegum pink all the time, as well as oversized red glasses), ridiculously influential Meg Bunch.

There are several bottles of gin and vodka out and I assume that eventually the venue will be moved to a restaurant but we never budge. Sixty-ish Meg Bunch sounds like a little tweety bird when she speaks— which is strange coming out of a woman over six feet tall—and between her and the sub-audible Vicki Tunbridge-Yates, conversation isn't too easy to follow.

"Oh! You know Thomas Land!" Meg chirps after I mention His Royal Brown Nose's name in passing.

"Yes. We used to work together."

"And now look at him! Editor-in-chief of *Boy!* My, my!"

How am I supposed to react to this? I look around . . . at her fawning entourage, at the floor, at the bottles of liquor, at Vicki's pigeon-toed feet.

"Yes. I'm being left in the dust," I say.

"Oh no! You mustn't think like that," Meg says. "You've got to give it the old rah-rah college try." She punches the air (it wouldn't have moved a floating tuft of gossamer, had it landed).

She persists in attempting to inspire confidence in me, all the time affectedly sucking on some kind of small thin cigar, which she handles like a Nazi interrogator in an old movie.

Meg Bunch says to me: "Now Tommy Land married Trisha Lambert. That certainly didn't hurt. What you need to do is get out more often, go to events and circulate . . . You and Leslie should come to one of my salons."

I glance at Leslie. She raises her eyebrows and smiles.

"That might be nice," I say. But Meg Bunch strikes me as possibly the most insincere person alive; she might invite her limousine driver to her salons too, but if he showed up she'd open up the door an inch and tell him nobody was home.

"Oh, you must come!" she tweets as she stubs out her cigarello into an ashtray. Her trademark Louise Brooks bob doesn't budge.

One of the other Versailles people—she's Alexa Van Deusen's cousin, it turns out—brings up Mark Larkin.

"Now that boy is a real comer!" Meg says, her face lighting up.

"What about the bow tie though?" I ask.

She goes on in unintelligible fashionese for a minute, something about clean silhouettes and stark palettes, and I tell her, "Well, it's not the look for me."

Meg gives me the once-over; thinking I'd be naked with Leslie in no time, I'd come over in jeans and a bulky but throughly convincing Berkeley sweatshirt.

"Anyway, Marky comes to my little soirees and maybe you two can iron out—pun intended, I assure you–your sartorial squabbles publicly."

Mark Larkin goes to Meg Bunch's salons? (Were her soirees and salons the same events?) I didn't even know there were such gatherings! Marky Marky Marky . . . who else called him that besides this bubblegum pink-crested chattering booby? At the *It* meetings I'm not invited to, is he Marky?

"Well, Meg, you invite Leslie and me, and we'll come over."

"Oh, please *do!*"

An hour after I show up, the others leave, except for Vicki, who either is staying over at Leslie's or is too pigeon-toed to elevate herself off the couch. I help Leslie clean up the bottles, glasses, and bowls of chips and dip.

"So if we get invited, you'll be my date?" she asks me.

"Of course I will."

"We'll be a *succés d'estime*, I'm sure." (*Succés d'estime:* more magazine-speak. She's using the phrase incorrectly but if I tell her, she might break a glass over my crown.) She smiles brightly and looks very pretty . . . she smells like gin again.

Vicki is on the couch—is she paralyzed?—facing away from us, watching a rerun of something. I reach for Leslie's hand to hold it, rub my fingers over her palm, and fiddle with the ring that Vicki's brother had probably spent over $10,000 on. I want to grind Leslie against the refrigerator and kiss her . . .

But she pulls her hand away—I don't even make it to the fingers over the palm part.

"Do you feel bad?" I ask her, assuming that because Vicki is completely inaudible, she's probably also deaf.

"Yes. I feel bad."

"Because of Colin?"

"No. I feel bad because of Ivy Kooper."

"I see."

"She's really so very sweet."

{   }

AFTER TWO retouches I hand in my positive book review to Mark Larkin. The book is *Black and White and Red All Over*; it's the autobiography of a grouchy cigar-chomping blacklisted 1930s-50s screenwriter who had slept with about fifty gorgeous actresses ("I got the rewrite over to Veronica Lake's bungalow on Wednesday morning and by Thursday I was banging her every night") and now, at age eighty, had decided it was worth telling (or lying about, since they were too dead to sue).

The usual course of action is: I write something myself or edit something, my editor suggests changes, I make them, then we route the copy from assistant editor to assistant editor, so that Liz Channing, say, or Willie can suggest changes, spot flaws, tighten things up. It's a foolproof system, designed to mold everything into the *It* format. Then the copy flows upward, to the likes of Betsy and Jacqueline and others, and by the time it's been fact-checked and proofread, it's airtight, dust-proof, and very, very standard.

My phone rings one day—it's an interoffice call, I can tell from the ring—and I pick it up.

"What the bloody hell is going on?" a male voice spits out.

My first thought: this is Colin and he's going to challenge me to a duel in Belgium, where it's legal. But it isn't Colin.

"Ollie? What's wrong?"

"I asked you what the bloody fuckin' hell is going on here?"

"I don't know what you're talking about. Calm down."

Was it him using my bed to do Liz? But wait. . . . I should be mad at *him* for that.

We agree to meet in Stairway A and walking over there I rub my nose and make sure it's intact . . . one broken one is enough.

He's angrily holding two pages of copy in his hands, curled up into a tight cylinder, something you'd threaten a dog with.

"You reviewed *Black and White and Red All Over!*" he says.

"Yeah . . . so?"

Why is it so annoying to him? Maybe the cigar-chomping author is an American relation . . . but I'd given it a good review!

"Here, Zeke, explain this!" He stuffs the paper in my hand and it takes a few seconds before I can focus in on it. It's slugged REVIEW: B W & R ALL OVER.

I read it and think: What's the big deal? . . . it's mine . . .

But it *isn't* my review! It takes a few sentences to discern this, so alike is our style. It's his.

"Can you explain this?" he says. He's still angry but he can tell from my aghast groan and the two shivering pieces of paper that I'm innocent.

"Who told you to review this?" I ask him.

"Theodore Bloody Roosevelt, that's who!"

"And he never told you I was doing the same thing?"

He shakes his head and asks me the same question. I tell him of course not.

"That cunt!" He crumples up the two pages and tosses them into a big green recycling bin.

"You assigned Oliver Osborne to review Jess Auerbach's book?"

"Yes."

Mark Larkin is reading *The Economist* . . . a pile of other magazines stands on his desk, waiting for his perusal.

"But I was assigned that too."

"This was your idea, Zachary, so you can't blame me."

"How is this my idea?"

He looks up and tells me that Regine Turnbull was under the impression I'd once suggested to her, via Sheila Stackhouse, that more than one person should be assigned to certain smaller pieces, so as to encourage competition and incentive. And it comes back to me: when I saw the Ethan Cawley galleys on Mark Larkin's desk, I thought that he'd been assigned it too, for *It*.

"You simply cannot do this to people," I say.

"Well, Regine thinks it's the best idea you've ever had."

When I told Willie this story he wasn't surprised. He reached into his in-box and showed me an article by Gabriella Atwater, a frequent *It* contributor based in California. The article was a two-pager on Rachel Carpenter.

"Join the club," he said.

{   }

"ZACK?"

"It's me."

"You haven't called for a few days."

"You haven't called *me*."

"What's up?"

I tell Ivy what's up, which isn't much except for my usual grumbling about work. I ask what's up with her and, though I'm all ready to tune out and not listen to something about her girlfriends' boyfriends' best friends, she begins to gripe about work, too: it's a short blast, maybe thirty seconds worth, nothing like my typical forty-minute jeremiad, but it is something new. Apparently her article on Neuro Euro-Rubbish has suffered so many changes in the routing process as to render it "totally unreadable, totally not mine" (her words). "They put the word *manqué* in and the word *faux-* and *wunderkind*," she complains. "I would never use those words! Would you? I'm not even sure I know what *manqué* is! And who the hell is Peck?"

I try to calm her, telling her that she, by getting her first piece published, albeit in *It*-mangled form, is herself somewhat of a *wunderkind*. "So the story is going in, right?"

"Yes it is. And it's got my byline too." She doesn't sound too proud about this. She mentions that, since some articles can be read on *It*'s website, millions of people all over the world can just type the search words *manqué* and *faux* and then find her name in seconds.

I get to the point finally: "So do you maybe want to come over?"

"Now?"

"Yeah."

"It's kind of late."

"You've come over later than this." But it's a done deal—she's staying put—and I find myself twirling the phone cord.

"I'm too upset, I think."

About Leslie? . . . Is this what she's upset about? I'm desperate for Ivy, just to be with her soothing presence. My nature has one good angel and ninty-nine bad ones but at that moment it's the loudest and most long-winded angel I've got going and might very well filibuster the others into submission.

"What are you upset about?" I ask. If she mentions the infamous Pernety Exit with Leslie I've got my answers prepared. But it's not to be.

"About work," she says.

{   }

TO: POSTZ
FROM: LISTERW
SUBJECT: our vanishing work force

guess what

Even though we can talk to each other directly now, we've resumed e-mailing. There are a few reasons for this: (1) Mark Larkin usually has his door open and might hear us (Willie has even said he can read our minds); (2) We're used to it, as far as communicating in the office is concerned; (3) it's more conspiratorial.

TO: POSTZ
FROM: LISTERW
SUBJECT: Re: our vanishing work force

I'm looking for work beyond these rusted gates of eden

I look up at him and he has a funny smug expression, perhaps what Babe Ruth looked like a split second after he hit the home run he'd supposedly called.

He continues:

sent my c.v. everywhere newsweek time conde hachette juggs leg show
my dumpy dimpled buttocks is outta here jake!! maybe

But if he's going, who would I have? Ollie and Liz? They're my friends but they're sneaking quickies with each other although nobody but me knows and they don't know I know. Ivy? My pipe dream of a captain's paradise had tumbled over into a hovel of burnt Lincoln Logs.

Before I can e-mail him good luck I realize he might not get a job at any of these places. Perhaps other companies aren't as obsessed with appearance as Versailles is, but still it counts for something. And, as they say: What have you done for me lately? Two years ago Willie's résumé was certainly respectable, his clips would have been more than impressive, not just his *It* articles but his freelance pieces for other Versailles magazines—he'd even had four small pieces in the "Out and About" section of *Gotham*, the only truly respectable thing Versailles puts out. But any decent Human Resources worker worth his or her salt would look at the dates and see he hasn't done much recently; they'd also see he was thirty-four years old and has been an associate editor for over four years. His plateau would jump off the page and nip someone in the nose.

And what kind of references would he get?

Mark Larkin wouldn't let him slip away . . . I think he enjoys having him around to torture. Betsy and Regine know he's valuable at *It* and also wouldn't want him to go. The ones who don't like him need him around for a whipping boy, the ones who do just need him around.

•   •   •

Usually there are a few things in each issue of *It* that make me want to hang myself with the nearest shoelace.

Mark Larkin has a feature in the April *It* (or is it March?), a nine-page piece on Miranda Beckwith, the twenty-eight-year-old soon-to-be widow of the ninety-three-year-old lanolin tycoon, Floyd R. Beckwith. It's the usual paint-by-the-numbers story: as Miranda Johnson she was a cheerleader in a small town in Texas, then a stripper in a bigger town in Texas, then—miraculously since she could barely type—Floyd Beck-with's personal assistant, then his home wrecker, and now his bride and sole heir, despite the four children and twelve grandkids from his previous marriage. There were the usual pictures: two nude shots of Dandy Mandy on a runway with grainy silhouettes of men's heads looking up at her, shots of Beckwith's kids (they're in their sixties) looking grumpy and hurt, shots of the new and improved Miranda, her hair up in a tight matronly bun, standing by Floyd's $30,000 wheelchair, the old man's face resembling a decaying apple core. In a photo on the opening spread, Miranda leans over and kisses Floyd as he sits up in bed, and you can make out their tongues coming out of their mouths and her nipples show through her modest white blouse . . . this is on purpose, this is the provocative *It* and Donna Reems touch.

Right after Regine's monthly letter comes the "contributors page." There's a small photo of a writer or photographer and then a brief summary of him or her and what they've got in that issue. Such as: "Zachary Post, who writes about actor Leroy White, is an associate editor at *It* and blah blah. . . . Post's interview with Pulitzer Prize–winning author Ethan Cawley ran in blah blah . . ."

On the April contributors' page, there is a head shot—Zelda Guttierez had taken it and it's richly textured and sepia-tone—of Mark Larkin. He doesn't have his glasses on and has assumed a scowl and is squinting his eyes ever so slightly. I think they must have put some makeup on too, there being no sign of his splotchy complexion.

"On page 50, Mark Larkin, the senior editor in charge of 'In Closing,' digs deep into the controversy swirling around Standard Lanolin CEO Floyd R. Beckwith, his bride and heiress, and his disgruntled, litigious family, and finds in it all the stuff of a classic American tale: avarice, love, sex, power. With his Teddy Roosevelt good looks and New England charm, Mark Larkin blah . . ."

Senior editor, it says. (He'd written the thing too.)

Is this permanent then, his "filling in" for Sheila? And how did she feel, I wonder, reading that?

I kept picking up that page, reading it, putting it down, picking it up again. I couldn't look at it, I couldn't not look at it.

It took me until three in the morning before I could fall asleep.

"Nothing yet," Willie says. "No bites."

"What about another magazine at Versailles?"

"I want to make a clean break, I think."

"Not even *Men?* I could see you there."

"How many articles about Ernest Hemingway, herringbone jackets, and the serene joys of angling could I handle?"

We're in the East Village Ukrainian bar that I'd been to with Ivy on our first date. (It was cold out that night but it seems a warm memory now.)

"You didn't tell TR you were leaving, did you?"

"Hell no. Why?"

"He just said—out the blue, I guess—that he thinks you've lost all interest in *It.* He said that you're going to wind up working with the copying-room dwarf guy."

He smolders for a few seconds, grips his glass very tight.

"What about you?" he asks me. He bends down to tie a shoe and I notice how thin his hair is. I've met his parents and they both have enviably full heads of hair, his sisters too. It's sheer worry eating away at him and clogging his shower drain.

"I don't know. I feel I'm just lucky to be there."

He finishes his shot of Wild Turkey in one loud gulp. "Lucky?! What about Liverpool and Berkeley and Plautus and R. J. Post, man!" (He knows all that is a crock.)

"Exactly. I'm in way over my head as it is."

He tells me that he's called a few places he'd sent his résumé to. But it was all "Don't call us, we'll call you" stuff.

"I don't know . . . I thought I was serious trade bait."

"Why didn't you tell me that you and Laurie broke up?"

He smiles out of one corner of his mouth. We haven't spoken about this yet.

"Oh, you know. I'm a fella, you're a fella, she's not a fella."

"You could have told me."

"Okay, I'll tell you: we broke up."

Should I ask him why? . . . but why push him into a corner where he'd either have to lie to me or admit he's going out of his mind?

"You know," he says, "you haven't told me all about you and Jimmy Kooper's bouncin' baby bubeluh."

"There's not much to say."

"It's over?"

"I think so."

"See! You *fella!* You didn't tell me either, fool."

"I did something stupid."

(I think that, were I ever to write my autobiography, each chapter would begin with the words "I did something stupid." *I Did Something Stupid* might even be the book's title.)

I tell him about the infamous Pernety Exit and all that's happened and not happened since.

"You really fucked up this time, didn't you?"

"Yes, I really did fuck up."

(That will be *I Did Something Stupid*'s final words.)

He slaps me on the back. It felt good for him to have me in his society, I suppose.

A few weeks later . . .

Laurie Lafferty sends me an e-mail, saying she has to see me right away. We meet in the lobby near the bank machine.

"I quit. I just quit," she says. "I told Kenny Lipman ten minutes ago." (Kenny is *It*'s head of research.)

"Which magazine are you—"

"No magazine! I quit wholesale. No plans." She pushes her glasses up her small freckled nose. She reminds me of Peppermint Patty from *Peanuts*. "I'm moving out of New York next week."

"To?"

"I have a few friends in Ann Arbor."

"Is it Willie?" Of course it is.

She nods, looks around, and asks if we can go someplace. We don't have coats or sweaters on but we go outside and walk around the block. It's coming on the end of winter and still brisk out, but the sun is shining, bringing copper and bronze tones out of the concrete and tall stone and glass buildings.

"He's insane," are the first words she says when we turn our first corner.

"Now, now, let's not overdo it. There's clinically insane, like with straitjackets and electric shock and lobotomies and then there's being a little bit off your rocker and—"

"He's way off his rocker. He'd be clinically insane but he refuses to go to a clinic or get help."

Trisha Lambert strides by (a new hairstyle in tow), acknowledging me with a dirty look, and fifteen yards behind her, twittering into a cell phone, is Meg Bunch, decked out in her usual pink, and her entourage, all interchangeable with each other.

"Listen, I love him," Laurie says, "and this isn't easy for me to say. Okay?"

Meg Bunch sees me and says hello, then zips on past.

"You know Meg Bunch?" Laurie asks me.

"I've met her," I say a little too casually.

"And she calls you Zeke?"

"Yeah."

"Anyway . . . I've got to clear out of here."

"Does Willie know about this?"

"I don't think he'd care if he knew."

When we make it around the block a limo pulls up and Martyn Stokes gets out.

"I'm living in the apartment now and he's at the Chelsea," she tells me. "When I move out, he'll move back in. But you know what? He thinks the phones are tapped, that the whole place is bugged."

"No he doesn't! He's just saying that. He told me that Mark Larkin can read our minds."

"He does believe it! I swear. He even hired electronics experts to check it out . . . he spent eight hundred dollars on it! When they told him everything was fine, he told me they were on the take."

"Jesus . . ." The next step would be the microchip or tiny satellite dish in his brain.

But this was sad. It was pathetic. He's losing it—that's plain to see—yet still he shows up at nine and stays until six every day. He sleeps an hour a night and speaks to the walls and furniture from midnight to 8 A.M. but he showers and brushes his teeth and puts on deodorant and new clothes every day. It's frightening: You might be a complete lunatic but as long as you can put together a costume and a decent routine, nobody will ever suspect. The man who sells me my paper every morning—who knows how many human skulls he has in his refrigerator?

We stand in front of the revolving doors and the sun gleams on the gold relief above the entranceway: depicted there are the twelve labors of Hercules . . . the sunlight spins it into life, and you almost smell Hercules cleaning out the Augean stable.

"And now," Laurie says, "he's got a gun."

Marjorie Millet and I are in the elevator one morning.

"So!" she says. We haven't been alone together since she told me about Jimmy Kooper and her.

"So . . ."

"Leslie tells me that you are quite some kisser, Buster."

"Please don't call me 'Buster'."

The elevator stops. Some dumpy loser from Accounts Loathable, holding a stack of manila envelopes, gets on, pushes the next floor up, then gets off at Accounts Deplorable.

"She told you that?"

"Yep. Said you were the best kisser she's ever kissed. Well, when she told me that, I said to her, 'He must be taking kissing classes at the Learning Annex since he was kissing me because he wasn't quite cutting the mustard then.' "

"You didn't say that!"

"No, I didn't. And as a matter of fact, she never told me you were a good kisser either or that you'd ever even kissed. But now I know. *Buster!*"

The elevator doors open on our floor, she waves at me and walks away.

⟩   ⟨

TO: KOOPERI
FROM: POSTZ
SUBJECT: Your fledgling career

This isn't really so bad. You should hold your head up and be proud. Really. Don't let it get to you.

We've just gotten in the copies of the new issue, and Ivy Kooper's Neuro Euro-Rubbish half-page is inside.

TO: POSTZ
FROM: KOOPERI
SUBJECT: Re: Your fledgling career

No no no no.
You're being nice for a change.
This is horrible. If I had time I'd go to the printing press with Wite-Out and cover up my name on every single issue.

I respond:

That's a lot of Wite-Out.
Listen. I was like this too. You get used to it. Just faux-get it!
Do you want to have dinner tonight? Maybe a movie?

It takes a few minutes before she writes back:

Too afraid to show face in public.

I e-mail her back saying if she changes her mind I'll be waiting for her call, which is the truth. (I did wait that night and the call never came.)

The next day:

TO: POSTZ
FROM: KOOPERI
SUBJECT: This just in! More bad news.

I just got promoted to editorial assistant.

It occurs to me to congratulate her, wish her well and welcome her aboard. But then I think better of it.

11

IT'S TIME.

I walk into Mark Larkin's office and for dramatic effect shut the door behind me. Sensing something unusual, he looks up from a few convoluted Boris Montague sentences scrawled drunkenly on Hôtel de Crillon stationery.

"Are you quitting?" he asks.

"Shut the fuck up."

He sits straight up, sets Boris's faxes aside.

"I still have that tape," I say.

"What tape?"

"You know what tape . . . grave robber."

"Oh, that tape."

"Marky, it's time to collect."

"You want *money?* I should have thought you were more imaginative than that, Post."

"I want my Leroy White piece to run. He's very big now. I want it to run on the cover."

"How powerful do you think I am here?"

"Pretty powerful. But I'd say I'm more powerful, this second. Can you imagine if I played the tape for Regine or Martyn Stokes?"

He pinches his nose with his thumb and index finger, maybe trying to work free some crust. "I'm meeting with Regine and Byron at noon-ish," he says. "I'll try. I really will."

"You better."

He mentions another story I'm working on—a story about Antony Beauchamp, an art dealer of highly questionable business ethics—but I insist that the White piece, already written and rewritten, be the one he pushes for.

"How about that Ivy Kooper?" he says as I get up to leave. "Working her way up the ranks. You must be awful proud."

"God forbid she should ever be successful here."

"Say, what's your take on this Todd Burstin fellow?"

This is the young gawky editorial assistant I thought was John Barsad, the guy out of *A Tale of Two Cities.*

"He seems like he'd fit in here," I say, "once his face clears up and his voice deepens."

"Let's say," he considers, "Will Lister moves on . . ."

"Moves on *where?*"

"Just moves on." (Is he going to fire him, make an offer like the *Zest* offer he'd made to Nolan, one Willie had to refuse or risk losing all dignity?) "Would it bother you to sit across from Ivy? I knows she's your lover. And these interoffice romances can get a little sticky. Or would you prefer young Burstin?"

"Where is Willie going?"

"Well, he certainly doesn't seem very happy here, does he?"

When Mark Larkin's fawning story on Muffy Tate comes out—it's the second feature, after the Tony Lancett cover story on Ralph Lauren (WHAT'S IT ALL ABOUT, RALPHIE? is the cover line)—he also has a story in that month's *Boy* about Lane Babcock, the young studly star of two recent independent movies. BELIEVE US: THIS IS THE NEXT JAMES DEAN, the big head shouts out across a two-page spread.

It's quite a coup for the puffy-faced *wunderkind.* Two features in two magazines in the same month. It is that which compels me to play the grave-robber card—and occasionally in my wrath I forget that I really don't have any tape.

And it's also his two features that compel me to . . .

To call up Alan Hurley, once an editor at *Appeal* but now an editor at

Gotham. This isn't one of those phone calls straight out of the blue where the person you call surmises—since you haven't spoken to him in a year—that you're calling for a favor. Periodically I call my B-list acquaintances just to Say Hello; that way when the Favor Call does come, it won't seem so obvious. Yet I still feel that even during the Say Hello Call they think I'm going to hit them up for twenty bucks.

Alan and I make chitchat for a few minutes—we always joke about the five dark offices at *Gotham* reserved for the eighty- and ninety-year-old writers who only show up once a year.

And now here it comes: "Listen, I just want you to know," I tell him, "that if you ever need someone to review books for you guys—you know, in the 'Books Considered' section—I can do it."

"Hmmm. I don't know. Novels? Or nonfiction?"

"Novels. I don't know enough history or politics to review nonfiction. I don't know John Adams from Henry Adams. But I know Henry James from Henry Miller." It's my notion that by downplaying my weak points, it tacitly highlights my few strong ones.

"I don't know, Zack. We have more than enough people."

"It seems you could always use a new voice in there."

"Well, I don't know."

"Will you give it some thought? You give me the book, I'll have a review tighter than a clam's asshole within three days."

"I guess I'll think about it. I don't know."

He says he has to go but I assume he's lying.

My desk has a black swivel chair just to the left side of it and it's rare when anyone sits in it. As I was speaking to Alan Hurley I kept an eye on the empty chair . . . with each "I don't know" of his, a dim fluttering shadow seemed to form itself, cell by cell and fiber by fiber, in the chair, until finally, when Alan said he had to go, Ethan Cawley was sitting only two feet away from me, pointing a spectral finger at me and laughing convulsively and soundlessly.

⟩   ⟨

I'M GOING crazy.

It seems that Leslie wants me to officially break up with Ivy so that she can then begin fooling around with me with a clean conscience, but

Ivy has already broken up with me (probably) and anyway, Leslie is engaged to someone. And I'm going crazy because I miss Ivy.

I call her up one night and invite her over and she says we should meet for dinner. Desperate to see her, I agree and then suggest—desperation tends to briefly drag out the romantic in some men—the site of our first date, the cozy Italian place downtown. But she mentions a restaurant in the thirties on Third Avenue.

I'm nervous walking there—it's one thing if she brings up Leslie Usher-Soames on the phone where I can squirm out of it without her looking at me. But if she does this from across a small table I might turn into sand.

"You look . . . different," I tell her when she shows up.

"You can't tell what it is?"

I look her over as we go inside. Everything seems the same, the long wavy hair, the figure . . . although the five pounds of baby fat are now down to about two.

She says, "Black is the new black."

That's it; Ivy is incorporating—besides magazine cover lines into her everyday speech—more black into her wardrobe. Now that she's no longer an unpaid intern and draws a decent salary for her age, she's wearing (I'm sure Jimmy and Carol Kooper help) some appropriate Versailles Inc. gear.

"When are you going to get the bottle of mineral water stapled into your palm?" I ask her.

We order our food and talk about work, which is our little way of avoiding the real stuff. At least she isn't talking about her friends and I'm actually listening to her—we stand on the same ground now—and I ask her to repeat herself if I miss a word or two. It isn't like being in school anymore; if she suddenly were to call my name and say, "So, Zachary Post, can *you* give one instance of Betsy Butler being both an utter witch but also a warm, considerate person, and can you compare and contrast her to Jac-*leen* Wooten?" I'd be able to respond reasonably correctly.

And yet . . .

I miss Daphne! I miss her girlfriend's best friend's boyfriends! Of course I have no idea who they are but I miss them. Ivy sits talking to me, about research she's doing for Jackie, about how she isn't getting along with her, and though I'm fairly rapt and leaning on every other word, I long for the other Ivy, the Ivy who doesn't wear black, who might never bounce around the office with a bottle of mineral water, who has a real life outside the cold ecru walls and hallways. The one I'd fallen for even though I hadn't realized I'd fallen.

When we leave the restaurant (she insists we go Dutch and I don't fight it) I ask her if she wants to come over and she says she'd told her mother she'd be home by ten.

"Now that you draw a paycheck, are you going to quit tugging on Mom's apron strings?" I ask her.

"Well, if you hear about a place, tell me. . . ."

Willie's fifth-floor bohemian dump on St. Mark's Place might soon be up for grabs, I realize; Laurie is going out of town and Willie is going out of his mind. He'll either kill himself or, hopefully, Mark Larkin. But I don't mention it.

"Should I take you home?" I offer feebly.

She raises her hand for a taxi.

"No thanks. I can get there myself."

{ }

TO: POSTZ
FROM: LISTERW
SUBJECT: unfuckingbelievable

you're not going to fucking believe this

i have to do research for teddy rsvlt! he just e-mailed me & told me to go to the library & do research
hold on

He e-mails me what Mark Larkin had e-mailed him.

TO: LISTERW
FROM: LARKINM
SUBJECT: What I need

Lister:
I need you to go to the library and find an article about investment banker Ferdy Gurvitz that appeared in New York Mag some time betw. Jan and May in either 1991 or 92. If not New York, then the

New Yorker or Gotham. And another article in the Wall St Journal, I
believe summer 1995 or 1996. Or maybe it was Fortune Magazine.
Or Forbes, autumn or winter 91 or 92.
Thnx,
Larkin

It isn't hard to absorb the insult of Mark Larkin's request, so auda-
ciously demeaning it is; the dates are so unsure, the sources so vague, it's
an impossibly tedious task Willie is being asked to perform. I look up
from my screen and his head is shaking, he's biting his lower lip and
breaking the skin.

"Take it easy," I urge.

He sits there trembling.

"It won't be so bad, Willie. Three days at the library . . . that means
three days not here."

"That fucking fucker!"

"Please. Calm down. Okay?"

He picks up his Krispy Kreme cup, dumps the pens and pencils
onto his desk, then stands up and hurls the cup at Mark Larkin's door,
which is half open. The cup hits the door and cracks into three large
chunks.

"What is this all about?" Mark Larkin says a second later, coming to
the door. He's grabbing his suspenders, sliding his hands up and down
them, and his ears are flushed.

"How dare you ask me to go to the library and do this menial shit for
you!"

"You work for me, Will. Don't forget."

I'm surprised that Mark Larkin, a physical weakling who probably
has trouble lifting his pants to put them on, would stand up to Willie,
four inches taller and eighty pounds heavier.

"I'm older than you!" Willie says. "I've been here longer than you!
I'm also a lot nicer than you."

"I'm your boss, you shouldn't forget that."

Willie's nose is almost in Mark Larkin's hair.

"Well, that's not a good thing."

"Then quit!"

"No!"

(There are two ways this can go. If Willie hits Mark Larkin, if he bashes his head against a cubicle wall, he's out of a job. If he doesn't, it's just more combustion, less sleep, and more insane delusions of tapped phones, cameras behind mirrors, and who knows what else.)

"I'm not doing this," Willie says. "This is what we have editorial assistants for."

"No. I'm asking you to do this because I trust you."

"You're asking me to do this because you hate me. Because you're afraid of me."

"Do you want me to tell Regine you're not doing this?"

Willie says nothing and Mark Larkin looks over at me and says: "Will you go to the library then?"

Oh no . . . I've been worrying I'd get drafted into this.

"Do I have to?" I ask.

"Don't do it, Zeke."

"One of you," Mark Larkin said, "is going and that's that, or else I'll have you fired."

"I'll go," I say.

"Could you move a bit?"

"Which way?"

"It's this dreadful belt buckle," Leslie complains.

"How's this?"

"Still not quite it."

"How's this?"

"No. Not now. I'm not ready for that."

I take my hand out from under her skirt.

"It's just not right," she says.

I sit up. Leslie's hair is in a ponytail as usual and is, despite me trying my best to muss it up, still perfectly lustrous and silky. I'm a mess, however . . . does the fastidious Saville Row poster boy Colin Tunbridge-Yates ever look this disheveled?

"I told Ivy that we were through, by the way."

"You did?" She sits up and flicks on the small lamp on her night table, then pulls down on her blouse—it had taken me twenty minutes of prying, poking, and cajoling to undo the top button. It might take a dump truck unloading a ton of soot on top of her to make her look even the slightest bit blowsy.

"Yeah. A few days ago on the phone. I told her I just didn't love her."

"Oh, that poor dear." (Pronounced "dare.")

I try to gently pinch her nipple through the blouse but she brushes my hand away as though it were a gnat.

"And I tried to comfort her and I kept handing her tissues and—"

"Wait. You said this was over the phone."

Oops!

"Well, uh, yeah. But then I met her someplace. In a bar. They keep a box of Kleenex there for such occasions. A good bartender should always have some tissue on hand."

(Yeah, a tissue of lies! And she'd caught me in one but I worked my way out of it.)

"I feel so bad for her. She's really quite pretty, don't you think?"

"She is."

"Do you not think she's praps prettier than I am?"

I examine Leslie. Though *praps* I haven't been able to dent her hair or panties, her lipstick is smudged. Her lips are so thin and pale though— she must not go through too much lipstick in the course of her life.

"No. I think you're prettier."

It makes me feel like a real rat, saying that.

"Well, you're right! I *am*."

I didn't get very far that night—some French-kissing and ear nibbling and she let me palm her breasts through her blouse for a few seconds. She didn't look much different when I left than when I'd come over but I knew that the groundwork had been laid for better things.

I was in . . . courtesy of some Kleenex.

⟩ ⟨

GETTING out of the subway one morning I run into Liz Channing.

She tells me about a feature she's working on; it's about the odious president of a Milan modeling agency that specializes in lithe and limber twelve- to fifteen-year-old beauties. The man had had his way with scores of these supple, irresistible *ragazze* and—this is where it becomes a man bites dog story—this was usually with the knowledge and blessing of the girls' parents. His first name, naturally, is Gianni.

"If this story doesn't get in, I'm quitting," Liz says.

"Are they sending you to Italy?"

"No. I've been doing all the legwork on the phone."

"You've been threatening to quit for some time." We cross a street and the big black transistor battery we work in comes into view, glistening and snake-slimy, clouds reflected in the black.

"How come you never threaten to quit?" she asks me.

"I wouldn't have anywhere to go."

"Sure you would."

We walk on for a few more steps, then I stop in my tracks and she stops too, a few feet ahead of me.

"I'm a lie," I say.

"What do you mean?"

"My whole life . . . the whole thing. It's all made up. It's like James Gatz except he had the mansion and the pool and the swank parties. All I have is a one-bedroom dump on Second Avenue."

I tell Liz that my father is a Wet Guy and my mother is a garment center bookkeeper who lives inside a piece of toast. Though I can't quite bring myself to utter the word "Hofstra," I do tell her I've never even seen the schools I'd supposedly attended.

"Wow! You've totally reinvented yourself!"

"From scratch. I don't know why I told you this."

"You might not be the only mythomaniac in our outfit."

"Oh." Seeing as I'm the Thomas Alva Edison of personal reinvention, the idea that there might be other Wizards of Menlo Park tinkering around on the floor—this doesn't sit too well with me. "Why? Who else?" I ask.

"Sometimes I get the feeling we're not who we say we are."

After buying our breakfasts at a deli we walk into the lobby.

"How are you and Ivy doing?" she asks me.

"We're not." I can't resist. "And how are you and Major Tom?" (Since the Christmas party we've dispensed with formalities and now when her husband appears in conversation it's usually in some kind of astronaut form.)

"You know, marriage is one-tenth inspiration and nine-tenths expiration," she says.

This would be the time, if I disliked her, to break out the high heel with the bubble gum on it.

"There's a nasty rumor afoot," she says quietly when we step into a crowded elevator, "about you and Leslie Usher-Soames."

I'm squashed against the rear wall by someone who smells like a gallon of Guerlain.

She says, "To put it bluntly: you're doing her."

However this piece of hearsay had hopped from desk to desk to Liz, Marjorie was probably the source from which it sprang.

"It's not true."

"You swear?"

"I swear."

"Good," she grins. "Because I don't know about her."

"What don't you know about her?" I ask.

"I don't know. She's just so . . . *her*."

"Laurie's gone," Willie says. "Yesterday was her last day."

This is news to me. I didn't know when she was leaving.

We're in his apartment, he's sprawled out on the couch, I sit at the wobbly table in the kitchen. "She's gone," he mumbles, massaging his face with his hands. Then he looks at the ceiling, which is flaking and crumbling, a berserk jigsaw puzzle.

"You'll get by."

"I wasn't getting by with her. I won't do it without her."

"Maybe she'll come back."

"She won't. It never happens in a mutual breakup."

"This was a mutual breakup?"

"Yeah . . . she was sick of me and I was sick of me too. Hey, do you think they paid her?"

"Severance pay?"

"No no no. Paid her to leave me?"

"No. I don't think that."

"But you don't know the truth, you don't know what goes on in there, Zeke."

In there? Does he mean in the office or in his mind? Somewhere on the premises is a gun, if Laurie was right, if Willie had indeed been telling the truth to her. Where was it? In a sock drawer, in the vegetable drawer in the fridge?

"Mark Larkin said that when Laurie left maybe you'll actually be a good worker again. And he added: 'But I doubt it.' "

"He said that?"

"Can you believe it?"

But Mark Larkin had never said any such thing.

"I had an interview with Human Resources," Willie says, going to the kitchen to pour two shots of Wild Turkey, both of which he drinks.

"Where? *Newsweek?*"

"No. *Our* Human Resources. Maureen O'Connor. She knew about me throwing the Krispy Kreme cup at the Rough Rider's door."

"Everyone knows about it."

"Well, apparently that kind of behavior is frowned on! Can you believe that?! Shit, before you know it, disgruntled postal workers won't be allowed to kill people anymore."

He goes on to tell me that Human Resources had asked him if he was unhappy and if so why; they asked him if he got along with his coworkers, if they were unhappy and if so why. They told him there were seminars on "Getting Along" that he could take — they were called "Attitudinal Adjustment Sessions"; there were therapists to see who specialized in these kinds of things, there were — this is a truly dreadful prospect — even group therapy counselors so that he, Mark Larkin, and I could air out our dirty laundry and then cry and hug each other. But he, Willie tells me, had only given one- to four-word answers: "No." "No problem." "That's not necessary." "We get along fine."

"And the clincher was," he says, looking through an empty shot glass like it's a jeweler's loupe (is he checking for a microphone?), "I shit you not, the clincher was the end. Maureen says to me, 'Have you put on some weight recently?' And I said, 'Yeah! I sure have!' And she said, 'And your hair's thinning, isn't it?' And I said, 'Yeah, it is!' And she picks up a pad and a pen and it was like a doctor writing a prescription. She hands me the paper and written on it are the phone numbers and addresses of a weight-loss clinic and a hair-loss expert. Can you believe that?!"

Willie might think his apartment is bugged and that people paid Laurie to leave town, but yes, I could believe it.

{ }

ONE FRIDAY evening I get an e-mail from Willie. But he isn't sitting across from me; the return address is: LAFFERTYL. He's at Laurie's old desk in the Black Hole.

I'M GOING TO KILL HIM, it says (and I don't have to ask who "him" is). But it doesn't merely say it once; it's about ten single-spaced pages of I'M GOING TO KILL HIM, margin-to-margin. At first I assume he must have written one line's worth of it, copied and then kept cutting and pasting, because what I'm looking at and scrolling hopelessly through is thousands and thousands of I'M GOING TO KILL HIM's. But then I see variations here and there, a spelling error, an extra space, and I realize he really did write the whole thing out.

I e-mail him back asking why but there's no answer. Mark Larkin's door is open and he's at his desk . . . any second Willie might run past me, charge into the office, and shoot holes in Mark Larkin's head and neck. But it never happens.

Over the past few weeks I've started saving some of Willie's e-mail, the messages such as these, and I save this one to that file. If someone ever puts a bullet in Mark Larkin's brain, I don't want anyone to think it's me.

"Do you remember Mark Larkin's first day at work?" Betsy Butler asks me. We're at the Greek coffee shop across from Crookshank's and this is the first time she and I have ever eaten together. When she had asked me out I knew something, most likely something bad, was up.

"I sure do. You don't forget things like that."

"I remember—I don't know if you do—coming over to your desk and telling you to get along with him."

"It hasn't been easy."

She tells me (mercifully it takes only three minutes) of her first ten years at Versailles, about some of the conflagrations and nasty politics and infighting she had to put up with. Now these people, she says, are her good friends.

"Do you ever think of leaving *It?*" she asks me.

Oh no. Is this the first budge of the shove out the door?

"Honestly? I never do."

"You're very valuable to us."

"Has Mark Larkin ever recommended running the Leroy White piece?"

"Oh yes! *Very* emphatically as a matter of fact."

"Well, that's good."

"See, Zachary, he's not your enemy."

I'm working on the Antony Beauchamp story, the keyboard on my lap, my feet up on my desk. Willie has called in sick.

Jackie Wooten comes by and says suspiciously quietly: "Meeting in the conference room." She looks pale. "Right now."

Footsteps, mostly high heels and pumps, click and clack down the corridors and I gently set the keyboard on the desk. The tone of Jackie's voice indicates something very serious, something unusual.

Mark Larkin comes out of his office. He wipes his glasses on a handkerchief . . . his eyes look misty.

"Could you not have your feet on the desk?" he says.

"Regine's not even in New York."

"But I am."

A minute later everybody, including the marketing and advertising people and Ted Tarrant, *It's* publisher, is crammed into the big beige conference room.

Velma Watts is the messenger bearing the bad news. She's wearing a bright purple dress and purple mascara.

"Sheila Stackhouse died yesterday," she says.

There are a few gasps and a sigh or two and I look at everybody . . . some immediately cast their glances downward, others up, some shake their heads sadly, some are doing what I'm doing: looking at everybody else.

"She died in her home and her family was with her," Velma says. "I spoke with her husband today and he said she died very peaceful."

Marcel Perrault crosses himself. Oliver and Liz are standing close together. Liz looks fidgety.

"We're going to pass around an envelope and Byron will create a nice card for the family, which I hope you'll all sign." The donations will go to charity, we're told; remembering Regine's roses and the dismissive, glacial message she had Velma write, the family might never want to see another flower again.

Mark Larkin takes his glasses off. He looks ten years older this way. He's not crying but his eyes are moist and he wipes the lenses again.

That lucky bastard, I think. He's now a—

"Mark Larkin," Velma says, "has now been permanently appointed senior editor. Regine called and said she'll be back in the office next Tuesday."

And then we all go back to work.

After the bad news, I have to talk to Jackie—she had announced her engagement to a doctor the previous week (her diamond ring is about the size of a yo-yo)—about the direction of the Beauchamp article. It's touchy, I've been told, because while Beauchamp was ripping off the artists in his stable in the seventies and eighties, some of the people he was selling to were Versailles big shots, people such as Gaston Moreau, Roddy Grissom, Sr., Corky Harrison, Regine Turnbull. I told Jacqueline that I knew better than to mention that, but hinted that it could be mentioned, accompanied by a quick, adroitly done aside.

"It's terrible about Sheila, isn't it?" she says.

"Yes. She was a good boss."

"And it's a big blow to Mark Larkin too, probably."

This doesn't make sense—if his being promoted to a full-time and not-just-until-Sheila-licks-the Big C senior editor is a big blow, then I could use one too.

"How is this a big blow?"

"I guess you didn't know. Well, don't tell anyone, Zachary, but Mark Larkin was lobbying Betsy and Regine for the Correspondent, Special: at-Large slot."

"But there is no such slot." (Tony Lancett and Emma Pilgrim are the only ones at-Large . . . we don't have any other people at-Large but those two, and they're Reporters-at-Large.)

"He wanted them to create it," she tells me, brushing her bony palm through her hair. "And I think they were going to do it too, but then *this.*"

Hence his misty eyes.

{ }

"WELL, THAT was good," Leslie says.

I pull the covers up to my neck. The walls close in a little, the ceiling moves down.

"Don't you think that was good?" she asks me.

I really do despise these instant postcoital thumbs-up/thumbs-down sessions. She's waiting for a four-star rave.

"Yes, that was good," I throw out to the sinking ceiling.

She nuzzles her face into my neck, slides her hand under the comforter and crawls it across my chest. Waiting for the review.

"I would say it was good."

She's still waiting.

But why would she say that it was good?! She didn't do anything, she didn't do one thing, except for that one simple thing . . . and that ruined it. Except for that and a few breaths when she moved her tiny waist an inch to the right, there wasn't much going on from her end and I too was far, far from spectacular. A real reviewer would have forgotten I was even in the film.

"I'd like to think we're going to do this again."

"Are you going to tell Colin?"

"I haven't thought about that."

"You know, I *did* break up with Ivy."

She sits up. It's pretty dark in the room and I can hear cars going up and down Central Park West, which is only about fifteen yards down the street from her brownstone.

"Well, Zachary, the thing is I don't see Colin every day. I don't work with Colin. He's not around me for ten hours."

"You've got a point."

"And aren't you glad to be rid of her?"

(I miss her a lot and would rather be sitting across a restaurant table from her than have you kneading my chest.)

"Well, it's good to be here with you." I feel something wet squooshing under my back and fish around for it.

"Where are you going to put that?" she asks me.

"I thought I'd just stick it to your night table."

I walk to the bathroom.

"No! Not in the bathroom rubbish tin. Could you put it in something first?"

"Such as what?"

"The bag in the kitchen . . . under the sink?"

So I walk to the kitchen and look for a bag under the sink.

"The bag's full!" I yell out. "What about a paper towel?"

"There are some above the microwave. But you should try to get it in the bag too."

"Then where does it go?"

"Into a big black plastic bag in the tall metal dustbin outside."

So I have to get dressed then. I walk back into her bedroom, still holding the offending dangling article, and pick up my pants.

"Well, don't bring it back in *here!*"

I go back to the kitchen, pull out a paper towel, put it on the paper towel.

"Where is it now?" she calls out.

"It's lying flat on the counter on a paper towel."

"Could you put some cellophane around it please? So it doesn't soak through?"

I find the cellophane and wrap it around the paper towel. "Okay, it's in the cellophane and the paper towel," I yell.

"Now please try to get it in that white bag."

I go back into the bedroom to put my clothes on.

"Are you coming back after?"

This strikes me as being very convenient, her pathological terror of spent prophylactics: I could put on my clothes, toss the thing out, and then just take off for home.

"Do you want me to come back?"

She giggles and asks, "Do you want to?"

I know I have to say, "I'd like to come back." And I say it.

"Then come back." She's on the bed, stomach-down but facing me, looking catlike and about to spring, and she keeps the comforter over her chest. Some streetlight comes in and there's a full moon out—her face looks very pretty. She bites a nail.

"Okay. I'll come back."

On the street below I dump the thing, so that it is now in a paper towel inside cellophane in a small white bag inside a bigger Hefty bag inside a large metal trash can. To my left all the cars, many of them taxis, stream downtown with their lights on. I wouldn't mind throwing myself onto the hood of one of them.

When I go back upstairs she's asleep.

During the act itself she did this one thing; she said something and this was why I was terrible our first time, why I didn't last very long.

She said (so Britishly, like Helena Bonham Carter or Kristin Scott Thomas): "Dahhrling . . ."

I've waited three decades to hear that.

"When will I get a chance to read one of your books?" she asks me a few nights later.

"My books? I haven't written any books."

"You don't have to play coy with me. I know."

"I swear. I don't write books." I try to take out the barrette that keeps her hair in a ponytail but she stops me with a slap on the knuckles.

"All right, anything you say . . . Lothar."

Oh, now I realize what she means: Lothar X. Criswell.

"You think I write science-fiction books, don't you?"

She jams her face into my ribs and giggles uncontrollably. "Ohhhh, I think I'm going to piss myself," she sniggers.

"I don't write sci-fi books. If you ever came to my apartment, you'd see I have no such book on my shelves."

She stops laughing and sits up stiffly and her expression changes.

"Stop nagging me about that. I'll come to your bloody flat one of these days."

"Okay."

"I don't like being told what to do. Do you think you're God's gift to women? That we should all follow you like pied pipers or lemmings off a ship to wherever you want us to go?"

"No, I don't think that at all. But I don't write science-fiction books and I never have. Okay?"

"Okay. But Marjorie isn't one to make things up."

Pied pipers? . . . lemmings off a ship? Jesus Christ.

*⁕{ }⁕

AN 11 A.M. edit meeting and everyone is in place: Betsy Butler, sitting at the head of a long table and wearing a gray cashmere cardigan, is leading it, and Velma, in a violet merino wool top and a black skirt, takes notes. Liz and Oliver aren't sitting next to each other as usual; they probably think that, because *they* know they're doing each other, everybody else does too.

"Okay. Jacqueline will be routing Tony Lancett's article on the senator . . . when?" Betsy says.

Jacqueline sets her long bony hands on the long table and the sunlight squiggles on her immense engagement ring.

"He faxed the first part this morning," she says. "I'll get the rest tomorrow and have it routing by Thursday the latest." Her eyes look at the ring for a second, then at the sun outside the window. Is she trying to urge it to shine brighter?

"Valerie Morgan got some great pictures in," someone says. "Pictures of the senator in drag and lingerie from his college days."

"How much does that thing cost?" Willie asks.

"The photos?" Betsy says.

"No no. That ring, Jackie. How much for a rock like that?"

"Oh," Jacqueline says, sitting up a little rigidly. "A lot. And it's Jacqueline."

"Over ten grand?"

Other people adjust themselves in their chairs and I begin to press on a pencil very hard with my thumb.

"Well," Jacqueline says, "that's really kind of personal."

"Over five grand?"

"I said it's personal." But you just know she wants to shout it out: TWENTY THOUSAND DOLLARS!!!

"How many places did you get it appraised at?"

"Willie!" Betsy says. "We're having a meeting!"

I look at Willie and give him a what-are-you-trying-to-pull-here look. He sarcastically mirrors it and I feel a stabbing pain in my gut and press harder on the pencil.

"Liz, how's your story coming?" Betsy asks with her glasses now down at the round tip of her *Potato Eaters* nose.

"It's all done," Liz says. "It's been done for a while now, Betsy." She taps the long table two times with a pen.

"Have you routed it?"

"Jackie said she put it in Regine's in-box. That was two weeks ago."

"That's the Black Hole of Magazine Calcutta, Liz," Willie says. "That's the Bermuda Triangle of Journalism. It's the Heart of Reportage Darkness, the Judge Crater of—"

I kick Willie's foot under the table and he says aloud to me for all to hear: "Why did you just kick me?"

Jacqueline says, "It's Jacqueline, not Jackie."

Betsy jots something down on her pad; I'm certain it says: "Talk with WL this PM."

Betsy asks Jacqueline to fish Liz's article out of Regine's in-box or out-box and take a glance at it, then maybe pass it around.

"*Maybe* pass it around . . . ?" Liz repeats, shaking her head.

I squeeze the pencil harder.

Betsy says, "We already have a lot lined up for the issue."

Liz interrupts: "I was told that it was pretty definite that this was going in."

"*Pretty* definite isn't definitely definite," Mark Larkin says with an arrogant Mussolini-esque thrust of his chin.

"It's definitely not," Liz says, again tapping the table.

I'm getting a headache: the tapping noises, the sunlight and Jacqueline's ring, this excruciating tension.

"If I can, I'll get it out of Regine's office and we'll have a look at it," Jacqueline says. "I'm sure she must have read it by now."

"You're going to get it, Jackie?" Willie says. "Or are you going to have someone else do it?"

"I'll have *you* do it if you don't shut up!"

Willie says to Liz: "I bet you she never even put it in there. I guarantee it. She killed it. It was never going to go in and she's lying."

Willie's theory certainly sounds plausible to me.

"We should take a look at it," Betsy says, making a bid to keep the peace or to find some trace of it first.

"Someone will get it out of Regine's," Velma says and we're all thinking: it might be under ten feet and thirty pounds of copy and magazines and newspapers and clippings and mail. Then Velma says, "But I ain't gonna be the one doing it, I'll tell you that."

People laugh and Willie says sadly, "I'll do it. I could use the exercise. But I still say *she* has it." He tilts his head toward Jacqueline, whose right hand now protectively filters the dazzles of her enormous diamond ring.

"How would you like to go to England, Zachary?" Betsy says to me a few minutes later at the same meeting.

"Me?" My first thought is: I'm being transferred to *Ego, U.K . . .* Nan Hotchkiss must need someone to polish her Filofax.

"*Squash the Toad* is coming out in America just in time for this issue," Betsy says. *Squash the Toad* being Daffyd Douglas's first novel, a big best-seller in England, Daffyd Douglas being a new client of Muffy Tate's, Muffy Tate being the new friend of the brand-new senior editor and would-be Correspondent, Special: at-Large.

"I'd love to go," I say. But my Spidey senses are cranked all the way up: England . . . Liverpool U. . . . I'm waiting for something here.

"Maybe it would give you a chance to visit some of your old haunts," someone says.

"Some of my old huncles too," I say and people groan appropriately.

I ask if Daffyd Douglas is coming to America to do a book tour, and Mark Larkin says that the twenty-five-year-old *wunderturk* doesn't want to come to the States presently.

"We could do a fax interview," I suggest. There's just something a little suspicious about this England offer. (I've never even been out of the U.S.A. before!) If a complete stranger walked up to me on the street and handed me $50,000 and said, "Here, keep it," I'd have the exact same feeling.

Betsy says, "He wants to do it face-to-face, Zack."

"Have you read the book?" someone asks me.

I can't lie about this one, in case everybody else at the meeting has read it. So I admit I haven't.

Betsy says, "Read it ASAP. Mark has Daffyd Douglas's bio in his office. Velma will work on getting the plane tickets."

"Okay," I say. "Sounds good. England." But I think my face might be pale. Something is up here.

"I'll be in the U.K. at the same time," Mark Larkin says. "Got some work to do on Lord Wincher. There are some rough edges that need smoothing out, I'm afraid." Lord Wincher is the slowly-dying life peer with the 400-million-dollar art collection and no heirs.

"Do I get to go anywhere?" Willie asks.

"Weren't you going into Regine's in-box?" Jacqueline snaps.

"Look, Jac-*leen*," Liz says, leaning forward and putting her elbows on the table, "it's my article. I'll either fish it out or just reprint it. And then I'll pass it around. Okay?"

"I think maybe we should wait," Jacqueline says, "and see what Regine thinks about it. Don't you think that's the best course of action?"

Aha! *Guilty as charged!* Jacqueline Wooten, that skeletal stuck-up Mt. Holyoke harpy with the blond Breck Girl tresses, never did put it in Regine's in-box! Look at her trying to stall! This attempt at a delaying tactic proves it for me, right there, and no other evidence is needed. Guilty!

But Liz doesn't see it. "But is it going in?" she asks. "Does it have a chance?" Her arms are folded across her chest, her hair is falling to one side.

Betsy says she doesn't know and Liz leans back in her chair and Oliver, who has been horrified by the poison circulating in the air, fixes his gaze at the long table.

"God, I hate this goddamn place," Liz says. She puts an arm back on the table, rests her head in a palm, and shakes her head. A sudden cool air of serenity steals over her and envelopes her. "I really do hate it."

Betsy doesn't like this rare open display of contempt but I think it's Liz's tranquillity more than her vocal protest that gets to her.

"Listen!" Betsy says. "We're all on this ship together!"

"Yeah, the friggin' *Lusitania*," Willie says. He cracks up for five seconds, then calms down.

The meeting is coming to a close and it's been a battle . . . the tension has been like a tide, rising, flattening out, then rising and roaring again. Betsy reminds me of my piece on Babar the Elephant Bar, a hot new nightspot owned by some Germanic Eurotrash club-meister. (And to my horror, I have to bring Ivy and Todd Burstin there, to show them how such a piece gets done.)

"What about your Starters piece on that Harvard club?" Mark Larkin is asked by Betsy.

"The Porcellian? Oh, I should have that done in no time. Certainly before I'm in England," he responds.

"Everyone's going someplace," Willie says aloud to himself, "and I'm stuck on this big blue marble, this island Earth, this kooky cockeyed caravan—"

"Ssshhh, ssshhh," whispers Betsy. She waves her hands, palms down, as though playing chords softly on a piano.

Mark Larkin says, "I have to get in touch with an old friend and former member. She—"

Willie interrupts. "The club doesn't have any women members. It never has."

Mark Larkin snorts, then asks, "How would you know?"

"I'm a Porcellian man, I'm ashamed to admit."

"So am I . . ." But he can't think of anything else to say.

"Oh, are you now?" Willie says derisively.

"It's noon," Betsy says. "Why don't we all take a break?"

At that second the pencil I've been pressing on breaks in two and the half with the point spirals across the table.

I walk out with Liz, Ollie, Willie.

"He's full of shit," Willie whispers to me. "He's a Porcellian man like Liz is a Dallas Cowboy."

"I'm gone," Liz says. "I'm gone."

"What's wrong with you?" I ask Willie.

"Plenty."

Five minutes after the meeting, Willie and I are out on the street, standing near the curb, right in front of the building. Cars aren't moving and horns blare and tempers are short.

"You're going to get me in trouble," I say to him.

"Well, we can't have that, can we?"

"Come on . . . you know this job is the only thing between me cleaning out swimming pools and selling frog-repellent."

"Maybe that's what you should be doing."

"It *is!* But I don't want anyone to know that."

"Don't worry. I'm sorry. I'm going . . . I don't know."

He rubs the gold stubble on his cheeks. "Wave to the people, Zeke."

He nods toward the traffic and I turn to my right and see a bus stuck in traffic, about twenty people on board.

"Just wave like you know one of them," he says, "and see if the person waves back. That woman with the scarf."

I point to her and begin waving and make a surprised hey-it's-you face. She smiles and waves back.

"Let's go back upstairs," he says. "Okay?"

It's impossible, ultimately, for me to be mad at him.

} {

MORE trouble . . .

A book I'd reviewed in the (I think) April issue was a modern rendering (a postmodern rendering, I should say) of *Macbeth*, set in the icy lonely wastes of northeastern Maine. My review, however, never mentioned a *Macbeth* connection.

I'm in Mark Larkin's office and Velma, Regine's Luca Brazzi, sits on my right. It's the same scene as months before . . . but now Sheila is dead and Mark Larkin presides as one of my judges.

"How could you not have mentioned *Macbeth?*" he asks me. "That simply astounds me."

"I don't know what kind of punishment she's going to cook up for you this time," Velma says.

Ice fishing in Maine in January? Would that be it?

"Well, the writer of the book," I say, "lives in New York so at least I don't have to go out to the fuckin' hinterlands again."

"Watch your language, please," Mark Larkin says, nodding over to Velma.

Something blazes right toward me in a bright white flash.

I say to Mark Larkin: "Do you remember your first day, when you didn't know how to get Regine her coffee? You said something about Velma . . . I don't recall exactly what but maybe *you* do."

He huffs a second, then moves his lips around for a moment.

"Have you read *Macbeth?*" he asks me loudly. "Don't you think you should have mentioned it? Or didn't you realize it was based on *Macbeth?*"

"I don't remember if I noticed it or not. To be honest, I may not have. Maybe some reviewers didn't catch on to *West Side Story* or *Kiss Me Kate* and—oh yeah! You said you weren't getting coffee for a Negress. Or something like that."

"Velma, I never said any such thing. And this has nothing to do with—"

I stand up and leave the two of them in there, Mark Larkin squirming in his slacks in front of Regine Turnbull's hired gun.

{ }

I PICK UP Leslie outside her brownstone at 9:30. I'm wearing the most expensive clothes I've ever worn, all of it with that perfectly creased radiance that shouts out BRAND NEW, all of it bought just for tonight, our first Meg Bunch salon.

(On the subway uptown, though, I find a tiny "INSPECTOR 903" tag in my new jacket pocket. Perhaps at this swank soiree, I imagine, Inspector 903 will seek me out, pluck me away, hand me a long stick, and tell me to clean some jerk's pool.)

Leslie, when she comes downstairs (it takes ten minutes, after I buzz her), looks wonderful in a lilac backless silk number and she wears a choker and glittery lilac stockings. She smells like lilacs too.

"Hey, do you want to go upstairs for a quick one?" I ask, taking in an eyeful of this shimmering amethyst, alabaster sprite.

"A jrink?" Leslie says.

"No. Sex. I lift your dress up, pull your panties down, my pants are at my feet like manacles and I look stupid but . . ."

"Please. We're running late."

Meg Bunch lives on Fifth Avenue in the Sixties. What a spread—it's been featured in *Here* magazine and was decorated by interior designer du jour Marion Bell, whose credo is "Garishness, Gaudiness, Glory!" Everywhere are tall mirrors and gleaming gold and spotless silver. The floors are shiny black and white marble tiles and looking down at them I can even make out my own eyelashes six feet away. Luxurious chandeliers make soft tinkling sounds and the leather furniture is black and although the lights are dimmed, each room glitters with tiny sparks of crystally light, from the glass in the chandeliers down to the marble tiles and across from the immense mirrors to the gold and silver furniture.

When we walk in I immediately espy Trisha Lambert's sleek six-foot-one frame and new geometrically correct Cleopatra hairdo among the crowd. You look at her and then bask in her refracted "Styles of the *Times*" glory.

I groan to Leslie: "I see someone and she doesn't like me."

"Nonsense! You're with me!"

"Ohhhh, I'm *so* glad you two could come," Meg Bunch chirps to us. She offers her cheek for me to kiss, I kiss it, she offers the other to kiss, I kiss it, she offers the first one again, this time I pass.

"Just toss your coats on anything, you two," Meg says.

I take Leslie's coat, a teal crinkly thing, and while she wades into the crowd of fifty or so, I try to find the bedroom. Passing Thomas Land I say, "Tom! Hi!" (I can't and won't bring myself to call that toadying bastard Thomas to his face.)

"Zachary, this is a surprise," he says.

"A pleasant one, I trust."

He smiles and after I pitch a few story ideas at him for *Boy* (all of them *It* rejects—why do the work if it's possible not to?), he slips away into a cluster of successful tall people.

Donna Reems, the photographer, walks by me with a brutish underwear model named Tony (known in the fashion business as "The Big Packet") and I ask her where the bedroom is and she points. Working my way down a narrow hallway covered with mirrors, to my shock and dismay I run into . . .

"Ivy?"

"Zack?"

"*You're* here?"

"Can you believe it? This is my first salon."

"Mine too. I fear I'm more saloon than salon."

She isn't wearing black, it's a relief to see, but has on a navy blue dress and her hair is in a braid.

"I'm only here 'cause of my dad," she says apologetically.

I want to say I'm only there because of my date but I say: "I figured as much."

"Are you alone?"

I feel my skin turn to translucent plastic and all the light shooting through me: I'm one of those instructional anatomy dolls and Ivy can see my bones, organs, muscles, and circulatory system.

"No, I'm not."

"I didn't think so." She casts an eye on my lungs.

"And you? You're stag?"

"No. I'm with Todd. The New Boy." Now she's staring at my larynx.

"Oh. You like him?"

"He can be a little difficult in a nerdy way but I didn't want to come alone, you know?"

"Yeah. I guess I do."

Three broomsticky women, one in a gold lamé dress and one in a sequin pantsuit and one in an ice blue not-much-of-anything, walk by and chandelier light ricochets off them and the mirrors and momentarily blinds me. Ivy checks out my pancreas and liver.

"Are you getting along with Leslie?" she asks me, no trace of bitterness in her voice.

I shrug and say, "I have to."

The rest of the evening is spent avoiding Ivy and avoiding Leslie, though I try to keep an eye on both of them, Leslie because I'm worried she might be having a little too much gin, and Ivy because I'm worried she might be having a little too much fun. Trisha Lambert shoots me three dirty looks (and this is someone I never did *anything* bad to, except I knew her husband when he was as much a nobody as I am now). I corner Todd Burstin and spend ten minutes with him, only to be disappointed to find that, although he's a little awkward and a bit too snobby for someone his age, he's basically pretty nice. The glasses he's wearing—small and oval and way too stylish—are not at all to my liking and his socks are ugly and don't go with his shoes; he has bad skin and his voice grates and—and . . . and I just want to pick up one of those thousand-dollar chairs and slam him over the head with it and grab Ivy by the hand and whisk her away from the whole dreadful scene.

"Have you met Hamish?" Trisha Lambert asks me when somehow I wind up in her little circle; she waves a palm to an impish bald gay Brit in a bright red plaid suit.

"No. I haven't."

Trisha introduces me and then makes a run for it. Hamish Courtnall is the art director of *Ego*, U.K. and has a nose like a baked potato.

"And how *is* Nan?" I ask, incredulous I can sound so phony.

Hamish tells me how Nan is a joy to work for, which I doubt: he probably thinks I'm a friend of hers so he's airbrushing the whole thing.

"You know," Hamish says, "I do think I've heard of you."

"Nan maybe mentioned me but—"

"I think we're going to reprint your article on Lane Babcock."

That wasn't me. That was Mark Larkin. He wrote that little butt-nugget of puffery.

"Really?" I say. My thumbs are locked tight in the crevices of my fists . . . I crack their knuckles and he hears them above the chatter and music. "I can't wait to see it!"

A little after eleven, Ivy slips out the front door, holding a black coat in her hands. I'm relieved that Todd isn't escorting her out but also depressed that I'm not either . . . then I see Todd leave too, almost tripping over his own feet.

"Did you have a good time?" Leslie asks in the taxi. We're going west through the park on a still, starless night.

"Not really, to be honest."

"Ivy looked pretty."

"She did."

"Not that pretty . . . a little stringy ackshilleh."

We ride silently for a while, then she asks: "Did you meet anybody?"

"A few people."

"Anybody important though?"

"A few."

She smiles and I see those two bad teeth way up in the back.

Meeting important people . . . that's the whole point and she knows it too.

"Can I come upstairs?" I ask her. She's opening her building's front door, standing three stone steps above me, her back to me. Her slender sparkling lilac calves look delectable under the faint flicker of the street-lights.

"I'm knackered."

"You sure?"

"You should just be a good boy and go home." She steps down, kisses me on the nose, then walks up again.

"Are you sure?"

"Yes. Quite sure."

She vanishes and I breathe a great big sigh of relief.

12

"KAFKAESQUE" is one of those second-tier magazine-speak words and phrases: "Grand Guignol," "cause célèbre," and, well, "and, well" are some others. My Leroy White article has been a Kafkaesque experience from the get-go. First of all, getting access to the man took months of wrangling with his publicist and agent. When his people finally consented to the article, I then had to reconvince Regine and others it was still newsworthy.

When everything was finally in place I flew (first-class) out to L.A. for five days; I was expecting to spend most of the time on the set with White, perhaps have dinner with him, possibly even pass an evening with his family at his house in Santa Monica.

I saw him for a total of twenty minutes, never for more than four minutes at one time. He was too busy taping his show to spend time with me, but was thoroughly apologetic about it. My notes for these three days read like: "2 P.M. LW: I'm sorry. Me: That's okay. Maybe in a few minutes? 5 P.M. LW: I have to go . . . I'm really sorry about this. Me: It's okay. Maybe dinner tonight? 8 P.M. LW: You're still here, man? Me: Can we get a few minutes now?. LW: I'm really busy. Sorry."

Five days of that, of me dozing off in his dressing room or drinking ten cups of coffee at a Hamburger Hamlet and knocking off every magazine published that month. He wanted to relax with his family at night so I was stuck in the hotel flicking channels, looking out the window, and taking long evening drives in my rented Cavalier. Somehow out of this (and eventually a long fax Q & A) I managed to piece together the thing. In the latest *It* flat plan (the boxy grid of articles and ads scheduled for an issue) for the issue we're currently working on, I see the words "LEROY WHITE." This is incredible to me! Finally. It's being given five pages and Jacqueline says they're going to try to schedule a Zelda Guttierez photo shoot. Okay, it's not Avedon, Reems, or Brooks but Zelda will certainly do. They better get this done ASAP, because the young actor who once stole scenes in *Foxy Brown* and *Slaughter's Big Ripoff*, the tough, tall soul brother with the gargantuan Afro and the barracudas swimming around in his boots in *C.P.T. Johnson Takes on the Man*, will be doing *King Lear* in England soon.

So my little bluff of blackmail seems to have paid off.

But what if Mark Larkin asks me for the tape?

⎰ ⎱

AND NOW the evening at Babar the Elephant Bar, where I'm to train Ivy and Todd in the craft of on-the-scene reportage.

I'm a little suspicious when my willowy heavy-lidded ex-something shows up without the gawky editorial assistant.

"Where's your better half?" I ask her just outside the momentarily exclusive Tribeca club. It's drizzling, foggy, and warm out.

"You're looking at it," she says. She's wearing all black, which I can't fault her for as this is, to use a magazine phrase, the "nightspot of the nanosecond."

In a flash these things occur to me: Young Burstin didn't come because he and Ivy are an item. Ivy has told him that she and I were once involved and it would make her feel uncomfortable, the three of us together. Young Burstin also would feel uncomfortable. Ivy realized that I, sensing how uncomfortable they both would be, would do everything in my power to make it even more uncomfortable. But I —

"Should we go inside?" she says, halting this out-of-control train of thought.

"Eventually." We stand around and observe the abominable trendy types moving in and out of Babar the Elephant Bar.

"Are you 'gettin' with' young Burstin?" I ask her.

"Do I have to answer this question?"

"Yes. You're under oath."

"Well, I will answer it then. I'm not."

Everything about my face probably changes, a slot machine rolling from lemons to blueberries.

"And are you 'gettin' with' Leslie?" she asks.

"I'm not. We just hang around together."

"I don't know if I believe you."

"I don't know if I believe *you*!"

"Are you telling me the truth?"

"Yes. Are you?"

"Let's go inside."

We do our job. The bronzed, blond Teutonic owner of the club—U.S. Customs should have prevented him from bringing all those umlauts in his name into the country—walks around in leather pants and a leopard-skin vest and no shirt and makes sure every patron is happy. Occasionally he emerges at the entranceway and the hateful velvet rope to make sure everybody waiting to get in is miserable. There isn't much to see or do and within twenty minutes Ivy and I are yawning our heads off.

"I just want to know," she says out of nowhere as we lean back on a cushiony couch, "what she's got that I don't have."

The answer is: attitude, but also connections, status, ambition, and, of course, Winston Churchill's cigar smoke. But if I tell her that, Ivy will hate me . . . if she hasn't already started to. Maybe, just maybe, there's at least a chance of salvaging her memory of me. And maybe there's a chance that she'll take me back, if the Post-Usher-Soames alliance doesn't ever come to pass.

"I can't answer that question," I say truthfully.

"You can't answer that question because you don't know or because you don't choose to?"

"I can't answer that question either."

When I walk home that night, after putting her in a taxi, I recall something about Ivy's first day at work: there was a big meeting that day and she hadn't been invited. The offices, cubicles, and hallways were empty and she was by herself. Later she told me that she'd sat down and leafed through a few magazines. There she was, all alone, abandoned, no bitterness, no attitude, not a jot of pretense. Feeling as I do now, I think that had I, for whatever reason, left the meeting and stumbled upon her that way, I would have fallen to my knees and proposed to her.

{ }

"YOU DON'T want to stay at the same hotel as Mark Larkin, I'm assuming," Betsy says to me in her office.

"No thank you."

She tells me that Mark Larkin is staying at Claridge's, that he'll poke around in London before going north to Lord Wincher's ancestral home, and then do some more poking back in London.

"Where will I be staying?" I ask her.

"How does the Hotel Royal Cambridge sound?"

"Sounds good to me."

"Regine thought that you should go to London to interview this Daffyd Douglas character, not me," I tell Willie.

"But?"

"Well . . ."

"Let me guess: Mark Larkin?"

"Yeah."

"He didn't think I could hack it."

I shake my head.

"You gotta be kidding me," he says.

{ }

IF THE most common dream is walking around naked in public, what would it feel like if that ever really happened, if you forgot to put on one stitch of clothing one day and then left your house? Perhaps you wouldn't be in the least bit worried because you'd be so positive that it was only a dream . . . even when they were arresting you and covering you with a sheet of newspaper, you'd still be convinced you were merely dreaming it all up.

"There's someone here to see you," Smitty croaks to me over my speaker phone.

"Who is it?" I'm not expecting anyone.

"Just get out here, will ya?"

I head down the corridors to reception. In three nights I'm flying to London (economy-class this time). Willie has told me (it turns out he's telling the truth) that Mark Larkin will be flying over on the Concorde. Willie is fuming about this but I'm just glad to be getting out of town for a few days; had they offered me a week on a garbage barge swarming with flies, I would have taken it.

I open the door that leads to reception and the elevators and Smitty tilts her head to the left.

There sits my mother holding a little brown paper bag.

It's like the naked dream . . . my nightmare is happening!

I've been through this scene hundreds of times . . . but now it's really taking place and I've forgotten the scenario.

"Hi, Zachary. Surprise," my mother says.

"Mom . . . what are you doing here?" I look around. There are three doors leading to the reception area and there are four elevators . . . if one of them suddenly opens I might have a stroke.

"Well, my boy's going to merry old London, England, and I just wanted to see him off."

"That's sweet of you. Do you maybe want to go outside and—"

A door opens. Two fashion neuters wearing orange and lime green walk out, see me with my mother and smile, then push the button for the elevator.

"Are those girls or boys?" she whispers, craning her little neck to check them out.

"Nobody has any idea. Listen, Ma, you know how the rule is that you're not supposed to call me or visit me unless something really tragic has happened . . . ?"

She hands me the little paper bag. I open it up and see tiny sample bottles of things inside—shampoo, a deodorant, toothpaste, a can of Consort hair spray, things like that.

"This is really nice," I say. "But I don't think—"

The elevator door opens and the two neuters get on and Jacqueline Wooten gets off and my heart sinks.

"Hello, Zack," Jacqueline says. She looks at my mother, then at me, and her precious dimpled smirk tells me she realizes who the old woman is.

"You must be Zachary's mother," she says, stopping by to rub it in.

"And who are you?" my mother, all of five-foot-two, asks her looking straight up at her chin.

Jacqueline introduces herself and then my mother, who remembers everything I tell her since I tell her so little, says, "Oh! I remember when you were just Jackie. Then you got that big promotion."

Jacqueline smiles and just as she mercifully takes her leave of us, Byron Poole, Betsy Butler, and Marjorie come out.

"Mrs. Post??" Marjorie says, almost lifted off her feet in disbelief.

"You must be Marjorie . . ."

"How would you know that?"

Despite my terror I detect Smitty jabbering away on the phone—*is she telling everybody in the entire building: "Zachary Post's mother is visiting! Everybody should get here right away!"*?

"That hair!" my mother answers Marjorie with her hand over her mouth, awestruck by its color, curls, and all-around magnificence. Then the two of them, the bookkeeper/mother and the associate art director/she-wolf, shake hands.

(I had told my mother—after the thing was all over—that I'd "dated" someone at work but had restricted my descriptions to name, job title, salary, and hair. Anything else, I didn't want her to know.)

"Seeing your son off to Europe, are you?" Byron Poole asks Mrs. Sally Huggins Post.

"Yes, it's his first time over there."

Mark Larkin opens the door . . . my mother might be slowly shrinking over the years, but it's only taking me a few minutes.

"Didn't he go to college in England?" Betsy says fairly loudly.

"What are you—" my mother begins.

"Listen, it's all water under the bridge," I butt in. I put my arm over her shoulder in order to steer her away. (And I'm thinking: okay, I'll tell everybody she's got Alzheimer's disease.) Out of the corner of my eye I see Mark Larkin waiting for the elevator. *What do I do?!* If I escort her out we'll be stuck for fifty flights with Larkin, Butler, Poole, Millet . . . but if I direct her toward the environs of my desk (which is right on the Hallway Highway), where there's little privacy, we risk exposure to Regine, Velma, and dozens of others.

The elevator comes and they get on.

But Leslie gets off. (I haven't told my mother about Leslie yet because there really isn't much to tell. And because, whatever sort of relationship it is, it's still going on.)

Leslie's eyes sparkle with the recognition: this is Zachary, this is a small old woman who resembles him, she therefore is his mum.

I introduce them but do so in such a way that all further talk will be forsaken: "Mom, this is Leslie Usher-Soames who works in our art department and who is incredibly busy right now, and Leslie, this is my mom, who is leaving."

"Such a classy girl," my mother says after Leslie walks away.

"She's okay."

"A little too classy. Maybe hoity-toity."

We're waiting for the elevator now.

"I want you to call me now," my mother says. "And don't be afraid to call collect. And it rains a lot there so I hope you bring—"

"Don't worry."

Oh no . . .

Mark Larkin didn't ever leave! He's still standing there! He's been watching us, listening, taking it in the whole time.

"Mrs. Post, I'm Mark Larkin."

The nerves in my jaw prickle.

"You're Zack's boss," she says.

"Yes, I am." He then—and it's a slobbery little exhibition—goes on to sing my praises for about two minutes, to tell her what a great worker and good guy I am, how I'm certainly going places . . . it's smarmy and obsequious and normally my Brooklyn-born mother would see right through it—but because it's all the news she has about me to chew on, she swallows it whole.

The elevator arrives.

Marcel Perrault comes out and just as he pegs the little gray lady as my mom, I nudge her into the elevator, my arm guiding her with force. I press the lobby button as hard and as fast as I can and keep pressing it until finally the door closes but . . .

Mark Larkin is in the elevator with us.

"Do you want to see our bookkeeping department?" I ask her, pushing the thirty-eighth floor. "We call it Accounts Deplor—"

"Nah. I get enough of that at work."

"I thought you lived in Palm Springs, Mrs. Post," my boss says.

Oh no. Oh no oh no oh no . . .

"Palm Springs!" my mother barks out. "I *wish*, Palm Springs!"

I mutter to Mark Larkin out of the side of my mouth: "It's Palm

Beach, okay?" (At least in the face of disaster, I can still stick to the story.) "What the hell are you following me for?"

"I find all this rother fascinating really," he whispers back. Then he says to my mother, "Palm Beach. Yes. Of course."

"I don't know what kinda stories he's telling you," my mother says.

(Alzheimer's, senile dementia . . . it's the only way out.)

Mark Larkin cocks up an eyebrow, whistles for a moment.

As they say in police shows: I'd been made.

{ }

I'M ON the way to Payroll because one of my regular contributors hasn't been paid (unlike the Stilettos of *She, Her,* and *Appeal,* I actually do use the stairs sometimes), and when I open the Stairway A door I see Liz Channing sitting halfway down the staircase, her back to me at an odd angle. I assume she's sneaking a cigarette. But she's not.

"Liz?"

"Please."

"Is something wrong?"

She looks back up at me, her face is blotchy and wet, she sniffles and says, "No. Everything's just hunky-dory."

"Should I go away?"

"I just handed in my notice. I gave them one month's more humiliation of me." She holds a crumpled wet tissue in her hand, covered with smudges of makeup.

"You should be happy. You're getting out of this swamp."

"I know. I should be beaming, right? When I told Regine, it was like . . ."

But she doesn't finish the thought.

"So they're not running the Gianni story?"

She shakes her head. "Fuck Jackie Wooten!"

"No thanks."

She squints and says, "I'd like to swipe that goddamn diamond boulder she's got on her finger and toss it down a manhole."

"It wouldn't fit, I don't think. Anyway, you should be happy. You're out."

"My marriage is pretty much in the toilet too. This is too fuckin' much at one time for me." A tear streams down her cheek. "Can I stay at your place when you're away?" she asks me. "Just for a few days? You know me. I'm sickeningly neat."

"Sure. But no gentlemen callers, okay?"

"Don't worry. Who would want to call on me?" She giggles and cries at the same time, and a snot bubble comes out her nose and then blows back in.

"You know," she says, "my article was killed because your Leroy White article is going in. So you *better* let me stay at your place."

I'm packing a brand-new suitcase—yes, I'm bringing all those sample bottles my mother unloaded on me—when the phone rings. I'd just had dinner with Leslie and then about three minutes of unathletic, uninspired sex at her place; she keeps saying "dahhrling" and I keep losing it, but she's not doing anything else so maybe it serves her right.

"Turn on your TV now! PBS. Hurry!" Willie says on the other end.

"I'm in the middle of packing."

"Turn it on!"

I walk over to the television and turn it on. In doing so I knock my passport off the bed and onto the floor. When I get back to the phone I hear Willie mutter, "This is just unbelievable."

"Okay, it's on," I tell him.

"Turn to *Duffy & Company*. Hurry."

I flick the channels and there, taking up most of the screen, is the head of the talk-show host, Chris Duffy.

"And I'd like to thank my guests . . ." he begins.

They cut to a staff writer for *The New Yorker,* then to the editor-in-chief of *The Village Voice,* then to Pete Hamill . . . it seems to be a panel about the current state of local journalism. I see my passport picture and it's looking at me and thinking: *God, we'd love to be on that panel, wouldn't we?!*

And finally they cut to . . . Mark Larkin.

". . . and I'd also like to thank Mark Larkin of *It* magazine . . . Mark's a senior editor there and an astute observer of the social scene . . . his work appears in *It* regularly. His column, 'Urbane Renewal,' will debut in *Gotham* next month and his collection of essays, titled *First Time as Travesty, Second Time as Farce,* is due out this October."

"December, Chris."

I pick up my passport and look at my picture smiling stupidly and then at the splotchy pink head with the enormous blinding white teeth taking up the screen.

"Can you believe this?" Willie says.

"Yeah. I can, I guess."

But no . . . the truth is I cannot believe it.

And then I hear two loud bangs and glass shattering.

Willie had shot his TV set.

"That oughta show him," Willie says.

PART III

13

THE HOTEL ROYAL CAMBRIDGE is a soggy, royal dump.

It isn't the fancy hotel it sounds like it might be and it also isn't a twee bed-and-breakfast overflowing with dusty hardcovers, fragile teacups, and precious Victoriana. It's a four-story (no elevator, just narrow stairs) dive just off Earl's Court Road and it's freezing cold, colder inside than outside, and there is rarely any hot water. The rasp of traffic and trains wheezes all day and night and the room is steeped in rot and mildew.

The bed is soggy, the breakfast is soggy, the staff is soggy.

When I complain to one of the Royal Cambridge desk clerks about the hot water in my room being colder than the cold water, he tells me they've been meaning to have it fixed. When I ask for how long, he says, "For a few months now."

There's no phone in the room and so I have to call Daffyd Douglas's people from a phone in the street. However, since everybody staying and walking around Earl's Court Road is a tourist, I often find myself waiting in the rain while people call Melbourne, Tokyo, Stockholm, Berlin, etc. All I want to do is call some office about two miles away! But still I have to wait, I have to stand outside and get drenched in the rain . . . but it really isn't so much wetter than my hotel room.

•   •   •

On my second day a note is slipped underneath my door—the "concierge" had written it. The note says: "When is the shoot? Please call ASAP." It's from Harry Brooks, who has flown over to photograph Mark Larkin's slowly dying lord—but since he's here anyway, the Important People figure, why not shoot my unintelligible Mancunian Peck's Bad Boy of the nanosecond?

I leave the hotel and wait ten minutes in the drizzle to call Harry's hotel, which turns out to be a real hotel, the Savoy.

"I've got Lord Wincher all day today," he says. "Do you think we can do it tomorrow really quick? Because I'm off to Germany the following day for him."

"For Mark Larkin??"

"No, no . . . the magazine *Him*."

(For a moment I think Hitler's brain has been cloned and that Mark Larkin had landed the Interview of the Century.)

"I'll try, Harry. I have to go." Behind me ten Swedes and Aussies with yellow and mauve nylon knapsacks grow impatient.

"What the hell is this Royal Cambridge joint you're at, Zack? Some hotel so swank the rooms don't have phones?"

"It's dank, not swank."

I drop in on the *Ego, U.K.* offices to use their phones and also to dry off. The office is on Longacre, blocks away from Covent Garden and the West End theaters.

A very pretty and very tall receptionist named Fiona, whose manner is so sleepy as to begin to lull me to sleep, lets me use an empty office after I show her my Versailles ID. I finally touch base with Douglas's publicist at Soft Skull U.K. Press. "We've been waiting for your call," the woman says.

She says she'll beep Daffyd "straight away" and so I hold on.

There are no books or shelves and there's no computer in the office . . . the lights are off and the door is ajar. A few seconds after putting me on hold, the publicist gets on and asks me to hold for "a bit" . . . she'll patch Daffyd through, she says. I wait about three more minutes and through the slit in the door I see Mark Larkin and Nan Hotchkiss pass by, heading for the stairway to the street.

"Oh, fuck!" I groan. I've been hoping I wouldn't bump into my nemesis. "Fuck fuck fuck!"

"Yeah well, fook you too!" a voice hisses on the line.

"Daffyd Douglas?"

"What's all the fook fook fook about?"

"Nothing. I just saw — oh, nothing. Look, are we going to meet? Today?"

"Be at the Occidental Lazy on Great Windmill Street in three hours. It's off Weegent Stweet." (Despite his less than modest upbringing, he somehow still has that upper-class British inability to pronounce the letter *R*, which either renders a person irresistibly cute or makes them sound like Elmer Fudd.)

I told him I'd find the place. The Occidental Lazy on Great Windmill Street.

I ask Fiona where Mark Larkin and Nan had gone. She tells me they're having lunch at the Ivy. Of course: the Ivy.

After buying an umbrella I take a walk, making sure to look the wrong way before crossing the wrong-way streets. (A few times already, cars have whooshed by me, just inches away.) All the time keeping an eye on my watch I walk to Jermyn Street, just south of Piccadilly. Mark Larkin, before setting off to London, had mentioned that he was going to have three Turnbull and Asser shirts made for him while in London. So I resolved to get four.

Inside the Turnbull and Asser store I try to remain as anonymous as I can, not wanting snooty salespeople to come over and start questioning me. I'm well aware I have no business being in here, but do they have to know it too?

I skirt along the darker boundaries of the store, avoiding eye contact but dazzled by stripes, textures, and prices, but once in a while I catch a glimpse of the other shoppers; I don't know if they're English or Italian or French but they're . . . they're *silver!* Their skin is tanned silver and their hair is silver or flecked with silver and the twinkles in their eyes are silver. There is silver in their clothes and their teeth, and even the black and red they wear somehow is silver. They have silver houses and silver cars and they go to St. Tropez and eat silver food at restaurants with reservations a year in advance and they go to masquerade balls in Venice dressed as silver.

"Can I help you, sir?" a salesman politely asks me.

"I don't think that's possible," I say and then I slip out.

• • •

Squash the Toad, I found when I read it, borders on the unintelligible. It's written entirely in dialect and was not easy to slog through—"thing" was "fing," "and" was "en," "stuff" was "stoof." The word "I" was "ah" (yes, lowercase)—this appeared a lot since it's written in the first person.

Douglas's novel is about two teenagers, a nameless boy (the narrator) and a girl, both part of the rave scene. Because I had little idea of what was being said (the book's memorable last line: "En so ah ha me new gear on, al naff en lithry en sootch, en em riddy en the long big impteh road is awayen me eddin sowf"), I have no idea what happens in the end. I think the girl may have died of an overdose . . . but at one point I was pretty sure that the boy had died, but then I realized that the boy was the narrator and was still writing, *roit?* (Douglas ends every fifth sentence with the word "roit," or "em ah roit?")

My one hope is that Daffyd Douglas doesn't really sound like that in person. I had gotten headache after headache with those Ethan Cawley tapes and I don't want to go through that again.

The Occidental Lazy turns out to be the Oxen and the Daisy, a small smoky chestnut-colored pub in Soho. It's about four o'clock and the sun slightly peeks through the ashy sky. Daffyd Douglas sits by himself at a small table, a pint of Guinness and a pack of cigarettes at the ready.

"One question. This Daffyd thing," I say to him right away. "Don't you realize by calling yourself Daffyd Douglas, the American reader's first thought is: Daffy Duck?"

"Ask me mum and dad about that."

Oh no . . . not another Ethan Cawley.

"What'll it be?" he asks.

I tell him Guinness is fine. He's younger than I and bigger and a lot squarer; his head, the shape of an ice cube, is shaved but some brown dots are coming in here and there . . . he resembles Sluggo from the old *Nancy* comic strip. But there's something likable about him, perhaps his utter lack of affectation.

He slams the pint on the table and I'm surprised that the glass doesn't break. "Your first trip to London?" he asks me.

"Yes, but don't tell anybody that."

I ask him the usual author questions, which writers he admires and which he doesn't, how much of himself he put into *Squash the Toad.* He's pretty forthcoming and, admirably, also loathe to insult someone else in print. He knows he has no chance to win the Booker Prize and says he would pay everything he had *not* to win it.

"So did you wead my book?" he asks, lighting a cigarette. (The son of a Welsh bricklayer, raised by his aunts in Manchester and Hackney, he seems to artfully segue from accent to accent, from drink to drink.) It is now about five pints later, for both of us, and rain taps and plunks the window just behind us.

"I did read it. I have to admit . . . I had some trouble understanding some parts of it. A lot of it."

"I lost track meself what was going on a few times," he jokes.

It's about six o'clock and we're preparing to leave. He's catching a tube to his girlfriend's flat in Fowingdon, he tells me. (Not until I get back to New York did the fact checker who worked on the piece inform me it's Farringdon, not Fowingdon . . . there is no such place as Fowingdon.)

We make an early appointment for tomorrow morning. Harry Brooks will meet us in Soho, outside the pub, and take a few pictures. I tell Daffyd he can buy some clothing and, as long as it's less than two grand, Versailles will cover it, but he says no thanks. My thought is: okay, *I'll* buy two thousand bucks worth of clothing and say he bought it.

"Listen, there is *one* fing," he says a little sheepishly.

Now, from experience I know when someone is about to be photographed for a magazine and they say "there is one thing," it can sometimes be a real doozy. One very famous actor wanted to be shot in a '65 red Mustang and then keep the car . . . and he got it. One actress, equally as renowned, wanted to be photographed naked under a chinchilla coat on a waterbed and she got that and got to keep the chinchilla, of course. "I'll do this shoot as long as I'm wearing the same dress Marilyn Monroe wore and we do it with me bending over the subway grating and it's blowing up the dress," one flamboyant clothing designer once said, and he got that too.

"Okay. What is it?" I ask Daffyd. I'm quite drunk now.

"I don't want to be photographed lookin' 'appy. Just make sure the picture makes me look . . . sort of bwooding."

"I don't think that will be a problem."

We stagger off in different directions, into the bleak brown drizzle.

As the soggy minutes pass, as I breathe in the leaden air, I get drunker and drunker . . . I reek of Guinness and other people's cigarettes and

Royal Cambridge mold. Somehow I find myself on Jermyn Street again. "Okay, I'm smashed," I reason, perhaps aloud, "maybe I'll throw some money down and have a few of these here bespoke shirts sewn up for me." And it won't be my money anymore—it's the Versailles money earmarked for the photo shoot.

It's dark out and I'm not walking too straight and the drizzle has turned into a hard rain. My umbrella is still on the floor in the Occidental Lazy and I'm sopping wet again.

I'm walking directly toward the store. I want to look in the window before going in.

I walk forward.

Oh . . . the store is closed.

I keep walking forward.

A sickening snapping noise sounds from inside my head, my nose goes through the window, glass shatters, alarms ring out deafeningly. Blood is flowing like it's pouring out of a turned-over carton of milk.

"Ohhhh, shit," I groan desolately . . . I almost start to cry. The glass is still breaking. *Chink-chink-chink*, it goes.

My first instinct is to make a run for it. My second is, since I'm running for it, hell, why not swipe a few shirts from out of the now conveniently open window display? But the sirens scare me into common sense.

I wait and the rain pours down. I pull my shirttails out and keep them over my nose. Blood is in my mouth and tastes warm, like stale gravy, and every once in a while more beads of glass fall, either to the street or inside into the display and it sounds to me like slot machines coughing up coins.

Three bobbies finally show up and what a pathetic creature I must be to them—forlorn, water-logged, and blood-soaked. I tell them the truth . . . and feel like an imbecile. (But I *am* an imbecile!) They don't believe me at first but then they realize that nobody, not even an American, would be idiotic enough to concoct such a story.

They're nice enough to drive me to St. Mary's Hospital, near Paddington Station, where I get some some stitches and a bandage (no, a "plaster") the size and shape of a brandy snifter wrapped around my nose—it's broken for the second time in less than three months—and where I'm given a prescription for fifty very strong painkillers.

So it was worth it.

VERY banged up, still drunk, and now very fucked up on codeine, I drop in on—as had been planned in advance—the Usher-Soames house, my collar and most of the other portions of my shirt streaked with blood.

I'm two hours late.

Their house in the Boltons, a little leafy eye-shaped eden, is bone-white and three stories tall, exactly as I've pictured it, and the surrounding houses are also the color of Leslie's skin; there are terraces with columns and balconies and fluttering lace curtains and curvy bay windows and at night, with the moon pouring fog-soaked light down the pillars and awnings, the whole place resembles an immense wedding cake. The Usher-Soames's residence looks right onto a church in the middle of the oval, St. Mary the Boltons, a cobbled seaweed-brown structure.

Being here is not like being in a city, it's like being in a cloud above a city.

But I'm not seeing or thinking straight when I arrive.

I push the buzzer and lean against the front door and almost fall into the foyer slapstick-style when the door is opened.

"Yes?" a tall pale man in a dark suit with a large spherical lump near his right eye says.

"I'm here to see the Usher-Soameses. Will you tell them I'm late?" I say to the butler. "My name's Zachary Post."

"I *am* Trevor Usher-Soames," he says, appalled at the sight of me. "And we're already quite aware you're late."

Only now does it occur to me: I should have called to cancel.

"What in God's name have you done to your nose?" he asks me as I reel in a few steps, holding on to the walls for support and getting my grubby handprints all over them.

"I broke it trying to get some bespoke shirts made. These tailors here . . . they can get kind of rough."

"Could you please wipe your feet on the mat?"

I backtrack, do a brief cha-cha on the fuzzy black mat, which has the family crest on it (or is it just a smiley face?), and then walk in . . . my shoes are wet and make loud squishy noises.

"Hyacinth?" Trevor calls out. While he calls out I try to check out the thing on his right cheek. "Hyacinth?"

Leslie had warned me that her parents were strange, old-fashioned, and stodgy, even by British standards, but she didn't tell me her father could summon forth flowers from their vases and weeds from the soil. Again he calls out: "Hyacinth!"

"I'm coming, Trev . . . please!" someone upstairs trills.

Down the staircase comes Hyacinth Usher-Soames, who, in her prime thirty years ago, might have been the spitting image of Carole Lombard. Now she looks like any rich conservative fifty- to sixty-ish British mother, round rosy cheeks, cream-colored brown hair with silvery accents, and lots of rouge . . . still the both of them are impeccably turned out, Trevor in his blue blazer, red vest, and yellow tie, she in a long black skirt, beige blouse, and pearls.

"My God!" she gasps when she gets an eyeful of my face.

"I don't usually look like this," I say. "May I sit down?"

They make me sign in—on a table near the front door, there is a large fusty book with gilt edges. For a second I think this might be for security purposes, this signing-in business, should some silverware or jewels be missing after I leave, but I flip the pages and see that the book goes back to the 1880s—every single visitor has registered his or her name here. Which means: *my name is now in the same book as Winston Churchill's!* And probably people like Lord Beaverbrook, Anthony Eden, Lady Astor, Evelyn Waugh, and Princess Di, and . . . and who knows who else?

I sit down across from them on one of their matching sofas (the print has exotic Asian flowers as big as human hearts) and describe my day to them; they keep saying, "Oh, dare!" and Hyacinth says at one point: "You seem to be having a rawther difficult time of it, don't you?" I—remember the Guinness, the pills, and the Massapequa—respond: "Fuckin'-A, right, I'm having a rawther difficult time of it!" Trevor coughs loudly at this and the golf ball dangling off his right eye wobbles a few times.

They offer me some tea and I accept. Hyacinth glides across the Persian rug to the kitchen to prepare it.

With her gone, Trevor brings up Colin Tunbridge-Yates.

"Are you going to visit him whilst you're here?"

Leslie had mentioned my visiting Colin as a possibility but this was so preposterous that I dismissed it out of hand.

"No," I tell Trevor, "I'm not really planning on it."

"Leslie and he seem to be having some, shall I say, difficulties? There's always some sort of row or other."

I am one of those difficulties, I want to tell him *whilst* jumping up and down triumphantly on the sofa and pumping my fists.

A thud comes from the kitchen and Trevor scratches his cheeks with his long fingers. He calls out, asks his wife if she's okay, and she calls back and says that she fell, that's all, Trev.

"Yes, they sure do," I say to Trevor, getting back to the difficulties and slowly sliding down the sofa toward the floor.

"I just don't know if he's the right one for her. She can be awfully difficult at times."

(Oh, man . . . he has no idea.)

He asks: "You do have other shirts, don't you?"

I look down at my navy blue shirt. Half of it is now brown, rippling with wrinkles and dampness.

"Just not on me."

Hyacinth glides back into the room holding a silver tea service, probably a family heirloom and something she could sell for a thousand dollars. She has thick calves and I see they're spotted here and there with black-and-blue marks; there are one or two on each arm as well.

"Leslie's been that way since she was a little gull, Trev," she says, setting the tray down on the table between the sofas, her ample bosom (which Leslie hadn't inherited) swinging pendulously. "She gets that from you, dahhrling."

(The mother says *dahhrling* too . . . this could get interesting.)

There are so many items on the tray, it looks as though she's about to perform surgery on my nose. I tally a china cup, a silver container for cream, a tiny gizmo for the sugar, a silver pot for hot water, a pewter pot for honey . . . and so on.

"How the hell does one go about doing this?" I ask, slouching over on the couch but then mustering the wherewithal to sit up.

"Will you please run him through it, Trev?"

Trevor leans forward and the golf ball is a few inches away from me—it's flesh-colored, dimpled, and craggy, and I would like to have seen pictures of him and of it when they were young: Was the thing getting bigger with time or was it always the same size?

He looks up at me and catches me examining it and I look up and start sipping my tea. Gnats are squirming around the bridge of my nose . . . it's the stitches making their presence known.

"Are you quite sure you're all right?" Trevor asks.

Who is he speaking to?

"I said, are you quite sure you're all right?"

"Yes, quite. Quite all right." By now I'm speaking with a British accent, sounding much more British than my hosts.

I sip the tea and feel something strange in it.

"What the hell—"

Part of my bandage has come apart and is swimming around in the teacup. I fish it out and see a little curl of blood on the surface.

"Where can I put this, mate?"

"I'm going out into the garden," Hyacinth says.

I dangle the tea-soaked bandage as though it's a fish I've just caught. It drips tea onto my pants and I stuff it into my jacket pocket. The room fades in and out, going from white to blue.

"Look, Mr. Usher-Soames, I'm not always this . . . what would be the right word? . . . uncouth."

"No, I suppose you're not."

"It's just that—"

"Leslie fairly raves about you on the phone. Several times a week, I daresay."

That's good. Maybe they'll trust her version of me rather than the genuine flesh-and-blood, knocked-out, sopping wet article they're probably anxious to deport from their living room and country.

A light comes on through a large window behind Trevor, where the garden is, and it gives a jaundiced tint to his scalp and ears.

"Does she always go out there when you have slobs over for company?" I ask.

"She goes there to be alone. Sometimes I think that garden is her entire life."

"You know, if your daughter marries Colin Tunbridge-Yates her monogram would be LUSTY? And if you did, it'd be TUSTY? And if your wife did, it'd be HUSTY?"

"Perhaps you ought to be going. I'm going to write down the name of our family doctor. If you mention my name I'm certain she'll see you straight away."

"Nah . . . I'm fine."

We hear a loud thud coming from the garden.

"That's Cinth . . . she's a dropper, always falling down."

Leslie had mentioned this to me, that her mother is a "dropper," but

I'd thought that it was British slang for something, like a teetotaler or someone with a betting addiction. But evidently it's exactly what it sounds like: she falls down a lot.

"Hyacinth?" Trevor calls out, turning so that the golf ball stares me in the face. "Is everything all right? Cinth?"

I begin peeling some of the loose bandage away from my nose.

"You're not drinking your tea."

"There's blood and shit in it. And, anyway, I prefer coffee."

"Hyacinth!"

He goes out into the garden and I want to lie down on the couch, curl up and drift off to sleep . . . so I do.

I wake up when a door shuts. But I don't sit up.

"Oh, dear," Trevor says, more to himself than to me. "Perhaps you ought to be going . . ."

"And why's that?"

"Because my wife has just died."

He phones for an ambulance and then walks me to the front door. He seems remarkably composed, considering his wife of forty years is lying dead in the rain and muddy soil a few yards away.

"I'm really terribly sorry about this," I say.

"I suppose these things must happen but. . . ." He cannot finish the sentence. (He had meant his wife but I was apologizing for me, my appearance and behavior.)

I'm leaning on the stand upon which the register sits. The book looks as though it weighs twenty pounds.

"So Winston Churchill's in here, isn't he?"

"Yes he is."

"What about Virginia Woolf?."

"She's not. Her sister Vanessa is."

"Wow. What about Lord Beaverbrook?"

"Yes. He's in there. Several times."

"Lady Astor?"

"Oh yes. Many times."

"Oswald Mosley?"

"Yes. Should you not be going?"

I open the door and rain thwacks the balcony above my dizzied head.

"Eisenhower? Kay Summersby? At the same time? Did they sleep in the same—"

"Please."

"Look, you can just put Wite-Out over my name on this register and we'll say it never happened, okay?"

He shuts the door behind me, not very gently.

I flag down a taxi on Fulham Road and tell the driver to drop me off on Pennywern Road, where the Hotel Royal Cambridge is. What I say to him actually is: "Yes, the Hotel Royal Cambridge, please," but he says, "Where the bloody 'ell izzat?"

It doesn't take long to get there but when we do, I'm out cold in the backseat and the driver is standing up, leaning over me, shaking my shoulders, trying to rouse me.

"Wake up, wake up," he urges.

"Yeah, okay. Thanks."

"Are you going to be all right, squire?" he says. I recognize in his kind eyes the gaze of a decent, humble human being looking at another human being who is an absolute wreck.

"Hey," I say to him. "I'm no squire. *You're* the squire."

"I'm 'ardly a squire, squire," he says.

"No. *You* the squire. *You* the squire."

I stagger into a phone booth on the corner—one of those classic red hulks—and pump a few pounds into the phone. It's about 6 P.M. in New York, I realize, and I also figure out how to dial overseas directly from the small print instructions in front of me, which eddy around a few times before settling into something readable.

I dial Ivy's number. The machine comes on.

"Are you there? Ivy? It's me. I'm in London and you won't believe this, I busted my nose again . . . Please pick up if you're there . . ." I wait and the machine hangs up on me.

It's a weeknight, I remember—she's probably still at work. So I put in more money and dial her number there.

"Jacqueline Wooten," the voice answers.

"Huh? Who?"

"This is Jacqueline Wooten. Who's this?"

I cannot resist and yell: "Jackie! You're going to die!!"

I slam the phone down (Jacqueline and Ivy's numbers are the same except the final two digits are transposed) and groan and feel faint . . . the bandage is drooping off my nose and getting in my mouth and I find myself chewing on it for some reason.

There are no more coins in my sopping wet pockets.

A card for an escort service—there are dozens and dozens of them over and around the phone—catches my eye. Paddling Pearls of Paddington. There's a line drawing of a big Nazi chick in a leather bustier with spikes and thigh highs and she's wielding a cat-o-nine-tails.

PADDLING PUNCHING FLOGGING WHIPPING BEATING HITTING SMACKING TORMENT SHREDDING BITING EMBARRASSMENT SPANKING DISCIPLINE TORTURE HURTING SLUGGING WHACKING RIPPING CHASTISEMENT CLAWING SPIKING SHAME SCRAPING TWISTING THUMPING GOUGING PUMMELING TWEAKING WALLOPING CONKING THRASHING SINGEING SWATTING CLOBBERING MANGLING PUNISHMENT AND GENERAL HUMILIATION £30

I was going to tell Ivy that I loved and needed her, that I wanted her back and would change, would work myself over from the ground up just to get her back into my life. I would utterly transform myself, be everything she wanted me to be—except deep down in the cockles of me, like a speck of dust with a hundred miles of twine wrapped around it, one molecule of the real me would be hiding and reveling in the trick I've pulled off.

Somehow—as in a slow dissolve—I'm back in my room and I flop onto the sagging heap of mildew that is my bed. Slowly the walls and ceiling turn into a gray mush and I sink in.

The next morning it takes a minute before I realize that the nightmare I'd just had wasn't a nightmare at all but was in fact the entire previous day.

After an ice cold shower—the water hitting the stitches agonizes yet invigorates—I get dressed and go downstairs to a phone booth and wait ten minutes.

When I call the doctor that Trevor Usher-Soames had recommended, I ask the receptionist if I can come over right away. When she says no, I tell her "I'm engaged to marry Leslie Usher-Soames, the daughter of Trevor and Hyacinth Usher-Soames, who died last night." After putting me on hold for thirty seconds, she then tells me I can come right over. It is not quite a Harley Street address but is close.

• • •

Dr. Miranda Currie has no idea that Hyacinth had perished the night before and when I tell her she says, "Well, I suppose one could see that coming, couldn't one? Always falling as she was." She redoes my stitches and after she's told the Turnbull and Asser story, she says, "Oh yes . . . I read about that."

"You did?"

"Yes. In the *Times*. This morning."

She asks me if the doctors at St. Mary's had given me anything for the pain. I lie and tell her they hadn't.

She writes out a prescription for fifty painkillers and a few minutes later I'm in the nearest Boots pharmacy. I get the pills, then cab it over to the Oxen and the Daisy in Soho.

Daffyd Douglas and Harry are already there, waiting outside.

"Where have you been?" Harry says when I get there.

"You wouldn't believe me. I'm only ten minutes late."

He gets an eyeful of my face — Dr. Currie had applied a new bandage — and says, "What, did a truck hit you or something?"

"I'd rather not talk about it."

"I only got here just now meself," Daffyd says.

"This is going to be quick," Harry tells us.

While he whips out his light meter and positions Daffyd against the facade of his favorite Soho haunt, I ask the author a few more questions and he cautiously fields them all.

While Harry measures and then starts clicking away I fantasize about: marrying Leslie and moving to London, taking over at *Ego, U.K.* when Nan Hotchkiss gets recalled (like tainted meat) to the States; I imagine living in that plaster wedding cake (after Trevor passes on), the creamy pillars and frothy white tiers, and I see Leslie milling around and bending over in the back garden, only a few feet from where her mother took her final spill. And then there's our house, our manor or cottage in the countryside somewhere (I'm assuming they've got one). And when all of it gets too unbelievable, I'll ring up Daffyd Douglas and we'll knock back a few pints and plunk down a few quid at William Hill's and pay some 300-pound Nazi vixen to spank and gouge us back into reality.

Daffyd Douglas tells me he's in the process of recording an audio version of *Squash the Toad*.

"Is that really going to help people understand it, make it more accessible?"

"Ah weally dunno."

"Could we have a few smiles, Daff?" Harry asks him. Remembering the author's request, I pull aside the photographer and tell him that Douglas wishes to be photographed bwooding.

"Okay. No smiles then," Harry says.

I ask Daffyd what his next book is going to be about.

"Went boys."

"What are those? *Went* boys?"

"Went. Like a car for hire?"

"Rent! Rent!"

He's going to write about a group of young male runaways who sell their bodies to older men and then slit their throats.

"Your typical cheery stuff."

"Yeah . . . *roit*."

I'm playing with the rolls of Harry's film in my pocket as Daffyd and I walk to Charing Cross Road.

"One thing I would like to ask you . . . How come you didn't want this interview to be faxed or done over the phone?"

"I might've preferred that. Christ, it would've helped you out too . . . your nose at least."

"But I was told you wanted to do this interview in person."

"I don't know why, mate," he says. We're on Charing Cross Road now and a bus screeches to a halt. "Sounds like someone doozent want you around, doozent it?"

{ }

AFTER HE descends into the tube station I walk to Longacre and the *Ego, U.K.* offices. Fiona, the gorgeous lethargic receptionist from yesterday, isn't there and instead there sits a plump young woman with a butch haircut, two nose rings, and very ruddy cheeks.

"Hi, I'm Zachary Post. I work for *It* in New York," I say to her, showing her my Versailles ID. "Is Nan Hotchkiss in?"

"Now."

"Yes, is she in now?"

"Now!"

"Yes! Right now! Tell her it's Zack Post."

She rolls her eyes and I start over; it goes on for another thirty seconds but the upshot is I'd mistaken her "no" for "now." Nan doesn't come in, she tells me, usually until eleven o'clock.

I tell her I'll return then and, walking down the stairs, I marvel at a life wherein you do not have to show up at work until eleven.

I buy a *Times* and go to a small sandwich shop right across the street and read all about . . . me. I've been imagining wedding announcements for Leslie and myself in the *Times* of London for months but never anything like this. Roddy Grissom had to be stabbed in the chest with scissors to get in the papers; me, I had to walk into the window of Turnbull and Asser.

I see Nan Hotchkiss walk by outside and follow her into her office.

"You seem to be making quite a hit in London, Zeke," she says, slapping her copy of the *Times* down on her desk.

"Jesus, I hope this doesn't get back to New York."

"Well, I certainly won't tell anyone." *What a liar!* She probably had stopped at a phone booth on the way and called twenty people. "Did they treat you well in hospital?"

"No, they didn't treat me too well in *the* hospital," I tell her as I sit down and check out her surroundings.

"If you stick around you might run into Mark Larkin. He's going to stop in for a bit."

"Then I won't stick around."

"Yes, he can be something of a wanker, can't he?"

My nose begins to ache and feel warm. I ask Nan about Fiona and she asks me if I "fancy" her.

So the Filofax-toting bloodhound had been in England less than six months but now sounds as though she'd grown up here.

"Nan, my hotel is a serious, serious dump."

"Which one is it again?"

"The Hotel Royal Cambridge. Betsy Butler arranged it for me. I always thought she liked me but—"

"Oh, that was my idea! I remember now. I mentioned it to Velma on the phone and she must have told Betsy."

We speak for a few more minutes about trivial things and I begin getting antsy—the last thing I want is to run into Mark Larkin . . . not with my nose all over the London papers.

"When are you coming to work for me?" she says out of nowhere. (Or maybe not out of nowhere but I just wasn't listening.) "We need good editors over here." Their launch issue had come out a month before and was neither well-received nor particularly well-done, though just how not well-done I wasn't impertinent enough to say. And besides, she's hinting at a job offer . . .

"You know, you told me that you'd recommend to Regine and others that I get your old job at *It*. Do you remember that? You told me I had important fish."

"Yes, I remember." Her phone rings and I hear the plump receptionist tell Nan over the speaker it's her husband on line three. She says, "I'll ring him up in a minute, Mary." She leans forward and says to me, "I did recommend you."

"But you also told Willie that. And Ollie and probably everybody else."

"Well, maybe I recommended them too."

"But Jackie got the job."

"Jacqueline. Yes. I put in a few good words for her too."

"I think that—" My voice breaks off.

"Yes? What do you think?"

"Nothing. I think absolutely nothing."

She was above me . . . she had the power. Maybe one day she'd hire me . . . as a senior editor, a deputy editor, as *something*. I couldn't alienate her now. It's a position I've found myself in since kindergarten: the ones I want to dump building blocks on, the ones I want to bite, hit, scream at, I can't . . . because I might need them someday.

Walking down the stairs to leave, I see a familiar face walking up. It's Hamish Courtnall, *Ego's* art director, who had mistaken me for Mark Larkin at Meg Bunch's apartment.

"We met in New York. At Meg Bunch's party," I say.

"Yes. Oh my. What happened to you?" He's looking right at where my nose would be.

"Nothing. I always wear this bandage except when I go to one of Meg Bunch's soirees."

"We're running your story next issue," he says as I take four more steps down.

"Which one?"

"The one on Muffy Tate."

I want to grab the potato-nosed elf by his ankles—which are about eye-level to me now—and drag him down the stairs, his head going *thump-thump-thump* each time his jaw hits another step, just like in *Pickup on South Street.*

"That's not my story," I say. "Okay? I'm me . . . I'm not the other guy."

And then I leave the building.

A few minutes later on the corner of Garrick Street and St. Martin's Lane I pull out my "Streetwise: London" map and try to set a course through Soho to New Bond Street. There being no way I ever show my battered mug on Jermyn Street again.

"What happened to you, old boy?" a familiar loathsome voice says.

I don't even look up.

"I broke my nose and I don't want to talk about it."

"Has Nolan Tomlin moved to London?" He laughs at his own joke, which is, I admit, not a bad one. "I'm surprised you need a map, Post. I should think you knew London rother well."

Now I look up. Mark Larkin has on a light blue cotton shirt with a pink collar and a navy blue blazer.

"I'm just trying to reorient myself."

"If you've nothing to do, you can walk me to my club."

He has a club . . . Mark Larkin is in some gentleman's club. A dark wood-paneled room, right out of Trollope's Palliser books, mahogany paneling and teak tables and mile-high ceilings and windows that airplanes can fly through and waiters in livery and plates full of mutton and glasses of sherry and port and men in tweed playing whist and mumbling incoherently. Mark Larkin belongs there and I would never get past the door, not because I'm a nigger or a kike but because I'm . . . me. I never even had a tree house as a kid but this son of a bitch belongs to some hotshot club. He *belongs.*

"Well," I say, "I'm going to Oxford Street." I'm hoping this is out of his way; wherever the clubs are, it seems they won't be in that direction.

"I'll walk you there."

We walk to Charing Cross Road and make a right. Somewhere along the way he says: "Well, I think I have enough at last to finish my story on Lord Wincher."

"When's he going to kick the bucket?"

"Not a moment too soon."

We're walking past Foyle's and he's on my right and occasionally our elbows touch. Were I not stuck with this pink blotchy ulcer, I could go into Foyle's and browse.

"I thought you liked him."

"Oh, I do, I do. But I will be in receipt of a swell little Alfred Sisley doodle upon his death."

"And you'll hang it over the roll of toilet paper or behind the towel rack?"

Up ahead I hear the hacking sighs and squeals of traffic on Oxford Street.

"Oh, I'll find someplace. I *am* moving after all."

"I was wondering when you'd get out of the East Village."

"I won't be terribly far, Post. Skeffington Towers."

To my left is a small winding street and beyond that are the porno shops, stores, and cafes of Soho. The sun is out finally, for the first time since my plane landed, but my nose aches dully.

"When you were at Liverpool," he asks me, "what did you read?"

"What did I read? You mean, what did I study?"

"Precisely."

"A few different things. Why?"

"And where did you live?"

"What does it matter . . ."

"It matters because I was just there. That's where I did my research on Lord Wincher. And I also got a chance to do some research on *you*."

I'm sunk . . . I'm a dead man. I'll be fired. He'll go back to New York, tell Regine and Human Resources and I'm out the door. They'll ask me: "So where *did* you really go to college?" and I won't even answer . . . I'll just get up and leave. Quickly I envision my next jobs: waiting tables, working in a copy shop or a coffee bar, cleaning apartments. Working someplace where I really belonged.

"So you know then. Big deal."

"When I saw that mother of yours . . ."

He stops, knowing that insulting my mother is beneath him. But he also knows that he doesn't have to insult her—she comes self-insulted, like a toy with batteries.

"I'm willing to swap," he says. "You give me the tape and nobody ever finds out about this."

"I don't make that deal."

Ahead of us ungainly red double-decker buses bound along on bustling Oxford Street.

"It seems like a good one to me," he says.

Of course it seems good to him: if I give him the tape then I have nothing on him anymore, but he still would have the information about me. So I'm safe. Making double skinny lattes and photocopying some idiot's screenplay is deferred, thanks to a tape that doesn't even exist.

"Don't even try it. If I ever give you that tape, it means I made twenty copies."

"Clever of you to choose Liverpool, Post."

"Thanks."

"And Robertson James Post?"

"What do you think?"

"No such animal?"

"Probably not."

We're now on a busy corner, where Charing Cross Road becomes Tottenham Court Road and Oxford Street becomes New Oxford Street. It's hectic and loud, taxis and buses and cars and people going every way, cars turning without slowing down and people moving and stopping in spasms and spurts.

"Perhaps I'll go to the British Museum," he says aloud to himself.

To my right about thirty yards away, just over the top of Mark Larkin's head, the word VICTORY in pearly white is coming our way. The sun turns Mark Larkin's hair into mustard and tumbleweed and my nose throbs. A small street sign indicates the direction of Bloomsbury and the British Museum.

"Maybe I'll go there too," I say.

I step off the curb, down into the street. VICTORY is actually VICTORIA, I see now, and is written on the front of the Number 8 bus heading west, coming right toward us.

"We should go there together," I suggest.

He takes a step into the street.

"So what club do you belong to anyway?" I ask him.

He's not facing me but is looking straight ahead.

He begins what might his last words on Earth: "Well, as it happens I belong—"

I step back onto the sidewalk and yell: "LOOK OUT!!!"

He does what I assume he would: he looks the wrong way, which is, practically everywhere else in the civilized world, the *right* way, that is, he looks to his left. But the bus is bearing down on him from his right and, with the sun shining so brightly, the driver doesn't see him. Mark Larkin, when the double-decker is just about to mow him down, then turns the other way . . . he steps back onto the sidewalk but the front corner of the bus sideswipes him and sends him flying onto his ass. Right at my feet.

He's okay. Perhaps an inch more out into the street or one tenth of a second without turning and he'd be mashed potatoes and ketchup.

A crowd of about ten people encircles him, still sitting down on the sidewalk. His face is dictionary red . . . he's huffing and shaken. Two men help him up and ask if he's okay and he brushes off his jacket and doesn't thank them.

He looks at me and combs his hair with his hands. His forehead is coated with sweat. I look back at him, say nothing, do nothing, show nothing.

There is a ghastly look in his eyes.

He's wondering if I just tried to kill him. And he doesn't know that the answer is yes.

{ }

NEWS IN BRIEF
Shop window broken

The windows of Tumbull and Asser were shattered late yesterday afternoon when a tourist visiting London from America walked directly into them. Zachary Post, 32, of New York City, suffered a broken nose and was treated at St Mary's Hospital, Paddington. It was the second time in less than half a year that Mr Post had broken his nose, he told police inspectors on the scene, but the first time he had ever done so shopping for shirts.

The windows of the famous clothier on Jermyn Street should be repaired some time within the next few months, a Turnbull and Asser spokesman said. Mr. Post's previous injury was incurred when he had a row with Nolan Tomlin, the renowned southern American novelist, he said.

14

"CHRIST, WHAT happened to you?!" Liz asks me when I step into my apartment.

"I'll tell you all about it."

I'd forgotten that she was staying there, forgotten until I walked in and saw the place looking immaculate. For a second I think someone has robbed the place and, rather than leave a turd on the floor as some burglars are said to do, had also done me the favor of straightening out the entire apartment.

I take a shower while she reads the *Times* clip I'd brought back.

When I sort through my mail Liz hits me with the bombshell.

"Willie's been relocated. To the Black Hole."

"Proofreading? Please tell me he's not proofreading."

"He's not. He's fact-checking. As a matter of fact he's sitting in Laurie Lafferty's old spot."

"Then who's sitting across from me now?"

"Nobody just yet."

"How's he taking it?"

"He comes in, he does his work, he leaves."

That was why they sent me to London—it all sinks in now. Mark Larkin was in England and I was in England and they made the move; Mark Larkin knew about it in advance, of course, and I did not. What was it that Daffyd Douglas had said to me? *Sounds like someone doozent want you around, doozent it?*

It was devious, it was brilliant. You have to give them credit.

{ }

MY FIRST day back I make a point of avoiding Willie because I don't know what to say. He's got to be seething with anger, about to blow to bits.

I'm going through my teeming in-box, catching up on things, when Betsy approaches me with an alarmingly solemn expression.

"Byron doesn't want to make a public announcement," she tells me in a voice a shade above a whisper. "He doesn't want a party atmosphere. He's resigning due to illness effective tomorrow."

"Oh, Jesus. That's terrible."

It doesn't take long to play out the musical chairs and the results I get are not happy ones. Byron quits, Marjorie takes over as art director, Leslie moves up. And with Leslie moving up, she would be through with me; how often do girls in the tenth grade go out with boys in the eighth?

"Do we know who's going to replace him?" I ask Betsy.

"Well, I'm sure you realize that nobody can."

I nod.

"But," Betsy goes on, "there are a few candidates."

"You've heard?" Marjorie says to me.

"Yes, it's very sad. Congratulations."

"For what? It's not a done deal yet."

"And if they *don't* give you the job . . ."

"Then I'd have to quit."

"Well, there you go."

"When it's time to rip the bandage off your nose," she offers, "give me a holler."

Leslie isn't even aware of her possible good fortune. She hurried to England to mourn the passing of Hyacinth Usher-Soames, who was buried with her gardening tools and some soil (as if there wouldn't be enough soil all around her). Leslie had sent me an e-mail before she departed, saying she appreciated my getting her father the roses. (*What* roses? Did I send him roses?)

It's my guess that after she arrived, after her mother had been laid into the ground she loved so well, Trevor, over a few Tanquerays and tonics and a plate of boiled eels at some plush hotel bar, would tell her the rest of the story.

And the pale vulture Colin Tunbridge-Yates would probably be hovering around too.

"So?" Willie says.

"So?"

"Come on . . . how was England?"

"The same as when I left it years ago."

"But you never left it."

With blow-by-blow detail I describe all that happened, finishing the story by telling him I now have enough painkillers to wipe out several elephants.

"Fact-checking sure can be fun," he tells me expressionlessly. We're near a window looking out over the Chrysler Building and sunlight winks off the silver eagle heads.

"Why don't you just do the honorable thing?" I suggest.

"Disembowel myself at a meeting?"

"No. Quit. Just get out and start over."

"No. They'll have to fire me." But it takes a lot to get fired at Versailles. There are so many other ways of getting rid of people: demotions, relocations, reassignments, and what they're doing to Willie now, forcing him to quit or lose face. It's like a rich family with a lunatic child: get the lobotomy done, stash the kid into a faraway loony bin, and never once talk about it again.

"Who do you think your new cell mate will be?" he asks me. "What if it's Ivy Kooper?"

"You've got to be kidding me! Is that really a possibility?"

"I don't know. I'm sure there are lots of assholes down in the office Asshole Pool."

"Yeah, that's where they found me too. Would they really move Ivy up so fast?"

"Well, she went to that fancy high school, didn't she?"

Nightingale-Bamford! I might be hoisted by that petard . . .

Out of nowhere Willie says, "At least I'm well-armed."

I flash him a feeble smirk and he says, "For purposes of self-defense only, I assure you. And I did buy a new TV set."

I don't say anything but I imagine him sitting up in a chair in the darkness every night, facing his front door and waiting for a knock, or a faint change in the light under the door slit, or a creak of the floorboards; maybe he thinks the CIA or FBI or the Inter-Galactic Dream Police will barge in any second. He probably sees mystical writing in the paint chips on his ceiling.

"You're still interested in knocking Mark Larkin off?" I ask.

"As much as I ever was. That bastard sent *you* to England and not me and then gave me the one-way ticket to fact-checking Palookaville."

"He knows I didn't go to Liverpool University. He knows all about my family, or lack thereof."

"How do we do it?"

"You had an idea once, remember? We were talking about the Beer Hall Putsch. You said, like, poison him or something?"

"Yeah, poison's good. An overdose of something. And hey! You've got all those painkillers now too!"

"But the police. If he takes five hundred Percocets—"

"What we do," he suggests, "is make it look like a suicide."

"It looks easy on paper. But how do we do that?"

"We just get him to write a suicide note first."

I'd been thinking about this on the plane back from England. But I want Willie to think we're making it up as we go along . . . or that *he's* making it up.

He says: "It doesn't seem so hard. He's got his memo pads and everything."

He fell right into it.

If only I didn't like him so much . . .

{ }

OTHER THAN a week-long fling with a waitress who'd been kicked out of her apartment, I've never lived with a woman before. But it's nice having Liz in my apartment. (She sleeps on the living room couch, I sleep in my bed.) When I wake up in the morning I make coffee for her and sometimes she brings me orange juice. We take turns getting the *Times*. It's a welcome change to hear something other than my own morning grumbles and snorts.

Her husband calls once a while. I always make sure to be out of the room for this. And Ollie calls too . . . I can tell it's him. She walks the phone into a corner and puts on a wistful expression. My guess is their relationship has cooled, that Ollie had assumed he was due for a whole big relationship and isn't so content now to play the role of dismissed *cicisbeo*. (She still doesn't know I know.)

There's a time of day in the office, usually between 4:30 and 5:30, that I call the "Dinner Call Hour." Husbands, wives, girlfriends and boyfriends call up to decide that evening's plans, when they'll be home, what to eat, which movie to see, etc. You can tell when this is happening: feet are on the desk and people are smiling, doodling, daydreaming. Liz and I go through this together now and it's fun being a part of the Adult Race for a change; I'll call her or she'll call me (even though we're only four cubicles apart) and we'll settle on Chinese or going out for Italian.

This whole thing is like a dry run for a marriage. But I know that when the real thing does come along, it's just not going to be this smooth.

{   }

I'M AT my desk, furious, looking at some copy of mine that Mark Larkin has virtually destroyed. He's overhauled the whole thing, even changed the font I'd used (from Courier to Dom Casual, that fuck!); hardly one word is the same and now there are phrases and words I wouldn't use if someone paid me (and someone *is* paying me): "roué," "moue," and "louche," for example. It's the Letter from the Editor and I'd done the June-is-busting-out-all-over motif. As I weigh going into his office to raise a fuss, he emerges, tells me he's going out for lunch, and strides past me.

I walk into his office. The sun is streaming in, turning the Mylanta masterpiece into something boiling, iridescent, and disgusting. Making sure to appear very purposeful, just in case someone walks in, I stand over his in-box, but I have a clear view out the door and nobody will catch me. I go into his e-mail and quickly write:

TO: POSTZ
FROM: LARKINM
SUBJECT:

Post: Do you still have any of those painkillers? I have an absolutely throbbing headache. Have had quite a few of them of late.
Thnx.
Larkin.

I send it to myself and hustle back to my desk. Where I write him back:

I have tons of them and don't really need them. They're yours.

I trot back to his desk and write to me:

Post: I appreciate it, really.
The more the merrier. Absolutely throbbing.

Back at my desk I sit down and reread Regine's letter . . . would twenty thousand readers cancel their subscriptions if they knew that some nobody from Massapequa had written it? My armpits are soaked but I feel good, I feel satisfied with my bravery. Such *cojones*! I read the copy twice and make some notes in the margins. Who really gives a shit about it anymore? It's as if somebody I didn't know had written it now, and "louche" really isn't such a bad word, is it? No petulant moues from *this* roué.

{ }

MARJORIE did get the job . . . that was a no-brainer.

There's a big lunch in her honor at Florian's in SoHo and the entire magazine staff is there . . . and some other Versailles people show up, Martyn Stokes and some of the three-piece-suit types with the million-dollar salaries and shares in the company. Her appointment makes the *Times* and it might be one of the few times she's ever read that paper.

Liz and Ollie and some others are at my table, along with some fashion assistants. Behind me is the Black Hole table and when I turn around I can see only Willie's shoulders: their table is in a dark corner and there are three pillars in the way. (It's like the "kids' table.") Sitting next to him is the Phantom, a proofreader whose skin is so pale you can see her veins from twenty yards away. She's quiet and seems spectral enough to pass through walls. Ivy sits across from me, three seats down, and when she catches me peeking at her she looks down and nervously plays with her napkin. Ollie and Liz are directly across from each other . . . maybe they're playing footsie or Ollie is trying to and Liz is pulling her foot away.

Ted Tarrant, *It*'s publisher, makes a little speech but—typical of his lack of social skills—never refers to Marjorie; instead he dwells on ad revenue, circulation, our growth curve. Betsy then stands up and tells us what a thrill it is for her to announce that Marjorie is our new art director. When Marjorie stands up, it is to as thunderous an ovation as 140 hands can muster. She isn't able to summon up a blush . . . surprising since she's usually so red, her hair, cheeks, skin and so on; this might be because she's imagined this very scene so many hundreds of times that for her it's already happened.

"Thanks so much, everybody," she says, looking radiant. She tells us the transition will be "seamless" and when she says that word I remember how (I still haven't figured this one out) one night I arrived at her apartment and she was tied up with a pair of black stockings. "How'd you do this?" I asked her and she replied with a laugh, "I didn't. The guy before you did." (I assumed she was kidding.)

We finish our desserts and coffee and it's time to head back to work.

I exit Florian's with Liz and Ollie and we walk toward the subway. Behind us sounds the clanky racket of car doors opening and closing and chauffeurs scurrying.

I turn around and see: Ted Tarrant, Marjorie, and Betsy getting into a limo, then behind them Mark Larkin gets into another one with Martyn Stokes and two of the three-piece suits.

Mark Larkin getting into a limousine. It's sickening.

The cars pull out and I see Willie standing under the restaurant's awning with the Phantom. A breeze blows Willie's thinning hair around. The Phantom puts on a pair of Wayfarers but it seems they're just hanging in the air, like something in a comedy movie about ghosts. Willie watches Mark Larkin's car slowly head up Sixth Avenue and he turns to me with a chillingly vacant expression.

He would kill him. That's what the look says. He would do it and he doesn't really give a damn if he gets caught or not.

{ }

LESLIE was away for one week. Versailles' policy is to give you five mourning days and that's it; if you need one more day, they come off your vacation days. If you don't use any mourning days over the course of a year, they don't roll over into the next year; so when Lori Crook's cat (she's our production manager—Lori, not her cat) died last year, Lori got five days off and when her twin sister died a few weeks later it didn't matter: she had shot her mourning wad.

When Leslie gets back I meet her at the airport and we take a Town Car (via Jihad Car Service) back to Manhattan. She looks drawn out and very pale—this could be from the long flight and, of course, her skin is normally pale—but she does look as though someone very close to her has recently died.

"How was it?" I ask as the car rumbles toward the LIE. It is past midnight and there's hardly any traffic.

"Awful," she says. "I never want to go through that again."

(Well, with one parent left she'd only have to go through it one more time.)

"I read your mother's obituary in the *Times* of London when I got back."

"The funeral was excellently done, I thought."

"I'm sure it was."

"Very much to the point. Not sentimental."

Silence for a while. And then she says: "I'm so glad you met her. It means rather a lot to me."

"I'm glad too. I mean, just think . . . one more day and it would have been too late for me."

I check to see if she's looking at me and if so, how . . . but she's not. Had I not shown up at the Boltons in such a miserable state, Hyacinth would still be alive. (I don't know if this is true but I've convinced myself that it is.)

But from the way Leslie looks and sounds I deduce: her father hadn't spilled the beans on me. Or not all the beans.

"She died doing what she loved," I say.

"Did you get a chance to see the garden?"

"No, I didn't, I'm afraid."

"Why was she out there at night?"

"I don't know. I'm not much in the way of a green thumb."

"No, I suppose you're not."

We drive past the dreary houses and shabby stores of Queens, a fried chicken hut covered with splintery wooden boards, a tire store with taped-up windows, a rug store going out of business. In the lobby of a drab old folks' home—or "manor"—a TV flickers blue and white light on four slumped over men either sleeping or dead. Far ahead, the lights of the World Trade Center, the Empire State Building, and the Chrysler Building twinkle into view.

I ask if she'd seen any old friends when she was in London.

"Yes. Quite a lot of them. And family too. There were over two hundred people at the funeral."

"Was Colin one of them?"

"Yes. Of course he was."

"Byron Poole quit," I tell her.

She looks at me, rests her cheek on an index finger, and says with suddenly re-illuminated eyes: "*Really?*"

"Yes. Due to illness."

"That doesn't surprise me. Sad though."

My eyes catch a familiar sight: my mother's building. The gigantic piece of toast is just a long brown smear but a blue TV light glimmers dimly in her bedroom window . . . a *Matlock* rerun.

"Has any announcement been made?" she asks.

"Marjorie got the job."

"That's really great," she says without the slightest hint of glee. Now, she knows there was no way *she'd* get the job—jumping over Marjorie was too impossible even to dream about. But still she envies Marjorie's good fortune, finds it unwelcome and irritating, and it's something admirable in her, that she can't even be bothered to disguise her distaste.

"I suppose she must be very happy," she adds. Her index finger leaves a little rose petal in her cheek.

"She's downright ecstatic."

"Any other sort of announcements?"

By which she means: *Have I, Leslie Usher-Soames, also been promoted?* This is the killing blow that will surely come; as soon as she gets promoted I'll be downsized out of her life.

"No. None yet."

The blue and silver lights of Manhattan float and flash in the air but then we're suddenly inside a dark airless tunnel.

{   }

"I HAVE to see you right away," Willie says to me.

We walk into one of the doorways that leads to the Black Hole. I always avoid going in there, afraid that, if both my feet were to touch the shaggy carpet, I'd never be able to extricate myself from the pile. The walls, desks, and chairs are black and the dim lights inside have the same eerie aquamarine aura of an Italian funeral parlor.

"He's a fraud," Willie says, out of breath and sweaty. "Mark Larkin went to Harvard one year and then dropped out! Shit, I don't even know if he ever graduated from *anywhere!*"

"Jesus, even *I* lasted three years," I say. (But the math isn't so simple; maybe one year of Harvard equals twenty of Hofstra.)

"This is fantastic!" he says.

I should be elated but I'm saddened in a way . . . the empty feeling you get when you know you should be thrilled but you feel nothing.

He tells me how he'd contacted an old Harvard chum, now a professor there. The friend had combed through the appropriate files and found that Mark Larkin had spent two semesters at Harvard and never even bothered taking his finals for the second.

"This is fantastic!" he says again, smelling blood, his nostrils actually flaring.

"What are you going to do with this?"

"I'm going right to the top, man."

"But Willie, see . . . he knows I'm a fraud. If you expose him, he'll take me down with him."

"You mean, we're just going to sit on this?"

He gazes off into space, lost and lonely.

"I'm sorry."

"Whose side are you on anyway?" he asks.

Is he seeing a conspiracy? Does he assume I've joined the team of Mark Larkin and the World versus the team of Him?

I tell him I'm on our side, his and mine.

He turns around, looks at his new work space, a small dark cubicle with some books in a sloppy pile, a crumpled up *Times*, some pens and pieces of paper. He can barely fit in there.

"Okay," he says. "I understand. I do."

He returns to his desk, squeezes into the chair, hunches over, and ruffles some paper.

Mark Larkin knows I'm a fraud and now I know he's one too. One cancels the other out. If I spill the beans on him, I'm as dead as he is.

But that's how I want him: dead. Him getting fired isn't good enough. I just don't want him alive anymore . . . anywhere.

"THESE ARE pretty serious charges," Maureen O'Connor says to me one sunny afternoon in her office.

"That's why it took me so long to come forward."

"Is there anyone else to corroborate this?"

"I don't know . . . I don't know."

Maureen O'Connor is *It's* Human Resources rep; she has jet black hair, eyes the size of eggs, and a forehead big enough to put advertising on; she's about six-foot-three.

"You tell me Mark is a racist," she says, "but what I need to know is, has he ever *acted* on it?"

"Like, you mean, prevented anybody's career mobility because they were African American or Latino or Latina or said something hurtful directly to someone because they're African American or Latino or Latina? I'm not aware of that, no."

"So it's just a case of him talking?"

"Yes. And frankly I'm sick of it. Nigger, spick, kike, all the time . . . If it's not blacks it's Jews and if it's not Jews it's the Irish—"

Maureen Mary O'Connor blinks just then. I continue:

"And it's terrible what he says. It's disgusting. If Lourdes Ballesteros or Seth Horowitz were ever to hear it . . ."

"Well, I'm glad that you finally came forward with this."

I stand up and peek back at the chair I'd been sitting in. There are small brass rivets going up along the back of it and I see one red rivet among the others and, three rivets above, another red one. I've heard this rumor for years and now I believe it's true: there is the five-foot-six rivet and the six-foot rivet; if a prospective female employee doesn't come up to the first or a male doesn't come up to the second, their chances of getting work at Versailles are slim.

Maureen walks me to the door of her office and opens it.

"I hope I've done the right thing," I say to her bashfully. "And please, Maureen, don't get me in trouble."

"Everything that goes on here," she assures me, "remains confidential."

IT DOESN'T take long. It's noon, only two days after her plane touched down at JFK.

TO: POSTZ
FROM: USHERSOAMESL
SUBJECT:
It's happened.

I don't even have to ask what It is. But I do, just to give her, I suppose, the exquisite pleasure of telling me.

What's happened?! Something bad?

Which perfectly sets her up to write me back:

No. Something absolutely terrific! I've been promoted!

As I write back to congratulate her I try to surmise how long it will be before she breaks up with me (as I do so, I can hear Colin Tunbridge-Yates's wings flapping overhead, blowing the dry dust around my carcass). I give myself two weeks, figuring it will be a few days before the announcement is made, a few more days before she realizes I have to go, and another few days before she can summon up the courage to go through with it.

But only one minute into my calculations, she writes me:

We have to talk.

And that evening she gives me my walking papers, telling me with icy light brimming in her eyes: "It's just not right."

That night I'm home and Liz is out . . . she's out with Astro-hubby having dinner in his neighborhood, her old neighborhood.

I've brought some work home with me. Mark Larkin needs some research done and I didn't want to go to the library in the daytime. The research is on Garson Locke, the ninety-year-old publisher; it's for a feature Mark Larkin is writing, one I hope he won't live to finish. What is never mentioned in meetings or between Mark Larkin and myself but is certainly understood is: Mark Larkin wrote a puff piece about Muffy Tate and then Muffy Tate became his agent. A collection of his essays was shopped around and Garson Locke, the president of Lakeland & Barker, purchased it. And now a puff piece is being done on Garson Locke.

After an hour of work I put everything aside. The place seems so empty without Liz. I've forgotten what living alone is like—to be honest, living alone wasn't so bad until someone moved in, and now being alone is terrible.

So I take a taxi up to Ivy Kooper's house.

I call her from a pay phone and to my surprise, she picks up, perhaps expecting someone else.

"It's me."

"Who?"

"Zachary. Can I see you?"

"I don't know."

"Please. I'm desperate."

"Have you been drinking?"

"No. Not one drop." Which is the truth, and I resent her thinking otherwise; it's an annoying stereotype that when a man makes a desperate phone call such as this one, he must be drunk.

"Where do you want to meet?" she asks.

"Just come downstairs."

I wait in her lobby and endure her doorman's demeaning stare. Ivy comes down in three minutes and she smiles embarrassedly at this scowling epauletted czar from Brighton Beach as she blows past him. She's wearing brown corduroy pants and a red checked Gap shirt, the top two buttons unbuttoned. We walk downtown a few blocks on Park Avenue, then sit on a bench on a traffic island that separates uptown traffic from downtown.

"I really would like to get you back into my life," I tell her as soon as we sit down.

"I think it's too late for this."

"I'll do anything you want. Anything. Plastic surgery, a soul transplant, you name it."

"This isn't—"

"I tried to call you from London."

"Yeah, you left a message."

"I was going to tell you . . . well, whatever . . ."

"Were you drunk then?"

"Yes. *Then* I was. But that doesn't mean I didn't mean it."

She stares straight ahead, toward Grand Central Station, and a breeze blows her hair into my eyes. "Did you and Leslie break up or something?"

"Yes. But that's got nothing to do with it." She shakes her head, smiles, and I resume. "Really, it doesn't. I think you should give me another shot."

"I can't."

"I'm worth another shot."

"You sure about that?"

"No."

We don't say anything for a while and then she says: "When I saw you leave the party with Leslie . . . that was like dying inside."

I feel so bad that I can't tell her I'm sorry. Instead I wait a minute and ask her, "Are you going out with someone?"

"That's none of your business, is it?"

"No. It's not, I guess."

"You know, you might be my boss someday. How smart would it be if we were going out and you were my boss?"

Well, she's right about that: that would be insane, ludicrous, impossible. But it uplifts me for a moment because: *if that's the only reason she can come up with for not being my girlfriend, then maybe there's some hope.* After all, she hadn't told me she despised the very sight of me!

"Please. Just give it some thought. I swear to you, I can be a good person. I can try."

She stands up, puts her hand briefly on the top of my head, and pats me. I'm hunching forward on the bench. She walks away, her hair frizzy and blowing around, and I must look like a bum, destitute, dejected, homeless, and hopelessly alone.

Somewhere in that conversation I was right on the verge of telling her about her father and Marjorie Millet. It was like undigested food coming back up into my mouth, chewed bits of steak and potatoes mixed in with sizzling stomach acid. I wanted to spit it out but it crept back down to its rightful place. I think I just wanted to show her the world was not such a great place, that heartbreaking, horrible things happened and were all the more heartbreaking and horrible because you could never—not on your worst sleepless night—imagine them happening. And that was about as good a place to start as I knew.

But I kept it to myself and thought, gee, I'm one hell of a great guy for doing that.

{ }

A FEW DAYS after Leslie told me to shove off I'm walking by her desk. (She hasn't moved into her own office yet.) I hear a familiar sound blast out of her mouth as she holds the phone up to it; it's two or three words spat out in a low quick spurt—what they are I can't make out and it doesn't matter. Perhaps she's saying "You're a shit" or "You twit" or "Bloody hell." But it's quite clear what is happening: she's fighting long-distance with Colin. They're back together again.

{ }

LIZ HAS packed her things at work, put all her personal effects into cardboard boxes, including a picture of her husband (something she hadn't ever taken down). Down came the little tchotchkes and souvenirs, the small black-and-white photos of Frank Sinatra, Dean Martin, and James Dean and a Derek Jeter baseball card.

She has no plans. She's just going to relax.

"Lizzie, you know we all love you," Betsy Butler begins. We're in the large conference room.

"Then why do I get this shitty going-away party and not a big dinner?" Liz asks with a gulp rippling her neck.

People are stunned and Betsy stammers a few words for a second and resumes:

"We all love you and are so, so sorry you're leaving."

"Jackie Wooten gets a big send-off at Casper's, Marjorie gets a big fete at Florian's, and I get a Yodel in the conference room."

Jackie butts in: "Liz, please. Can we just get through this?"

"I don't want any present," Liz says gathering courage and steam. "If you bought me something, I just don't want it. And the thing is, I don't even care about the size of this party. I don't! Because you don't mean it anyway. The envelope goes around and you might as well spit in the thing. I don't care about the cake."

As in a movie, everybody glances toward the not very impressive cake on the table, then looks back at the floor.

"I'm sorry," Liz says, her voice cracking a little. "I'm sorry. But this is a terrible, dreadful place to spend eight hours a day, five days a week. Anybody who stays here for longer than a month should have her head examined." She's getting choked up now, but also marveling at her own courage.

"You're all really, really mean," she says and then she turns around and walks out.

Tomorrow Liz goes to California for a week . . . she wants to spend some time with her parents, who only recently have found out about her separation.

She, Willie, Ollie, and I meet at a Tribeca bar, not far from the Hudson River, at around ten o'clock. We're seated around a rickety table and from where I sit I have a good view of a pay phone hanging on the wall. There are a few quarters in my pocket . . . but who is there to call? Ivy? Leslie? Marjorie? Not one of them has any interest in me. Maybe I'll call all three of them just to bounce into a triple play of rejection.

Willie does most of the talking and I don't hear a word of it . . . it's paranoid gibberish, a tape squeaking while it fast-forwards. Ollie looks at Liz but says little. I feel bad for him . . . I think Liz has lost interest and he's hurting. It might be dawning upon him that he wasn't the cause of a broken marriage but was merely a symptom of it.

I tell Liz she's done a great thing, telling us all off, but she's not hearing any of it. She's chewing gum ferociously, blowing bubbles and popping them crisply.

Willie resumes what sounds like a tirade against the government.

"Help me get a taxi?" Liz says to me.

She and I walk outside. It's a cool June night and the river murmurs and smells briny and decayed.

"Are you going to be okay without me?" she asks me.

"Sure. Why wouldn't I be?"

A taxi goes by and we don't attempt to hail it.

"I don't know. I worry about you."

"My mother worries about me. Don't waste your time."

"I guess in some strange masochistic way I'm going to miss it at work."

I understand her perfectly and say something about *Notes From the Underground* and toothaches.

"I'll miss you, you know," she says.

"Oh, you'll soon get over that."

"Yeah. Probably."

Across the river a cloud settles over the smokestacks of an abandoned factory.

"I better get going," she says. She puts two fingers in her mouth and whistles shrilly and it vibrates the bone of my skull. A cab stops and she gets in. She sprawls out across the backseat and flops her head down in the other corner and she takes off.

An hour later I'm walking with Willie toward his place. I noticed that he's giggling.

"What's so funny?" I ask.

"That's what I've been trying to tell you, Zeke."

"Explain it again." I'm too sleepy to have been listening to his ramblings.

"I've got what we need. The note."

He pulls from his wallet a small piece of memo paper . . . "From the Desk of Mark Larkin." There, written by an obviously agitated hand, is:

I cannot go on like this. It simply has to stop. I know what I have to do to end it. I've avoided taking this step but I have no other recourse. I'm sorry

"This is his suicide note," Willie says. We've stopped near an all-night store—run by either Arabs, Iranians, Israelis, Greeks, or Russians—that makes falafel, pizza, hot dogs, doughnuts, and bagels. Flickering red and green neon light sends stripes and circles all over.

"What is it really?" I ask him.

"He flipped out on me. He's gone paranoid," Willie says. I now hold the piece of memo paper in my hand, all to myself. "He thinks I went to Human Resources and complained about him being a racist."

"Did you?"

"Yes, I did," he lies. (So much for confidentiality.) "So he writes this note and leaves it on my desk in the Black Hole."

I read it again. And then again, this time in reverse. The wild and uneven scrawls read exactly like a suicide note. That ending: "I'm sorry" and the flagrant missing period. "I know what I have to do to end it." The absolute certainty, the wisdom of the damned. "It simply has to stop." He's had enough . . . every second alive has become unbearable and excruciating. "I cannot go on like this." Something like this must figure into every suicide's last words, and why would Mark Larkin be any more creative than an abandoned, depressed spouse or a construction worker blowing his brains out because he can't find any work? The actor George Sanders penned the best suicide note ever written, a true concise master-piece: "I was bored." Three words that sum up everything . . . only a moron would have to ask any more questions after that. I was bored. Give me a college writing class to teach: "I was bored" would be the only thing on the syllabus.

"This is just what we need," Willie says. "The bastard did the work for us. We just have to finish the job."

The carnival light flashes over our hands, simmers in the pores of our skin, and turns wickedly on the trembling piece of paper.

15

"TELL ME WHAT you think of it, Post," Mark Larkin asks as he literally drops his Garson Locke article into my lap.

"You really care?" I say.

He adjusts his cherry-red bow tie and heads down the hallway for the elevator.

"You two don't get along, do you?"

It's Todd Burstin . . . he'd been standing within earshot and I hadn't realized it.

"It's not really that," I say.

I look at the kid: tall, skinny, a mess of strawberry blond hair. Harvard again. The kind of kid who got beat up a lot when he was young and also the kind of kid who had it coming.

"I'm having a small article in Starters in the September issue," he tells me.

I pretend to listen to him and one out of every five words sifts in through the haze — if you only listen to nouns, I've found, you can get most of what people are saying. I hear: director . . . agent . . . film . . . Scorsese . . .

While he goes on something dawns on me: I should not be seen to hate Mark Larkin. It should be understood that he and I get along, that we've completely ironed out our differences and are now working together splendidly. I've got to put on a show, I realize; I've got to spew out the most convincing smokescreen I can. Todd Burstin continues: ". . . festival . . . actors . . . award . . ." It is imperative that this knowledge be disseminated, the quicker the better. I mean, there are film clips of Lee Harvey Oswald handing out "Fair Play for Cuba" leaflets in New Orleans! And if you look at a photo of one of Abraham Lincoln's inaugural speeches, you can see John Wilkes Booth standing around among the crowd . . . and he doesn't look very happy either.

Marjorie Millet sets a big red paw on a cubicle partition's edge and rests her chin on this hand.

"Where's your boss?" she asks me.

"I think he went out to lunch."

"I've got these for him."

She sets down a box of stationery, then sits on my desk, her rump to my left, her chest to my right.

"The invitations," she says.

"He'll be very happy to get them."

Mark Larkin is throwing a party, a "bash" he calls it, to celebrate a) his moving into Skeffington Towers, b) his general conquest of the world.

"Can I sneak a peek?" I ask.

I notice Todd edging away, knowing he's out of his element with these people ten inches up the masthead from him.

"Don't you go anywhere," I tell him.

I open the box and take out an invitation. There's a vintage duo-toned photo of Clara Bow in some short cellophane-like outfit. She looks groggy with ecstasy, intoxicated by the sex she's just had. THE IT BOY! it says in red Garamond bold italic above her head.

"Good job," I tell Marjorie. "Hey, you ever thought of maybe designing things for a living?"

"He went all out," she says. "These things cost—"

"I don't want to know."

She lifts herself off the desk and in doing so, her formidable rear end tumbles back into place.

"Mark's going to really like these," I say to her genially. She looks at me, slightly startled. This is my first salvo to the world; normally I would have said something like: "I hope he chokes on the invitations." But this is New & Improved Zack Plus.

She walks away and I say to Todd, "Where were we?"

He resumes and up wafts the fog all around me. I look through the invitations. I'd given Marjorie the guest list after Mark Larkin had given it to me—the bastard hadn't invited me and I called him on it so he had a change of heart. And—I couldn't resist—after adding Willie's name, I also added the Phantom's name and a few other C-list invitees, such as the dwarf copy-room guy, a male intern in the art department in the process of becoming a female intern in the art department, a demented mail clerk, and another undesirable or two.

"So what do you think?" Todd asks me after he finishes telling me whatever it was he was telling me.

Clara Bow's left eye gazes up at me with carnal lethargy.

"Sounds good to me," I say. "Todd, um, you wear a Gap khaki pant with a 32-inch waist and a 34-inch inseam, don't you?"

"H-h-how do you know that?"

I point down at the translucent tape (with the sizes on it) running up his leg. He laughs embarrassedly and walks away and I hear him peeling the tape off.

A few minutes later it dawns upon me that Todd Burstin is going to have an article in the magazine. This troubles me greatly.

And so the smokescreen goes up. I ask Mark out to lunch and, though shocked, he joins me. We go to a restaurant where I know at least ten other Versailles people will see us. When we leave I say, "We should make a habit of this . . . just getting out of the office," and he agrees. Two or three times a week we go to Max Perkin' at about 2:30, just when Tom Land and Trisha Lambert go for their daily lattes, just when Betsy Butler goes, just when many others drop in. Marky and I are becoming bosom companions . . . or so the world thinks.

I even tell him I know he didn't graduate from Harvard. At first he seems lost in consternation. But then he realizes it's only me who's speaking to him and he erupts in embarrassed chuckles.

More musical chairs. As long as people keep dying and getting fired and moving around, it's a game that won't ever end.

I'm standing in the fashion department, envying a yellow Hugo Boss shirt hanging on a rolling rack. On the other side of the rack are a few fashion people and Marcel Perrault.

"I heard who's going to replace Liz?" someone says.

"Oh?" someone else says.

"Yes, it's, like, *definite?*"

"Who eez it zen?" Marcel asks.

"Shawn Jefferson?" They murmur for a few seconds. Someone even repeats the name: Shawn Jefferson.

"It's about time we had, like, a man of color here?" one of them posits.

"I know zis Shawn Jefferson," Marcel says. "And she is not a man of color. She eez a white bitch."

Here are the vital stats: University of North Carolina, an internship at *Her*, editorial associate at *Appeal*, then associate editor at *Zest* for four years, and now *It*.

Another person to fear, *zis* Shawn Jefferson, is my first reaction, and then my usual second reaction: I wonder what she looks like.

"How would you feel about working with Ivy Kooper?" Mark Larkin asks me. A neon beer clock sheds a dim golden light on both of us. It's two weeks after Todd Burstin pulled the tape off his new pants.

"Are you serious?"

He lifts his martini glass to his lips and sips. A silver film lingers a moment, making his lips seem even more fish-like.

"I am indeed serious. She's a comer, don't you think?" A lightning-quick Teddy Roosevelt smile.

It's 7:30 at night and we're sitting at a bar two blocks away from Grand Central Station. This place—it might have been where circus performers and comics with parrots went to unwind after doing *The Ed Sullivan Show* across town—is popular with the business people at Versailles, who like to knock down a few before getting on their trains back to their dreary lives in Connecticut and Westchester. Nothing has changed in here in decades . . . the air is haunted by fifty-year-old cigarette smoke.

"I would prefer it if you didn't promote her in my direction," I say.

"You realize I'd have to tell her it was you who nixed this?"

I knew he would say that!

I'm halfway through a vodka and tonic and suddenly I don't want another drop of it.

"She can be promoted," I say. "She definitely *should* be. But I just would rather not sit opposite her."

"You're an idiot for getting involved with someone at work."

"I know that."

"An absolute idiot."

"Where else is there to meet someone? And what are you into anyway? Boys? Girls? Ferrets?"

"That's my business. I try to separate business from pleasure."

He takes another sip and three broad-shouldered men in suits enter the bar and walk past us. Jimmy Kooper is one of them and he stops when he sees Mark Larkin.

"What a surprise," Jimmy says.

Suddenly this has become a scene in a very poorly constructed play; I was just nipping his daughter in the bud and then he immediately entered, stage left.

Mark Larkin and Jimmy Kooper shake hands and it's obvious that Mark Larkin's slight bones are no match for the crushing pressure of the bullying attorney's grip.

"I thought you journalists and such went downtown to get shitfaced, with models and artists and novelists," Jimmy says. All buddy-buddy.

"You know Zachary Post, I'm assuming . . . ," Mark Larkin says.

Jimmy Kooper looks me over and tries to remember who the hell I am. Among the eight thousand or so people he's met in his life, into what file, into what synapse, had he placed me? Clients, clients' husbands, former neighbor, creep in the sixth grade who once tried to kiss me, someone I see when I buy the newspaper, the asshole who dated my daughter for a few days . . . *Oh yeah, that's it!*

"We've met," he grunts and then he catches up with his fellow double-breasted bullies already seated in the back room, which is dark, smoky, and grainy.

"Did you arrange that for effect?" I ask Mark Larkin.

"No, that was a coincidence. Most gratuitous, don't you think?"

"You mean 'fortuitous.' Look, I don't want to work with her and I don't want you to tell her that I nixed it."

He stands up, daubs his lips with one of the yellowed cocktail napkins that have been lying on the bar for four decades.

"You ask a lot of me," he says.

He walks out. The entrance, three steps beneath street level, is two swinging zinc doors, each one with a small diamond-shaped window; I see the back of Mark Larkin's head through one of them. I look all the way to my left and see Jimmy Kooper and his colleagues, looking like fuzzy ghost images seen on a broken television. I swing my head back to the right and to my surprise Mark Larkin is looking at me through the window. He sees me see him and then he walks away.

I think I know why he had hung around—the bastard wanted to catch a peek of me being miserable by myself.

But not much he can do really bothers me anymore. It's like a dying parent not giving you five bucks. In a week or two, you knew, you're getting everything.

❧ ❧

IN MARK Larkin's empty office, I send myself more e-mail.

TO: POSTZ
FROM: LARKINM
SUBJECT:

I'm worried about Will Lister. No, not worried, I frankly admit to being rather frightened of him, Is he the violent type?

Larkin

When I dash out of his office to answer this fretful query Leslie walks by, clutching a cardboard box full of her personal effects. Wearing heels (unusual for her), she seems a good ten feet taller. She's getting her own office, is getting it, in fact, this very minute. Behind her two building maintenance men lug a desk, not the standard metal job I've been dealing with for four years, but something elegant, expensive, and antique.

She looks in my direction and smiles with tremendous agony for a second, not from the burden of the cardboard box, I think, but from the burden of having me for a memory.

Well, she may be through with me but I'm not quite done with her.

I call a nearby florist and ask them to send a dozen roses to Leslie right away. I have them write "Congratulations from a Secret Admirer" on the card.

The roses are in her new office in twenty minutes and so am I.

She's moving things around, getting settled in, adjusting things an inch or two. The window looks directly onto another office building; her view isn't great and this pleases me.

"This is cozy," I say.

She's deciding where a picture, probably a Constable print, should go.

"You know, perhaps we can still be friends," I say.

"Of course we can." She doesn't look at me . . . now that she has her own office, her snotty mode has more oomph to it.

"The flowers got here quickly."

"They're from you?" She turns only her face around.

"Yes. That looks perfect there," I say about the picture, a pastoral British scene with a church, clouds, hills, and stag. The thing is being hung about two feet too low on the wall.

"Do you think so?"

"Yes."

She looks nice in heels, they make her look tougher, give her a much-needed sense of menace.

"Perhaps a little higher?" she asks, sliding up the picture a few inches.

"No. Down. You should leave it right there."

And she listens to me.

Two minutes later she comes at me at my desk with a flushed face, angry swagger, and wriggling finger. I'm in for it. She has an office, I have a cubicle; she has an ornate walnut desk, I have steel or tin or something; she has paintings on her wall, I have schedules tacked to dull ecru cloth.

"I don't want any flowers from you," she spits out.

"I understand. It's over . . . I really don't know why . . ."

I'm a stain on her—she's trying to rub me out and although I disappear for a while, I keep resurfacing.

"It shouldn't have happened," I say. "You know, I sure wish it hadn't. That's why I got the flowers."

For one instant her face, squinched up like a red fist, goes slack; she doesn't like hearing me insult our relationship, although it's okay for *her* to do it. Then her face tightens up again.

"I don't ever want you *thinking* there's a chance we'll ever pick up where we left off," she says. "Do you understand?"

"Leslie, that's the very last thing I want."

She spins around, almost balletically, flounces her dress, and stomps away.

And right at that moment I know for a fact that, yes, this woman will one day be my wife. There's no doubt about it. And I think she knows it too.

No wonder she's so angry.

· · ·

"I'm fired," Willie says.

"Again?" He's told me so many times that he will be fired, is about to get fired, was fired . . .

We're in the bathroom on our floor—he told me he had to see me ASAP and then led me into there.

"This time I mean it. I just got canned," he says. To his left hangs the electric hand dryer. "They're giving me a week, until we close this issue. Then I have to clear all my things out. But I don't really have many things anymore. I might have to borrow some stuff from you just to make it look more dramatic."

A baseball-sized lump creeps up in my throat and I say, "I'm sorry."

"What am I going to do with my life?"

"I don't know."

"Who else will have me?"

"There are a lot of other places out there."

"McDonald's? Starbucks? Kinko's?"

"Come on . . . don't think it has to be that bad."

He really does think he has to be a fry chef or make copies of other people's résumés, people who, unlike him, have a chance. He's been robbed of everything, self-confidence, self-esteem, self-respect; if not for the fear of sounding trite I'd also say his very self, because there just isn't that much left of him.

"Did Mark Larkin do this?" I ask.

"Of course."

"I suppose it's not too much of a shock though, is it?"

I try to tell him that six months collecting unemployment benefits sounds like a dream vacation but he says: "It's not as if I'll be in St. Tropez for six months, dude. I'll be in my apartment with nothing to do."

And I know what that means. Self-torture and torment. Insanity.

I ask if there had been one final straw that had broken the camel's back.

"I don't know," he says. "A final straw? Well, I threatened to kill him. That might have done it."

(This must be what it's like when you find a million bucks in a brown paper bag on the street.)

"You threatened him to his face?!"

"I did . . . I did it to his face and with other people around. And I used e-mail. I guess that was it."

(Now there are ten million bucks in the bag.)

But no! It might be Monopoly money because:

I inch closer to Willie and say, "But now you *can't* kill him. You'd be everybody's first suspect."

"I don't care what happens. Everything is pretty much done for me."

"Jesus, I don't know what to say," I say, which sounds good enough.

"You'll still be my friend, I hope?"

A rope tightens around my chest and keeps tightening.

Willie leaves the bathroom and I go into a stall. It's a good thing that only God can witness some things and what a sight we absurd, insane mortals sometimes must be for Him, looking down at the very tops of us: the teenage boy holding a porno magazine and whacking off, a woman doing her face up with makeup for three hours and telling herself aloud she's beautiful, a man in boxer shorts conducting an imaginary orchestra with a soup spoon, a naked couple talking baby talk to each other, all this seen by the Almighty in foreshortened form, our heads as big as medicine balls, our feet the size of matches. And what a sight I must be now, sitting on a toilet and crying, tears and snot pouring out. Every few seconds I spin the roll of toilet paper and I make strange noises, like *glllllrrr* and *bliiihhhhhh,* and the tears keep flowing.

But I stop right away when someone walks in.

⟩   ⟨

THIS CARD has been up my sleeve for a while and it's time to play it.

"Hey, Leslie, what's a 'went boy'?"

We're in a crowded elevator early one day, going up to work.

"A went boy?" she asks, having no idea what I'm saying.

"Yeah."

There are about ten other people in the elevator. Leslie has been looking very pretty lately and presently is wearing a sage green dress that hangs loosely off her shoulders by two straps as thin as dental floss. Her promotion becomes her magnificently.

"I have no idea," she says on the subject of went boys.

A few people get off and some more get on.

"I know it sounds like a joke," I resume. "Like, you know, what's a Grecian urn?"

"I really don't know what you're talking about."

"That author I interviewed, Daffyd Douglas? I just remembered that I mentioned your friend Colin to him."

"You did?"

"Yes. And he'd heard of him! He told me that he was doing a novel about 'went boys' and that he knew that Colin hung around—what is it?—the Tottingbridge Cart Road tube stop and frequented went boys. But I have no idea what went boys are . . ."

"Rent boys," she says. "Rent boys. Tottenham Court Road."

"Yes, that could've been it."

The door opens on our floor and she gets out. She stops in her tracks and turns back and puts two fingers on her little mouth. It's the most pensive I've ever seen her look.

∗{   }∗

To: POSTZ
FROM: LISTERW
SUBJECT: AS IF ANY MORE EVIDENCE WERE NEEDED, FINAL PROOF OF MY SPECTACULAR DEMISE

Zeke, i'm sleeping with the phantom

TO: LISTERW
FROM: POSTZ
SUBJECT: Re: AS IF ANY MORE EVIDENCE WERE NEEDED, FINAL PROOF OF MY SPECTACULAR DEMISE

Why are you doing that?

To which he responds:

just to rub it in

∗{   }∗

IVY GLARES at me paralyzingly and asks: "Is it true?"

We're in a tiny windowless room, beige walls, beige ceiling, beige carpet. She'd directed me in here and then asked me her question out of nowhere, no segue or anything. A fan stands in the corner, revolving and buzzing.

"Is what true?" I stall.

"You prevented my promotion. Is it true?"

Lying would be the easy thing to do. But if there's one person in the world I didn't want to lie to . . .

"Sort of, yeah. In a way. But I—"

"I can't believe this!" Yelling and whispering at the same time.

She stands there and shakes her head and some stray hairs blown by the fan get into her mouth.

"Don't cry. Please," I implore.

"I am not going to cry."

"I would feel very uncomfortable working with you. Can't you understand that?"

"But this is my life here!"

"You'll move up. You know that." I want to put my hand caringly on her shoulder . . . but she'd swat it away.

Sure enough tears begin to well in her eyes.

"I can't believe this horrible place means that much to you," I tell her with a quavering voice.

"*Means that much to me*?! Listen to you! Do you hear yourself?!"

"But I thought you were better than that. This isn't the real world we're in, you know. I mean, it better not be . . ."

People pass by outside the room.

"Who did get the job anyway?" I ask. "Todd?"

"Yes." Now the tears stream freely and she wipes them away with her wrists.

"If this means anything, I told Mark Larkin you should be promoted. Okay? You will move up here, there's no question."

She dips her head; her heavy-lidded eyes sink into the beige ether and almost vanish, then she picks it up and looks at me with her dusky eyes.

"Well, at least *he* got the job," she says with a weepy giggle that sets off alarms all over.

"Huh?"

The fan turns and her wavy brown hair blows over her eyes and she rakes it back with her hand.

"We're sort of going out," she tells me. Then she starts crying again but also giggling, wrenched between being distraught for herself and overjoyed for her tall, bony, preppie, clumsy, pale, zitty boyfriend, who now will be sitting only a few feet away, facing me.

Todd moves in a few hours later and if not for Ivy's scene with me, nobody would have told me about it. This in itself is a slap in the face. Where was Betsy to call me into her office or Velma to drop an unsubtle hint in a hallway?

"This desk is pretty rickety," Todd says as he sits down in his chair to get the feel of his new surroundings.

"It was good enough for Willie and for Nolan before him."

He grips the metal on each side of the desk and squeezes it. He resembles a pilot checking out a brand-new cockpit and so I ask him, "When is takeoff, Captain?"

After seeing Willie, now pushing 250 pounds, sitting in the same spot, Todd looks like an upside-down broomstick with wire-rim glasses dangling beneath the straw.

"What's Mark Larkin like as a boss?" he asks.

"He can be difficult, but in the long run he'll be the best boss you'll ever have. And a good friend too." It pains me to go through with this charade sometimes. I'd even had lunch with Teddy Roosevelt the day before, at Le Capon. It was humiliating; he treats waiters and waitresses like ants.

Todd opens some drawers, gets the feel of the place.

A few hours later Ivy drops by to say hello to him. She is kind, magnanimous in defeat, she says everything she should say under the circumstances. When she turns around to leave I look up from whatever it is I'm pretending to read and catch her eye. For one moment it is as if we're the only living creatures in the world and everyone else is gone, the world is ours and ours alone, we have the earth's cities and islands all to ourselves . . . but still we have absolutely nothing to say to each other.

{ }

SOMETIMES I'm not as chickenshit as I might seem. The day that Willie told me he was fired, I went into Mark Larkin's office to try and save him.

It's still morning and he has the blinds down. The room has an amber hue now, tints of brown and maroon, as if the air, furniture, and rug were soaked in a dark liqueur.

"I feel this is a big mistake," I begin.

"I admit I didn't take into account your feelings when we made the move."

"We? You, Betsy . . ."

"And Regine."

"What about just giving him a leave of absence?"

He leans back in his chair, folds his arms behind his head in a grandiose "boss" gesture, not a shrewd move as his armpits are very moist.

"You want me to *un*-fire him? Do you know how weak that would make me look, what a dangerous precedent that would set?"

This is one of those times when I could just wring the life out of him and when I would be greatly upset when he finally died because it would mean an end to the joy of wringing. Yes, he was saying, giving Willie a leave of absence might be wise but I can't do it because it would make me, Mark Larkin, look weak. Jesus, he has to be a real hateful bastard to live with himself.

"It's not fair. He's a good guy," I say.

"Good guys don't threaten to kill you."

"I don't know if I agree with that."

He stands up and walks to the window, almost disappearing in a shadow of syrupy amber. This is a great office, big, well-appointed, a tremendous view. I could easily live in here. He shuffles his fingers down and then up the blinds, then splays a few slats apart, letting some light in. Through the opening I see the tram slinking over to Roosevelt Island.

"Only a few people ever really make it in life, Post, don't you think? And the rest are . . . sort of dwarves."

I say nothing. A big speech is coming and I'm dreading it.

"I mean *really* make it. I may think I'm important because I'm a senior editor at this obscenely successful glossy magazine but then Regine Turnbull is editor-in-chief and *her* salary is ten times mine and she lives on Sutton Place. And Regine is sitting in her chair right now stewing in her Chanel because Martyn Stokes owns her. But do you know who Martyn Stokes, who makes three times *her* salary, had lunch with last week? The Vice President of the United States. Wow. The second most powerful man in the free world. But as they're sitting there in the Vice

President's office all of a sudden the phone rings. The man had to go get the President a cup of coffee. Regular, no sugar."

"So we're all dwarves then," I say. "A president gets eight years if he's lucky and then what? He's stuck at home going over his ghost-written memoirs and he's got to be photographed with a shovel breaking the ground for his library. The dwarf in the copy room has it better, if you ask me. He's in the world."

He sucks some air between his teeth and twiddles his fingers along the blinds . . . stars of yellow and white shoot in and run through the room, across the walls and on the floor. Then he pulls his fingers out and everything disappears into abrupt blackness.

"Willie might be your friend, he might be a good writer and a good editor . . ."

"But?"

"But . . . he's just not one of us."

"But we're not one of us!" I say. "Don't forget that!"

He smiles an eely, sickening smile, pained but somehow resolute, as though little pieces of broken glass were embedded on his tongue.

Then he laughs and says: "Well, I'd say now we are."

{ }

LIZ AND I are on the phone, I'm at work and she's at home, my house. It's the Dinner Call Hour.

"When you get home, I have some news for you."

"What news?"

"When you get here, I'll tell you."

When I hang up, Todd Burstin's phone rings, two quick beeps. An interoffice call. He cradles the receiver with his neck, puts a foot on the desk, taps the desk with a pencil. He might actually be a fairly decent kid despite his background—a rich family, boarding school, trust funds up the wazoo—and I've yet to discover anything annoying about him. He doesn't chew loud, he doesn't make strange noises, he has no bothersome facial gestures. But I have to admit: even this easygoingness is getting to me.

"Well, there's always a movie," I hear him burble.

My cheekbones begin to cave in. I try to listen but hear only verbs and conjunctions: eat . . . go . . . see . . . and . . .

I stand up and walk to where Ivy sits, a tiny cramped cubicle not far from the Black Hole. She's on the phone too and when she sees me her entire skeletal structure perceptibly tightens.

I quickly walk back to my desk and see that Todd has readjusted his position. There's no way that Ivy has told him about us . . . or is there?

He hangs the phone up with conspicuous gentleness, perhaps thinking that if I don't hear him hang up, only one second later I'll forget he'd just been on the phone.

"You got a girlfriend?" I ask him.

He looks at me and shrugs and I say, "Sure you do."

When I get home that evening Liz has cooked dinner—filet mignon, corn on the cob, salad, and even apple pie. For the first time ever in this apartment, the table is set . . . who even knew I had a tablecloth anywhere? Somehow she'd found one.

"I'm going back to the astronaut," she tells me.

"When?"

"Tomorrow. Or the next day. Depends on how much packing I can get done tonight."

"Pack slowly then."

The food tastes great and she looks nice.

"I guess it makes sense," I say.

"You think so?"

"It's your marriage." I drain a glass of wine in ten seconds.

"I wish I knew for sure I was doing the right thing . . ."

"You are." But who knows if I mean it?

"I hear you and Mark Larkin are burying the hatchet," she says. "Coffee every day."

I have to keep up the show and so I can't say, Yeah, I'm burying it right in his temporal lobe. Instead I say, "We're trying to get along."

"That's too bad."

"I have to tell you this . . . I know about you and Oliver Osborne."

I'd caught her in mid-chew and a chunk of something goes down the wrong pipe.

"How do you know?"

"A heel and some bubble gum."

"Damn it!" It certainly isn't very pleasant finding out you're not nearly as clever as you thought.

"Well," she says with a smile, "I had my little fun. It's over and done with. Maybe it's time to have babies."

"That'll be interesting." I picture her cradling a baby, feeding it, her husband looking lovingly at her in their East Side apartment, a stroller, a crib and the rest of it, and Liz thinking: *Okay, so now how the hell do I get out of this mess?*

After dinner, she starts packing. She hadn't moved that much down to my place, just some clothing and a few books.

"Ivy was the only good thing that's ever happened to me," I say out of nowhere. I'm on the couch and she's walking around, gathering things.

"I don't know if I believe that."

"You gotta give me credit: I fucked it up like a real pro."

"There are plenty of others out there."

I hear Willie saying: McDonald's, Starbucks, Kinko's.

"Is there maybe some way you two can reconcile?" she asks, cramming some socks and pantyhose into a duffel bag.

"And then there's Leslie Usher-Soames," I say.

"Please!" She holds a black bra as nonchalantly as if it were a pair of sweat socks. "Don't even consider that again."

"I could say the same thing about you and your husband."

She stuffs the bra into the bag, zips it up with zest, and says in a very friendly but crisp tone, "Would you maybe please go fuck yourself, okay?"

{ }

No, it isn't very pleasant finding out you're not as clever as you thought. Sometimes an empty can hits you on the head, goes *clunk,* and you realize: Wow, I'm a real moron, aren't I?

As a veritable guardian of Mark Larkin's office, I'm privy to all his comings and goings, to his routine. I know his patterns and he seldom varies from them: in at 9:20, out to lunch at 1:00, etc. Therefore I feel comfortable going into his office and sending myself e-mail from him; I know he'll never catch me.

I've begun to enhance and embellish our newfound friendship. I'd send a sentence from him like: **"That Shawn Jefferson sure has a pair of legs on her, doesn't she, Post?"** and send in return: **"Does she ever! Fine pins on her. Up to her nape."** Or from **"LARKINM to POSTZ: Yankees looked tres pathetique last night."** To which I'd respond: **"Bosox still** haven't won a World Series since the Stone Age, Bossman, and the Yanks have won, what? 200 in that time?!?!"

And so on. All very chummy, palsy-walsy stuff (with an emphasis on the palsy.) "Don't know what I'd do without you here sometimes, old boy," he "wrote" me once, to which I responded: "Please, Mark . . . don't get all weepy on me."

I've never had a friend this close in my life!

So one day late in June I'm in his office and I'm writing an e-mail to POSTZ ("Simply adore the Sagaponack article, Post. A scene stealer.") when a green arrow comes on over his "mail received" box. The sun is coming in behind me and I feel a little sweat on my neck.

I double-click and see the e-mail is from MILLETM.

I look up, out the door of his office. Nobody is around, not a sound, not a shadow. I click and open the mail.

I'm in my office thinking about you and my panties are sopping wet. I want your cock inside me.

And *clunk* goes the can on my crown.

How could I have been this stupid?! What a total idiot! There's a luke-warm wooziness in my bowels.

I respond:

I'm as hard as a rock picturing your prodigious bosom majestically swaying to and fro underneath me.

(My impression of him talking "dirty.") The sweat on my neck, although the sun is shining on it, feels like ice melting down my shirt.

Cut the poetry and come into my office. I want you so bad I can taste it.

Marjorie is still the same, I see, except she doesn't have to resort to the thrill of Stairway B anymore, now that she has her own office.

I'm dying for it.

I write back:

No. Can't right now. Something's come up.

To which she responds (as I know she would):

Then if it's up, bring it to me, Big Boy.

(Mark Larkin must have laid the law down to her: Marjorie is now using punctuation and capital letters . . .)

Now, I have to admit, this is slightly amusing to me. Some men may pay young musclebound hunks to do their wives in front of them while they flog themselves or something, the idea being: well, you can do this better than I can so I'll just sit back, relax, and enjoy the show. Like getting the kid down the block to mow the lawn. But what exactly am I doing here? I'm impersonating the man I hate most and sending erotic e-mail ("**I want to slosh around in your tremendous moistness**") to the woman I most desire. There's a touch of farce in all this and I'm reveling in the irony of it all, except . . . *except I ain't gettin' any!* It's just me bending over a computer with sweaty palms and a pounding heart. Oh, if only Zeus-like I could transform myself into the white swan of Mark Larkin and flutter into her office, kick the door shut with my talons, and ravage my skirt-suited scarlet Leda and shudder my swanny loins all over the equally swanny Versailles rug. But this farce has no climax.

"I cannot talk right now," I write her, ending the futility.

Back at my desk I feel a cramp in my stomach and double over.

Then I stand up, grab some paperwork, and amble down a hallway and make it into Marjorie's office.

She's calmly eating a ham sandwich on rye with lettuce.

"What is it?" she asks me.

"Who's designing the Sagaponack article?"

"It hasn't been assigned yet. I think it will be Vanessa."

"Oh. Vanessa's really good." I sound sarcastic though.

"You don't want Vanessa doing it?"

"No. I said she's good."

Why have I come here? Because I know she's aroused, as horny as a dumb dog, wet as she can be without dissolving into her chair . . . I know she's dying for it (she had written that she was, after all) and I know, furthermore, what she's like when she gets this way. She's like me. Everything else stops.

I close the door behind me.

"What are you doing?"

"Come on, Marjorie."

"What is this?"

"Let's go. Right now. Come on."

"You want to fuck me, Buster?"

"Yeah."

"No."

"No?"

She shakes her head, takes a bite of her sandwich.

"You're rejecting me?"

"I sure am. And if you persist I'll call security." She puts her hand on the phone and a few bracelets slide noisily down her wrist.

"Okay, then," I say. "It was just an idea."

Now I knew. *I knew, I knew, I knew!* I knew that Mark Larkin would die very soon. It was like betting on the sun coming up.

In the bar near Grand Central Station, the son of a bitch had crowed about separating business from pleasure. Add this to all his other personality crimes: he's a hypocrite.

But I felt, that night as I tossed and turned in my bed until dawn, so . . . so *stupid*. Stupid because I hadn't seen it, because the whole Jimmy Kooper thing might have been a lie, a smokescreen. And stupid because I was now conspiring to murder someone for the basest, worst, cheapest reason: jealousy. Moron loses broad, other man gets broad, moron kills other man. Such lack of originality! The most tired, played-out, hackneyed motive in the the world, from jungles to towns to cities, from amoebas to whales. My previous motive was pure, shrewd, noble; it made sense: kill the king and inherit the throne. Something right out of *The Golden Bough*, isn't it? But now things have been perverted . . . suddenly it's a crime of passion. It's no longer the brain, now it's the gut, or the balls. I'm just some jealous low-down obsessed mug after all.

But . . . big deal. He still has to go.

} {

COLIN Tunbridge-Yates, gaunt wings spread wide, slowly floats through the office, lost.

"Looking for Leslie?" I ask him in a dark hallway. Two silhouettes, he and I. "Down there, make a left, then another one."

"Cheers."

Not only is he wearing the same pinstriped suit he had on the other time I'd met him, but he also has no recollection of ever having met me.

I make a point to stroll by Leslie's office and there I espy Colin, Leslie, and Shawn Jefferson (blond, blue eyes, a delicious golden brown complexion) together.

I duck my head into the office and say to Colin, "You found her, I see."

"Yes. Cheers."

One look at Leslie tells me all the information I'd come for. I might as well be looking at the needles in a polygraph test.

Later there is a large meeting and Leslie arrives a half-hour late—everyone knows her on-again/off-again, out-of-town again/in-town again boyfriend is on again and in town. The timing is perfect: Regine, Betsy tells us, is moving my article on Sagaponack toward the front of the book, giving it two more pages, and moving back and cutting two pages from Tony Lancett's article on a performance artist who's going to kill herself live on European TV. It's a glorious moment for me, and my new buddy Mark Larkin even pats me on the back, that doomed pompous hypocritical fuck. Leslie is seating herself and tending to a wayward pleat in her skirt exactly when this happens. Color flashes in those pale cheeks of hers, I swear it.

As I leave work that day, I go by her office.

"So Colin's in town, I see."

"Yes, that he is," she says. "Oh! Congratulations."

"For?"

"Your article."

"Oh, yeah, that . . . but I've got so many other things in the works right now." I know she won't ask me about any of them, which is good, as there aren't any.

I said, "So you never told Colin about us . . ."

"No, as a matter of fact, I haven't. How could you tell?"

"I understand why you wouldn't tell."

"I didn't think it was important enough."

"Well, if it's so unimportant and won't mean anything, then you could tell him. Right? What harm would it do?"

"Your logic sometimes . . ."

She smiles and it's a nice one. Not a fang in sight and apparently genuine.

With Colin hovering around, I figure, I've got a good chance to twist myself back into her life. The more he's around, the better my chances are; if he moves in with her, then she'd hijack the moving van and move in with me. If he shows up at her window with the intention to elope, she'd drag the ladder to my house.

We talk about work-related things for a while and then it's Leslie, not me, who detours back into the personal.

"So are you with anybody, Zeke?"

"With anybody?"

"There are all these rumors floating about . . . you know, you and Liz Channing?"

Wow! I'd never even counted on this one. Of course! Liz and I were living together, people know that, but it's evolved (or degenerated) into something other than Liz on the couch and Zack in the sack. This has fallen out of heaven, ricocheted into Leslie's brain, bounced into my lap, and has sent my stock soaring.

"There's nothing to these idle rumors. Mere innuendo."

"I don't believe you, not a'tall."

She shuts down her computer and begins gathering together her personal effects, preparing to leave, so I say, "I gotta go."

"Do you want to wait up?"

"I'm in a big hurry. Sorry."

What a walloping knockout I've just scored!

{ }

WHAT SORT of going-away party did Willie Lister have?

None.

I asked him out to lunch that day but he said no, he had too many loose ends to tie up.

At 5:30 I went to the Black Hole, thinking he might still be there, but he was gone and his desk was bare. There was that eerie fluorescent glow, funeral parlor blue and green floating over the black desks, carpeting, and walls.

He's gone.

And we won't be in touch for a while.

That's the plan.

{ }

MARK Larkin's party. His bash.

A spanking brand new two-bedroom apartment in Skeffington Towers, on the twentieth floor. Freshly painted walls, brand new furniture, everything smells new. A sweltering night in early July, unbreathable damp air, but inside the air conditioners are humming and soothing. People are everywhere, magazine people, book people, agents, publishers, artists, writers of fiction and non-fiction, illustrators, ingenues, photographers, a model here and there, a hunk, a has-been, a hack. It is rumored that even Boris Montague is here . . . but nobody who makes less than five million dollars a year knows what he looks like.

Are all these people here because they like Mark Larkin? No. It's better than that. They're here because they're afraid of him.

The first person I see is Meg Bunch. The bubble gum pink outfit, the perfect Louise Brooks do — it's uncanny how she always manages to look exactly like herself.

I circulate. I make small talk, smile, and laugh it up.

Liz, her astronaut, and I chat for a while. Her living with me isn't brought up. He seems happy; I'm not sure about her.

Thomas Land and I exchange polite grimaces. He's wearing Armani and it's brand-new, not a wrinkle. Why not just wear the goddamn price tag too, I'm thinking. But I do notice a gray hair and let out a chuckle that no one hears above the throbbing music.

The first time I bump into Mark Larkin, we shake hands and I say, "Great party, boss." For the first time since I've known him, he looks drunk. His face is flushed, his eyes are drooping, and he's teetering on his heels.

At about 10:30 I see Alan Hurley, my *Gotham* connection. He either has a new girlfriend or the old one has gained weight. We speak for a few minutes and he assigns me a book to read. He's all done up in tweed, standard uniform for *Gotham* . . . but it's 90 degrees out and 90 percent humidity. Tweed, this guy has on.

At around 10:45 I see Willie out of the corner of my eye, the Phantom on his arm, she looking as vaporous as ever.

I slip through the crowds, slink around the cliques, and glide past the lonely wallflowers, like a hockey puck sliding around, dashing between legs, bouncing in all directions off the boards.

The dwarf copy-room guy is here, I see. Talking to the demented mail clerk.

Near a plush leather couch I've seen advertised many times on the back page of the Sunday *Times* TV section, I run into Willie.

"Everything's a go," he whispers to me.

"Be cool," I advise. But then I say, "You've got—"

He quickly flashes me the suicide note. From the Desk of Mark Larkin.

We separate and I resume being the life of the party. It occurs to me: *tell Willie not to do it.* Call it off. It's absurd. But I do nothing, say nothing. Maybe he'll call it off on his own.

Marjorie is here, laughing it up and flirting with everyone, up for grabs. Leslie and Colin quietly hover around the periphery, looking as though they've signed a pact not to have fun.

I talk alone with Leslie for ten minutes. She's drinking, getting drunk, then is drunk, and her skin and eyes light up the immediate vicinity. Our hands touch for a moment.

"You know, I miss you sometimes," I tell her.

"And I miss you hideously," she says.

She walks away and I thank God and British Airways for Colin's visit to the States. Nobody has ever missed me "hideously" before and it feels good.

More mingling, more insipid conversation: Meg Bunch, Roddy Grissom, Sr., editors and art directors of *There*, *Men*, *Boy*, and more. I score many points with Heather Miller, the editor-in-chief of *Zest*, who looks just like Shirley Temple. She offers me $500 for a sidebar on some subject I have no interest in. Alexa Van Deusen, the Stiletto now running *She*, somehow engages me in a dialogue for two minutes. I run into Martyn Stokes and Corky Harrison and we talk magazine gibberish for quite some time.

A few minutes after midnight I slip out the door and walk down twenty flights of stairs. I explore the stairways, see there's no trace of a video surveillance system, see that there's a covert way out of the building that doesn't take you past a doorman but that lets you out on a sidestreet. I walk back up and resume my circulating. Velma, Trisha Lambert, Shawn Jefferson, two New Boys and a New Girl. I run into Willie near the kitchen, he's got a bottle of Rolling Rock in his grip, and I tell him about the exit. He slips away.

The crowd is thinning now.

I do reruns: Meg Bunch, Betsy, Alan Hurley, etc.

Jimmy and Carol Kooper leave and he bangs his shoulder against mine and doesn't say he's sorry. Bedraggled by liquor, Mark Larkin shuffles to the door to see them off.

"We're going in the same direction," I tell Marjorie. "Let's get a taxi."

"Not if you —"

"I won't."

"Promise?"

"Scout's honor."

"Get my coat."

I walk into the bedroom and pick through the dozen or so coats left on the bed.

(Is Willie underneath the bed, I wonder . . . ?)

Marjorie and I are leaving. Closing the door behind me, I turn around (only twenty or thirty people are left) and see Mark Larkin, almost knocked out, talking to a rich, respected publisher . . . the man is tall, bald, and bearded. He must have thought the party was black tie because he's wearing a tux . . . or else he's just come from the opera. Mark Larkin slowly turns to me and I do something I hadn't planned on: I blow him a slow, silent kiss good-bye.

Marjorie and I walk a few blocks before we get a taxi and her heels echo against the buildings we walk by . . . the streets are empty save for us. The air is hot and rancid and my lungs are parched.

I tell the driver to let us off at her house first, which is actually out of my way.

"Well, that was exciting," Marjorie says in the cab.

"You think so? Get any phone numbers?"

"I do all right."

"You were practically breast-feeding that big bartender."

"He looked thirsty."

Silence for a few blocks.

"What time are you heading back to his place?" I ask.

"What do you mean?"

She's on my right, her head is against the window, and her black-stockinged legs are close to my feet.

"He told me. I know."

She swallows . . . the old giveaway.

"He told you what?"

"Enough crap, Margie. Enough lying. Jesus, I don't care anymore.

After Jimmy Kooper, who cares? That thing the other day in your office . . . I was just . . ."

Her slitty green eyes close serenely for a moment, then open.

"I'm off married men. It's not my—I'm not cut out for the mistress thing."

"So you rebound to that pretentious, arrogant prick?"

But I have to be careful here. The smokescreen.

"I thought you didn't care anymore. And besides, you two seem to be getting along handsomely lately."

The taxi stops and she says good-bye but I get out too. I make sure to get a receipt. Proof, just in case.

"What are you doing?" she says when I get out of the cab. "You promised you wouldn't try anything."

"I won't. Can we get a drink?"

"We've had drinks."

"Please . . . I won't touch you. I just don't want to be alone."

We're having this conversation right in front of the entrance to her building . . . the doorman, seated on his stool and bathed in sallow apartment lobby light, is watching us.

We get a drink at a nearby bar and don't say much and I walk her back home.

She gives me a maternal peck on the cheek and says good night and from outside her building I watch the elevator door close on her.

So many alibis . . .

I go home and toss and turn and then take a few tranquilizers to sleep. Is he dead yet or is he dying, I keep thinking. Has Willie pulled it off or chickened out? Which one should I hope for? While 15 milligrams of Valium work their wonders, I call Ivy. It's 2:54 A.M.

She answers, perhaps thinking it's Young Burstin.

"Hello . . ." she says groggily.

"It's me, I think."

"What time is it?"

"It's late." My room is pitch black, except for the sapphire glow of a digital clock. I'm groggy now too, floating on all that blackness and blueness.

"What is it? Is something wrong?" she asks.

"No. I just wanted to hear your voice."

It takes a few seconds before she responds.

"This is hardly my voice," she says.

"But it's you."

"I'm asleep."

"I've got nothing. I'm very scared."

"I'm asleep . . ."

"Okay. Me too."

I wake up at about 11:30 the next day, a Sunday, and turn on the local all-news channel. Nothing.

I take another pill and sleep until dusk. My shoulder aches where Jimmy Kooper had bumped into it and my skin looks gray and flaky.

When I wake up I turn on the TV again . . . it takes a half-hour but finally the anchorwoman says that Mark Larkin, a senior editor of *It* magazine, has been found dead in his apartment on East Sixteenth Street. Only last night, she says, he'd thrown a big party. Investigators are examining the contents of a note.

Police are treating it as a suicide, she says, and then it's on to the weather.

16

AM I going to get caught?

George Leigh Mallory had to climb Mount Everest, he said, "Because it's there." Well, once he climbed it, it wasn't there anymore. Instead he had to wonder: *Okay, now how do I get my ass back down again?*

Some people have to climb mountains for peace of mind, some have to paint landscapes, do volunteer work, hang glide, plant trees, pray.

Me, I had to have someone killed.

The thing to do is be myself. Act normal. A nervous wreck who always trembles, slobbers, twitches his eyes—were he to murder someone, the next day his hands would be as steady as cinderblocks, his lips would be dry, he'd never once blink.

I just have to act normal.

So what would Zachary Post do in this situation, normally? If I woke up one day and turned on the TV and found out that my boss and one-time enemy had committed suicide?

"Mom?"

"Zachary?"

"Have you seen the news? My boss is dead."

"Was he the one on the subway tracks?"

"No. That wasn't him."

I tell her what I know from the news on TV.

"Who knows? . . . This might be a good thing?" she suggests after offering a minute's worth of condolences.

"A good thing?"

"Well, I guess there's a job opening up now . . ."

When your mother backs you up, it always makes you think you've done the right thing.

What else would I do?

Would I call Marjorie? This one is hard to figure out. Had I not known that Mark Larkin and she were "involved," I would call. For all I know, though, she may have discovered the body. But: *How would I even know there was a body to discover?* So I should call. That was acting normal.

"Marjorie . . . Have you—?"

"Yes. I know."

"How did this happen?"

"How? Sleeping pills. The question is why."

Sleeping pills?

"Well, he sure was wasted the last time I saw him. Maybe it only took one sleeping pill to do it."

"I found the body. And the note."

There's something so perfect to this. I'm on the phone feigning shock but smiling and soaking it up.

"You did? I'm so sorry."

"Yes. He was facedown. He had green lounge pants bottoms on. J. Crew, drawstring. He was completely white."

Then she says: "You didn't kill him, did you?"

Be myself. When she'd said "sleeping pills," I was alert enough not to correct her and call them painkillers. Be me.

"Yeah. I killed the son of a bitch all right. Hey, I was with *you* after the party. Maybe *you* killed him."

"It's just so weird. Jesus, my luck with men . . . it just keeps getting worse. Oh well. Single again."

"Marjorie, I have to say it: you don't sound too upset."

"To be honest, I was just starting to dislike him intensely. And then, this."

・　・　・

And of course, the most important call. To Willie. But he calls me first.

"Zeke, have you heard?"

"I was just about to—"

"He's dead, man."

"I know. I know."

"He killed himself. He left a note, they say."

"I know. This is incredible. Can you believe it?"

"No. Not really."

I'm talking to a man, I know, who thinks his phone is tapped, his room is bugged, who thinks the insects in his sink are toting cockroach-cams. This has to be done by the book, not one little wry aside.

"Sleeping pills, I heard," I say.

"Really? Who told you that?"

"Marjorie. She found the body."

"She did?"

"Yeah. I haven't told you this but . . . they were dating."

Silence for a beat.

"Why would Mark Larkin kill himself, do you suppose?" Willie asks me. "The dude had everything going for him."

The news is on with the sound turned off. For the thirtieth time, the all-news channel plays the same tape: an exterior shot of Skeffington Towers, panning up from about thirty yards away and then back down, then cutting to two men carrying a stretcher out, finally a still photo of Mark Larkin, eyes wide, puffy cheeks, calling to mind a marshmallow dipped in Pepto-Bismol. It's the sepia photo from *It's* contributors page. His "rugged Teddy Roosevelt good looks."

"Who knows?" I say. "Maybe there was an inner agony that he, who always kept his feelings to himself, never let anyone see. On the surface: cool, intellectual, detached. Inside: anguished, tormented, a volcano. At once placid and volatile. In a word: hell."

"Yeah. Maybe that's it."

"Bye."

"Bye."

And then a night of bad dreams: cold jail cells with vermin in every corner, endless appeals before judges (most of them Trevor Usher-Soames), visits by priests, rabbis and imams, conjugal visits with Marjorie, lethal injections mixed up in a Williams-Sonoma $400 blender, and of course, brutal rapes by tattooed toothless linebackers in the shower. And a final meal—*coq au vin*, a coffee milkshake with chocolate syrup, a Bombay Sapphire martini.

} {

"WELL, WE all know why we're here," Betsy Butler says. "Velma is going to read something from Regine. But I'd like to speak first," she continues. "Mark Larkin was . . . well, I can't honestly say that he was a friend. But . . ." She's struggling, trying to explain exactly what he was but at the same time be polite. "He was an integral part of this magazine. A driving force. He may not have been the easiest person to get along with but . . ." But *what*? He may not have been the easiest person to get along with but he shouldn't be dead? She can't even force herself to say it. She wraps it up: "I think it's safe to say that he'll be missed around here. Zachary?"

Huh? What? Why this? All eyes suddenly turn to me.

"Zack," Betsy says, "do you want to say anything? You worked for him."

"Yes. I would. I have to admit when Mark first started here . . . I really didn't like him. I guess we were fiercely competitive. That's him and it's me and, for better or worse, it's the nature of this place. And we're different. We *were* different. But maybe we weren't so different after all and that was the problem. Ultimately we resolved our problems. And I can say that, if he wasn't a friend, he was ultimately someone I knew I could always rely on, who I could go to. The thing is, I had no idea he was so tormented. And I feel terrible about it. Had I known, I could have done something. Or tried to."

(As I'm speaking, I feel this is a speech that's taken two weeks to craft and retouch. But it's all impromptu, including the very slight choking up at the end. Okay, maybe it's not "Friends, Romans, countrymen," but give me some credit.)

The floor is turned over to Velma, who reads from a fax sent from Claridge's in London.

"Mark Larkin's presence will be sorely missed at *It*. His imagination, his discerning wisdom, creativity, wit, and brilliant incisiveness are as irreplaceable as he himself was irrepressible. We all will cherish his memory and he certainly will not be forgotten. And now let us move on."

Betsy says, "Oh. We're going to work a half-day today. Everyone can leave at one. I know we're all upset and we might need some time."

Oliver whispers out of the side of his mouth: "Nicest thing the cunt ever did, topping himself in a slow work week."

{ }

A DAY later.

I'm at my desk. Young Burstin is across from me, pecking away with hummingbird velocity at his keyboard. Mark Larkin's door is closed . . . it hasn't been opened once so far this week.

"Here you go, Zeke." Leslie smiles briefly and hands me a 10 x 13 manila envelope with a red string and walks away. Written on it is: "For ML's family. A gift. We'll figure out what to get." I take out ten bucks from my wallet and shove it into the already considerable pile. Normally Willie and I would remove a fiver (or more) but I'm thinking: What happens if I get questioned for the murder? I could say, with a polygraph measuring every flicker of activity, No, I did not kill him. And I'd pass. But if some smart homicide dick asked me, "Did you take ten dollars out of the manila envelope?" if I said no, the needles would melt.

I retie the string, pass it along to Todd.

"What are we getting the family?" he asks me as he puts five dollars in.

"Flowers, probably."

"It'll certainly be a lot of flowers."

"I'm sure the Larkins have room for it."

"You mean the Liebermans."

"The Liebermans?"

"His real name was Lieberman. His father sells Hondas outside Philadelphia."

In a flash: Gatsby/Gatz on the raft in a swimming pool, a slow-motion billowing of blood, everything shimmering aqua blue. There I am, fishing around for the corpse with a Wet Guys net.

"I'm sure they have enough room," I say to Todd, "whoever they are."

The Liebermans. Oh, well.

"How did you come upon all this inside info, Young Burstin?"

"You know . . . I just did."

That afternoon four building maintenance workers open Mark Larkin's door and begin removing things: the desk, file cabinets, the horrible painting, bookcases. Fifty times on TV I saw EMS people take the body out of the building and now this. Post-it notes, a stapler, a three-hole punch, paper clips.

It takes a half an hour and the room is empty. Not even a rug.

He's dead.

And no policemen poking around. Leopold and Loeb are in their low rung of Hell, offering me high fives.

When the maintenance men leave I walk in. It's like being an ant inside the drawer of a file cabinet, it's so sterile. The blinds are gone. The late afternoon sun drifts in and buildings are glazed with red and orange. The air, stripped of human life, is so fresh it's almost dizzying, like pure oxygen.

I'm going to get away with this. I'm going to get what I want.

The next morning I'm in Betsy's office, surrounded by Velma, Jacqueline, and Betsy. I'm wearing a black suit.

"I think the first thing we want to know," Betsy says, "is if you're okay."

"I'm okay."

"Are you sure? Human Resources tells us that in situations like this, people can have trouble coping. There are therapists who—"

"I'm fine. I don't need to speak to anyone about this."

In the simple old days, I reflect, Human Resources (when it was still called Personnel) hired people, transferred people, sent up gals from the steno pool . . . now they rock you, burp you, spank you.

Velma takes over.

"We do have a problem, however. We need to replace Mark Larkin."

Act normal. Be myself.

"Didn't Regine say he was irreplaceable?"

Velma says, "No, she said he was irrepressible. She never said irreplaceable."

"I think she said he was irrepla—"

"*Please!*" Betsy says. "We need to hire an editor here. We're missing a body and we have to find one."

"And am I inside that body right now, Betsy?"

Jacqueline and Betsy glance at each other.

"You might be," Betsy says. "We're also considering Shawn Jefferson. But that doesn't leave this room."

"It won't," I assure them.

Shawn Jefferson?! They couldn't do that to me, could they? I recall *The Treasure of the Sierra Madre,* when all the gold is blown back up the mountain and Tim Holt and Walter Huston are reduced to delirious laughter.

"Regine was also thinking that Nan Hotchkiss might be interested," Velma says. Jesus, who else is up for the job? The demented mail clerk?

"All good people," I say. But that isn't me. "Me" would say (and now I do say it): "Look, I know I can do the job. I know it. I was here longer than Mark Larkin, I've been here longer than Shawn Jefferson. And I'm just as capable as Nan Hotchkiss. You want an editor, you want a body, I am that body. Right here."

"That's good, Zack," Betsy says. "Confidence is something we need to see. Who knows? Had you shown such confidence before, you might have been promoted ages ago."

For a few weeks, I am told, I will assume Mark Larkin's duties. But not his title. And I'm not to move onto the sacred ground of his office. That still has to be decided.

The day after my temporary promotion I run into Willie in a hallway. He looks a bit different. I immediately know what it is: he's been sleeping better.

"What are you doing here?" I ask him.

"Just hanging around."

"Uh-huh."

Tucked into the waist of his pants, pinched in tightly into his expanding gut, is a gray Glock 9-millimeter pistol.

∗{   }∗

"IT'S HARD to believe, isn't it?" Ivy says to me a day after Mark Larkin's body was discovered.

"I know. I saw him just two days ago."

"Why do you think he did it?"

We're in a hallway, near the bathrooms.

"Honestly, I have no idea. He seemed happy."

"Maybe having to work so closely with you?"

I make a face. "Come on."

"Admit it to me . . . you hated him."

"I loathed him. It doesn't mean I'm happy he's dead."

"Oh yes it does."

"Speaking of stiffs, what's up with you and Todd? Everything going smoothly?"

"Pretty much . . . We even talk about moving in with each other."

"It's kind of soon for that, don't you think? And you work with each other. You'd be seeing each other nine hours a day here, then fifteen hours a day at home and all day on the weekends. It's a good way to quickly kill a relationship."

"Well, we were talking about it, that's all."

And maybe I'll find them the apartment, help them move in and pay the rent until they no longer can stand the sound of each other's eyes blinking.

Perhaps I had the wrong coworker killed.

} {

LESLIE comes over to my desk and says, "Admit it. You did it."

"Yeah. I killed him."

"It was one of the first things I thought of when I heard. First I thought Willie did it. Then that Zeke did it. It's brilliant."

"But it's suicide."

"Yes. I suppose it is. But it's still brilliant."

This is all said flirtatiously, her little waist practically in my face at my desk. Colin must be making her miserable, both three-thousand miles away and close-up on his visits. Maybe some animal part of her—if she has one—smells the blood on my hands, the fresh kill, and she's drawn to me.

"You going to visit me in prison, Leslie?"

"That might be fun." She clicks her tongue two times and rolls her eyes. It's too bad that when her clothes are off she's as supple and yielding as a closed mussel.

"We can drill a hole through the window in the meeting room."

"Now, now." Her expression changes, goes dull.

Still herself.

∗{ }∗

THE FUNERAL was in Pennsylvania and Velma went as our sole ambassador. It was true: Mark Larkin was once Mark Lieberman and his father sells Hondas.

The *Times* ran an unimpressive three-paragraph obituary and there was no picture. It was one of those obits when you're sure the person had died of AIDS: "MARK LARKIN, IT MAGAZINE EDITOR, DIES, AT 28" was the hed and the last sentence was: "He is survived by a father, Herbert, his mother, Estelle, of Ridley Park, Pennsylvania, and a younger sister, Tina." (Of course if I died people might say the same of me: male, magazine editor, under 40, never married, no kids.)

A memorial service was held in the east thirties at a church and I attended. As usual with Versailles functions, everyone was decked out in black, but this time we had an excuse other than fashion. Martyn Stokes was there, so were Land and Lambert, so was Alexa Van Deusen. Marjorie wore Jackie O. sunglasses. She wasn't crying. Nobody was.

Betsy spoke and so did Martyn. There was a lot of coughing.

Ivy and Todd sat together and did not hold hands and I caught Leslie sneaking a peek or two at me.

As we were leaving I pitched a story idea to Alexa Van Deusen and she seemed to like it.

∗{ }∗

"WHAT, YOU won't get me coffee?" I say to Young Burstin.

"I . . . I just don't know if that's in my job description."

The phone rings. An outside call. I jauntily pick up the phone on the first ring, banging it so that it jumps up and flies into my hand.

"Zachary Post," I say.

"Zachary Post?" a gruff voice says.

"Yep. This is he."

"Yeah, Mr. Post, this is Detective Tom Marino from Midtown South. I hope you have a moment?"

"I have a moment. Sure." My mouth is cotton dry by the word "sure."

"This is about the Mark Larkin death," he says. (He said "death," not "suicide." And he pronounces it "Mawrk Lawrkin.") "First of all, let me extend my condolences."

"Thanks, Detective."

"Did you ever supply or furnish the deceased with any kind of medication or medicines or pills?"

"Pills? Yeah. I did as a matter of fact."

"Do you remember what kind exactly?"

"They were painkillers. He had headaches." I wait a second and then groan: "*Oh, no . . .*" As if just realizing that those pills were the very means by which he'd committed self-slaughter.

"Mr. Post, do you remember exactly what kind of pills they were? I need to know wh—"

"Percocet, I think. And something called Vicodin."

"Can you maybe give me a ballpawrk figure how many?"

"Well, I didn't give the pills to him. I gave the bottles to him."

"How many pills, sir?"

It's amazing that I can still speak with my mouth this dry.

"Ballpark? I'd say, a hundred or so. Please tell me it wasn't those pills that he . . ."

"The empty vials were found in his trash basket. In his bathroom. Yeah, it's what he took to kill himself."

"I thought he took sleeping pills."

"He didn't."

"Jesus . . . I feel so terrible . . ."

Nothing on the other side except some gum chewing.

I ask: "Am I going to get in trouble for this, Detective? I mean, it was like, he asked me for the pills one day and I said, sure, here, take 'em. I wasn't using them."

"There's no trouble. We're just tidying up a bunch of loose ends over here."

"Okay. God, I feel so terrible."

When I hang up, the handset is soaked.

A *bunch* of loose ends . . . ?

That call wasn't unexpected. I did expect it. Yet I still hoped it would never come.

The jig might not be up but it's lifting slightly. I know I'm going to hear from Detective Tom Marino again. I just know it. And I can't let the fact that he sounds like an idiot fool me into complacency.

Immediately there are two e-mails waiting to be read, I see.

TO: POSTZ
FROM: KOOPERI
SUBJECT:

You want TB to get you coffee?! Not fair!

And then a surprise . . . Willie's in the building again.

TO: POSTZ
FROM: LISTERW
SUBJECT:

you wanna go get a bite?

I write back to Ivy:

He can fight his own battles, can't he?

And to Willie:

Something weird just happened. Let's talk. ASAP.

I lean back in my chair and consider the possibilities. Why was Marino looking into things? Maybe they do this for every suicide. It was agreed that Willie would not dispose of the vials—that would be too conspicuous, a suicide taking a hundred pills, writing a note, but also finding the time to dispose of the bottles. Not even the prissy punctilious prig Mark Larkin was that anal retentive.

I get an e-mail that says:

We should talk about this.

And I write back:

A homicide cop named Marino just called. About ML. The jig might be up.

The very instant I click on SEND a big shadow steals over me. It's Willie at my desk.

"I'm replying to you right now," I tell him.

"I'm right here."

I look at my screen. I'd just written to Ivy, telling her, not Willie, that the jig might be up . . .

"What very weird thing just happened?" Willie asks.

Willie and I stroll the aisles of Crookshank's, going from socks to ties and back again. In British spy movies they always wind up in the park, avoiding the possibility of being listened to. This is our Hyde Park, I suppose.

"This cop named Marino . . . he found the vials."

"So? We knew—"

"It just makes me nervous."

"But this is how we planned it."

"It's just a little unsettling. You know?"

"The coward dies a thousand deaths, pal o' mine, the hero dies but twenty or thirty."

Is Willie setting me up? This occurs to me, that every second of the past year he has been ingeniously plotting against me, faking insanity, pulling me down and down. But no, he's too crazy. Or is he?

He has a pair of gray cashmere socks in his hands. There are little golden tennis rackets and white balls on them.

"How can you be so cool about this?" I ask him.

"There was a girl I knew at Harvard named Jennifer. Very pretty, very popular. But she'd resolved to remain a virgin until she married. She just wanted to save herself for Mr. Right. So Jennifer let boys do her up the back way. The Toblerone Turnpike, if you will. And *anybody* could do it. And a lot of boys did. I mean, dozens and dozens of guys did it. But that was years ago and by now I imagine she's married and she still had her maidenhead intact on their honeymoon night and her husband thought he was getting a chaste, untainted, untarnished angel. So there."

"The point being?"

"The point being, she was fucked. The point being, *there was no point.*"

I think what he meant was: he, Willie, was fucked. His life was over anyway. So why should he worry about anything?

"I don't really need these," he mutters to himself as he puts the socks back on the rack.

"What did you mean before, the jig might be up?"

"Huh?"

It's Ivy, at my desk. The e-mail I sent to her by mistake.

"You wrote me tha—"

"Right, right. I thought I was—oh, just forget it."

She rubs the dimple in her chin and says, "You said something about a homicide cop . . . ?"

I put a pen down and say, "Ivy, I thought I was writing to Willie. But I was writing to you. There's a policeman asking questions about Mark Larkin. All right? It's nothing."

"Willie? Willie doesn't even work here anymore."

Was I hallucinating Willie? Was I talking to myself when I thought I was talking to him?

"Ivy, it's nothing!"

I may have sounded like her father scolding her, so sternly did I say it. She tucks her fingers in her pockets and walks away.

The next day we get the new issues in, June or July or August. Starlet Du Jour is on the cover, a pale blue sky overhead, cobalt-blue waves bob around her. Miss Nanosecond is naked but bubbles of white sea foam prevent the picture from being too naughty. To her right are some cover lines, among them:

LEROY WHITE IS THE NEW BLACK
BY ZACHARY POST

Now, I know I should be overjoyed. Not only did my piece finally get in, not only is it six pages (two and a half are Zelda Guttierez photos of Leroy White wearing Armani, Canali, Zegna, Valentino), not only is it a nifty cover line, but my name is on the cover too. For the very first time. Two thousand miles away, people who knew me when I was seventeen years old will see my name and wonder: *Hmmm, could that be the same Zachary Post . . . ?* A few months ago this would have sent me blasting off through the ceiling and the ceilings above that ceiling. Plaster and dust would be flying. But now? It's my name in red, size 16 Garamond bold, against the blue of the Pacific. A half an inch to the right of the *t* in Post is a chevron of white foam and Starlet's bronzed elbow. *Hmmm, could that be the same Zachary Post?* I pick up the issue and I feel the heft of Chanel, Polo, Absolut, Hermès, Cartier, Revlon, and BMW ads, and I can smell the perfume. It's not Zachary Post, no, it's just his name in hundreds of infinitesimal dots of magenta and yellow against a sea of a million infinitesimal dots of cyan. It's not the sea or the sky or the Girl of the Moment but millions and millions of tiny dots. That's it.

{ }

THE FIRST big meeting without Mark Larkin takes place four days after his untimely demise, and bones and muscles which for months have felt so tense that they were about to crumble and snap have now slackened. I think that I've gotten back at least five years of the ten that Mark Larkin took off my life.

It's a good meeting, enjoyable, friendly, productive. It's an hour like this—taking about ten minutes to pass—that makes the business I'm in worthwhile. We're all intelligent, well-read, funny, clever people. In what other job would I have found coworkers like this? There are none of the slumped-over, sleepy-eyed, matted-haired, reeking slackers I would have met working in a Starbucks or Kinko's.

Everything clicks. I make suggestions and Betsy takes note of them or other people make suggestions based on mine and the ball keeps rolling. I come up with an idea for a story and even suggest that Young Burstin do it. I make a joke and someone rolls up a piece of paper into a ball and tosses it at me and with great aplomb I bounce it off my head to Ivy, of all people, who then, as if this is volleyball, passes it to Jacqueline, who spikes it onto the floor. One of the three hottest directors in Hollywood has consented to an interview for a feature article and yours truly has just been given it. A trip to Los Angeles and this time I mean business. No waiting around in a trailer or in my hotel room or reading twenty magazines at the Hamburger Hamlet.

And so on. Until . . .

Until Shawn Jefferson comes up with two brilliant ideas for stories.

"Boy, I wish I'd said that," I say the first time. "Boy, I wish I'd said that too," I say the second time.

"Shawn, don't forget to print out the Pierre Modot piece this afternoon and pass it around," Betsy bids her.

"Sure," Shawn drawls. "I'm having a late lunch out today so it'll be about three o'clock or so."

Supposedly Shawn doesn't know that she and I are up for Mark Larkin's job. To her I'm just another coworker. For me this honey-skinned great-granddaughter of slave whippers is an obstacle, a blond boulder on the road. Someone to be nudged aside.

So after the meeting, after I go to a greasy coffee shop and sit at the counter and soak up all the box scores in the *Daily News*, I go back to the office and poke around on my computer. I go into a file; it's the piece that Shawn is working on, a three-page article about a snobby young French art dealer recently transplanted to New York. (It's mostly about his apartment, not him.) I take a sentence such as "The soft light seeps in through the slats and settles on Pierre Modot's Louis Quatorze armoire, playing in the coffee-like swirls of centuries-old mahogany" and, with a few clicks here and a few pecks there, turn it into as ugly a sentence ("The soft light seep in into them slits . . .") as can be created by someone capable of stringing words together and spelling. And, yes, I fuck up some of the spelling too.

It works. Poor Shawn just prints it out without going over it first and by the time it makes it to my in-box, it's a spider web of pencil print; five or six people before me have caught the mistakes and commented on the abominable grammar. I correct the spelling of "mahoganny" (none of those five or six geniuses had noticed it) and delete an unnecessary preposition (one that I hadn't even put in!) and pass it around for the other editors to mark up beyond the point of legibility.

Yeah, I feel bad about it too. Mark Larkin at least had it coming. But a rat's got to do what a rat's got to do.

{ }

"MR. Post?"

I know who it is on the phone. Instantly. This time he's calling me early, not even 9:30 in the morning.

"Who's this?"

"Detective Tom Marino, Mr. Post."

"Oh. Hey. What's up?"

I slurp some coffee, giving him a clamorous squall of not-guilty non-chalance right in his ear.

"A few things, Mr. Post. Can you possibly tell me the exact break-down of medicine you might have given or loaned to Larkin?"

"Well, I couldn't do that now, Detective. Maybe when I go home I can find the vials."

"Well, he had the vials in his house. We got those. I just need to know how many were left."

"I don't know if that's possible. I'll try." *Pzzssssscchhhh* . . . another long loud pull of coffee. (Actually there's no coffee left now—I'm making the noise with my lips and some saliva.)

"Mr. Post, was the deceased into, you know, *kinky* sex?"

"I . . . I don't know. How would I—"

"Did you and him ever talk about that kind of stuff?"

"No. We didn't. I have other friends for that."

He coughs into the phone. A smoker, maybe two packs a day for fif-teen years.

"Yeah, I'm sure you do, Mr. Post. Do you know anyone that Mr. Larkin might've spoken to about this?"

"Marjorie Millet. They were boyfriend and girlfriend. She works here."

"Yeah, I know that. Yeah. Okay."

Of course he would already know about the extent of the relation-ship between the deceased and Marjorie. She found the body . . . they must have been in contact. But why, why, why was Marino inquiring about kinky sex?

"Am I allowed to ask why?" I say sheepishly. "I don't understand."

"You don't understand *what?*" Marino snarls. (I've always noticed it, the contempt the police have for civilians and victims, for anyone other than other policemen and criminals.)

"Wasn't it a suicide? That's what I heard. And what's this about kinky sex?"

"Mr. Post, let's just say that there were *objects* or *an object per se* that might indicate something other than *what you heard.*"

Bells go off, ringing and dinging. "Okay. But I can't add to anything other than what I've told you."

He gives me his phone number. I'm to call him if I can figure out anything regarding the pills.

"We'll be in touch," he says.

I walk around the office, four times. I return to my desk and stare at my computer screen, then take four more spins around. Gradually people filter in, take their seats, hang their raincoats over their chairs and slip their wet umbrellas under their desks, nibble on their muffins and croissants.

Betsy is reading the *Times* in her office, fiddling with the crossword puzzle, her glasses almost dangling off the edge of her nose. I walk in and sit down only a few inches away from her.

"Zack . . ."

"This is what I'm doing. I'm getting the key from Velma and I'm moving into Mark Larkin's old office. It's mine now. I'm moving in and I'm calling the maintenance guys and getting furniture put in. I'm doing it in three minutes. If you and Regine don't want me there, then you can drag me out by my hair. Or get security and have them throw me out of the building."

She pushes her glasses up to the bridge of her nose, looks at me.

On the top of her in-box is Shawn Jefferson's copy . . . there's hardly anything visible now beneath the scrawls of gray, brown, and red marks.

Betsy says, "Okay. You've got the job. But wait. Let's just wait before we make the announcement. Okay?"

Okay. I'll wait.

TO: KOOPERI
FROM: POSTZ
SUBJECT: Great news!!!

I'm telling you and only you this and please keep quiet about it.
I'm going to be promoted to senior editor.

TO: POSTZ
FROM: KOOPERI
SUBJECT: Re: Great news!!!

Congratulations.

TO: USHERSOAMESL

FROM: POSTZ
SUBJECT: Great news!!!

I'm telling you and only you this and please keep quiet about it.
I'm going to be promoted to senior editor.

TO: POSTZ
FROM: USHERSOAMESL
SUBJECT: Re: Great news!!!

That is good news indeed.
Shall we go out and celebrate then.

{ }

SOMETIMES nature conspires with your real life and provides the perfect
dramatic background. You're scared of something and it actually thun-
ders outside. You're mad at someone and the sun turns blood red. When
it doesn't, when your girlfriend of ten years decides to break up with you
on a glorious sunny spring day, things just don't seem right or real.

It's pouring out and fog is everywhere, like one monstrous clump of
steel wool clinging to buildings, sidewalks, and sky. Everything is gray
and black, running like paint thrown from a bucket.

It's seven at night and I'm at Midtown South, the police station.
Built like a refrigerator, Detective Tom Marino is huge, six-foot-five and
250 pounds, with an enormous bumpy head pitted with acne scars.

"So you figure out the pills yet?" he asks me when I sit down in front
of him. He regards me with utter contempt.

"No. It's about the kinky sex thing."

"Oh yeah?" His chair squeaks.

"Did you find something . . . on his person? Or up his person?"

"There was some kind of foreign object in the deceased's rectum, yes."

"Was it a bow tie?"

He rubs the thumb of his enormous left hand under his chin two
times, as if trying to smudge something out.

"You tell me," he says.

Marino and a partner put their raincoats on, pick up some umbrellas,
and dash out of the station. I zip up my jacket and walk to the corner
and find a pay phone, which, of course, doesn't work. I walk three

blocks in the downpour before I find one that does. My clothing is sopping wet . . . my feet are soaked and I'm cold. I can barely see anything, it's so wet and foggy and black.

"Willie."

"Yeah . . ."

He already sounds resigned.

"They know. They're coming to get you."

"When?"

"Now. Right now. They'll be over there any minute."

"Oh, well . . ."

Rain slashes down and down and crawls over my hair and face.

"What are you going to do?"

"I guess . . . the usual thing that one does," he says.

"Please, I mean, are you going to—"

"Don't you worry, amigo. I'll make sure you're off the hook."

By the time the two policemen got there, Willie had blown his brains out in his bathtub.

17

Leslie Usher-Soames, Zachary Post

Leslie Forsythia Usher-Soames, the daughter of Trevor Usher-Soames and the late Hyacinth Usher-Soames of London, England, is to be married today to Zachary Allen Post, the son of Sally Huggins Post of Sunnyside, Queens, and Robert Post of Massapequa, Long Island. Judge Hector Ortiz of the New York State Supreme Court will officiate at the Puck Building in New York.

The bride, 28, is a graduate of St. Martin's College of Art and Design in London and was recently assistant designer at It magazine in New York. Her father is Director, Business: European of Versailles Publishing, Inc. Mrs. Usher-Soames died earlier this year gardening.

The bridegroom, 32, is a senior editor at It. He attended Hofstra University. His mother is a bookkeeper at Tip-Top Togs, a clothing manufacturer in Manhattan. His father is co-owner of The Wet Guys, a chain of leisure-activities supplies dealerships.

Miss Usher-Soames, due to a company policy that forbids

married couples from working at the same magazine, will become assistant designer at She magazine. She has chosen to retain her name.

You bet your ass she'll retain her name.
Because there's no way I'm losing that hyphen.

* {   }*

AFTER THE police call me at home to tell me Willie is dead, the first thing I do is call Liz.

"I have something terrible to tell you."

"Yeah?"

"Willie's dead. He killed himself."

I can tell her hand is over her mouth.

"Can you please come down here?" I ask. "Please?"

"I don't know."

"He murdered Mark Larkin. He forced the pills down his throat and the police knew about it."

"How did they know about it?"

Liz didn't even care that Willie had killed Mark Larkin. She simply cut to the chase: How did the police know?

"Because I told them. They were going to find out anyway."

I picture her in her bed on the East Side, her astronaut hubby lying on his back in absurd pajamas (little attaché cases and dollar signs on red silk?), Liz sitting up with a book on her lap, rigid yet trembling violently.

"Can you please come down here? I need your help."

But no. I couldn't inflict it on her. Not all of it.

Liz and I identify the body together. It's a gruesome sight . . . probably. She and I walk into the morgue together and it's exactly like on TV: a dismal gray room, long shadows, creaky noises. A dentist's office smell. An Indian man in a stained white smock—the stains look more like his curry dinner than squirts from body parts—whips a sheet off a table and there he is, already on his gray way to whiteness.

All I look at are Willie's big feet.

"Yes. That's him," I say.

"It is," Liz seconds.

We walk outside together. It isn't raining anymore. Liz's skin seems pulled tight against her cheekbones and jaw.

"Did you look?" I ask her.

"Yeah. There wasn't much of anything there."

I tell her to go home, that I'll call the family.

I wonder if she suspects I had something to do with this.

Now there are phone calls to make.

I take a Valium and when my hands warm up to a reasonably normal temperature, I begin.

"I have some terrible news, Mr. Lister," is how I preface it, stammering all the while, after I tell him who I am.

When I break it to him there is silence, broken by an anguished groan that barely makes it to his mouth up from his gut.

"I'm sorry," I say.

"He wasn't very happy, I know," his father finally recovers to say. "I tried to get him to seek help but . . ."

"Yes. I did too." But am I telling the truth?

And then the other news.

"There's something else, sir. He murdered someone. He killed someone and the police were going to arrest him. So he committed suicide. I'm sorry."

This time no silence, just the groan . . . it shivers the tiny hairs on my ear.

"Was it Mark Larkin?"

"Yeah."

He laughs a swift satisfied *hmmph*.

I was glad he didn't start crying. I don't know how I would have dealt with that.

Two days later Liz and I drive in a hearse to La Guardia and then watch the coffin being boarded onto a plane. It's very hot out and very sunny and the heat floats up from the tarmac and turns the plane into silver jelly.

"You've met the family?" she asks me on board.

"When the parents came to the office I met them. One or two times."

"That's how I met them. The sisters too? Kristin?"

"Yeah, I met Kristin." And she was very pretty too. I don't want to admit it but I'm looking forward to seeing her again.

Liz and I are both reading magazines, of course.

An hour into the flight she asks me: "Are you going to get Mark Larkin's job?"

"I've already got it."

She shakes her head, then lifts the window shade until the sun blinds us, then shuts it.

"Any luck getting pregnant yet?"

"No. Not yet."

I flip the pages. An anorexic model in a black satin bra, her ribs almost poking through the skin; a close-up of perfect feet in high heels as black and slimy as an eel; a gold Rolex on a wrist, a burgundy Mercedes parked in an empty piazza under a magnificent Tuscan sky.

"Oh, dear, dear, dear," Liz says to herself. "What will become of us . . . ?"

It was just the family—the parents, the two sisters, and an uncle—and us at the funeral. The day was sweltering. What was worse for Willie's family: Willie having died so young or Willie having murdered someone? Were they grief-stricken and embarrassed or merely grief-stricken? I don't even know if the rent-a-reverend who performed the service was ever informed of Willie's status as a murderer.

The stone said William R. Lister—not Will, his byline name, or Willie, his friend name. For some reason as I stared at his name I thought of his article about the Chelsea Hotel; it had won an award but he'd had to get on his knees and beg for it to run.

There were gravestones at the cemetery two-hundred years old and, with the sun burning down, they seemed to be sweating. The grass was well tended to in some places but was wild and brown elsewhere. Willie's spot is near the street running by the cemetery and I could hardly hear the words being said above the growls of traffic stopping and starting.

Kristin Lister, as blond as her brother and dressed in black, looked very pretty. She's tall and has a nice figure and is going for a graduate degree in medical illustration. Her eyes were blue and twinkly but she wasn't crying. I would like to see her again sometime.

I'll wait a few weeks, I figure, before I'll call Mr. Lister up and casu-

ally remind him that I'd laid out the money to transport Willie's body to
Ohio.

Flying back to New York the next morning I want to lean over to Liz and
whisper: *If you can't have your best friend kill your worst enemy, then what
good are friends? That's what friends are for, right?*
    But I'll never tell anyone.

❧   ❧

THAT'S what friends are for.
    Willie did get me off the hook. He left a note — Detective Marino
never told me its contents in full and I was too scared to ask — and he
took the fall.
    (Did he write it before he got in the bathtub or when he was in it?
Was the gun in the other hand when he wrote it? That old ugly tub in
the kitchen, from the 1920s or so, streaked with grime and green. But
Willie went out with class. The bathtub was filled with champagne — it
was the Cristal that the ever-elusive Boris Montague had given him for
his European wild goose chase months ago, when Willie returned with
nothing but a handful of dots.)
    Marino looked at all the e-mails, between Willie and myself and
Mark Larkin. I was never in any trouble. Long ago I'd — jokingly, mind
you — told Willie where to shove Mark Larkin's bow tie. How was I to
know he'd really do such a thing? Marino looked at Willie's threats,
looked at my burgeoning friendship with the deceased. It all played perfectly.
    The case is closed.
    It wasn't even the top story on the news, thanks to a glitzy triple mur-
der on the East Side the same day. A rich plastic surgeon (many socialites
among his clientele) killed his wife, her lover, then her lover's son, with
whom he'd been having an affair. He'd tried to kill himself but the gun
jammed. This is the kind of story we'll be hearing about again; maybe
Emma Pilgrim or Tony Lancett will write about it for *It*. Or maybe I will.
    But Willie's story did make a little noise. The theme: Golden Boy
Goes Insane, kills rival who surpassed him. Jealousy. Obsession. Lunacy.
Murder. The *Post* mentioned that he'd recently gained a lot of weight.
    How they found it I don't know but one local station played a brief

portion of the tape of Willie playing football, the tape he'd shown me about ten times. There he is, swarming over people, knocking them down, banging them silly, his long yellow hair wagging all over the place, mud flying, rain falling. There he is, smoking a cigarette on the sidelines.

"Oh, he shouldn't be doing that," a voice says.

{ }

THE *Times* wedding section sometimes runs a picture of the happy couple, all smiles, a rosy future. Sometimes, however, they just show the bride, sometimes no photo at all. Leslie and I had sent one solo shot of her and also one of the two of us. For our announcement, they didn't run any picture.

I measured myself against the other grooms in the paper that day. Two doctors, a congressman, a slew of lawyers, a few stockbrokers. Okay, I wasn't in their league. But then there was the owner of a candle store, an assistant manager of a tile shop, a few graduate students, two losers who worked for their parents. So, despite Tip-Top Togs and The Wet Guys, I did okay, I figured.

I did it. I pulled it off.

Senior editor at *It*. Not too shabby.

{ }

OF COURSE I had to tell Leslie about my less-than-stellar upbringing before she read about it in the newspaper.

(I also came clean to Betsy, telling her that the Mark Larkin episode had had me wringing and cleansing my hands.)

At the appointed time for this Leslie was flying off in a rage regarding the company policy dictating that she change her job. She'd never heard about it.

"Do you know about this?!" she spits out furiously.

"About . . ."

"Betsy Butler told me. A couple at Versailles cannot—*cannot*—work at the same magazine together. I have to move. Or *you* have to! Did you know about this?"

"I do remember now something about a company policy. But it hadn't occurred to me. I swear to God."

Her cheeks are flushed and eyes are glowering.

"Well? Who's going? You? Me? Who's going?"

"I-I-I've been at *It* longer, honey."

She slumps down into a chair and curls up her legs so that her elbow rests on her knees. Tears are forming.

"This is just unbelievable," she cries.

I might as well take care of the other thing now . . .

"There's something else I have to tell you."

(You think I really didn't remember the company policy? *Come on!*)

After that matter's been taken care of, I'm sitting on the couch with her. She's cried her eyes dry. My arm is around her.

"We'll be happy, won't we?" she whimpers into my shoulder.

"I hope so."

"Watch. We'll be so bloody happy it will make everyone else completely miserable."

"Sounds good to me."

"You'll just keep getting more important and so will I and we'll simply be fabulous together. In two years I'll be art director at *She*. We'll make Tom Land and Trisha look like the wankers they are. And they'll *have* to invite us to dinner."

She pulls her face up from my shoulder and says, "We'll make it work, old boy. I know we will."

"I'd really prefer it if you didn't address me as 'old boy,' sweetie."

It's the morning of my wedding day. I've slept only two hours the whole night and even that came ten minutes at a time. No boisterous bachelor parties with strippers and blow jobs for me—just a sedate dinner for three (Ollie, Liz, and myself) at a cozy oyster bar on Cornelia Street.

It's eight in the morning and I'm sitting up in bed staring at the wall. All night long I'd been thinking of Ivy. Sweet Ivy, lost to me.

The buzzer rings. I hardly notice it. It buzzes again. I walk to the door and press the button and say, "Huh?"

"Przrn," a voice cackles through the static.

"Who is this?"

"Yr przm."

Your prism? But I didn't order a prism.

I buzz the person in, whoever it is.

I listen to the elevator creak toward my floor and stare into the oatmeally haze of the hallway. Who is it? The Fates? The Furies? The Grim Reaper about to lop off my scrotum with his scythe?

No. It's Marjorie Millet and when I see her take a step toward me my heart pounds. She's wearing a black fur coat and her hair is exploding with each step she takes toward me.

"Your present, sir," she says when I let her in.

She kicks the door shut behind her, whips open the coat. Here she is in all her ripe, plump, splotchy, burning hot Marjorie-ness. Black lace, black stockings and garters, a rosette bobbing amidst the cleavage.

Into the bedroom. We sound like pigs being slaughtered with deliberate cruelty. The room is quaking.

Am I dreaming? But I don't have to pinch myself . . . because she's pinching me, biting me, clawing me. I am not dreaming.

But . . .

There's no satisfaction. We grind and thrust but it won't happen. I'm at the very edge . . . but it doesn't happen. And—I'm certain of this—*she didn't let it happen*. She was torturing me. Again.

"Enjoy your marriage, Buster," she says when she whisks her way out of the apartment. Leaving me trembling, cold, and raw.

{ }

TREVOR USHER-SOAMES came to New York for the wedding, as did five of Leslie's friends, one of which, to my jealous chagrin, Oliver Osborne (my best man) was chatting up mightily at the reception. Trevor made a brief toast and I listened to it with my teeth grinding so hard I thought they might turn to powder. He was as diplomatic as he could be under the circumstances; after all, hadn't I recently killed his wife and wasn't I now kidnapping his daughter? In typical oblique British fashion, he damned me with the faintest praise imaginable, referring to our alliance as "a terrible surprise" and "awfully unusual." I was to be "a not entirely unwelcome addition" to their illustrious family and he was sure that we would be "abhorrently content" for some time to come.

While Leslie and I were planning who to invite and who not to, she mentioned that her brother, Nigel, would not be able to attend.

"Who?" I asked, slightly stunned.

"My older brother. Have I not ever mentioned him to you?"

"No. Never." A vision seen as clearly as the A-list and B-list inches in front of me: the sumptuous wedding-cake house in the Boltons and the elegant country estate (Moldywood, Withergland House) crumble like sand castles under the wheels of a truck

"Why can't he come?" I say trying to appear composed.

"He's insane. Absolutely stark raving mad."

This doesn't surprise me.

"Is he institutionalized?"

"Oh God, yes."

But just as I'm in the middle of my sigh of relief, Leslie adds: "But he is getting better, they say."

My father and his wife and my mother attended the ceremony although, as far as I could tell, there was no exchange of eye contact between the two parties. "Your mother won't mind me and Sheila coming," my dad said. "Your father and what's-her-face won't mind me coming," my mom said. It had occurred to neither of them that I might mind all three of them being there.

I saw Trevor chatting with my mother for ten minutes at one point, he, impeccably groomed and splendidly dressed and silvery from top to bottom, looking down at her blue-white hair; she, as well put together as she possibly could get, looking straight up at the golf ball (perhaps he'd even powdered it for the occasion) dangling near his eye. This strange confluence of silver and blue . . . it was like looking at steel being polished.

"You're a bastard but I do wish you luck," Trevor said to me as he was leaving.

Bob Post slipped me an envelope and winked two times as he did so. Sheila kissed me many times on the cheek.

In the envelope was $5,000 in cash. His brother Jimmy (Wet Guy II) gave me one wink and $2,500.

It took only four nights in a St. Martin casino to lose the better part of this largess, all at the craps table. (You can take the boy out of Massapequa but . . .)

It took only two hours on the beach for Leslie's skin to be so badly burned that she never set a toe on the beach again. She wouldn't even glance in its direction from our hotel room, in which she spent the rest of the week recovering. She ran a fever, had diarrhea. A doctor came and told her to rub balsamic vinegar on herself three times a day. She did not want to be touched. The air conditioner gave her terrible chills and by the week's end she looked like a badly bruised pomegranate.

I spent my days shuttling from the beach to the room to check on her, then going to the pool and then back to the room, then to the beach. I'd say I averaged about seven banana daiquiris a day. Leslie didn't join me in the casino at night and has no idea I lost all that money.

(A week later I discovered that a wedding ring did not help her conquer her fear of semen. She detests "spunk," detests the very idea of it. She also doesn't like kissing, clutching, bumping, spooning, and groping. Talking dirty isn't even an option—there's little to talk dirty about. Were it a choice between "doing it" and eating cauliflower, I have no doubt she'd be nibbling away, a peck a minute. It's a good thing I saved the card for Paddling Pearls of Paddington.)

Late one day at the beach after knocking back two drinks on my chaise longue, I'm staring at the sunset, the crimson fire slowly dissolving into deep lustrous blue. My toes are in the sand, my feet are wiggling in and out of the sand, playing with that cozy gritty sensation, my mind is verging on utter numbness. The chaise longue has been baked with my sweat—the sun was brutal and relentless. I notice a man jogging along the shoreline, going from my right to my left. From my vantage point I can see the footprints he leaves with each step . . . his feet thud down into the wet sand and leave beige tracks that speckle the shore. Clear blue water ripples in and begins to tow away the footprints. I could swear to God, as I hear behind me kettle drums chinking and glasses tinkling and water splashing from the poolside bar, that it's Willie running. Willie young, robust, brilliant, sane. Then he disappears where the shoreline curves out of view. The sun is now mostly in the water, just a corona of bright orange yet to sink in, and all the footprints are gone.

{   }

MARJORIE HAS MADE her last appearance in these pages; it is now time for Regine Turnbull to make her first.

Lunch at the Four Seasons. Here I am with Regine and I'm having a

Bombay Sapphire martini and *coq au vin*, acting as if I do this every day for lunch (yesterday I had a tuna melt and a Dr Pepper at a counter in a coffee shop). The Tiny Terroress looks like a million bucks and if there's one stray lock on that frosty hairdo of hers, I'll lick her plate clean. (I'd probably do that anyway.)

"It's really been a long strange trip for you, hasn't it, Zack?"

"It sure has."

I'm still tan from St. Martin but starting to peel around the nose and forehead. Perhaps I look like I really do belong in this opulent setting. But I think the busboy has me figured out as someone who should be in the kitchen doing the dishes.

"You started out . . . Where was it again?"

"I started out at *Here*."

"And then where was it?"

"*Zest*. And then *It*. And here I am. From *Here* to *It*-ernity."

We chuckle, sip our drinks. She's got a Tom Collins working. As well as a necklace that's hurling sparks at my eyes.

I note a familiar face six tables away. Ethan Cawley, all in white, is sitting with two other people. A waiter wheels a silver and gold cart to his table, drops a match onto a burner, and a ball of flame bursts up.

"The first time I met you, Zachary," Regine tells me with as big a smile as she ever offers anyone, "I thought to myself, This boy is going to make it."

Maybe Regine is mistaking me for someone else. Mark Larkin possibly?

But does it even matter?

I redid my office—*my* office—from the ground up. Enough of that dark austere oaky look. This isn't a stodgy British men's club, this is the office of someone who edits a glossy, very popular, shallow magazine. The paint is new and is, appropriately, glossy white and the floor is black marble tile and you can see yourself in it, should anyone ever venture to drop in on me. (Few people do.) No more anvil-like desks that look like they belonged to a 1930s prairie schoolmarm—I've got chrome and glass, silver and some gold, and chairs that wheeze with delight when you sit in them.

And I've moved things around, positioning the desk so that I can see the space just outside my door . . . so I can see the two people who work for me: Todd Burstin and Ivy Kooper. They're ten yards away from me and only a few feet from each other. Ivy looks great, does good work, she fits in well but not too well, she's razor-sharp and has good ideas and I feel a miserable pang every time I think about her for more than ten seconds.

They both work very hard for me.

Are they sending e-mail to each other? Once in a while I hear them giggling, on the verge of hysterics . . . sometimes I want to step out, ask what's so funny, and then giggle along. Other times I'd just like to throttle them for being so goddamn happy.

They probably despise me.

Twice Ivy has cornered me and asked: "So what was the jig up about that day?"

"Nothing. It's business. It's nothing."

I think she knows.

I did it. I pulled it off.

My Rolodexes get plumper by the day; I steal names and numbers off of Regine's Rolodexes whenever I can. It's like feeding a ravenous lion slabs of raw meat. I flip the cards now and instead of a pizza parlor showing up, it's a director, a model, a senator.

Maybe it's not a corner office but it's big enough and I fully intend to have a corner office one day.

On a sunny morning I'll raise the blinds all the way and take in the view. Stone, glass, iron, sky. The sunlight floods in and bathes everything yellow and white. The other buildings seem utterly unpeopled, I can't even detect a shadow behind the million windows. Slices of metal and stone stretch toward the sky, lit up to scarlet by the sun . . . the light shoots off the glass, it's a maze of blazing mirrors. Over Queens and Brooklyn a long loafy cloud of smoke is slowly dispersing. Bridges ignite to sulfurous yellow and platinum white. The Chrysler Building is as red as a smoldering ember and its chrome eagle heads stare out with their eyes furious and aflame, gazing fire in all directions.

The whole city is on fire.

I did it. Son of a bitch, I did it.